DANCE OF THE LIGHTS

DANCE OF THE LIGHTS

Stephen Geez

Fresh Ink Group
Roanoke

DANCE OF THE LIGHTS

Fresh Ink Group
An Imprint of:
The Fresh Ink Group, LLC
PO Box 525
Roanoke, TX 76262
Email: info@FreshInkGroup.com
www.FreshInkGroup.com

Edition 1.1	1995
Edition 2.0	2003
Edition 3.0	2011
Edition 3.1	2016

Book design by Ann E. Stewart

Cover design by Joe Posada

Photo by Alysha Carwile

Cataloging-in-Publication Recommendations: General Fiction;
Grief (Fiction); Relationships (Fiction); Retirement (Fiction);
Foster Care (Fiction); Old Age Romance (Fiction);
Tarpon Springs, FL (Fiction); Slipstream Fiction;
Contemporary Fantasy Fiction

Library of Congress Control Number: 2010940032

ISBN-13: 978-1-936442-00-3

In memory of my sister, Tanya

The songbirds still sing

Acknowledgements

Thanks to the following wondrous souls:

Team Leader: Ann E. Stewart, Managing Director, The Fresh Ink Group, LLC

Production Team: Joe Posada, Alysha Carwile, Patsy LaFave

Content Team: Lucas Cale, Beem Weeks, Mark Allen North

Support Team: Kent D. Casey, Todd Tessin, Tom Stockbridge, Marshall Shearer MD, Mary Watson, Susan Stewart, Tracey Bibby, Dillard Greenwell

Member Team: All of *you* who subscribe to the newsletter updates and free stories at www.FreshInkGroup.com, and especially those who support our members by buying books. It keeps us going when you spread the good word.

CHAPTER 1

They came from every direction, floating down from trees, wafting on breezes, threading their way among tropical plants, through tall grasses, and into the sandy clearing. They rose up out of the still waters, small ponds, canals, and winding little streams among the trees here in Tarpon Springs. Tiny pinpoints of light so small they might be specks of glowing dust, they shined every color imaginable, constantly changing, sparkling and twinkling in hues of magenta and fuchsia and turquoise, yellow and cobalt and violet, chartreuse and copper and sapphire and tangerine and more.

A regal old toad, big and fat, looked on absently. Nearby, several small lizards sunned themselves, peering about lazily for a chance insect to devour. All looked utterly unimpressed by the show no human had ever witnessed. Then came the sound of gentle breathing from inside the end of a giant hollow log, nearly four feet across the opening and worn smooth by years of exposure. A smallish boy of twelve or so was napping inside.

More shimmering lights joined the swarm, swirling around each other in a translucent whirlwind, forming shapes that shifted and twirled in a frenzy like some spider-bit villager dancing the tarantella, fighting the fever that threatened to engulf its desperate victim.

Three-dimensional images appeared, faces forming and dissolving as butterflies spun off, flitting through sunshine to fade into showers of sparkles carried off into the sky. Tiny creatures strutted away on a zillion legs while birds circled and dived. The solemn eyes of a cat peered up, then spun away into more lights and more faces and more shapes. An armadillo danced a jig, swaying forward and back, swishing his tail this way and that, prancing in rhythm to the pulse of the Earth. Still more faces passed through and swirled away: old men and ladies, children and babies, dark and brooding souls, laughing tots, worried widows, teenagers with eyes gleaming of youth, mothers and fathers and grandparents and grade-schoolers—all appeared in the air, sometimes lasting seconds, sometimes forming and disappearing all in an instant.

The toad looked away, but peering from the inside the log two big brown eyes watched with awe. Barely awake, Kevin Riner spied faint traces of a shimmering, all-colored ribbon snake as it darted by and dissolved into stardust that sparkled into the sand. He yawned and rubbed his eyes, then looked again into the blinding yellow sunshine that baked everything it touched, wavy lines of heat rising from dark surfaces. It made no sense; the harder he looked, the more difficult the lights were to see—like trying to decide the ever-changing color of a twinkling star in the velvet night sky. Still, dots spun off and floated away, scattering here and there, sinking into the ground, plunging into cool waters. They glowed from dark depths in a flowing spring cut hundreds of feet through porous limestone, splintering into a million tunnels where last year's rain filtered up to ripple in bright sunlight yet again.

Kevin climbed out of his private refuge and stood blinking in the afternoon glare, his eyes playing tricks, the lights nowhere in sight. A lizard scurried up a tree trunk; a beetle trundled across the sand. He listened to all the familiar sounds, the buzzes and chirrups and hums and tweets of all the creatures who lived here where he came when he needed time alone in a world that belonged only to him. Nobody but Kevin ever came to this spot, not since last year, the summer of 1989, when the only two families with kids moved from the fading trailer park he called home. He decided to head for the condos on higher ground along the main channel not far from the trailer he shared with his mom. Maybe Frank would be home.

Frank was pretty cool for an older guy, even if that patch of gray hair he combed across his balding pate looked a little silly. He didn't seem to mind if Kevin hung around while he tinkered with his vintage Corvette, worked in his flower garden, or relaxed in the shade under those cypress trees by the water out back.

Kevin started down the sandy path, stopping one last time to look back. Maybe he saw a purplish twinkle out the corner of his eye, a silver sparkle in the weeds, the pinkest glimmer dashing between his feet. He turned several directions, always thinking he glimpsed something at the periphery, but the lights were gone, nothing to see but a toad gazing indifferently, and the glare of hot Florida sunshine in Kevin's private sanctuary hidden amid the reeds down by the cool, clear springs.

He turned and ran toward Frank's.

Frank Tanyon hovered around the flower bed in front of his condo, hoping to glimpse his new next-door neighbor, giving wide berth to the movers and that little firecracker of a woman finding fault in all their efforts. Kevin stole quietly up from behind to stand beside the old fellow and watch.

"Is that her?" Kevin whispered.

"I'm not sure. I will say, though, that I'm a bit disappointed." He watched a long divan being brought down the ramp. "I was hoping for a nice, congenial neighbor, maybe a learned old gentleman for trading stories and lies, or a nice unattached lady who makes lemonade and enjoys an occasional dinner out." Frank threw up his arms in disgust, then smiled and leaned over to elbow Kevin in the ribs. Whispering in the boy's ear, he concluded, "Instead, I get a shriveled up old hag who's rapidly working her way up to the rank of all-out bitch."

Kevin snickered and nudged him back, understanding his disappointment. Units A and D were owned by retirees with homes and cottages up north, not used more than a few weeks per year. Frank lived in Unit B, but ever since his friend and long-time business partner in Unit C died the year before, Frank passed his time as the only person in a big deserted place. He had just about given up hope that the developer would ever put up the other buildings originally planned.

"So what's wrong with this one?"

"Just watch." Frank walked over to two of the movers and offered to help. The woman made a bee-line from the truck, intercepting Frank and snapping orders for him to stay out of the way. The movers shook their heads resignedly as the old fellow retreated to watch again from the flower beds with Kevin. "So what do you think?"

"Bitch," concluded Kevin.

"Bitch," Frank had to agree.

Beverly Herndon gripped both armrests as the jet descended toward Tampa. Long past any chance to turn back, the recent widow regretted that moment of weakness when she'd foolishly decided to sell her home in Michigan and settle for a condo where aging snowbirds flock to pass their final days in air-conditioned oblivion. Mired by grief and loneliness, she'd dismantled her life in a desperate bid to spend more time with her only daughter, a young woman busy finding her own place in the world. Worse, this move would put her way too close to Loretta, her meddlesome older sister, an overbearing toxicant best suffered in small, infrequent doses.

Beverly swallowed hard during landing, her heart racing in anticipation as the plane taxied to the gate. Linda would be waiting in the terminal, her ever-present camera poised to capture the moment, a picture of happy reunion masking the inevitable: a brief interlude reveling in the illusion of better days, then the onset of pervasive loneliness, this time leaving her trapped far from home.

Propelled down the cramped walkway, she scanned the waiting faces.

"Mama!" Linda called, a flash of familiar blond hair pushing through the crowd. Beverly summoned her best smile just in time for the shot.

Click.

Linda never looked more beautiful, the 24-year-old's blue eyes sparkling, her tan face aglow. For an instant it seemed this might work after all, that Beverly could find ways to share a not-too-intrusive part of Linda's life while gradually discovering new ways to live her own.

"Hey, sweetie," was all she managed to say before the tears came. She found herself in Linda's arms, the daughter now holding the mother who'd held her so many times.

"It's okay, Mama," Linda whispered.

Beverly dabbed her eyes with a tissue, then struck a regal pose for another snapshot before they strolled arm-in-arm toward baggage-claim. "Is the truck here yet?"

"Just arrived. Aunt Loretta's out there supervising the movers."

Beverly chuckled at the thought. "They'll be happy to get done and get away from her."

"Oh," Linda teased, "you wouldn't have her any other way."

"At least she proves that some things in the world never change."

Finding the right carousel, they stood off to the side and waited for Beverly's bags.

"So did you find out what's holding up the money?" Linda asked.

"Well, sort of. I sure wish I'd asked a lot more questions when your father was alive. Bless his heart, he always wanted to handle everything himself—the man's job, he called it."

"He did watch out for us," Linda said quietly, her eyes wistful. "He just didn't expect we'd be on our own so soon."

Beverly looked away, and she found herself surrounded by indifferent strangers all crowded into this unfamiliar place, too many things changing too fast, the future she never imagined eclipsing a past still too bright to examine, even as it sometimes grew too dim to recall.

"So what did you learn?" Linda asked quickly, maybe sensing how easily Beverly tended to lapse into that overwhelming sense of helplessness that had marked so many of her days these past five months.

"Well, it seems your father already knew Uncle Chuck was sick *before* they sold the company. I never believed he really wanted to retire, but his heart just wasn't in it anymore, not with knowing Chuck would no longer be a part of something they'd built together from scratch. When Chuck died, he did intend to leave us his estate. The reason your father sued the bank was because they stalled probate and refused to pay it out. I don't think it was the money he cared about so much as that he owed it to Chuck not to let them steal his life's work."

"But how are they getting away with that?"

"Without your father knowing it, Chuck had put everything into a trust and foolishly gave the bank control. He didn't want to burden us with handling his affairs as he got sicker, and he was afraid the state would take it if he had to be put into a long-term care facility."

"But doesn't the will beat that?"

"The bank's claim is that it's invalid since Chuck relinquished his authority to name an heir. They lost in circuit court, but now while they appeal, the bank continues to bilk the principle for administrative costs while *our* lawyer is charging a fortune in legal fees. Stockbridge says I already owe his firm nearly two-hundred thousand, win or lose."

"Wow," Linda whispered as a buzzer signaled the conveyer. They grabbed the bags and headed for Beverly's sedan, which Linda's roommate, Sherry, had driven down the week before. They loaded up and, with Linda at the wheel, escaped the parking-garage gloom, bursting through a curtain of blinding glare and into the warm Florida sunshine.

"Maybe it's time," Linda suggested, "to seek some independent advice."

"I think you're right, but for today I'm going to forget about it and enjoy my time with you."

Linda reached over to squeeze her mother's hand, and Beverly knew that living close enough to touch her like this, even for a moment, on those days she needed her most . . . well, giving up everything else will have been worth it.

"Hey, I've got good news," Linda said, turning south toward Tarpon Springs. "My boss said I can stay on for another year, so I don't have to take the other job up in Tallahassee this fall."

"But will he let you take more pictures?"

"Oh, I'm in no hurry for that. The research department is a good way to learn the newspaper biz. Besides, you just got down here."

"You don't have to decide right away, do you?"

"Oh no."

"Then we'll talk about this some more. And don't think I moved down just because *you're* here," Beverly insisted, smiling over at Linda. "I'd heard Florida's got better homestead protection in case all those crooked bankers and lawyers bankrupt me."

Linda chuckled, which satisfied Beverly, who didn't want her daughter to realize the shades of truth lurking beneath her joke. They rode along in contented silence for a while, Beverly studying the area and trying to imagine when all this would someday come to seem familiar.

"There's Lake Tarpon," Linda said, pointing at the picturesque scene appearing on the right. "Try to keep Sunday open next week. Sherry and I are renting a pontoon boat so we can party with you and Aunt Loretta. There's a park at that end where we can barbecue and sit around feeding cat food to the giant toads."

"Did you say toads?"

Linda wagged her brows. "You'll see."

"Well, I'll just have to check my social calendar and try to pencil you in."

"Practice batting your eyelashes, too, in case we find some foxy guys to flirt with."

They turned off the main road and headed back toward the condos, pulling up to where Loretta stood glaring at several exasperated movers. Linda grabbed her camera as she stepped out. "Come on, Mama. One more picture."

Beverly positioned herself amid the mayhem. As Linda focused, a voice said, "Hi, neighbor."

Click.

The first photo of Beverly Herndon, just arriving from Houghton Lake, standing in front of her new home, and some guy named Frank managed to sneak his grinning mug into a corner of the shot.

Kevin walked up the path behind the mobile-home park. He passed one boarded-up trailer at the end and went up to his own from the back, surprised to find his mother's car gone. Maybe she got a chance to work an extra shift at the drugstore again, something she would never turn down. They needed the money.

Heading around to the other side, he picked up a plastic milk crate, placed it upside down under a window, then stepped up and stood on his toes, peering into the dim interior. Rats! Mark was in there, snoring quietly on the couch amid the clutter of beer cans and snack wrappers. Not much older than twenty, he looked like a sleeping Satan. Those piercing eyes, scraggly goatee, and jagged scar down one cheek always made Kevin feel creepy. A bourbon bottle stood empty on the side table. A broken lamp sprawled across the floor.

Kevin hopped down, moved the crate away, and went to the rusty shed out back. He pulled open a bent door and squeezed in among the broken lawnmower and piles of junk, then reached into a torn box and removed a toilet paper roll, disappointed to find only two or three squares hanging from it. He frowned, went back outside, and looked toward the small patch of woods behind the park, but the idea of relying on bug-crawly leaves, well, just didn't seem like it would do the job. Deciding to take a chance, he went around to the front and fished a key from his pocket, opening the door as quietly as he could, then easing inside.

Struck by a blaze of sunlight, Mark rose up, staring with one open eye. "Get outta here, you little shit!" He threw his bottle at the door, barely missing the boy.

Jumping out, Kevin slammed the door and fled down the path. He should have known better than to try to come home before his mother. She always acted as a buffer between him and that unemployed jerk who sort of moved in over the winter.

Stopping short of the clearing where Frank lived, he sat down and tried not to cry, wiping tears away in spite of himself. His belly cramped and uncomfortable, he urgently needed to use a bathroom. He wiped his face on his shirt and sat very still, trying to calm his breathing, hoping that Frank had returned from seeing his accountant—"Money-grubber," as he liked to call him. He headed past the small pond, crossed the stream on a makeshift log bridge, and walked across the yard toward the entrance to Unit B. The moving truck was gone, but he could hear voices and sounds from inside Unit C for a change. He rang the bell twice, waited, then rang again, holding his belly with the other hand, his frustration threatening to bring more tears.

Finally Frank pulled up and stepped out of his car. "Hey, hoodlum. What's up? Couldn't find any liquor stores to rob?"

"Frank, can I use your bathroom?"

"Well, it'll cost you a quarter." He fumbled with his keys, got the door open, and let the boy in first. Kevin wasted no time dashing down the hall.

After the second flush and sounds of running water, Kevin emerged feeling a lot better. He had combed his longish, silky brown hair, feathering back the slashes cut over each ear. Frank waited at the breakfast nook with a cold beer and half a turkey sub in front of him. Across the counter, he'd set out a cold Mountain Dew—Kevin's favorite—a whole ham and cheese, and a basket of corn chips.

"Come on, pest. I don't like to eat alone, ya know."

Kevin climbed up on the stool and started chomping, scarcely taking a breath, glad that Frank always had extra munchies and stuff around. He always found Mountain Dew in the refrigerator even though he had never seen the old man drink one.

"So is your mom late?"

"Prob'ly. She's still saving up for school." As long as he could remember, his mother had been pursuing an ever-elusive cosmetology certificate to become a licensed hair dresser.

"Good for her." Frank had asked him to bring his mom for dinner several times, but she always declined, and Kevin steadfastly refused to let Frank come to his trailer. He'd spotted the older guy driving by once when nobody was home, but Frank never mentioned it, probably understanding his young friend was ashamed of where he lived. So far he'd managed to keep Mark secret, afraid that if Frank found out, he'd consider his mother trash and might not want Kevin to come around so much.

"So how's your new neighbors?" Kevin had finished the sub and started working through the last of the corn chips.

"I don't know yet. That woman we met doesn't live there. She's the sister of the one who bought the condo—a lady named Beverly. I tried to help them when they were moving everything inside—even got myself invited in by her daughter, uh, Linda—but the other two obviously didn't want me around. That sister, Loretta, acted suspicious of me, watching my every move like I might steal something. Linda kept trying to be friendly and get me into conversations with her mother, but Beverly never did warm up. She's a sharp-looking lady who seems nice, anyway, so I guess she just felt overwhelmed and didn't want to have to deal with me. I bowed out after a while and left them unpacking."

Frank watched while Kevin cleaned up the mess.

"You didn't eat yours! You want me to wrap it up?"

"Naw, just toss it. I'm not hungry anyway."

While Kevin wiped off the counter, he asked, "Hey, Frank, you got some work you need done? Like weedin' the flowers or something?"

"As a matter of fact, yes—and watering, too. I have to go over this stuff from Money-grubber by tomorrow. Why don't you snag yerself another Dew and get me a beer; then I'll meet you outside."

Over the next few hours, Kevin weeded and watered and raked and pruned and picked, occasionally feeding crickets to the toad who lived under the edge of a small bush by the gutter downspout. Frank lay sprawled in a chaise-longue while he went through papers, playing with his calculator, frowning occasionally, making notations, chatting with Kevin, and keeping an eye on the condo next door.

By 6:00, Kevin had dragged the hose and sprinkler out to water the lawn, so Frank packed up his things and rolled the chair back inside. He pulled a cell-phone from his briefcase, then walked over to Beverly's door and knocked, pretending to make a call while Kevin watched curiously. Linda answered the door with Loretta peering over her shoulder.

"I've got the pizza place on the phone now. They need to know what you want on yours. Anchovies? Rattlesnake? Octopus? Wildebeest?"

Linda laughed. "Anything but mushrooms. Mom doesn't agree with them."

Loretta frowned and announced, "I have to be leaving, now. I'm volunteering in Seminole."

"Come on, Aunt Loretta, Frank's buying!"

"No, I've got to go." She turned and called, "Beverly, I'll be by day after tomorrow. Hopefully your car will be here by then. Remember to keep checking your phone to make sure it gets turned on."

While Loretta headed toward her car, purse clutched tightly, Linda shrugged and sheepishly told Frank, "Well, you better make it a small pizza."

"I'll tell you what, I'll hose down the kid—" He gestured toward Kevin watching from the flower bed. "—And meet you and your mom on my deck out back—say, fifteen minutes or however long you need?"

His offer accepted, Frank hastened to set out all the accoutrements of a patio picnic. He urged Kevin to take a shower and put on one of the outfits he'd bought him for changing after dirty-work, the housekeeper knowing that any boy-sized clothes in the wash belonged on a shelf in the garage. Kevin unlocked the small refrigerator under the backyard bar, then helped him light some mosquito coils before fetching some clothes and following him inside, each grabbing one of the bathrooms. Ten minutes later, they stood in the hallway, inspecting each other. Agreeing they were just two too-handsome dudes, they went out to await the ladies.

Linda and Beverly came out back and joined them on the deck. They, too, had made a hasty effort to clean up after a day of unpacking and moving dirty boxes around. Frank introduced Kevin as his youngest friend. When the pizzas arrived, everybody discovered they were hungrier than expected. Beverly seemed a bit uncomfortable at first, but she finally relaxed and joined in the aimless chit-chat that Frank endeavored to keep light and easy. Everybody included Kevin in the conversation, treating him just like another grown-up, so for a while he got to feel pretty good about himself, worries about going home again forgotten.

A cool breeze blew in from the coast, a lovely evening with beautiful sunset visible off to the right, colors splayed across the springs. They all sat mesmerized for a while before the ladies got up to go. Linda explained that her mom would be staying with her in Tampa that first night, bedding and such still not having been found among the boxes. They declined Frank's offer of a linen loan, so the guys walked them to their car and wished them a good night.

Kevin thanked Frank and, before it got too dark to see his way, headed down the path toward home. He came out behind the trailer and saw his mom's car, so he took a deep breath and let himself in.

He found his mother sitting on the couch crying, a purplish bruise under one eye, bleeding from a split lip.

Mark was gone.

CHAPTER 2

"Come on, Linda, vacate that bathroom!" Sherry insisted. "Don't make me late for work. Your mom's been ready half an hour now."

"All right, all right." Linda emerged looking quite stylish for somebody anticipating a long day reviewing wire reports in a dingy newspaper city room, then walking around a dirt field taking pictures of the Car Dealers' Association charity fund-raising carnival. "There'll be two good-lookin' Herndon babes out this morning," she explained, "so I had to dress to beat the competition."

"Give it up, girl," warned Sherry as she rushed to claim the open bathroom. Poking her head out the door, she added, "Beside your mom, won't nobody notice you!" She got the door closed just in time to deflect a pillow snatched up and thrown from the couch.

"That's all right, sweetie," interjected Beverly. "If anybody flirts with us, you'll be the one he's interested in."

She'd understated her odds of attracting appreciative men's eyes. Fifty-some years had taken the same distinctive beauty her daughter enjoyed and given it a more dignified, distinguished, yet soft and graceful style. Oh, she showed a few faint lines in her face, but those beautiful, vivid-blue eyes of hers always outshined them, sparkling in the light. She'd swept her hair up in loose waves, letting it fall gently to her ears, set off by several golden tear-drop earrings on either side. She also wore slacks, but with an open-collared blouse of shiny chartreuse. A small, golden butterfly clung to her right collar, and two more festooned the azure handbag that hung by a strap from her shoulder. She boasted several breathtaking rings on each hand, her favorite a cluster of diamonds and sapphires atop a base of cut amethyst that her husband, Marshall, had given her for their 30th wedding anniversary just months before he died.

Too early for brunch at the nearby plaza, they drove to a 24-hour deli-restaurant. As they talked, they reminisced about breakfasting like this back in Michigan during Linda's frequent trips home from the university in Ann Arbor. Sadly, what used to be casual jaunts out together had started to be tainted by concern for Marshall's health and the legal obstacles that troubled him. Then when Linda followed her friend Sherry to Tampa to pursue her career, they realized how much they would miss their spontaneous trips to the store or stopping for a bite to eat.   "If those omelets don't get here soon," Linda said, "we'll get caught in traffic."

"You've got a long day ahead of you, so don't try to come out to my place tonight.

Get some rest. I'll have things organized by the time I'm ready for bed."

"I just wish Loretta was around to help you today."

"Good Lord, I don't. After listening to her constant complaining about all the ungrateful people she devotes her time to, I'm ready for a break."

"Oh, Mom, you know she means well. There's something about old spinsters who aren't getting any."

"No, it's just Loretta. From the time I could walk, she always tried to meddle, from telling me how to dress to how to act. Then when we got older, she used to compete for my friends, too, sticking her nose in until they stayed away from both of us. Oh, I love her—but that doesn't mean I like to spend all day with her."

They had heard Loretta's version many times, that Beverly never kept up on her responsibilities, always letting just anybody make important decisions. It fell to Loretta to worry for both of them.

The waitress finally showed up with two huge omelet platters. After several bites, Linda smiled mischievously. "So, what do you think of that Frank feller? He does order a mean pizza, huh?"

"Oh, he seems very nice. It looks like he'll be a good neighbor as long as he's not coming over bothering me all the time."

"Well, I want you to wait a few weeks before you go jumping his bones."

"Linda!"

"Okay, be old-fashioned and get married first."

Beverly felt a sinking deep inside. She had known this feeling since Marshall's first heart attack, an undercurrent of fear that all too often gave way to overwhelming helplessness and loss. No, Beverly would have new friends—she might even really like another man someday—but she would never marry again. She would never allow herself to get so close that any man would ask.

"Now, let's not turn this into something it's not. He's just my new neighbor, is all."

"Your *new* neighbor is right. Mom, this move is a new beginning for you, a chance to relax and just let whatever happens happen. Be open to any and all possibilities!" She spread her arms and gestured expansively, grinning.

"Yeah, well, I just don't want all these retired guys down here thinking I'm on the prowl."

Linda brought up Frank again several times during the drive out to Tarpon, but Beverly assured her there would be nothing romantic going on. After they pulled into the driveway, Linda got out to open the garage door. Frank's started powering open at the same time. Noticing the silver compact, he grinned and walked over to talk.

"Good morning! I hope you ladies enjoyed your slumber party—you know, pillow fights, prank calls, talking about boys and all that."

"Lordie," Beverly returned, "I just can't keep up with these kids anymore. The prank calls have gotten expensive, too. Now it's 900-numbers."

Linda added, "Yeah, and look who's got the calluses on her dialing finger." She made a show of inspecting her mother's hands.

"I hope you two will forgive me, but I'm late for a meeting with my accountant. I just wanted to ask Beverly for a tremendous favor." He raised his eyebrows and cocked his head. "Will you do me the honor of accompanying me to the yacht club's dinner-dance tonight?" He hastily added, "I know it's very short notice, but I haven't known you long enough to ask any sooner."

"Well, my clothes all need to be dry-cleaned . . ."

He interrupted, "Oh, it's *very* informal. The outfit you're wearing would be perfect. I'd be proud to show up with you on my arm."

Linda caught her mother's eye with a knowing look. "No pressure, Mom. Just say yes and let the man get to his meeting."

Beverly graciously accepted. "If you'll promise to remember that I don't know anybody—and this old girl hasn't been getting out much in recent years. I've forgotten how to act around people, you know."

Frank bowed and tilted his head. "It starts at five, but we can show up any time before seven and still make dinner. If you're home this afternoon, I'll check in so we can synchronize our watches." With that, he was off, leaving Beverly feeling a bit overwhelmed.

Linda grinned and put her arms around her mother from behind. "He likes you," she whispered.

Beverly looked across the road at a single white crane standing in the shallow canal. He looked so lonesome there, all by himself, staring vacantly into the water. "I'm afraid you might be right."

"It looks like I'll have to go back to Cheboygan and see what's going on myself." Frank paced from the filing cabinets to the window twice before stopping to look out from his accountant's second-floor office.

"You could do that, or you could wait two more weeks until I get the numbers from last quarter. I can crunch them in about two days." Frank's Money-grubber was his old friend Henry, who used to take care of most of his corporate accounting when he kept an office up in Milwaukee.

"Maybe you're right. Showing up in the middle of everything could stir up a hornet's nest. I want to have the latest info so I know what I'm talking about."

Frank dreaded spending time in Wisconsin again. Five years ago he'd retired, turning operations and sales over to his partner Jack Taylor's sons. Retirement seemed like the right thing to do. Jack and Frank had spent more than twenty years building up a successful printing company, starting with one reconditioned offset press and handshake credit from their suppliers. Graduating from menus and fliers, they moved more into contractual jobs doing labels, stickers, bar codes and, eventually, appliqués for the auto industry. They continued to expand, adding new clients, several more facilities, and the latest equipment. Frank proved himself the marketing whiz who could finesse clients and contracts. Jack ran a tight, profitable operation that could produce anything Frank promised, always on time, and of the highest quality.

After Jack's oldest son, Doug Taylor, graduated from college, they opened a consumer print shop for him to manage. Specializing in everything from photocopying to wedding announcements, it proved very successful. They had opened two more by the time younger son Junior graduated. Eventually, with eighteen stores from Milwaukee to Ann Arbor, five production plants, and more than a hundred employees, they began grooming Doug to take over running the company. When Jack's prostate surgery and cancer scare coincided with Frank's long-overdue divorce, the partners decided to head for a warmer climate and enjoy the tropical fruits of their work. Doug assumed responsibility for all corporate management while Junior ran the consumer print shops.

Because Frank and Jack were equal partners, each owning half of the company stock, they acted as the board of directors and made Jack's boys salaried employees. Profits continued to grow for the next three years, leveling off in the fourth just about the time Jack died. Jack's ex-wife and their two sons inherited thirds of Jack's stock, or one-sixth of the company each, then started pestering Frank to sell them his half, citing unnamed investors who would finance their acquisition. Frank chose to keep his interest for at least a few more years. He wanted to generate some capital for new business ideas he had been pondering, and figured it would be good to let them accumulate some capital of their own to avoid investors and keep as much stock as possible in the family.

Then what started as a friendly arrangement grew increasingly tainted by financial issues. Casual phone calls started turning into pitches for "board" approval of expensive, ill-conceived expansion or advertising experiments, the most recent a diatribe from the family matriarch, Marta Taylor, arguing that Frank had been carried by Jack's talent and hard work. She felt that her family was entitled to Frank's shares at a fair price, and he should be happy to get that.

That is when the company, still under the tutelage of Doug and Junior, had begun to slide. Up-front costs soared, debts grew, and the company showed a first-time-ever loss. Now Jack's family was sending him confusing financial data, and not even being cooperative about that.

"If I'm going to do this," Frank said, "you might as well come with me."

The accountant ran his fingers through the few remaining gray hairs on his head. "But if I show up with you, they'll really have their backs up."

"That's what I mean. I got a feeling it's gonna get hairy either way; I might as well have ammo with me. I may just need to stay there and take over if they're running it into the ground."

"Or robbing it. You know it looks like they're covering something up."

Frank looked out the window for another moment, then came back over to the desk and took his personal planner from his briefcase. "Open your calendar, Henry. They've got a reason for putting me off two more weeks. Let's show up and see if we can figure out what it is."

"Sorry it took so long, sweetie," announced Ruth Riner, Kevin's mother, as she came into the trailer with a brown bag. "I had to drive clear up to Nelson's. Audrey wasn't working tonight, and that old man wouldn't cash my check."

"Did you get the Mountain Dew?" Kevin asked as he cracked the ice from a blue freezer tray and filled a plastic tumbler.

Ruth unpacked the bag, setting out six quarts of malt liquor, a bottle of Kevin's favorite soda, chips, bread, and a carton of generic cigarettes. "Mama's not gonna forget her little guy."

Kevin made hotdog sandwiches just the way she liked them—a lot of mustard and a touch of ketchup—then set a plate in front of her. Ruth set her cigarette in the ashtray and rubbed eyes, wincing with pain from the one still slightly swollen.

She misted up and announced, "Oh, sweetie, I sure do love you takin' care of me and all, just the way you do." She jumped up and wrapped her arms around him, trying to pick him up in a bear hug like she used to, but discovered he had grown too heavy for her. He hugged back until she let go, then put the condiments back in the fridge. He always felt a little awkward and embarrassed when she started getting maudlin.

"How you gonna explain that black eye at work?"

"I'm not goin' to work tomorrow. I'm gonna call in sick and spend the day with my little man. I'll be able to cover it up with make-up after that. Remember, if anybody asks, I bumped into the cabinet."

In spite of having eaten with Frank just an hour before, he munched voraciously, pausing only long enough to wash mouthfuls down with Dew. Ruth watched, nibbling chips and drinking beer, but ignoring the rest of her food. "So what do you wanna do tomorrow, sweetie? You just name it."

Without looking up, he mumbled, "How about if we clean this place up?"

She watched him eat for a moment, lit another cigarette, and replied, "Okay! We'll get up first thing in the morning and get right on it. You can take charge."

She finally ate one of the hotdog sandwiches, giving the other to Kevin. He wolfed it down, then cleaned up the mess while she parked herself in front of the TV and started her second quart of beer. When Kevin joined her on the couch, she slid over, put her arm around him, and pulled him against her. He rested his head on her shoulder and relaxed for the first time that night. They watched funny shows, sometimes laughing, sometimes making fun of the actors, until he faded into sleep.

He woke up several hours later and found his mother dozing with her head on the arm of the couch, an empty quart bottle on the floor, the ashtray piled with butts. He fetched a blue sheet, spread it over her, cleaned up the ashtray and put the empty bottles under the sink, then stood beside her, looking down at her while she slept. The trailer-park street light cast an orange beam through the window and across her face. He looked at the bruise and the split lip. Standing very still, he watched her breathe. His lower lip quivered and a single tear started down each cheek. He wiped his eyes, leaned over and kissed her gently on the forehead, then slipped down the hallway and into his bedroom.

He let her sleep past noon. When she finally got up, she complained about a severe headache. She took several pills and refused Kevin's offer to make her something to eat. After lying on the couch and puffing down two cigarettes, she finally got up and disappeared into the bathroom. By the time he got her to help start cleaning, it was after 4:00 and her enthusiasm for the job—if she ever had any—was gone. She opened one quart of beer and drank it while she half-heartedly helped straighten up. Then, over the next few hours, she steadily drank her way through all three remaining quarts. The drunker she got, the more she clung to Kevin, hugging him and telling him how lucky she was to have him as her little man. When she got her purse to go down to the corner for more beer, he tried to go with her, but she wouldn't hear of it. "I'll be back in a few minutes, sweetie."

After an hour, he carefully locked the door and walked down to the store. Audrey, the cashier, told him his mother had left quite a while before. Kevin went back home and waited. After another hour, her battered old car drove up. Mark and his mother came in holding hands, both fairly drunk. Ruth looked at Kevin and acted surprised, as if she had forgotten he would be there.

"Look who I saw outside the store, sweetie!"

Before he could reply, she turned and told the interloper to sit, then pulled the small paper bag from Mark's hand and went to the counter, took out two tumblers, wrestled with the ice tray, and poured liberally from the vodka bottle in the sack. She rooted around in the refrigerator, finally settling on Kevin's soda to top off the drinks. She turned on the TV, lit a cigarette from her purse, and joined Mark on the couch with the drinks. They ignored Kevin as he busied himself cleaning up the mess she had just made. He tried to sit on the floor and watch TV, but Mark started kissing on her, and Kevin felt too angry to concentrate on the flickering image.

Mark drained his cup and stood up, pulling Ruth with him. He walked her down the hallway, disappearing into her bedroom and closing the door behind them. Kevin heard his mother squeal and giggle a few times, so he turned up the TV as loud as it would go and sat on the couch, furious. Not long after, Mark emerged from the bedroom stark naked, walked over to the counter, and picked up the vodka bottle. He started back toward the hallway and noticed Kevin glaring at him, open-mouthed, from the couch. "What are you starin' at, faggot? Get your scrawny little ass outta here!"

Kevin jumped up and ran out the trailer toward the path, leaving the door banging against its broken hasp.

"This is so beautiful," she whispered—as if loud noise might make it all go away.

Beverly and Frank stood on the veranda along one side of the yacht club's meeting house. They looked across Tampa Bay, toward the open gulf with its string-sculpture bridge glowing golden in the sunset. A small storm off to the north refracted shades of violet and red in swirling clouds, punctuated with occasional flashes of heat lightning as a warm breeze blew through Beverly's hair. She put her hands on the rail and looked wistfully at a large sloop that floated by, tacking alee to make its way toward a marina in the bay. Frank put one of his hands on the rail beside hers just close enough so they touched. As they stood there quietly drinking in the panorama, two other couples strolled out to join them. Everybody knew Frank, all graciously accepting Beverly like a cherished friend. After several more couples came out to the rail, a waiter started circulating with glasses of champagne and frosty mugs of dark beer.

What a splendid setting, a beautiful evening with wonderful people, yet Beverly never felt more alone. These were not her people. This was not her town. This man beside her—she hardly knew him at all—he was not her man.

She missed Marshall so very much. For most of her life, the two of them had been a team. *Marshall and Bev . . .* It just rolled off the tongue like those two names naturally went together. *It's time to get on with your life, Bev,* she thought. *It hasn't been perfect so far, but it's been damned good. Marshall would tell me to kick up my heels and have some fun for the both of us. Linda . . . Linda's right. "You've still got a lot of livin' in you, Mom,"* she told me. *She always lives life to its fullest—like it comes natural. I just wish it were easier for me.*

She looked up at Frank's face. He seemed somehow to be paying attention to her, even while a fellow yachtsman regaled him with tales of recent fishing escapades like snagging a big porcupine fish, fully bloated, and having no idea how to remove it. Beverly smiled and tried to look interested. Frank reached down and stroked her hand gently, then took it in his. When the storyteller moved to another group, the waiter brought them fresh drinks. Beverly hesitated to take another champagne, but decided it might help her relax.

Frank took her on a tour of the yacht club. They peeked into the grand ballroom where the dinner buffet was being set up, then strolled through the building, admiring artwork, enjoying views out giant plate-glass windows, appreciating the craftsmanship of antique appointments decorating smaller meeting rooms. They walked out on each of the piers to see the more impressive ships, Frank relating anecdotes about the foibles of their owners. They paused a few minutes while he helped a rather tipsy fellow dock his 39-footer. Then he showed her the empty slip where his beloved *Fine Print* would be had he not left it in Destin this month to have a temperamental engine overhauled.

Eventually, they wound up by themselves at one of the gazebos on the waterfront, surrounded by tropical trees, palm and cypress and a giant weeping willow, and beautiful flowers with delicate aromas wafting on the gentle breeze. They sat on a bench facing the bay and gazed silently at the refractions of setting sun splaying colors through the storm clouds on the horizon. *Marshall would have liked this.*

All at once, Beverly again felt awkward and uncomfortable—like she was cheating on her dead husband. She'd let grief come between her and this wonderful man who simply wanted to enjoy an elegant evening in her company.

Frank caught her eyes with a look that seemed to say he would understand. He seemed such a nice man—funny and smart and charming and so self-assured. "It's been a busy week for you; surely you must feel a bit overwhelmed," he whispered.

She shrugged and managed a wan smile. "Yes, it's been quiet the last few years, but you've made my move here so much easier—not just your help, but how you've tried to make me feel at home."

After some gentle prodding, Beverly opened up a little and told him briefly about her husband, he had sold his company and been embroiled in legal disputes, and his subsequent battle with declining health. She tried to describe how she had struggled since his death, trying to spare her daughter the grief of dealing with probate and lawsuits and such. He asked if she would like to hold off signing any legal paperwork or paying off those people until he could look over her papers. She agreed, somewhat surprised at herself. For a woman who always reserved a modicum of suspicion for everybody and everything, she felt strangely safe with Frank. Her intuition said here was a man she could trust.

Turning the tables, she made him recite a brief history of his life, his rise to business success, losing his sister—his last remaining relative—to breast cancer nearly ten years before, and his tumultuous marriage. More than twenty years Frank and Marie had been together. His college sweetheart, he married her, then became a workaholic, trying to be successful and give her the life he thought she deserved. They had been reasonably happy for the first decade or so despite her penchant for spending foolishly and embracing various unusual religions, philosophies, and behavioral fads.

In the later years, though, the situation had become increasingly difficult for him to manage. She blamed him for their inability to have children—despite numerous medical opinions to the contrary. She became addicted to diet pills and tranquilizers, took to binge drinking, wrecked cars, fell prey to scam-artist "friends," and ultimately had several affairs, not bothering to be discreet. She started disappearing for days at a time, finally calling from her new boyfriend's place at Laguna Beach out in California to tell him it was over.

Although she had asked for the divorce, once the proceedings got underway, her phalanx of lawyers and witnesses fought a vicious battle, portraying her as a victim, chasing after every asset and dollar they could get. He ultimately settled for paying a lump sum and ten years' support, only recently expired, that cleaned out his savings, home, cars, and smaller business interests. He survived with his half of the printing company, the vintage Corvette, an apartment lease she had signed during one of her binges, and some well-calculated investments since. She had refused ever to talk to him after that, their only form of contact being her endorsements on the backs of his checks. He admitted he'd kept loving her long after she stopped deserving it, remaining loyal until she refused even to let him try. After losing his print-company partner and lifelong friend, Jack, he was left an aging man with no family—only memories and a few regrets.

He asked Beverly about her family. She explained how Marshall had been the last survivor in his, and that she and Loretta were the last in hers—except for Linda, the sparkle in her life. She told him how Loretta had been engaged five times—near as she could count—but had never made it to the altar. Employed half-time as a nurse, Loretta spent the rest of her time in volunteer work trying to buy friendships from people who only took advantage of her. When Beverly talked about her daughter, her face softened with pride and radiated love. Linda had been the perfect little girl— Daddy's princess—who excelled in school, collected and nursed stray or wounded animals, and had a talent and passion for photography.

"I couldn't have got through these last few years without her. We've come full circle. Now *she* worries after *me* all the time!" Beverly laughed and looked across the water. They sat quietly for a moment; then Frank reached up and brushed her cheek lightly with the back of his hand . . .

"All right, you two! It's time to eat. Let's get to the banquet room!" It was Larry, the tipsy fellow who'd had so much trouble docking earlier. They walked back and joined the crowd in the beautifully decorated dining room. They sat at a large round table, set for ten and boasting a gorgeous floral centerpiece. Animated and friendly, everybody shared stories and jokes. Sometimes Beverly still felt overwhelmed—out of place, alone, even slightly afraid, but Frank seemed to sense this and made every effort to be the attentive escort. They received several invitations together—an informal dinner, a weekend on the yacht, an evening around the barbecue—but Frank begged off, citing a pending business trip that would have him out of town for an indeterminate period.

After waiters cleared the tables, the lights darkened and the room filled with the twinkling of a million miniature white Christmas lights. A musical group took the stage, filling the air with hauntingly beautiful melodies and harmonies.

People drifted off to chat with others, refresh drinks, or dance. Frank looked over to Beverly and grinned mischievously. He looked so handsome in his light-green polo shirt and tan chinos. Well over six-feet tall, a little on the slim side, he had a muscular build and short salt & pepper hair, except for that shock combed across his thinning pate and a small tail in back. His deep tan, perfect pearly teeth, and shiny hazel eyes somehow made him look gallant and charming. They sat quietly, drinking in the music.

After several songs, Frank took her by the hand and led her onto the dance floor. He put his arms around her and started to move gently back and forth. Feeling awkward and stiff, she tried her best to follow. He felt strong and had a nice, musky fragrance mingling with the scent of his aftershave. Pinpoints of light sparkled in every direction. Velvet chords cascaded from the speakers, building layers of beautiful music. Ribbons of breathy sax riffs floated around the room, encircling the two of them, lifting them as they flowed with every rivulet of sound. When she danced, Frank stayed right there in sync. When she relaxed, he led, supporting her in his arms, taking her with the rhythm. Beverly sensed the tension slipping away. Maybe it was the champagne, or maybe just being so tired, but all at once she felt tears in her eyes, and she buried her face in his chest. He danced them to the outskirts of the crowd where she stood trembling while he held her tight.

The twinkling lights seemed to swirl around the dance floor. The music flowed in and out of her, taking with it all of the pain and fear that weighed so heavily in her heart. This night, right there in the ballroom of some Tampa yacht club, in the arms of a man she barely knew, the sounds and the lights and the smells and his strong arms all conspired to carry her away.

Even after the music stopped, they stood there together in the dark corner, surrounded by sparkles while he held her close.

CHAPTER 3

Splash!

Sherry swam out several yards and turned, treading water, then raised her arms and eyebrows in the look of, *Well, what are you waiting for?* Linda stood on the edge of the pontoon boat, clad in a fluorescent-orange bikini.

"Is it cold?"

"Naw! Come on in. Don't dive, though; it's not very deep."

Linda turned and mugged at Beverly and Aunt Loretta sitting on the bench seats at the other end. "What do you think? Pull up anchor and skedaddle out of here before Sherry can get back?"

Loretta scowled. Beverly smiled and bent over the rail, grabbing the anchor rope like she really intended to pull it up.

Splash! Linda hit the water, too. "Come on in, Mama! It's nice."

Beverly sported a one-piece swimsuit patterned with a brilliant floral design, plus sunglasses and a newly-purchased straw hat tied with pink ribbon. Loretta wore shorts, a mannish polo shirt, deck shoes with short socks and, reluctantly, a similar straw hat with yellow ribbon. An obvious pair of tourists.

"You, too, Aunt Loretta. Just take your stuff off and get in. Nobody cares if you do a little skinny-dipping."

Sherry added, "Maybe you two can lure a boat-load of guys over here for us. Let's get this party kicking."

Loretta just scowled. Beverly walked over to the ladder and sat on the edge, dangling her legs in the water. "It *is* nice," she observed. "I'm used to that cold water up in Houghton Lake. Used to be, I could only stand to lake-swim during a month or two in late summer."

"Swim around the whole lake, for all I care," Loretta remarked. "I'm fine." With that, she sat back and opened one of her magazines.

Beverly joined them for a while, then climbed the ladder and fished her towel from the travel tote she had brought. "You should have brought a swimsuit, Lor; it's so pretty out here."

It *was* a beautiful day: warm sunshine, a soft breeze carrying the scent of flowers across the smooth surface of a blue, spring-fed lake, and lots of big pretty birds circling in the air or perching on branches along the shore. To Beverly it seemed idyllic, complemented by the vision of two beautiful young women playing and splashing nearby, one of whom she loved with all her heart.

I should have moved down here sooner, she thought. *I'll never live away from my little girl again.*

"What did Stockbridge say about that?" Loretta asked, interrupting her younger sister's reverie.

"Huh? What?"

"What did the lawyers say?"

"Everything's moving along all right."

"Well, how much longer is it going to take?"

"I don't know, Lor. He's working on it."

"Well, I think you oughta tell him—"

"I'm not telling him anything until I get copies and see what it's all about." Right after Marshall died, the distraught new widow had let down her guard, allowing Loretta access to too much information. Now living so close, she feared having to deal with her sister's nosiness even more.

It would be different if she thought Loretta's intentions were good, but there always seemed to be an element of self-interest in everything she did. She had hounded Marshall to invest in various schemes of hers, but after listening patiently to her proposals, he always gently turned her down, later confiding to Beverly that she just didn't understand how to set up and run an enterprise. Finally she moved to Florida, ostensibly to have more opportunities for charity work with the elderly, but really to chase a man—a former co-worker from the convalescent center where she'd practiced as a registered nurse. After he rebuffed her, she stayed in the south, hoping her prospects would improve.

"Well, why don't you let me come over and look at—"

"It's *handled*, Loretta."

"But you don't know what—"

"Frank is going to advise me. He knows all about this stuff."

"Frank? Frank!" Loretta was aghast. "But you hardly know him. He's just a stranger. You can't trust him—"

"Loretta, let me handle it. It's nothing you need to worry about."

"You two play nice, now," interrupted Linda, climbing the ladder. She stood dripping on the deck, running fingers through her hair. The sun glistened on her wet skin and highlighted her beautiful blond locks. Sherry climbed up, dug several towels from a tote stashed under the seat, and handed one to Linda.

Loretta sat back and pretended to read her magazine. Linda pulled up the anchor, swishing off the mud while Sherry started the engine.

Beverly fished out a hairbrush and sat on the bench opposite Loretta, combing out the water. "Have you ever been out on Lake Tarpon before, Loretta?"

"No, but it sure is pretty."

With that, they headed off on their tour, the tension broken, but not entirely gone. They cruised around the east end of the lake, near some condos, admiring the houses on the rise, watching cranes and a huge heron wading in the marsh along the shore, laughing at the comic antics of a pelican balancing on a pole.

Snapping occasional photos, Linda pointed out that only two miles that-a-way is where her mother now lived. Eventually, they headed toward the camping and picnic area, nosing up to a wooded embankment punctuated with cypress knees jutting from the water. Linda pulled them in with a branch and tied off the anchor line.

"Before we unload the goodies and stuff," Linda instructed, "let's get the senior ladies on shore and find some of them big toads."

She handed her aunt and mother up onto the bank, reminding them to be still and keep quiet, then stalked around the picnic area set off by cut railroad ties and floored with pebble-gravel and wood chips. Spying her goal, she reached down into the undergrowth and snatched up the biggest toad Beverly had ever seen. Squealing with delight, she held him up, one hand around his belly. He looked as big as a bas-ketball—especially with those long legs hanging down. The toad seemed uncon-cerned—until he sprayed a long and impressive stream of urine. Not surprised by this common defense, Linda held him away from herself, pointing the toad's ammunition into the brush. Everybody laughed except Loretta, who looked rather disgusted. Re-ally, a slimy toad; who could think it was cute?

Linda held him up and talked silly-talk to him—"You're such a pretty toad, yes you are!"—before heading off for some nearby picnic areas to find cat food. Back in less than a minute, she put a handful on the ground, cautioned everybody to hold very still, and set the toad down next to it.

He sat there for several minutes, apparently enjoying the warm sun on his back. Beverly was used to seeing small toads in Michigan, but this one looked absolutely impressive. She noticed that his skin, though covered with a plethora of "warts," boasted a beautiful and intricate pattern of browns and reds, almost iridescent.

Blrrup!

Linda giggled and whispered, "Didja see it? Didja see it?" Sherry giggled, too.

Blrrup! He did it again. Linda snapped his picture, delighted with her shot.

"Oh Christ. I'm watching a toad eat cat food," Loretta remarked, rolling her eyes.

They spent the afternoon grilling and snacking on jumbo shrimp and crab legs— "On the grill?" Loretta asked—and enjoying each other's company. When Linda and Sherry set off in search of more toads and subjects to photograph, Loretta tried again to talk about money. Beverly kept changing the subject.

"Well, you better not let that Frank get into your business," she advised.

Beverly didn't respond. She was watching the biggest toad of all as he sat under the edge of an oversized fern, gazing unconcernedly at the two women.

He seemed to be just about as interested as Beverly in Loretta's advice.

"Nice boat, Frank!"

"You like it? She's my baby. It was all I could do to afford her after my ex cleaned me out."

Rob Buchanan, private investigator—offices in Milwaukee and Cheboygan—stood on the pier admiring *Fine Print*, Frank's 69-footer. Like a lost puppy, she'd found her way home from Destin, one of her twin in-board engines overhauled and humming as much as a big diesel can hum. Frank stood on the foredeck, pointing toward the gang-plank.

"You got bedrooms on this thing?"

"Four staterooms, four heads, a shower, and a sundeck that's rumored to be addictive." He handed the investigator up and offered him a brief tour. In the larger room, he introduced him to Kevin, the boy on his knees unpacking boxes and putting supplies into a cabinet.

"You a private eye?" Kevin asked. Short and bald, overweight and overdressed in this heat, he looked unkempt, more like a criminal.

"Yep, that's what we's called sometimes."

"I hope you help Frank save his company."

Rob looked at Frank questioningly, investigators being reluctant to comment about cases except to their clients.

"Yeah, me too," Frank added. "I need the money—the boy's labor is *not* cheap."

"And he works me to death, too. I'm thinking of reporting him to somebody."

Rob smiled and gestured at the satchel under his arm. "Well, I *do* have some things you'll find *very* interesting. If you'd like to get started—"

The two men went up and sat in deck chairs opposite each other. Rob pulled a sheaf of papers from his satchel. "Well, I still got a lot of digging to do, but your instincts was right. They're pulling a scam on ya."

Kevin brought up two frosty beer bottles with one hand, a bowl of trail mix in the other, a jar of macadamia nuts and bag of cheese puffs under either elbow. He set all the goodies off to one side.

"What service!" clucked the investigator.

"Yeah," Kevin retorted, "I'm trying to impress the old geezer to give me a raise."

Frank added, "Yeah, he's all right—but I have to keel-haul him sometimes to keep him in line." After Kevin saluted and disappeared, Frank continued, "So whatcha got?"

"Well there was thirty-eight vendors on the list you gave me. I started with the ones where they spent the most money this year. The first two didn't seem like nothin' strange, but after that it started gettin' real interesting." He took a long draught of his beer and wiped the sweat from his forehead. Frank sat quietly and waited. "It seems one outfit outta some town near Ann Arbor is getting all of your paper-stock business now—more than eleven-mill a year. At that level, you'd think they'd be a corporation, at least. Turns out it's just a DBA, filed with Washtenaw County *doing business as* Pittsfield Paper. It's run out of an upstairs room in Depot Town with no phones and no employees. Guess who's the principals?"

"All three of 'em?"

"No, actually, just Mrs. Taylor and somebody named Elijah Rumsey."

"Rumsey? Seems like I've run into that name somewhere before. Elijah doesn't sound familiar, though. Elijah Rumsey . . .""

"I don't have much on him yet, but I did find the boys' names on other DBAs. Plus, the ink company is a Michigan corporation—also filed to do business in Wisconsin. Not one of 'em actually have all three names on them."

Frank stood up and walked to the rail, his face creased with thought. Rob drained the last of his beer and poured some nuts into his grubby hand, downing the whole mouthful at once.

"Hey, Frank!" It was Larry, the ever-tipsy fellow who had needed Frank's help docking *Lorna's Egg Money* that night of the dance. "How's it hangin'?"

"To the left, Larry—to the left."

Larry sauntered by as Kevin came down the pier carrying three large sacks, having trouble seeing around them.

Frank headed down to help, asking Rob if he was ready for another beer. He grabbed the sacks so Kevin could trot back for more supplies. Frank set them aside, went to the galley, and headed back up, handing a bottle to Rob as he sat down. "How many?"

"Well, we checked twenty so far—the biggest ones anyway—and found twelve smelling bad. And that's not to say somethin' ain't been arranged with any of the legit ones, either. Three of 'em—" He turned the list toward Frank and indicated the ones with red check marks. "I called the ones that used to get your business and pretended to be from these new companies. All three of 'em, somebody came on like they knew who I was. I acted like it was a mistake and got off real quick. I didn't want to call any more before talking to you 'cause I didn't wanna tip too many of 'em off."

"Yeah, that's good." Frank rubbed his jaw and looked out across the bay, still thinking.

"I guess it's pretty obvious your partners is just setting themselves up little businesses to be the middlemen. They's buying your supplies and stuff, then selling it to your print company at big markups."

"Yeah," Frank agreed. "Not only do they make a big profit for themselves, but they cut me out of making anything from the company at the same time. I wonder if this is a ploy toward offering to buy me out."

"What better way to do it than knock its value way down—even put it in the red for a while to make you squirm. They buy you out cheap—or even stick you with some bills—then turn it around and make it profitable again after you're gone."

"Damn, Money-grubber was right. A lot of those vendors came *up* with us—good, honest people trying to make a living—some with us from the beginning. It just didn't look right to see all those new names in the ledgers."

"What do you want me to do next? Keep runnin' down the ownerships?"

"Yeah—but don't call any more of the old vendors. I'll check a few myself. I know which ones'll be straight with me if we're discreet. You keep running down the ownerships, dates of establishment, and such. Start a run on tax, regulatory, and license records for all thirty-eight, too. I need a complete list of who's a scam, and it wouldn't hurt to see if any look dirty other ways."

"You got it, boss. I'll be needin' more scratch." He fished out a detailed invoice and slid it across the table. Kevin came up and cleared the empty bottles, disappearing again below deck.

"When are you heading up?" Frank asked.

"Tomorrow morning. I'm gonna hit Tampa tonight and try to find some of that Florida nookie."

Frank looked over the invoice. "I'll have it wired up to your office in the morning—should be there before you land."

After the investigator left, Frank sat back and rubbed his jaw some more. Kevin stole up quietly and sat across from him. After a moment, Frank smiled and asked if everything was loaded.

Kevin nodded and looked at Frank curiously, shading his eyes from the bright sun. "Frank, what's nookie?"

Frank was looking him over, Kevin suddenly self-conscious. Hey, it's not like he's too young to know.

"It's a woman who fools around with you—you know, just sex—not like when you're in love with her."

Kevin thought about that for a minute. That must mean his mother is nookie if she lets Mark do it with her. He didn't like the idea of that, not one bit. "Did you find out what you needed?"

"Yes, I did. They're ripping me off—big time. It doesn't seem to be anything blatantly illegal, though."

"Well, just make 'em stop."

"It's not that easy. The boys run the company. They're the ones who make those decisions."

"Then fire 'em."

"Well, it takes a majority of the board to fire an officer—and I'm not a majority. I only own half and they control the other half. I'm not sure what I can do about it now, but I'll figure something out. I just need to get a handle on what's going on first."

"You're smarter than they are, Frank."

Frank looked at him and smiled. Kevin had been coming around since Frank's retirement to Florida. Afraid of being a pest at first, he'd finally decided the older fellow did enjoy spending time with him. Kevin used to regret not knowing his own father, but then he'd decided the man must be no good and that was for the best.

"Let's go, hoodlum. I'm taking Beverly and her daughter out for dinner tonight. I need to get cleaned up and make some calls."

They secured the boat and headed up the pier toward the club. Several seagulls circled over them, searching for scraps of food.

Tipsy Larry, sitting on his forward deck, watched them until they were out of sight.

Kevin stood on the milk crate and peered into the window. His mother's car gone and no sign of Mark, he went inside. The house sure smelled funny, an unfamiliar scent mixed with the all-too-common odor of alcohol. His mother hadn't left a note, so he called the drugstore and learned she'd not shown up all day. He went back to her closed bedroom door and knocked, quietly at first, then louder. He pushed his way inside and found nobody, but that stench got really strong.

He noticed an odd collection of paraphernalia on the dresser: a plastic tumbler with some dirty liquid in the bottom, a bent coat hanger with a burnt cotton swab twisted around the end, and a small glass container with a rubber stopper in it. Several tubes protruded from its neck, one flared at the end with a burnt silver screen in the top. A sticky, brown, dirty-looking film coated much of the inside. He had seen this on TV. Mark was getting his mom to smoke crack.

He carried everything to the kitchen sink, poured out the liquid, then put the other items into a paper sack and rolled it up tightly. He went outside, set it on the sidewalk, crushed it under his foot, and walked to the other end of the trailer park so he could put it in the far trash bin, burying it under a lot of debris. He hurried back inside and started to straighten up.

In his bedroom, several things looked amiss, like maybe it had been searched. Panicked, he pulled his dresser away from the wall, lifted the heat-vent cover off, and reached inside for the small plastic box. It was empty, his money gone. There was supposed to be more than $300 in there—money he had saved from his earnings with Frank. Furious, he stood up and kicked the dresser. He paced back and forth several times, then replaced everything the way he had found it.

He went back out to the living room, opened all the windows, turned on a fan, and sat on the couch to wait—for his mother, for Mark, for whomever would come home first. He knew his mother would never steal his money—even if she had known where it was. It had to be Mark. He took Kevin's money so he could buy more crack so he could get high and make his mother get high so he could get more nookie and just keep messing up his mom's life.

Kevin would do something about it—what, he had no idea—but this would have to stop.

Dinner at the yacht club proved quite a treat. Afterwards, they strolled outside along the waterfront and down to the piers. The sun had set, so the soft glow of orange and yellow lights hidden discreetly in recesses lit their route as Frank led Beverly and Linda to the *Fine Print* for an after-dinner bottle of wine.

With all three seated above deck, he dimmed the lamps, revealing a darkening velvet sky full of twinkling stars, a thin sliver of moon accenting the perfect backdrop. A gentle breeze had finally stirred after such a hot, still day. Soft splashes punctuated the quiet, snappers feeding on insects attracted to lights along the pier.

They chatted about many things, with Frank seeming especially fascinated by Linda's exploits seeking the Pulitzer Prize-winning photograph and her mother's tales of life on the lake up north. Clearly sensitive to Beverly's feelings about her lost husband, he let her tell the stories she felt like sharing, careful not to pry too much about any particular topic. Finally, Beverly asked if he had any opinions to offer about the papers she had given him.

"To be honest, Bev, I think your attorneys are trying to bamboozle you. My first advice is not to sign or agree to anything. They're trying to settle now because they know the gravy train is about to derail, one way or another. A friend of mine tells me that, in Florida, those trusts can be transferred to the heirs of the beneficiary—without the discretionary stipulations—simply by petitioning the probate court. Then any parties that challenge it have to demonstrate that their interests—in your case, the bank and lawyer—are greater or more in line with the intent of whoever set it up. They wouldn't have a chance in hell of getting anything except a few bucks for administrative and legal costs—and I think they know it."

Frank poured more wine for Linda and continued, "Problem is, that's Florida law. I called a lawyer I know in Michigan and asked him to have his clerk see if it's the same up there. He said he thinks it is."

"So I should wait a little longer," Beverly asked, "and see what he finds out?"

"Yes, and there's two things you should do in the meantime. First, we need to fax a notice to Stockbridge tomorrow morning—and send a copy by registered mail—telling him not to take *any* more action on your case. You need to draw a line so he can't keep billing hours to you."

"Do you think he's been overcharging so far?" Linda asked.

"No question. He's claiming more than a hundred-thousand in costs for something that should have been a fraction of that. Later, we can refuse to pay his bill and let him sue you. Then the burden of proof will be on him to justify the reasonableness of the hours he's claiming."

Beverly thought for a minute, then asked, "What's the other thing I should do?"

"Well, you need to go through all your personal papers—everything Marshall stashed away, too—and find anything and everything that shows the relationship between Charles and your husband. You may need to argue the *intent* of that will and trust fund. Personal letters, notes, any references to his intentions for that money—in the absence of anything stronger, that should be enough."

"I'll help, Mama."

Frank added, "You can take your time on that one. We may be able to pressure them without having to go that far."

"Thanks, Frank. I wish somebody had explained it to me this way before."

"Everybody involved—even the ones supposedly representing your interests—have a personal stake in delaying and driving up the costs. It's time for *you* to take charge."

Yes, Beverly thought, *it's time I take charge.*

They chatted a while longer, then listened to fish lapping the water. Wisps of cloud floated in front of the fingernail-crescent moon, casting refracted and broken beams every direction, reflecting every possible shade of violet across the sky. It got late early, so they closed up to go home. Linda lived fairly close and had her own car there, so Beverly rode back with Frank in his Corvette.

Outside the condo, they said good night. Frank took her hand in his and squeezed, not letting go, then put his arms around her. Tense at first, she relaxed and rested her head against his chest. He held her tighter and gently stroked down her back with one hand. It made her tingle all over, rippling out in soft waves that both surprised and reminded her how wonderful it can feel to be held this close.

"Frank!" screamed Kevin. "Oh, Frank!" He burst from the woods and tried to talk, but he started crying.

Frank grabbed him by the arms and forced him to make eye contact. "Kevin! Kevin, what is it? What's wrong?"

Beverly stood by, feeling helpless.

"She's in jail. She called me from jail." He could hardly catch his breath to talk. He wiped tears from his face and continued. "My mom called from Pinellas County Jail and said she was arrested. She was cryin' and I couldn't hardly understand her.

She sounded all funny."

Frank put an arm around him and held tight. "We'll find out what happened and see what we can do."

Beverly whispered, "Don't worry, Kevin, Frank won't let you down. He's good at taking care of things. It'll be okay."

They walked him into Frank's place. Still sniffling and wiping his face, he sat on the couch. Beverly went to get some drinks, pouring the boy a big glass of Mountain Dew, while Frank called information for the number of the jail in Clearwater. Beverly sat with Kevin while Frank went in the other room to make the call. For ten minutes she kept the boy talking, asking about his favorite TV shows and music and such.

Finally, Frank came out looking somewhat frustrated, but putting on a good face. He sat in a chair and explained, "Well, she's okay. She got in some trouble with Mark and has to go to court the day after tomorrow. I won't be able to find out much until tomorrow. Kevin, I want you to know I'm going to look out for you *and* your mom."

"You can count on that," Beverly affirmed.

"Listen, you stay here tonight. That's what the guest bedroom is for—for when *friends* stop by and stay however long they want. Why don't you dig some of your clothes out of the cabinet and go wash up. I'll get a bed ready so you can get some rest."

Kevin stood up and started to go, then stopped and looked at Frank again. His lower lip quivered ever so slightly. "Thanks, Frank."

"Hey, you would do the same for me, wouldn't you, hoodlum?"

Kevin nodded, lingered for a moment, then went out to get his clothes. Frank watched, not saying anything. Kevin came back through, carrying a bundle down the hallway and into the bathroom.

Beverly whispered, "Frank, what happened?"

"I don't know; they wouldn't tell me much except that she'll be arraigned the morning after next." He shook his head and looked down the hallway.

"For what?"

"They're charging her with murder."

CHAPTER 4

The next morning seemed a blur for everyone. Up very early and on the phone, Frank lined up a lawyer for Ruth, arranged to have funds wired to Investigator Buchanan's office, canceled his plans with a friend from the yacht club, and left instructions for Money-grubber to have a letter drawn up ordering Stockbridge to cease any activity on Beverly's claim, then to have it couriered to his place for Beverly's signature. He checked with the jail again to confirm visiting hours and policies, called his house-keeper to give her the day off, rescheduled an appointment with his broker, and arranged for his bank to confirm his liquid funds in case he needed bail or lawyer money.

Frank looked up at one point and saw Kevin watching him. The boy had never looked so fragile and scared. He sent him off to the guest bathroom to take a shower. Just then, Beverly called and told him breakfast would be ready soon, could they come over in fifteen minutes? Grateful, Frank asked for twenty and headed for the shower in his own private bath.

Beverly had a full spread laid out with fresh fruit, warm toast under a cloth napkin, miniature sausages on a platter, a pitcher of orange juice alongside a glass of milk for Kevin, and omelet fixins ready to cook. Confirming that both liked cheese, onions, and peppers, she quickly turned out three big, fluffy beauties and joined them at the table. She assured Kevin that he should only eat as much as he wanted. Frank wasn't surprised when he out-ate them both, wondering that surely he must have hollow legs.

Frank took Kevin to the living room while Beverly straightened up. He explained that visiting hours didn't start until 1:00, but that they needed to go see lawyers and take care of other things in the meantime. "Do you want to stay here with Beverly until visiting time, or go around with me?"

"I want to know everything going on."

"Sure, sure. Your mom needs your help—our help—now, and you're smart enough to handle yourself okay. But if you change your mind, you just let me know. You can tell me *anything* you want to say, okay?"

Kevin nodded. Frank knew he could ask him to jump off a bridge right then and he would—that's how much the boy trusted him. "Do you want to invite Beverly to come along in case there's something she can do, too?"

"Yeah, I like her a *lot.*"

They took her car, since the Corvette was a two-seater. After several stops, they wound up at a law office. Mr. Mogill came out to greet them, then led them to a big, wood-appointed office and offered refreshments. He looked toward Kevin, then back at Frank. Frank told him he could talk freely.

"Well, I confirmed it. She's to be arraigned tomorrow on a charge of open murder."

"Murder?" Kevin's eyes went wide.

"What have you found out?" Frank asked.

"Apparently, there was a robbery at a suspected crack house early last night. One man wound up dead of a gunshot wound; another is in critical condition—which means it could turn into two murder charges. Arrested in a car just a few miles from the scene were a Mark Sisk and a Ruth Riner—" He looked over at Kevin. "The car was registered in her name. A gun and good-sized quantity of what appears to be crack cocaine, plus a baggie of marijuana, were recovered from the vehicle. No statements were made. Both parties requested attorneys. At this point, that's about all I could find out."

"What's the next step?"

"Well, if you—if she wants, I'll interview her, file a notice of representation, and talk to the assistant prosecutor. I won't learn much until after the arraignment tomorrow morning."

"How much?" Frank asked.

"Well, I get two-hundred dollars an hour, and I'll need to start with a ten-thousand-dollar retainer. Once we see what we're up against, we can talk about a package. Until then, I don't know."

"Can we have a few minutes?" Frank asked, glancing toward Beverly. The cost had surprised her, but Frank already made the promise, and in an instant he knew no amount of money would be worth letting down his young friend.

"Certainly. Take your time. Just signal my secretary when you're ready."

After he left, Frank explained to Kevin that his mother might be eligible for a public defender, but that he was willing to pay for a private attorney—at least through the arraignment—until they could assess the situation. "How do you feel about this guy? Do you have confidence in him, or should we talk to some others?"

"I think he's good," Kevin answered. "You decide, though, Frank. I don't know about this stuff."

"We can always replace him later if we aren't satisfied."

When Mogill came back, Frank told him he would need to have Ruth agree before he would pay a retainer. Mogill said he would go over that morning and meet with her privately.

"We're hoping to go see her at one when visiting hours begin," Frank explained.

"Hmmm. That might be a problem. You're not related to the boy—er, Kevin—are you?"

"Uh, no." Frank hadn't really thought about that being a problem.

"They're not going to let a non-relative bring in an undocumented minor. If you like, I can have her execute an affidavit during our meeting."

"Yes. Yes, definitely."

That settled, they agreed to meet afterward for lunch at a restaurant on Clearwater Drive.

They drove back to Frank's and picked up the letter for Stockbridge. Beverly signed, and Frank faxed it from his office in the condo. He made copies for himself, Beverly, and Money-grubber, then packaged it for overnight delivery and called for a pick-up, leaving it in the box out front. Beverly called to update Linda while Frank talked with Kevin about staying at the condo for a while—until they could get things worked out. He wanted it to be clear that all important decisions would involve them both.

Since they had time to spare, they went by the trailer so Kevin could pack up some of his clothes and possessions. Police must have entered with a search warrant, tearing up or scattering what they didn't destroy, the floor piled with debris.

Kevin took one look and froze. Beverly went over to the kitchen and started putting things back into cabinets. Frank and Kevin worked their way into his room and sacked up his clothes, an album of photographs, his video game and cartridges, and other meager treasures. He took some things from his mother's room, including a shoe box of papers gathered up from the floor. They locked the doors and put the sacks in the trunk, Kevin trying not to look back.

During the drive to Clearwater, nobody could think of anything to say. Kevin sat in the back seat by himself, usually looking out the side window.

Beverly finally interrupted his reverie, turning around to look right at him. "Kevin, I haven't known you nearly as long as Frank has, but I want you to understand you can count on me, too." Kevin glanced toward Frank's face in the rear-view mirror, then allowed a hint of a smile. "Is that okay?" she asked.

He nodded. "Frank was right about you."

"Oh?"

"Yeah," Frank interrupted. "I told him you're a rare jewel with a heart of gold. Hoodlum said he already knew it, but that he was glad *I* could tell, too."

They met Mr. Mogill and ordered some sandwiches. The lawyer gave Frank a copy of the affidavit and assured Kevin that his mother was okay. "I want you to know she did *not* kill anybody. I won't say she didn't make a big mistake—she had no business going out with that guy or getting involved with illegal drugs—but she *was* at the wrong place at the wrong time. She wouldn't even talk about her case until I assured her you were all right and that Frank would look out for you. She's looking forward to seeing you this afternoon."

"So what's the bottom line?" Frank asked.

"Well, she wanted me. In fact, she was *very* grateful you had sent me."

"Good." Frank took a check from his wallet and handed it across the table. It disappeared faster than a playing card in a magic act.

"The arraignment," continued Mogill, "will be a simple reading of the charge. I'll ask for a low bond so she can get out of jail. The prosecutor will ask for no bond or a very high bond. Hopefully, the judge will set something reasonable and allow us to post ten percent. You need to think about how high you're *willing* to go. He'll set a date for preliminary exam within the next two weeks. Until then, I'll be dogging the prosecutor and the detective-in-charge to see what they have for a case. Obviously, we want to have it dismissed at that point. If not, we'll see if we need to cut a deal or go to trial."

"What else can we do now?"

"Trust me to take care of business."

A full docket of arraignments took place before the magistrate in a small, sterile room crowded with families, two reporters, and a photographer. Mr. Mogill was nowhere in sight.

One-by-one, prisoners entered wearing orange and blue jumpsuits. Each stood next to an attorney at a podium, heard charges read, then put a plea of "not guilty" on the record or had their lawyers indicate that they would "stand mute." Most were allowed bond, usually in the $250 to $500 range.

Mogill came in through a side door and approached Frank. "We're ready now." Ruth came in, flanked by uniformed officers on each side. Manacled at the ankles, her wrists cuffed, she looked at Kevin, managed a weak smile, and mouthed the words *I love you!* She looked disheveled, her hair tangled and unwashed, no make-up at all. The photographer snapped several shots.

Mogill indicated that he would represent Ruth Lynn Riner, waived a reading of the charge, offered that she would stand mute, and requested examination. The magistrate set a date for a week from Tuesday.

An assistant prosecutor asked that bond be denied. Mogill made an eloquent speech about Ruth's standing in the community, support of friends like Frank, and her need to care for a son. He argued there was no risk of flight or danger to the public. The magistrate glanced toward the reporters, then denied bond. Led away, Ruth looked back at her son just before the steel door clanged shut.

Mogill went over to the trio, motioning them to sit back down. He stood next to them and whispered, "Let's see what happens with Mark Sisk."

Mark came in dressed in a similar jumpsuit. An attorney identified himself as a public defender. A "stand mute" was entered for him and, during the discussion about bond, Mark gave Ruth's address as his own. The photographer snapped several shots, then packed up and left. Bond denied, he shot a menacing glare at Kevin as he was taken away.

Mogill led them out into a hallway. He told them it had gone much as he expected. In the meantime, they should try to keep Ruth's spirits up, visit, send letters, and deposit a small amount of money in her jail account so she could buy toiletries and snacks. "She's fairly distraught now, worried about Kevin. Keep showing her that he's doing fine so she can concentrate on helping me with her defense."

Mogill left to take care of other business he had pending in the same building. Kevin continued to remain stoic. They walked out to Beverly's car, Frank taking the wheel and suggesting they find someplace for a light, early lunch. Kevin sat in back again and continued to be quiet, but he turned and buried his face in his arms against the side window. Frank headed across the causeway toward the beaches, then stopped at a small place and whispered to Beverly that he would get some fast carry-out and be right back.

Alone together in the car, she talked quietly to the boy. "What you did in there was wonderful, Kevin."

He raised his head and looked at her questioningly, wiping his eyes. "What did *I* do?"

"You were there showing your mom support. You made it look like you were confident in Mogill and that you believed everything would be okay. You can't imagine how much she needed to see that." Kevin considered what she was saying. "It's okay to be scared or even cry sometimes, but you need to be brave, too. She's pretty lucky to have you."

"I just wish I knew everything *would* turn out okay."

"That's the way the world works, sweetheart. Life sometimes offers cruel surprises, but what matters most is that you stick by the people you care about—who care about you—and make the best of whatever comes your way."

"Like Frank."

"Yes, just like Frank. Give me a hug?" she asked. Across the back of the seat, she held him tightly, whispering in his ear, "One thing is pretty obvious: he sure cares about you." She felt his hug tighten for a moment before he let go and sat back. He wiped his face again and looked more content than he had since he'd run up, hysterical, two nights before, interrupting Frank and Beverly's embrace.

"Burgers all around!" Frank announced, climbing back into the car. He looked carefully at Kevin and, apparently satisfied, started the engine and drove out along the shore. They stopped and took their lunch to a bench where they sat quietly and ate, with Kevin tossing bread crumbs to the growing flock of squawking gulls. They all laughed as he started throwing pieces up for them to catch in mid-air. Afterward, Kevin packed up their refuse and put it in a nearby barrel.

"Are we in a hurry?" he asked. "Can I walk down and see what's there? I've never been here before."

"Get lost, hoodlum. Try to be back in less than half an hour, though. I need to call and cancel tomorrow's trip up north."

Kevin took off with all the enthusiasm of an explorer in a new land. Frank gazed at Beverly for a moment, then quietly apologized for dragging her into such a mess.

"You didn't drag me into anything, Frank."

"In this day and age, most people don't want to get involved."

"Many of us are blessed," she observed. "Others need someone to lend a hand. Back in Michigan I used to be a foster mother whenever they needed a short-term home for abused or neglected kids. Marshall . . ." She looked off into the distance. "He used to say as long as our home was big enough, then our hearts certainly had the room." She looked at Frank and smiled.

"With Kevin . . ." He paused, having difficulty finding the words. "Well, the little hoodlum's been coming around, looking for attention, trying awful hard ever since I moved here. He was only about eight years old then."

"He doesn't have to try hard with a pushover like you."

"I always thought I would be a good dad—you know, at least better than *my* father."

"You *are* a giver, Frank. I like that."

They looked at each other; then Frank leaned over and kissed her, both surprised by the depth and intensity as she kissed back.

Beverly whispered in his ear, "Oh Frank, I never expected . . ."

They kissed again, long and deep. Waves lapped against the rocks. Circling gulls squawked for more bread crumbs. Bringing squeals of laughter from the beach, the warm breeze that flowed across the water carried a scent of brine around and through them.

Kevin peeked from behind a big pile of rocks and smiled.

CHAPTER 5

Beverly and Kevin stood haplessly outside the condo. After another minute, Frank emerged, still angry, but relieved.

"It's okay, they're gone," he announced. "You can come in."

Frank's place looked a mess. Furniture had been moved, drawers emptied, papers scattered about.

"What did they steal, Frank?" asked Kevin, peering about, his eyes wide.

"Apparently, not much. All the big stuff is still here—the TVs, stereo, my computer and stuff—though I think my disks are gone."

"It looks like this is where they came in," Beverly observed, examining the door-wall that leads out onto the deck. It had been jimmied off its track and pushed aside.

Kevin started to pick things up, but Frank said to wait for the police. Beverly offered to make the call while he checked the other rooms for missing items. By the time police arrived, the only things he couldn't locate were business records and miscellaneous computer files—including his favorite sailing-the-seas disk.

The police took down some basic information, photographed the doorwall, and suggested Frank contact his insurance company. Skittish and flinching at every loud sound, Kevin helped Beverly start cleaning up while Frank made several calls, eventually finding somebody who would come out and repair the door. Linda stopped by to see her mom and wound up pitching in to help, chatting a lot with Kevin, asking him all about himself, keeping his mind off yet another worry.

After a while, Frank pulled Beverly off to the side and explained, "You know, this must have something to do with my investigation of the company. They're playing hardball and trying to slow me down. I was planning to go up there with my accountant tomorrow, but decided to postpone it, what with—" He gestured toward Kevin.

"You go do what you need to do, Frank. Kevin can stay with me. We'll keep an eye on your place while you're gone."

"I can be back tomorrow night—the last flight gets in at 9:50."

All four continued to work until well after dark. Frank kept thinking how much he hated to ask for help—to need help. He could do this himself. He could do it with Kevin. Yet, somehow, it felt better to have Beverly and Linda there, too. Not much more than a month ago, he didn't even know these two.

Eventually, all four wound up relaxing on the deck, the door repaired, interior back in order, Frank packed for his trip. The adults sipped a light cabernet souvignon while Kevin slurped his recent-vintage Mountain Dew.

Fireflies—lightning bugs, they were to Frank—winked at them from everywhere. Across the water, just at the limits of their sight, they danced in the air, caught up in a swirl of colors, joined by a million pinpoints of light in every imaginable color, casting a glow that gave pause to the curious creatures in the night.

Around the conference table sat Frank Tanyon, President Doug Taylor, Vice-President "Junior" Taylor, and their mother, shareholder Marta Taylor, plus Frank's personal accountant Henry Wanamaker and two company bookkeepers. A large, modern meeting room, it featured three walls covered by framed samples from some of the more impressive jobs produced through the years. The fourth wall boasted a full-length plate-glass window overlooking a small stream running alongside some woods. A blue-glass building stood off to the side, through some trees—another company's headquarters sharing the same prestigious corporate park at the outskirts of Cheboygan.

They spent more than an hour reviewing the numbers; then Doug sent the bookkeepers out. "That's our current status," he concluded.

"It sucks, Mr. President," observed Frank.

"Look, Frank," Doug continued, "the whole business has changed a lot since you retired. Costs have skyrocketed, the competition has grown—"

"There are more than ten new competitors," Junior interrupted, "within the customer radius of our consumer stores."

"We're busting our butts up here to make adjustments," Doug added. "Costs are rising too fast, and we can't discount any deeper without going further into the red."

"How do you propose," asked Frank, "to cover the deficit? How much is that, Henry?"

Money-grubber flipped through some pages in front of him, scratching his head with a pencil as he answered. "By the time you factor in the end-of-year tax liabilities, it will be a lot more than the one-forty grand that's showing here. Plus, more than two million in equipment falls off the depreciation chart over the next eighteen months. Without any capital expenditures—equipment upgrades, building improvements, new investments or what-not—that's really going to eat your bottom line."

"How much, Henry?"

"Well, could be more than a million dollars this quarter alone."

Frank stood up and leaned across the table toward Doug. "What's your plan, Doug?"

Doug and Junior faded back—even squirming a little in their seats. "Well—" Doug started, but he paused when his mother shot him a sidelong glare.

"What's the plan, Doug?"

Marta joined in. "Sit down, Frank. The boys are working on a proposal."

Frank sat down, leaned back in his chair, and crossed his arms.

"Go ahead, Doug," she prodded.

"Well, we need an infusion—a big one. With some new cash flow, we could do a massive upgrade—a new print-plant, several new stores—"

"We've got the site all specked out," inserted Junior.

"An extended line of credit," continued Doug, "with a general upgrade on equipment that falls off the depreciation tables."

"From where, Doug?" asked Frank. "You got it stashed under your mattress?"

"Well, we've got two options. We could bring in an investor—which means severely diluting all of our individual stock holdings—or you could sell to us and walk away. You get to cash out without any new risk and before we incur any more losses. It's going to take a rebuilding period after that."

"How, Doug?"

"Well, we—the three of us—would sell off forty-eight percent of your stock to investors and pay you off. That way, we would still retain control, bring in some new cash and new credit, and keep the company intact. It would preserve what Dad—what *you* and Dad spent your lives building up."

Henry looked at Frank with a sidelong smirk. "You would need to have this all lined up real fast to pull it off before the end of next quarter," he pointed out.

"What if it doesn't happen right away?" Frank asked him.

"Well," Henry estimated, "I'd say by then it'll be a choice between paying vendors, covering payroll, or avoiding delinquency on the taxes."

"We *could* pull it off in time," interrupted Doug. "We've had investors ready since the first time we made you an offer."

"Who?"

Doug squirmed. Marta interjected, "If a formal proposal is to be made, full disclosure will occur at that time. Until then, your best option is to cut and run—at which time our investors become *our* concern, not yours."

"In the meantime, the longer I wait, the worse things get. How convenient."

"I'm sorry the market has changed so much, Frank," apologized Doug. "You just don't know what it's like in the trenches anymore."

"Look, Frank," Marta said, "we don't need a decision right this minute, but it's obvious what you need to do. Don't make us go the route that gives control of the company to some stranger. We'll have a corporate appraisal done and pay you par value for your stock—all we need is a thirty-day carrier. It's the smart thing to do."

"No, it's the *scared* thing to do. The *smart* thing is to fix what's broke—and what's broke is the management of this company."

"Frank, according to the by-laws—" Marta began.

"I know the by-laws. Your husband and I wrote them when it was just two best friends with a lot of ambition and a willingness to work hard for our success. If his heirs had shared that same dream, then those by-laws would still work. Sadly, they don't."

"But that's what they are, and you can't change them without a majority—"

"I said I know, Marta. Let me point out three things for you." Everyone fell quiet while Frank paused for effect. "First, consider *my* offer, which is the same as yours. I'll buy out the shares from all three of you, based on the same kind of appraisal, at the *end* of this quarter."

"That's a *lot* of money, Frank," pointed out Doug.

"Let me worry about that. You're not the only manipulator in this room. Second, you turn the company around *now*—by the end of this quarter. That'll not only give you a higher appraisal for the buyout, but it just may prevent me from wrapping all three of your butts up in lawsuits, regulatory investigations, and possible criminal charges."

"Get real, Frank," admonished Marta.

"I *am* getting real, Marta. This is the *real* deal, right now, on the table. You have no idea how much I've got on you already."

All three registered shock.

"What's number three?" Doug asked.

He put his fists on the table and looked for a moment at each of them. "Remember who you're dealing with. Your father and I built this company from scratch. I can do it again without you. Most of your big customers, most of your vendors—the real ones, not the dummy businesses you've set up as middlemen—most of these people know and trust me. I think I could make a convincing case to them that you're going under and that maybe their loyalties should be with the man they trusted from the beginning."

Marta jumped to her feet. "Listen, you bastard. You know as well as we do that you can't afford to let this company go under."

"I can afford it more than you. Remember, as shareholders *and* corporate officers—not to mention members of the board of directors—every one of us is personally liable for company debts. If you want a pissing contest, my bladder is bigger than yours. You'll have to bail out first—at a big loss."

Henry chuckled. "Touché," he whispered, packing up his papers to go.

Frank picked up his sheaf and strolled toward the door, Henry right behind him. He turned and surveyed the stunned group at the table.

"Take my offer, or play games with me, people. If you decide to play, we'll see who blinks first."

Frank and Henry parted company at the Tampa International Airport. Frank picked up his car and started the 45-minute drive out to Tarpon Springs, frustrated by several construction slow-downs along the way.

This impatience was new for him. Normally content to relax and listen to his car radio, he'd forgotten how it feels to have somebody waiting at home, a sensation both reminiscent and refreshingly new. He felt pretty good about how the meeting went, and he looked forward to telling Beverly about it, but mostly he needed to see Kevin and be assured the boy was holding up. Then he could send him to bed and relax with that truly remarkable woman who lived just one convenient door away. He would hold her in his arms and continue what they started the day before on a bench in a park by the water under birds who circled in the warm Florida sky.

Beverly met him on her porch with a lingering hug. She asked if everything went okay. He smiled and nodded. Once inside, she offered him a drink.

"I could use a beer," he remarked. "I'll run next door—" Before he could finish, she produced one. *She stocked up on my favorite beer!* This had to be a sign. "Is the brat in bed—did he give you any problems?" he asked.

"Well, actually, there *is* a problem." She sat next to him on the couch. "Now don't panic, Frank, but they took him away."

"What?" He jumped to his feet. "Who took him? Where?"

"A caseworker came by first thing this morning—not long after you left. Apparently, regardless of the mother's wishes, if you're not a blood relative, it's up to them where he lives. They were all set to let him stay with you until the next court date, but you had left the state. The affidavit Ruth signed didn't mention me. I was a nobody that you—according to how it looks on paper—dumped the child on before running off to take care of your own business."

"I should have taken him with me."

"No, we should have had Ruth do a second affidavit. We just didn't think of it, what with the break-in and last-minute plans and all."

"Where is he? What did they do with him?"

"He's okay, Frank. I've been working on it all day. Right now, he's in a foster home in Holiday—not even five miles from here. It took a lot of finagling—and for once, Loretta was a great help with her contacts in the system—but they gave permission for him to call me several hours ago. I assured him we would have him back real soon, and that he should just relax and take it easy for now."

"Damn! On top of everything else, he must be worried to death."

"He never had any doubt that you—you or I—would get right on it and find a way to bring him back. His biggest question was just how long it would take."

"What do we do?"

"Well, I went down and filed an application to have myself approved as a foster parent. I started the paperwork for you, too, but you need to go down there at eleven tomorrow."

"I'll be there."

"Now, here's the thing. It takes as much as three weeks—even with Loretta's connections walking it through the system. *But*, in Michigan I'm still a registered foster parent. I spent the day getting my documentation together, having all the pertinent info faxed, filling out all the forms. I even went through the interviews already, and had Linda come down for a reference. Every step of the way, I made it clear that the fastest possible way was the only way I would accept. The supervisor took over and is handling us personally."

"Good girl!"

"She was impressed by my concern for the impact all this is having on Kevin. Ruth made the front page of the Tampa paper, by the way."

"So, how long will it take?"

"*Should* be by the end of the day tomorrow—next day at the latest."

Frank sat back and sighed. He realized his hand holding the beer was trembling slightly. He felt a lump in his throat like he'd felt that night he knew his marriage had ended once and for all.

"One more thing: "He said, Tell Frank I—well, you know . . . I said, Tell him you love him? He got real quiet and said, Yeah, tell him that."

Frank whispered, "Thank you, Beverly."

"It wasn't altruism, Mr. Tanyon. With or without you, that kid needed my help, and my help is what he got."

He reached up and gently brushed her cheek with the back of his hand, then walked over to her stereo, turned on an FM station with soft jazz, held out a chivalrous hand, and invited, "Would the lady do me the honor of this dance?"

She giggled, pretended to check the dance card on her wrist, then announced, "If you promise *not* to behave yourself, I'll pencil you in right away."

They danced *several* songs, in fact, floating around the room, finding a tempo set more by their breaths, the pounding of their hearts, the tingles that rippled across their skin, the rhythm of Tarpon Springs. They danced down the hallway, beyond the sounds of radio, on a band-length that traveled around the world and out beyond the stars as they came together to become a whole greater than each part, exploring and finding new feelings and greater passion than either had ever known possible . . .

Twice, they found it that night—not counting the next morning.

CHAPTER 6

"I'm sorry we missed the brunch, Mama. But you know I wasn't gonna let him stay out there."

"Goodness, no. You? An abandoned doggie by the side of the road? If you had driven by and left him there, I'd *know* something was amiss. We'd have missed the brunch anyway while I drove straight to the police to report that aliens had taken over my daughter's body."

Riding in Linda's car, they pulled up to the condo. Beverly apologized again, adding, "I wish I wasn't in such a hurry to get back. Frank couldn't get any later flights, and I refuse to let him leave Kevin in an empty house."

"Will he be back in time for the court date?"

"He flies in late tomorrow afternoon, and the exam isn't until eleven the following morning."

Beverly put together a snack tray of cheese and crackers and lunch meats. Linda sat at the breakfast counter and watched. "Good Lord, woman, your pantry is stocked! You sure didn't feed *me* like that."

"Well, that boy eats day and night. Frank says he's got hollow legs."

"I think it's wonderful how you two have shared looking after him. Frank still doesn't have approval yet?"

"Well, it's a lot more complicated than it used to be with all the background checks. But they *did* okay overnights with *my* permission. I just hope Kevin doesn't start staying over there *all* the time. I really like having him around—he's such a helpful little gentleman. What a sweet boy."

"Did that lawyer have anything new to say?"

"Only that it's all circumstantial evidence on Ruth. They've got a lot on Mark, including the victim who died several days later having *named* him. The lawyer says Ruth might not be bound over on murder, but she probably won't be able to get out of some lesser charges."

They paused quietly for a moment.

"You know," Linda recalled, "when we went to the aquarium in Tampa the other day, Kevin showed me the little key ring he's got with your key and Frank's key added to his trailer key and some kind of meta-warrior key symbol. He was so proud that you guys gave him those."

"Yeah, we might not even ask for them after he moves back home with his mom," chuckled Beverly. She sobered for a moment and added, "*If* he ever gets to live with her again."

Linda got up and refilled Beverly's soda. She came back and sat quietly.

"What is it you wanted to talk about today, hon?"

"I got a job offer."

Beverly looked surprised and pleased. "All right, Flashbulb! Is it taking pictures?"

"Yeah, it's that Tallahassee job I was going to be up for in six months. The guy is leaving earlier than expected for a plum job on the west coast, so they want me as soon as possible."

"Good girl! You've got some planning to do—fast."

"Well, I didn't accept it yet. I said I'd let them know by the end of the day tomorrow."

"Well, what's the delay? It's what you've been wanting."

"Yeah . . ." Linda paused, then explained, "But not this soon. I wanted to spend some time with you down here before I go running off deserting you again."

"Nonsense. You take that job and don't think a thing of it. We can do day-trips or weekends. Good Lord, girl, I'm getting tired of having you around all the time. Go on. Get outta town. I'll come see you so often you'll be trying to get rid of me."

Linda thought for a moment, then added quietly, "Oh, Mama, I just know I would miss you. I've been so thrilled to have you within easy harassing distance."

"Linda, ever since you were a little girl, you've wanted to do this. I wouldn't be happy if I thought you passed it up for me."

The sound of Frank's garage door opening could be heard faintly in the background. A moment later, Beverly's door chime rang. "You've got a key!" she yelled. Frank and Kevin let themselves in. "Don't be expecting an old lady to jump up and down, opening doors for no good reason."

Frank came over and took a cracker out of Beverly's hand. He put the whole tray in the refrigerator and announced, "Ha! We got here just in time. Let's go to the brunch. I'm paying—" He turned toward Kevin and whispered, "—For my own. Let these two cover theirs. They eat too much."

Kevin grinned. "Yeah, who're you kidding? I can eat more than all three of ya!"

They loaded into Linda's car and drove down for the brunch buffet, lingering afterward over coffee, juice for the kid.

Linda asked what Frank's plans were up in Wisconsin the next morning. "Are you going back to your company?"

"Nope. I'm letting them stew. I've got moles with eyes and ears everywhere. They're in a panic, trying to undo all the stuff they set up to rip me off. Until they contact me about my offer—or threats—I'll just leave 'em hang."

Beverly nudged Linda. "He's enjoying this, you know. He gets calls from Mr. Buchanan, the investigator, every day, then chortles about all the espionage going on."

"Anyway," continued Frank, "tomorrow I'm meeting with some of my old customers. The few I've talked to agreed to make noises about withdrawing their business. I'm going to meet with several more—it's much better to do it in person—and do a little planning. They know I'll make it worth their while when I regain control, but they're good people who would help me out either way."

They waved off a waitress hovering around with a coffee pot in her hand.

"Well," Beverly announced, "Linda has been up to some subterfuge of her own. She's planning to run off and leave us."

"Oh, Mama, I said I still haven't decided."

"Yeah, well, I refuse to have anything to do with you if you don't move out of Tampa right away."

"Where you goin', Linda?" Kevin asked.

"To a staff photographer position in Tallahassee."

"Bravo!" Frank practically shouted.

They talked on and on about all the wonderful things to do up there, promising over and over to visit. The chef packed up the fixins while the staff cleaned the empty dining room around them. The busboy glared at them several times while Linda gazed at her mother and wondered just how she could leave her once again.

With Frank, she thought. *That's how I can leave her again.*

A familiar-looking lady who stood next to one of the cameras with a microphone in her hand kept glancing over toward where Kevin sat with Frank and Beverly in the front row. They had been waiting more than an hour, sitting through an armed-robbery proceeding, waiting for Ruth Riner's case to be called.

Mr. Mogill came in, spotted the trio up front, and came over to join them. He leaned over and whispered, "Good news. All he's asking for is second degree—two counts."

"That's good?" Frank whispered back.

"Yeah," Mogill continued. "It takes it down a big notch and moves us out of the death-penalty range. He's also going to try to load her up on lesser charges, though, probably to keep bargaining heat on her. I'm expecting possession of two categories of drugs—marijuana and cocaine—use of a firearm during the commission of a felony, aiding and abetting, and so on. It looks like they're going hard after Sisk. Witnesses place *him* at the crack house on previous occasions—but not her—and he's the one who bought the gun."

An officer signaled Mogill, so he took a seat at the table up front just as Ruth entered through a door off to the side.

When Kevin saw his mother, his heart started pounding, his hands trembled, and he had to fight to maintain his composure. He managed a weak smile when she looked over at him, mouthing *I love you* to her just as she had to him during the arraignment.

Ruth got bound over for trial on all the charges the prosecutor requested—including the murder counts. The judge continued the denial of bond and set a pre-trial date for September 26th. The cameras duly recorded it all, then turned to get shots of Kevin as Ruth's supporters got up to leave. Mogill got in the way and shielded him as best he could, but a print reporter and one camera crew followed them out, trying to get a statement from the attorney. He waved them off and ushered his charges into Beverly's car, then poked his head in the window. "Believe it or not, it *is* going well. We're in a position to bargain now. Have faith."

As they headed back toward Tarpon Springs, Kevin watched out the window. Beverly kept an eye on him in her cosmetic mirror. Frank watched them both.

A news bulletin about the Clearwater crack-house killings came on the radio. Frank quickly cut it off.

On a glorious Sunday morning, Frank, Beverly, Kevin, and Henry Wanamaker boarded the *Fine Print* to celebrate Frank officially becoming Kevin's guardian, subject to six-month review or a change in Ruth Riner's status. While Frank and Kevin unpacked the fishing gear, Beverly relaxed in a deck chair, looking cool and comfortable in shorts, sandals, and a light, airy blouse pulled up and tied at the midriff for an effect somewhat more provocative than usual for her. Henry wandered around, looking worse than a tourist in gaudy plaid Bermuda shorts, his brown socks climbing substantially up pasty white legs.

Linda came down the pier carrying two tote bags and a basket. Frank helped her aboard and stowed her gear. The captain Frank had hired for the day announced they were ready, then cast off and piloted the *Fine Print* into Tampa Bay. Everybody admired the seashell-shaped public aquarium overlooking the water before they turned and cruised toward the bridge and out into the Gulf of Mexico.

"What do you think, Linda?" Kevin asked, showing her his new clothes. He wore oversized baggy shorts, a baggy heavy-metal t-shirt, Buccaneers cap, and monstrous basketball shoes emblazoned with fluorescent colors. "Man, you guys sure know how to shop." She pretended to swoon over her "handsome dude," sweeping him around in a dance until she managed to embarrass him.

"Thanks again for taking him shopping," Frank told the ladies. "With school starting in a few weeks, it never occurred to me he needed clothes." He leaned closer, like sharing a secret, but spoke extra loud. "Last night I caught him wearing his new swimsuit in front of the mirror, striking muscle-man poses."

Linda squealed and tried to get him to pose for her, too. Red-faced, he slinked off, supposedly to pester the captain about how to use the radio and navigation instruments.

Frank leaned over toward Beverly and said, "He's starting to show signs that he's, you know, maturing. Sometimes he seems like such a kid, and other times he's so serious and grown up. If his mother winds up spending serious time in jail, I'm going to find myself living with one of those animals they call *teenager.*"

"Does he have any close friends?" Henry asked.

"No, not really. We're too far from the subdivisions for him to have access to other kids. The other day, I left him at the video arcade on Highway 19 while I spent some time at the bank. When I went back, he was having a ball with a group of boys about his age. I didn't have the heart to drag him away, so I went in and gave him some money and told him to call whenever he wanted to be picked up. He was gone all afternoon."

"He needs a bicycle," Beverly announced. "If he had a bike, he could pedal up to places like that and make friends."

"That's a good idea," Frank agreed. "He's been detailing my 'Vette all week. Maybe I'll reward his work with some wheels of his own."

"Did you pick a fund for him yet?" Henry asked.

"A fund?" Beverly asked.

"Yeah, and *he* helped me pick it out," Frank replied. Then to Beverly he explained, "The foster-care checks, I'm putting them into mutual funds so he can start saving for college."

"What a wonderful idea!" Beverly clapped her hands.

Standing against the rail, Linda asked, "What did he pick?"

"Well, he now has a hundred-twelve shares of Dillard-Select/Balanced. They invest in five other funds balancing blue-chips, medium-sized company stocks, communications in emerging countries, and municipal bonds for security."

"A smart choice," Henry remarked, ever the Money-grubber.

"I've got to tell you," Frank added, "he impressed the hell out of me. We sat there for three hours with the calculator, prospectuses, and yield tables. He practically took charge. It turns out the kid is a math wizard, too."

Henry nudged Beverly and smirked. "Reminds me of Frank at that age." Frank just smiled.

They all watched several large boats pass, waving at the people on deck. Kevin came back to join them, enthusiastically greeting everybody who floated by.

"How goes the moving plans, Linda?" Henry asked.

"I'll go up there next weekend and look for an apartment. I'll come back most weekends over the next few months and take my time moving. I've still got six more months on the lease with Sherry, so there's no rush."

"That way she can *come see her Mama,*" Beverly added, talking baby-talk.

"You know it, old lady; I gotta keep checkin' up on you."

"I want to move in with you," Kevin announced. "These two lock me in a dark closet and make me eat bugs. Please take me with you."

Linda went over behind his chair, put her arms around him, and announced, "Then I could buy you clothes and fix up your hair and baby you—just like what I did with my dolls when I was little."

"Hey, wait a minute—" Kevin protested.

The hum of the engines dropped lower as the *Fine Print* slowed down. The captain had spotted mahi mahi; time to set up for trolling.

Soon Beverly got the first strike. The captain tried to help her, but Frank waved him off, letting her struggle by herself. Everybody called out encouragement and instructions, but ultimately she landed a beautiful, iridescent maize-and-blue bull with the characteristically pronounced knot above his eyes. It weighed in at twenty-three pounds—not a big one, but a respectable first catch. Over the next two hours, everybody caught two each, with Kevin winning the derby when he reeled in a 36-pounder. He got it up to the top of the water, but Frank had to help him lift it into the boat. Held up beside him, the fish nearly rivaled the boy in size. Linda snapped pictures throughout.

Click. Click. A close-up of Frank, caught gazing at Beverly with a twinkle in his eye. A shot of Kevin struggling to pull in the big one, turning his head for a brief moment to look at the camera, bursting with the pride of victory on his face. A shot of Henry sprawled flat on his back, trying to control a flip-flopping fish. A shot of Beverly screwing her face up in revulsion at the little squid that three not-so-chivalrous fellers insisted she put on the hook by herself.

Click. Click. A shot of Frank with his arms around Beverly, showing her how to hold the rod, lingering longer than necessary, looking strong and protective, like he never wanted to let go.

Click. Click. Linda caught off-guard, pulling in a fish of her own, a photo snapped by that mischievous Kevin who had watched how she operated the camera, framing the shot with a surprising flair for composition and timing.

Click. The greatest mother in the world, surrounded by people who loved her, smiling and content, radiant and alive.

CHAPTER 7

"So what's the big surprise you've been hinting about?" Ruth Riner spoke into a telephone, her face appearing on a video screen. She wore the orange-and-blue jumpsuit, but at least her hair—always a source of pride in her appearance—was combed and styled as best as she could without the tools of her wannabe-trade. Showing a hint of make-up, she looked all the more like the mother Kevin remembered. Frank hovered behind him, not wanting to infringe on these brief precious moments during prisoner visitation.

Kevin clutched his own phone, grinning mischievously. "The surprise is . . ." He paused for dramatic effect. "We got you a big package of books and stuff for getting your cozzumtology license! Linda went somewhere and signed you up for correspondence class. Frank got it all set up with the jail so we could bring 'em in."

Ruth practically squealed with delight. "Oh, Kevin, that's wonderful!"

Kevin beamed with pride. "You can study, take the tests, and mail it all in. Then all you have to do when you get out is go down there and do your last test actually fixing some people's hair. They'll help you get a job, too."

"Oh, sweetie, you're gonna be so proud of me. I'm gonna get nothin' but perfect scores. You watch." She looked past her son at Frank and smiled, nodding her gratitude. "You thank Linda for me now, too. Oh, they've all been so nice."

"Beverly got me a bunch of school clothes—" He modeled his outfit for a moment, Ruth nodding her approval. "And Frank got me a Roto-bike and a mutual fund for college and he's even teaching me all about how to run his company." He thought for a moment, then finished, "That's pretty complicated, but I'm learning fast, he says."

Ruth misted up, reaching out like she could touch him, and whispered, "Oh, honey, it's so much easier knowing that you're okay." Tears crawled down her cheeks.

"Don't cry, Mom," Kevin whispered, misting up himself. "You work on gettin' your certificate for now."

A distorted voice interrupted them, coming through the phone line. "Visits are over for Tessin, Stapleton, and Riner. Visits are over for—"

Ruth was led away, turning her head to wink one last time at her son. Frank put his arm around Kevin's shoulders and steered him through the crowd.

The boy wiped his face with his hands and looked satisfied.

Frank, Henry, Kevin, and Clarence Roux, business broker and management consult-ant, sat around the dining-room table at Frank's place. Ledgers, logs, printouts, tax and sales records, client lists, packages of advertising and samples, and other miscel-laneous records from the printing company spread around them. All four had ten-key calculators, running tape. Henry extrapolated depreciation tables based on various scenarios. Frank kept tabs on asset estimates while Kevin subtotaled various docu-ments that Frank passed over to him. Mr. Roux worked on a master ledger while the others fed him information. As fast as they could keep up, he kept asking very specific questions, sending Frank or Henry into the piles to retrieve more data.

Eventually, they all wound up sitting back, watching Mr. Roux put the final touches on his calculations. He tore the tape off his machine, shut it off, noted a few numbers on the form in front of him, and looked at the other three. "There are a lot of ways to calculate the value of an ongoing business enterprise," he explained. "Ob-viously, the lowest number would be if you were to cash it out, sell its assets, pay its debts, and walk away. A successful, ongoing, profit-making enterprise, though, is worth a lot more than the sum of its parts."

Henry nodded in agreement. Mr. Roux continued, "Frank, you did a good job pulling together estimates of actual costs from your vendors, assuming you could go back to a direct relationship and cut out the dummy enterprises set up by the Taylor family, but extrapolating an anticipated quarterly and annual profit—as you've seen today—is highly speculative and open to interpretation. If you were to take over the company again, any analysis would devalue it some just because of the change of power. Right now, it's running smoothly under its current administration—as it were—and a buyer, unless he intended to clean house and outright take over all man-agement functions with his own team, would be more wary of a company that came under new management right before the sale."

Frank asked, "You mean it's worth more with them in charge than it would be under me?"

"Yes," Mr. Roux replied, "as far as calculating its paper value. Obviously, if you have a buyer who knows the situation and is comfortable—or even likes—the change, then it has no real effect. But you need a paper number to work from for now. So I've tried not to discount that in this figure." He gestured toward the sheet in front of him. "If you revamped the vendors and restored the profitability that you could rea-sonably anticipate, then a conservative estimate is—" He passed the top sheet over to Frank, indicating the bottom line.

Frank grinned at Henry and read aloud, "Eighteen-point-seven million."

Henry's eyebrows shot up. "Just remember," he deadpanned, "that I'm one of your dearest and most loyal friends."

"*Dollars?*" Kevin asked, standing up and leaning over to see the sheet.

"It sure ain't clams," answered Frank.

Henry scratched his belly and pointed out, "Frank, that's damned near ten mill you'd have to come up with to buy out those stinkin' snakes."

Frank rubbed his hand several times through what was left of the hair on his well-tanned pate. "What about the banks, Henry?"

"Three, maybe four-mill—tops. You're looking at venture capitalists, selling off private stock, or going public."

Frank waved off the latter suggestion. "There's no way I could set all that up and be ready for a public offering in time. If I cash out, I could only cover somewhere near a half-mill myself, so I guess I need a rich buddy or two willing to take a minority stake and let me make 'em some profit." Frank looked off in thought. "I'd have to stay up there probably six months to a year until I could get new management set up to run it without me."

"What about those two investors we talked about?" Henry asked. "They said they're available to meet you any day this week."

"How about tomorrow? Let's meet on the *Fine Print* and, if things are going well, we can take a little cruise and relax—show 'em a good time."

Mr. Roux interjected, "I'll bring them out. And if that doesn't pan out, let me know. This would be a good opportunity for someone with the scratch. The people I run into look for plums like this—and they know how to recognize one. They wouldn't have all the concerns about instability—as long as you convince them you can run it straight without losing any momentum."

"Yeah," Frank agreed. "You keep your eyes open; just don't talk it up yet."

Everybody sat quietly for a minute. Finally, Kevin broke the silence.

"Wow. Eighteen-point-seven million *dollars!*"

The next morning, Frank gathered up various papers and packed his briefcase. Kevin came out of the bathroom, combing his hair after a shower.

"Oh, look who finally came home," Kevin remarked, wagging his eyebrows.

"So I was out late—"

"Yeah, *real* late. I heard you sneak in after five, but I didn't hear your car drive up." He put a finger to his mouth and posed like he was deep in thought. "Hmm . . . You must have been somewhere within walking distance. Hmmm . . . I don't think it was the trailer park. Hmmm . . ."

"You just mind your own business."

"Now what could you have been doing next door until all hours of the morning?"

"We were sharing our love," Frank said, "in a personal and intimate way."

"Yeah, well," Kevin returned, "that's not what Lonnie calls it."

Changing the subject, Frank snapped his briefcase shut and asked, "Where will you be today?"

"I'm gonna meet Lonnie at Tarpon Mall to see the dollar movie. If he doesn't have to get home, we'll probably come back here and play video games or whatever. He wants to see where I live, and I told him we could go by the trailer park, then hang out back by the springs."

"Well, I don't know about me—it might be only be a few hours, or if we take the boat out I might even be past dinner-time. You've got enough money on you to eat—for both you and your friend—if you need to, don't you?"

"Oh yeah, no problem."

"I want you to write Lonnie's number on the message pad. In fact, get his address and put it down, too, in case of emergency."

"Sure, Frank," Kevin agreed, going over to write it down.

"I'll keep my cell-phone on in case you need to call. Otherwise, you're on your own."

Frank tousled his hair, Kevin punched him on the shoulder, and Frank disappeared out the door. Kevin watched through the window as he met Beverly coming up the walk. She wore her robe, carrying the newspaper. They chatted for a minute, then embraced with a lingering kiss. Kevin smiled and nodded his approval.

Yeah, he knew where Frank had spent the night.

Frank and Henry came down from the upper deck just as Clarence Roux walked up to the gang plank with two other men. Surprised, Frank recognized tipsy Larry, who owned the 39-footer down the pier.

"Gentlemen," Mr. Roux began, "I'd like you to meet Larry Rumsey and his brother, Elijah Rumsey."

Later that morning, Linda stopped by and picked up Beverly. They planned to have lunch, then head down to Seminole to meet Loretta. Only two days before Linda needed to report for her new job, they wanted to spend as much time together as possible, plus give Linda a chance to say good-bye to her aunt, Frank, and Kevin.

"It's not like you won't be back in a week or two," Beverly pointed out.

"Yeah, but now that the time has come, it sure feels like a big change—just like when I moved down here."

"Yeah, it's hard for me to send away my little shutterbug, so this'll just be a good-luck and see-you-soon."

"Hey, let's celebrate with lunch at the sponge docks—starting with a big basket of garlic-shrimps." They headed out a back road, along a small canal. Linda continued, "We had such a short time living in the same area, though. I got spoiled fast."

"In this day and age, a few miles don't mean much. As long as you don't move to the moon, we'll *always* be able to spend time together. You'll be pushing my wheelchair around someday—if your walker isn't too hard to handle."

A raccoon darted across the road!

Linda hit the brakes and swerved to avoid him.

The wheels caught gravel on the shoulder, causing the back end of the car to whip around. Out of control, they flew sideways into Cypress trees at the edge of the canal, flipping and slamming into—

A loud bang, the explosion of shattering glass, and the door folded in on Beverly. Crushed under sharp metal, her left leg screamed in agony, then went numb, then suddenly ice cold.

A million pinpoints of iridescent light in every imaginable color swirled up out of the canal, enveloped Beverly for a brief instant, then curled into a tight whirlwind and snaked down into the wreckage, stirring a shock of blond hair before disappearing from sight.

"Linda! Linda—" Beverly gasped, suddenly tired, so very tired, fighting to stay conscious.

And the lights reappeared, dancing feverishly for a moment, reflecting a dervish of changing shapes and images against cloudless blue sky before retreating into the murky depths.

Somebody squealed . . . voices, strange noises.

Beverly tried to reach for her little girl, but she couldn't move.

"Be still," someone said. "We'll get you out."

A siren, pounding and grinding, gusts of cold air, hands pulling at her, frantic shouts, more pulling, a stiff blanket, slipping away, strange words, shivering, slipping . . .

Another voice, sounding off in the distance: "What about the other one?"

"Still no vital signs—"

Everything went dark, a colorless void slipping into the blackest depths, enfolding Beverly with a harsh, biting chill.

CHAPTER 8

Kevin and Lonnie exited the theater, unlocked their bikes, and pedaled down the street to a fast-food restaurant. They ordered greasy lunch, each paying for his own, and took it outside to sit at one of the tables.

"The part where his head blew up was pretty cool," Kevin critiqued, "but most of it sucked."

Lonnie agreed. Nearly a year older than Kevin, Lonnie would be in eighth grade when Kevin started seventh the following week. He sported longish light-red, almost blond hair and more than a few freckles scattered randomly on his face. Slight of build, he stood an inch or two taller than Kevin and favored similar baggy outfits like most of the boys at their middle school. Lonnie tended to be shy, but he opened up if given time to feel comfortable. His passion for anything having to do with robotics and computerized automation could override, when the right occasion arose, any remnants of his bashfulness. He was somewhat self-conscious about his changing voice, a source of frustration that squeaked all the worse when he became flustered. He and Kevin vaguely knew each other in school, but had hooked up recently at the arcade.

"He shoulda killed 'em all when he had the chance," Lonnie summed up.

"You want to go out to my house and play Cyber-Squash?" Kevin suggested.

They finished scarfing down their fries, cleaned up their refuse, and pedaled off.

"Wow, this is nice," Lonnie pronounced when they entered. Who else lives here?'

"This is Frank's place. The trailer I told you about is my mom's. She took off for a while, so I stay with Frank, just me and him. He's pretty cool."

Probably sensing Kevin's reluctance to explain, Lonnie didn't press him for details. They helped themselves to liberal doses of chocolate-almond ice cream while flipping through various cable channels.

When Kevin got up to use the bathroom, Lonnie said he needed to call his mom and check in. Kevin came out several minutes later and found him still talking quietly into the phone. He looked at Kevin with an odd expression and repeated, "I said it's okay. There's nothing to worry about." He paused, listening, then continued, "No, not now. Don't worry about it. No. I'll be home before dark. Bye." He hung up.

"What's wrong?" Kevin asked.

"Nothin'. Come on, let's go back to the mall."

Still puzzled, he locked up, got on his bike, and followed Lonnie down the road, trying to keep up. "Wait up! What's wrong?"

When Lonnie finally stopped, Kevin pulled up beside him. They stood there next to water, the croaking of a nearby frog the only sound for a full minute.

Lonnie looked away, embarrassed. "My mom doesn't want me around you. She just found out your mother is a drug addict who's in prison for murder. Is she?"

Kevin bounced his front wheel up and down a few times, then looked across the water. "My mom's in jail because she went out with a guy who tried to rob some people and wound up shooting them. She's gonna get out after she goes to court. She never hurt anybody."

"Wow!" Lonnie thought about it for a minute. "Anyway, I gotta go. My mom said to get right home." He quickly pedaled away.

Kevin turned his bike around and took off as fast as he could the other direction. Lonnie stopped and watched him for a moment, then turned and started after him. He called to him several times, his shouts ignored. Kevin followed a sandy trail back through a wooded area by the springs, slowed but undaunted by the soft ground. He leaned his bike against the giant, hollow log and climbed inside. Lonnie walked his bike the last few hundred yards, trying to be very quiet. As he approached the log, he heard Kevin inside sniffling. Finally, Lonnie climbed inside, too.

"Get out of here," Kevin ordered. "Go home. Stay away from me."

Lonnie sat there anyway. "It's all right, man. I just freaked. Don't worry about it."

Kevin wiped off his face, embarrassed now, and didn't say anything. They sat there quietly until Kevin's breathing had slowed.

"It don't matter," Lonnie said. "Mom freaks about everything. Ever since my dad split, she stays on me all the time."

"When did he leave?" Kevin asked.

"When I was in sixth grade. He was a real piece of shit—drunk all the time, beatin' on me and my mom. She had to call the police on him when he picked up my baby sister and acted like he would throw her against the wall. Mom just don't trust nobody no more."

"I don't even know who my dad is," Kevin explained. "My mom said it doesn't matter anyway. She's pretty cool and all, but she was going out with another piece of shit named Mark. Frank got her a good lawyer, though, and she'll get let go."

They sat there another minute, then Lonnie asked, "How do you know Frank?"

"I've been working for him since third grade. He always takes me places and stuff, kinda acting like a dad."

"Is he married?"

Kevin grinned. "No, but ever since Beverly moved in next door he's been acting all puppy-lovey. She goes all over with us and stuff, and Frank stays over there sometimes when they wanna have sex."

Lonnie grinned, too. "So why didn't they put you in the youth ranch?"

"Beverly was a foster lady, and she got Frank to be a foster dad so I could live there. If Frank goes out of town, I stay over at Beverly's. Her and her daughter Linda like buying me clothes and stuff. Linda got my mom her books so she can be a cozzumtologist when she gets out, and she got me this wallet—" He took out the half-sized leather fold-over of which he'd grown so proud. "She's the one who's gonna teach me all about taking pictures."

"Hey," Lonnie suggested, "show me your trailer."

They had to walk their bikes through deep sand until they emerged at the back end of the trailer park. As they let themselves in, Kevin explained how the police had torn everything up. A short, overweight lady with dirty hair startled them by banging on the door. She waved a lit cigarette at Kevin and informed him his mother was now two months behind on the lot fee. She needed her money soon or she would have the trailer towed away. He told her he would pay it, but she would have to wait a few days. She stalked off.

Lonnie suggested, "Let's go back and play Cyber-Squash."

While they walked their bikes back down the path, through the sand, past the hollow log, and across the makeshift bridge over the spring, a county Sheriff's cruiser sat parked in Beverly's driveway.

Two uniformed officers knocked repeatedly on the door before giving up and driving off.

After offering seats to Elijah and Larry Rumsey, Frank went below deck to fill their drink orders. When he came back, he handed an envelope to Henry and said, "Here's that info you wanted."

Henry opened it, read briefly, then folded the note up, stuffing it in his pocket. "Thanks," was his only remark.

"Man, what a coincidence," Larry started. "Me and Eli been looking for some ventures to get into. When he came down from Michigan to check on a couple things, he mentioned your company. When he said your name, I told him, Shoot, I got a berth down at the club by him. He's a friend of mine."

Eli interrupted, "Yeah, I had concerns about the situation, especially after Henry here mentioned there was some dispute over control, but when Larry vouched for you—he said you're really on the ball—I said, Hey, let's check it out."

Over the next few hours, Frank kept their drink glasses topped off, going long on liquor and short on ice. The hotter it got, the more they drank. Frank presented an overview of the company, carefully choosing the information he divulged. Occasionally, one or the other would refer to the information Henry had provided them previously.

The sun beat down relentlessly, the air very still. No mention was made of taking the boat out. Frank just kept pouring drinks and talking. He dwelled for a while on equipment depreciation, doing a poor job explaining his projections for upgrading and replacing. At one point, Eli cut him off and clarified that he liked the plan to computerize and automate the offset presses in the consumer shops.

Frank shot Henry a knowing glance. That was information Henry had never shared with them, a discussion only with the Taylors, and it had appeared on a set of graphs stolen from Frank's condo during the break-in.

Eventually, Larry steered the presentation toward price and timing. Frank grinned and told them stock might be available for a private transaction at the end of the following quarter.

Surprised, Eli asked, "Oh? I thought you were in a hurry. Why the delay?"

"Well, the good news is, you can buy in a lot cheaper then. Right now, the total worth is already undervalued, but I've got a plan that'll drop it way down from there."

Henry nodded in agreement. "We're talking a third of that."

"Wow, how are you going to do that?" Larry asked.

"We plan to break the backs of the other shareholders. I won't go into the details, but while they're up there trying to clean up the operation, I've got the whole company sabotaged. By halfway through next quarter, the bottom will fall out. They'll lose their shirts and have to sell out so fast they won't know what hit 'em, just to recover any money at all. I have it set up so the whole company will go under, if necessary, and be replaced by another I'm already setting up. All the big customers, the vendors, most of the key employees—it's wired. Don't tell anybody, but I'm stringing the others along until the company is worth almost nothing." He sat back and took a long drink of soda water disguised as something stiffer.

Henry endorsed Frank's assertions. "Just hold off three, maybe four more months and you can buy in real cheap."

Sherry arrived home from work and checked her voice mail, which included an urgent message to contact the Tampa Police Department. She called and learned a car would be sent over within fifteen minutes. The dispatcher wouldn't explain. After what seemed like hours, she opened the door to two uniformed officers who asked if they could sit.

Sherry sat across from them. "What's this about?"

"Is this the residence of Linda Herndon?"

"Yeah, yes. Er, for now anyway. She's getting ready to move. Why?"

"And you are?" One of the officers took out a small notebook and wrote down her name. The other one inquired about Linda's relatives, noting the names of Beverly and Loretta. He asked if she had Loretta's address, phone number, and place of employment.

Sherry dug out Linda's phone book and handed it across to the man taking notes. "What's this about? What's wrong?"

Finally, the officer who had been doing the writing explained, "I'm sorry to tell you, but I'm afraid your roommate has been involved in a fatal car accident."

"Oh God, no . . ." Tears started down her cheeks.

"Linda Herndon was pronounced dead at the scene. Beverly Herndon was airlifted to Central Hospital."

"Is she okay? How bad is she hurt?"

"I don't have that information, ma'am. A relative will need to contact the hospital for that."

They both waited a minute while Sherry paced around the room, trying to regain her composure.

"Are you okay? Do you need us to stay with you for a few minutes?"

"No. No. I'll call Loretta."

"You're free to call Ms. Marlowe if you want, but we'll still call it in and have the local police send a car around to notify her officially."

"We're very sorry, ma'am," the other officer added.

With that, they left. Sherry sat on the couch and cried hard for several minutes. Then she picked up the phone.

Just coming in from a community committee meeting, Loretta answered the phone and listened while Sherry explained what had happened. Her heart pounding, her eyes blurry from tears, Loretta managed to call information and get the number to the hospital. After a long, frustrating merry-go-round of being transferred and put on hold, she finally talked to somebody who confirmed that Beverly had gone up to surgery. She grabbed her purse and headed for the door, then paused, looking at the phone.

She went back, looked up Frank's number in her directory, and called.

Kevin was outside saying goodbye to Lonnie, confirming plans for the next day, when the phone rang. He rushed inside and grabbed it, expecting Frank to be checking on him. Instead, he heard Loretta, who sounded groggy and half-asleep. He couldn't predict when Frank would be back, so she had him write down the name and number of a hospital in Tampa.

"What's this about?" he asked. Loretta paused, then blurted out what had happened. Barely able to speak, Kevin promised he would tell Frank, then hung up and sat down, lost in the gravity of bad news.

Linda's gone, he thought. *Linda's gone forever.* He tried not to cry, but there was nothing else he could do.

He had known Linda for such a short time, yet every moment he had spent with her had made him feel like a grown-up. Sure, she teased him about being a "little man," but deep inside he loved it. Linda had planned to show him how to use a camera. She even promised to tell him secrets about girls—how to ask them on dates and to make them feel special—and to teach him how to dance so he would be confident at that first big school social. Somehow, it wouldn't have been embarrassing to clomp around like a goof in front of Linda.

He remembered her childlike wonder at every little thing. When they had gone bike riding together up toward Holiday, she stopped a hundred times to point out and explain things only she seemed to notice. When he showed her his hollow log back by the springs, she paused to talk to the toads and other critters.

She had taken him out to Tampa once, stopped by her apartment to show him where she lived, then treated him to supper and the kind of slasher movie most girls don't like. She told him he would be the little brother she never had, and anybody who messed with him just better watch out.

He started to smile at the thought—Linda for a big sister would be excellent!—then he flashed on an image of her lying dead in the twisted wreckage of her car.

Swept away by a wave of nausea and fear, he trembled and wept for a world that had just lost too much, and for the critically injured mother who might have trouble thinking of any good reason to live.

"Kevin, what's wrong?" Frank found him sitting on the living-room couch in a daze, his eyes swollen and red, his answer like a series of blows knocking the wind out of an old man.

Kevin offered him the paper, as if this proof made the unthinkable real. Frank rushed to the phone and called the hospital, confirming only the basics, then called the local county sheriff's department and talked to an officer, learning more about the wreck.

Frank sat in a dining-room chair and put his head in his hands, feeling the tears blind him. He heard Kevin crying and looked up to see the helpless boy watching from the couch. He went over and put his arms around him. Kevin buried his face in Frank's chest and cried.

After several minutes, Frank went and got a towel. He wiped Kevin's face, then his own. He kissed Kevin on top of the head and whispered, "I need to get to the hospital and check on—to be with Beverly."

"I want to go, too."

Frank took a deep breath, then agreed.

It was a long, frustrating drive, compounded by rush-hour traffic and construction delays. They took turns misting up, never giving voice to their thoughts. Frank reached over and squeezed Kevin's shoulder, holding on for a while.

In the bright glare of the emergency room, amid the bustle of people buzzing about, Frank managed to learn nothing new. He would have to wait until the doctor was available. After a while, Loretta came in looking pretty haggard. She stiffened when Frank hugged her hard, but she let him, then sat with him and Kevin to wait.

By 3:00 a.m., Kevin dozed fitfully in the chair, leaning against Frank. Loretta went to the coffee machine for yet another dose of caffeine, came back, and sat across from them. Frank had given up harassing the desk nurse for information. Finally, a physician came out. The nurse pointed him toward Loretta.

"Are you the Herndon Family?"

"Yes!"

"I'm Dr. Bentley. We had to remove the toes from her left foot and do a lot of repairs to her left leg, including the insertion of pins to help support shattered bones. Her left arm was broken—a clean break at the radius—but we set that and put it in a cast. We're still concerned about the blow to her head, but the swelling has shown signs of subsiding. Other than that, she has a lot of bruises and contusions. Oh, and we stitched up a three-inch gash across her rib cage on the left side."

Loretta collapsed into the chair and shook her head repeatedly.

Frank asked, "Does she know about her daughter yet?"

"I don't think so, but that'll likely be one of the first things she asks. It's probably best that she hear it from one of you or, at least, when you're present for emotional support. You should all get some rest, though. I doubt she'll wake before noon."

"Will she get better?" Kevin asked, now wide awake.

"Well, son, in time she probably will. She'll have to learn to walk again, and maybe need a prosthesis, but if all goes well, she'll get by." He looked sad. "Her hurt is going to be a lot bigger than her physical injuries, I'm afraid."

They thanked him and walked reluctantly out to the parking lot. Frank kept looking back, feeling like he didn't want to leave her in there. They stood by Loretta's car for a moment. He said, "I'll call and find out where—what the procedures are for Linda. Beverly will need help with funeral plans and such. Who do we contact to let know what happened?"

"I'll call the people she knew in Michigan," Loretta answered. "I guess Sherry will cover her friends down here. I'll check with her and see."

"I'll arrange notices in the papers up there and here in Tampa," Frank added.

They stood there awkwardly for a moment, then said good-night and went their separate ways. Kevin slept during the drive back. Frank's emotions drifted between shock and helplessness.

Headlights passed, obscuring unseen faces, people driving here and there, everybody taking care of business, many going home, all caught up in their own lives as they passed indifferently by Frank and his profound grief in the dark night.

CHAPTER 9

"Are you Ms. Marlowe?" Two uniformed officers stood at the door, one holding a large paper sack.

"Yes. Come in."

"Ma'am, we're sorry to disturb you so early."

Loretta glanced over at the clock—5:17 a.m., more than an hour earlier than she was used to waking up. Pulling her robe tighter, she offered to make some coffee.

"No, thank you."

"We don't want to intrude. We just need to make an official notification for the next-of-kin and turn over some personal property."

They told her their names and showed their identification. Everybody sat down.

"I understand you were notified by Ms. Sherry Lubinsky about your sister's accident?"

"Yes, that's right."

"We understand that Ms. Herndon—Beverly Herndon has not yet regained consciousness."

"Yes, but that's because they have her sedated. She had surgery and came through it okay."

"Oh, good," both remarked.

There was an awkward pause for a moment, then the officer holding the sack gestured toward his partner. He explained, "Uh, ma'am, we have personal property recovered from the vehicle. Shall we turn this over to you?"

Loretta looked away for a moment. "Yes, that would be fine."

"I'm sorry, but we need to go through it all and check each item off before you sign for them."

The one holding the sack opened it, reached in, and handed over a typed checklist on a clipboard. As one officer read, the other removed each item from the bag and handed it to Loretta. These included various things from the glove box, an umbrella, jumper cables, a small tool pouch, several women's magazines and a photography magazine, an envelope of personal financial papers—some pertaining, apparently, to some kind of lawsuit—a waterproof hat, five CDs, a package of breath mints, more than a dozen kinds of make-up, Beverly's purse, Beverly's wallet containing $276.24, identification and photos, Linda's purse . . . Linda's wallet containing . . .

Loretta turned her niece's wallet over in her hands, then lowered her head and covered her face with one hand. The officers sat there quietly. Finally, Loretta opened the wallet and flipped through the photos, staring blankly at each through her tears.

Flip. Marshall, Linda's dad, dressed to the nines for his retirement celebration; he was so proud and so looking forward to spending more time with Beverly. Flip. Beverly, sitting on the dock at Houghton Lake, mugging for the camera, holding her hat against the wind. Flip. Flip. Sherry and several more friends, toasting Linda's move to Tampa to start a new job and an exciting new career. Loretta, accepting her community-service award last year, smiling for the crowd.

Flip. Flip. Frank, arms around Beverly, hugging her and gesturing to the large fish on deck, Beverly laughing from the excitement and proud of her catch. Flip. Kevin's face up close, intensely curious, studying the shipboard radio, exploring the mysteries of his universe. Flip. Marshall again, giving her a thumbs-up from his hospital bed, only two months before the attack that killed him. Randall, Linda's boyfriend from college, waving from the boarding ramp in the airport terminal before going off for volunteer work in foreign lands.

Flip. Flip. Beverly, close up, smiling, love in her eyes while her little girl snaps her photo. Flip. Marshall and Beverly, posed in the studio, documenting their devotion on their final wedding anniversary.

Flip. Flip. Flip Flip. Linda, cap and gown, posing outside the auditorium, flanked by her proud parents, ready to take on the world.

Frank fought demons and dragons and fell from great heights and felt cold and hot, then cold again. He couldn't escape and didn't know which way to go and didn't know the answer and didn't understand the question . . .

He heard sounds—real sounds—there in the room. He climbed up out of his sleep just enough to see what they were. Kevin sat on the side of his bed, clad in gym shorts and t-shirt—the way he always goes to bed. The curtains look dark. The clock says 5:20 a.m., 5:20 a.m., 5:20—Damn, Linda is gone . . . is she? Beverly is hurt . . .

"Kevin."

He must be crying. Yes, his face is wet. He's not saying anything. Frank felt like he was sinking. None of this could be true. Spiraling out of control, he reached out.

"Kevin!" Frank took his arm. Kevin looked into his face, lost, helpless, confused. Frank sat up, pulled Kevin closer, and put his arms around him, protecting him from the world, wishing he could protect him from the hurt inside.

"Did I—did I wake you—wake you up?" Kevin asked, breathing hard, not quite catching his breath.

"It's all right, buddy."

"Did it—did it really happen?"

Frank squeezed him harder and whispered, "I'm afraid so."

"What are we gonna do?"

"We'll stick together, you and me, and we'll help Beverly, whatever she needs."

"What about Linda?"

Frank squeezed him again and paused. "We'll remember her and make her a part of us always."

They fell silent for a moment.

"What if Beverly don't get better?"

"She will, Kevin, because we won't let her forget the good things she's got." He softened his hug until Kevin settled in comfortably beside him. "We'll find a way," he whispered.

They drifted in their own thoughts until Kevin's breathing slowed and his eyes closed. Frank looked at the clock again. He pulled the sheet so it covered Kevin, too, then stroked his hair several times and left his hand resting on the boy's shoulder. He closed his eyes and drifted off.

They were chasing him, and he felt himself falling and couldn't figure out the answer and didn't know the question and couldn't escape and couldn't see whose face stared back from the mirror.

He reached out, but touched empty air.

He listened, the answer stark silence.

Where are you, Beverly? I can't hear you . . .

CHAPTER 10

"Are you holding up all right?" Frank asked Sherry, talking into the phone. Showered and shaved, he should have felt somewhat better, but his exhaustion and the pain of the night before kept pulling him down.

"Yeah, I guess. Susie came and stayed with me. She had to go to work, but I called in and took the day off. My boss was real cool."

"Good. Don't worry about the expenses. We'll find a way to help you out."

"It's just so hard—" She paused, struggling with her emotions. Frank could tell she was fighting back tears. "So much of the stuff here is hers." Susie went in her room last night and put away her things and closed the door. I just couldn't look in there. Her bed wasn't made—like she was just up to get a—to get a snack or something—like she would be right back—"

"Hang in there, hon. We'll help with her—you know, with her things."

"I'm getting a lot of calls wanting to know where to send flowers—what the funeral arrangements are. I don't know what to tell them."

"We need to talk to Beverly."

"She's still not awake yet?"

"No, I just checked. We're heading up there in a few minutes."

"She still doesn't know . . ."

After they said their good-byes, Frank tried dialing Loretta's number again, but got her answering machine message, the same cheerful "not home right now" that had been on there since before the accident. Kevin brought the morning paper to Frank, opening it to the "Local" section and pointing to the headline and photographs. Linda's car, badly smashed, was turned on its side and partially wrapped around a tree, several large pieces of debris scattered on the ground. Linda's photo appeared below, apparently from her driver's license, the blurred, poorly shot image an insult to the vibrant young photographer who routinely captured magic on film.

"Did you read it?" Frank asked.

"Yeah. It says they think she swerved for a raccoon, but wound up killing it anyway."

Frank refolded the paper and laid it on the dining room table.

"Are we going to the hospital soon?" Kevin asked.

"Yeah. I wish I could get hold of Loretta, though."

"She's next door at Beverly's. She's carryin' stuff out and putting it in her trunk."

I tried to help her, but she wouldn't let me."

Frank went outside, Kevin at his heels. Loretta was locking Beverly's front door, the trunk of her car already closed.

"You need some help, Loretta?" he asked.

"No, I'm done. I just picked up a few things that needed to be taken care of." She did not offer to explain.

"Well, why don't you come in for coffee or something. I've still got a couple of calls to make—and I want to order some flowers to pick up on the way to the hospital. We can follow each other."

"No, no thanks. I think I'll just go ahead."

Back inside, Frank watched her through the window while she drove away. *She acted like she'd been caught in the act,* he thought. "Kevin, why don't you put on one of your school outfits so you look nice for Beverly?"

Kevin went off to get dressed while Frank ordered the flowers. He called Henry to update him—or tell him there was nothing new to report, anyway.

They stopped for fast food along the way, eating as they drove.

"What's Beverly gonna say, Frank? I mean, what do we do?"

"I don't know, buddy. She'll take it hard, I'm sure, but she needs to fight to recover. We can't let her get so down that she doesn't care about herself."

For most of the drive, Kevin watched out the window, lost in his own thoughts. Frank tried to concentrate on the road, but nothing seemed real anymore. Everywhere he looked he saw people and drivers and shoppers and pedestrians and roller-skaters and bicyclists, but nobody knew, nobody paused, nobody seemed to care.

Linda was gone.

Beverly lay unconscious in the hospital, yet everybody just went on about their business like none of this even mattered.

It *did* matter. It mattered a lot.

They had to wait several more hours at the hospital. An uneasy tension began to grow between Frank and Loretta. All she would offer were short answers or blank stares whenever he tried to converse. Kevin sat by, feeling uncomfortable, worrying about Beverly, numb about Linda, confused by the behavior of these adults. Frank mentioned that it might be good to narrow the funeral options in advance so Beverly could make her wishes known through simple choices rather than considering open-ended questions.

"*I'm* familiar with this area. I'm sure I can recommend someplace nice."

Frank tried to placate her, acknowledging her turf. "Good, then you can probably help find a nice cemetery close to Tarpon Springs."

"We'll work it out." She walked away, ostensibly to get more coffee. Frank walked over and sat with Kevin. They looked at each other, acknowledging a situation awkward at best.

Eventually, a physician came out, asked for Loretta, and said Beverly was awake—very drowsy, but awake. Frank and Kevin stood up, but Loretta turned and told them she would go in first. The physician shrugged and asked if Loretta was the next of kin.

"Yes," she answered quickly. "I'm her *only* living relative."

"We'll be waiting right here," Frank offered, motioning Kevin to sit back down.

Loretta followed the physician down the hallway, leaving Frank standing there rapidly progressing from worried to agitated to angry.

"Bitch," Frank mumbled.

"Bitch," Kevin agreed.

CHAPTER 11

She felt herself floating, pitching and slipping like a ship in a storm. When she opened her eyes, the bright glare swirled around her, making it hard to focus, hard to see, hard to understand. She felt tired and sick to her stomach. Her entire body ached. Her leg—something didn't feel right there. What about her leg? It felt like a balloon, blown up too large, ready to burst, trying to float away with the wind, blown off the swaying ship, caught in the swirl of those bright lights.

She remembered the little girl who fell and broke her foot, crying for big-sister Loretta to make things better. Better would never come easy, though. There would be pain, a trip to the emergency room, a mean doctor making it hurt worse—but Loretta would be there. As long as she held on to Loretta, she would come through okay.

Loretta. *Loretta!* Yes, Loretta was here now. She would know what to do. Yes, Marshall would come to rest down here. New Port Richey would be very nice—especially a pretty cemetery with pretty flowers near the water. Loretta would know what to do.

Linda should have a say—what was that about Linda again? Oh, no, she's hurt! She's not coming back. Mama can't help her . . . Beverly started crying softly. The ship rocked, nausea rising up in waves, balloon ready to pop, lights swirling and threatening to carry her away.

"Don't cry now, little sister. You need your rest. I'll take care of everything."

Of what? Oh yeah, a funeral. Linda's dead. *Linda's dead!* That can't be. That just can't be.

Oh, baby, hold on. Mama will come get you . . .

The blinding lights swirled faster and faster until they swept her away.

Beverly awoke to those infernal lights again.

Frank sat close by with that kid.

Frank— Florida— Yes, she was in Florida, but something seemed wrong—*very* wrong. Linda was gone.

It was Florida.

Beverly shouldn't be here. Linda shouldn't be here. Everything would be okay if Florida just never happened.

Frank reached over and held her hand.

The kid sat by, looking helpless.

The lights were too bright.

Florida had turned way too bright.

Frank exhaled, releasing some of the tension, then realized he was gripping the wheel too hard and grinding his teeth. "I hope she likes the flowers we brought," he said.

Kevin clenched his mouth and nodded. Frank pulled a slip of paper from his pocket and examined it for the umpteenth time—name and address of funeral home, name and location of cemetery. The physician had said that Beverly might be able to attend—in a wheelchair—the following Saturday, five days hence.

"She was pretty much out of it," Kevin offered.

"Yeah," Frank agreed, "but she didn't have to let Loretta make all the decisions."

"Loretta's just trying to help."

"There's a difference between helping and taking over."

Kevin thought for a minute. "I've seen her stand up to Loretta when she wanted her own way."

"Yeah, but—" Frank shook his head. "She's not in much condition to stand up to anybody right now. I just wish I knew what to do."

Frank drove on, wondering about having the funeral on a holiday weekend, pondering Kevin's upcoming first day of seventh grade next Tuesday, feeling uneasy about Beverly's lack of interest in him and Kevin there in that overlit, antiseptic hospital room.

What about the fight for his company? What about Beverly's lawsuit for the rest of Marshall's estate? How would Ruth's court date—now just a few weeks away—turn out, and what would happen to Kevin then?

How would Beverly ever find it in herself to laugh again, knowing her precious Linda was gone forever? How could he protect her from ever being hurt again?

How could he protect himself?

"Well, it's not real dressy," Sherry continued, "but she liked high-quality yet simple styles, nothing too fancy."

"Yeah," Loretta agreed. "I think this looks good. It's how she usually dressed."

The two women stood in Linda's bedroom, the first time Sherry ever felt like an intruder, the last time she would ever be asked for opinions on what her friend should wear. Linda's unmade bed sat off to one side. The knickknacks and souvenirs and loose jewelry and spare set of keys waited quietly atop her dresser, as if Linda might need them ever again. The walls boasted scores of photos, framed prints big and small, documenting and displaying important moments in her life.

"Where does she—did she, uh, keep her papers—you know, her financial records, checkbook and such?"

"Um, I think most of that is in here." Sherry opened one of the drawers in the chest. "Plus, there's some out here." She led Loretta down the hallway to a closet.

Together, they packed several cartons and carried them down to Loretta's car. Not only was Linda gone, but the pieces of her friend's life were being carted off, too.

"That's all I need for now," Loretta announced. "We can take our time cleaning out the rest of her stuff."

Good. Sherry had reached her limit for today. She wanted to believe Linda might still come home—maybe, well . . . no, *Let's just close her door for now* . . . but—*please.*

Before she left, Loretta wrote out the funeral information for Sherry to pass along to other friends.

Sherry waited for another wave of tears to pass before going back into Linda's bedroom to put away the loose items from the closet. She stood there a moment. So many faces looked out from those pictures. So many faces . . . smiling at her like they didn't know, couldn't understand, wouldn't feel the profound loss Sherry felt every minute since the officers first came to her door—a permeation sometimes vague and surreal, sometimes overwhelming.

All those smiling faces . . .

Smile! Randall, mugging from behind an armful of books in front of the student union. Marshall and Charles flashing the big check they got when they finally sold out to retire and relax and savor the fruits of their labor, to spend time with family and friends. Smile. Beverly carrying a huge, roasted turkey to the table that first Thanksgiving after Linda moved to Florida—the one when she dragged her new roomie back to Michigan for some of Mama's home-cooked goodies.

Smile, and lots more smiles. Her friends and co-workers at the paper celebrating with that young, red-headed guy after he accepted the offer to go west and become a TV correspondent. A smile and a scowl. Beverly pointing at that big old fat toad next to a pile of cat food, Loretta standing behind her doing her best to look bored and disinterested.

Frank piloting his yacht, hand on the tiller, the gallant sea captain mugging for Beverly's little shutterbug.

Kevin, that mischievous little scamp, holding a shhh-finger to his lips, pointing at Frank's beer where somebody had arranged a squid tentacle reaching for a drink.

Sherry, her best friend, dirty and disheveled after lugging one end of that big old chest up the stairs and into Linda's bedroom the day she moved in.

Focus, aperture, click. Linda, taking a picture of herself in the mirror, playing with a new lens, pleased with the odd angle and interesting composition, framed and displayed, a portrait of herself, a face in the crowd, the centerpiece of her room, surrounded by the smiling faces of the people she had loved.

CHAPTER 12

Frank sat in a chair beside Beverly's hospital bed. He held a pad on his lap, an awkward man, trying to reach out, the picture of sadness in a room filled incongruously with brilliant flowers. The fire he'd once discovered in Beverly, the warmth she always exuded, the glow of her charm, that sparkle in her eye—all seemed muted, far off in the distance, out of focus, lost to the world.

"Norman and Peggy Sullivan," Frank read, "Bob Alden and Doris Dibbiel, and JD Pluchartz also said they would arrive sometime Thursday night. You can see them and many of the others at the funeral home if you're up to it—if you want."

"Yes," Beverly remarked numbly, "I would have expected the Sullivans—and, of course, Bob and Doris, but that's awful nice of JD. It must be hard for him to get away . . ."

"Your phone hasn't stopped ringing. Kevin and I have taken turns covering it—"

"Kevin . . ." Beverly thought for a moment, as if remembering who Kevin might be. "How is the boy? Is he doing all right?"

"Well, he's, you know, he's hurt by—"

"What about his mother? Is she still in jail?"

"Yes—" Frank started, only to be cut off again.

"You said more cards came today?"

"Yes. Would you like me to read them to you?"

"If you want."

"Well, you got one from—"

A nurse came in with a tray full of small cups. "It's time for medication again. Excuse me," she said to Frank, setting the tray on the side table next to a pitcher of water. "How are you feeling this evening, Ms. Herndon?"

"Well, my leg still hurts an awful lot. I can move around easier now, though."

The nurse gave her some pills and a cup of water, watching carefully to make sure she managed to swallow them all. "Drink another one, hon. You need to keep pushing the fluids." The nurse left, and Frank started to read the first card.

"Who's that from again?" Beverly asked.

"It's a sympathy card from the Haywards. They—"

"The Haywards . . . yes, how are they doing?"

"Well—"

"This all seems so unnecessary," she interrupted. "There's no reason to send me cards. Why won't these people leave me alone?" She closed her eyes and refused to continue, eventually drifting off to sleep.

I'm not reaching her, thought Frank. *Why won't she let me in?*

"I'm sorry, Ms. Marlowe," apologized the funeral director. "The injuries to her face were too substantial. We're not satisfied with how, uh, with the cosmetic restoration. I must recommend that the lid remain closed both during visitation and the ceremony—even during any private time set aside for the family."

"Well, then," Loretta decided, "let's keep it closed." She looked away for a minute, then added, "That's too bad, though. Sometimes it's a lot easier when you can see for yourself."

Beverly lay awake, unsure of the time, not caring if it was day or night. The room looked darker than it had earlier, a lot quieter, too. For the first time, she noticed the fragrance of the flowers. Blossoms surrounded her, little cards attached to plastic sticks, a pot wrapped in purple foil.

She remembered, and felt herself sinking again.

"Are you awake?" came the voice.

She ignored it, closing her eyes against the world. Her leg still felt like a balloon. If she lay very still, that feeling would fade away, the room would fade away. . . .

Florida would fade away.

"It's okay. Nobody else is here."

Linda. Linda? Sweetheart, where are you? "Linda?" she called out.

"Shh, be quiet. I'm right here. It's okay, Mama. I'm right here."

Beverly opened her eyes. There in the darkness sat somebody in the chair. "Linda? Is that you, baby?"

"Yes, I'm here, Mama."

Beverly started crying, reaching out for her little girl. "Oh, Linda. I thought you were gone. They told me you were gone." She lowered her voice to a whisper, talking through her tears. "I never believed them. I knew you couldn't be—couldn't be gone."

"I'm here now, Mama. Are you okay? How do you feel?"

"My leg. It's my leg. Something's not right."

"They had to operate on it—put in some pins. It'll heal okay. You lost some of your foot, though—the front part."

"Oh! Well, as long as *you're* okay."

"Mama, you need some rest. Why don't you go to sleep?" Linda leaned over and hugged her.

Beverly whispered, "Oh Linda, I love you so much."

She whispered back, "One more thing, Mama. Don't tell anyone I was here. Just go along with them. If you don't tell, I'll come back. I won't let you be alone."

"I knew you wouldn't. I just knew it."

"I love you, Mama. Always remember that . . ." Linda's voice faded away.

Beverly looked again, and she was gone. All that remained were flowers with cards on plastic sticks and colored foil and an empty chair beside a tray holding a pitcher and cup.

A light from the hallway cut a gentle swath to the corner of the room, flickering occasionally before fading with Beverly into a deep, peaceful sleep.

CHAPTER 13

Henry hovered nearby as Frank moved among the funeral-home crowd one last time, preparing to leave. Neither had never met any of these people prior to this week, but because Beverly had told so many of her friends about him, Frank found himself welcomed and accepted. Because she had requested that visitors not come to the hospital, they loaded Frank with cards and messages of love and support for her.

"You about ready?" Henry asked when they reached the outer lobby.

"Yeah. I have to be there by five, and I promised Kevin we'd swing by to pick him up on the way. I need to check on the workers."

Driving separately, Henry led Frank out to the condos. Frank parked in the garage, then locked up. They walked over in front of Beverly's place where Kevin diligently supervised several men building one wheelchair ramp to the porch and another continuing to the door step. Pleased with the progress, they left the workers to their task.

All three loaded into Henry's car and set out for the car dealership on Highway 50 in Brooksville to pick up a new minivan. The saleslady demonstrated its wheelchair lift and lock-downs before Frank went inside to sign some papers. Henry waited outside while Kevin jumped into the driver's seat and pretended to cruise the highway. Henry admired the instrumentation through the window, then inspected the lift. Kevin walked back and watched while Henry operated it several times.

"He sure is doing a lot for her," Henry said.

"He's in love," pointed out Kevin as he made the lift go up and down for the umpteenth time. "He's got it bad."

Frank dropped Kevin off at Lonnie's house, then drove into Tampa to see Beverly at the hospital. A physician was examining her leg, so Frank offered to step out, but Beverly indicated he should stay, gesturing toward the chair against the wall.

The physician continued, "Yes, I think I'll discharge you tomorrow. I'm going to refer you to a specialist with an office out closer to where you live. You'll need to see him daily for as much as a week; then he'll determine a schedule for follow-up—that's assuming there are no complications."

"How much longer will I have to wear this brace?" she asked.

"Well, that'll be up to him, but I would guess several months—at best. He'll probably have the stitches out in about ten more days, though."

"What about my foot?" she asked.

"It's healing fine, too, but I hope you understand it will be some time before you can put any weight on it. I'm sure you'll need physical therapy so you can learn to walk with it—especially to balance on it."

He closed up the bandages and refastened the braces. He nodded to Frank and left.

"Hey, Beverly," Frank started. "It sounds like good news."

"Yeah," she replied with little enthusiasm.

Frank slid his chair over to the bed and pulled a folded sheaf of papers from his pocket. "I have some messages from people at the funeral home. Would you like to hear them now?"

"Okay."

As he read them, she nodded or made small remarks about the senders, but her reactions showed indifference. Frank felt uncomfortable, distant and distanced, looking for her to betray her feelings, good or bad. Even her grief seemed to have faded into vague obscurity.

"You know," he pointed out, "if you get out tomorrow, it means you can go to the funeral."

She looked at him for a long time, seeming like she just noticed he was there.

"I don't plan to go," she finally answered.

"Well . . ." He wasn't sure how to respond. "I guess if you don't feel up to it, that's okay, but a lot of people have come for you."

"I don't know if I'll feel up to it or not. It's just that—well, it all seems so unnecessary."

Frank sat for a minute, then asked, "What do you mean?"

She shrugged slightly, but didn't reply. After another awkward moment, Frank changed the subject.

"I had a ramp installed at your place. You can test it tomorrow."

She looked at him with an odd expression, then remarked, "Oh, you mean the condo."

"Yeah, of course."

"Frank, I don't know if I'll be—well, if I'll be staying down here or not."

He stood up, gulped, then sat down again, trying not to show his panic. "Why not?"

"Well, I just don't know about Florida. Nothing good has happened down here."

Hurt, Frank leaned forward and looked into her eyes. "I happened down here," he whispered softly.

She gazed back, then looked away. For a brief instant he saw her—he saw Beverly. He saw the woman he loved, but then she was gone.

"Well," she explained, avoiding his last comment, "it all depends on Linda."

"I thought you decided to have her laid to rest down here, and to have Marshall brought down to be buried beside her."

She shook her head, looking somewhat confused, then adamant. "You just don't understand, do you? You just don't understand."

Frank felt her slipping away. "Tell me, Beverly. Tell me, and I'll try to understand."

She shook her head and looked away. "I can't."

"Come on, Bev. I care about you—you know that. I'll do anything in the world for you."

"Oh Frank, you're such a sweet man, but I can't tell you. It's a secret."

"What's a secret?"

She thought for a minute. "Well . . . Will you promise not to tell anybody else?"

He moved even closer and took her hand. "Yes. You know you can trust me."

"It's just that— Well, Linda's not really dead."

Frank felt the pain well up inside him. Could she be so consumed with grief that she had lost touch with reality? Could her head injury have created a bigger problem than the physicians realized? He pictured the casket, draped in flowers, surrounded by people. He pictured the photo in the newspaper, the crumpled car being examined by a fireman, hoses snaked across the pavement. He remembered that phone call, hearing the horrible news. He looked at Beverly's injured leg, the faint marks on her face and arm, the shaved area on her head, evidence this was not some bad dream.

"I'm sorry, Beverly, but she is. I know it's hard to—"

"She is not! I don't want to hear it. I told you that in secret, so you just better keep it that way."

"But Beverly, I—"

"Go. Go on. Get out of here. I need my rest. I have plans to make. Go on."

He stood up. She pulled her hand back out of his. "But Beverly—"

"Go on, now. Go back to the funeral home and tell everybody I'm just not up to attending. Send them my best."

With that, she rolled over on her side, facing away from him, wincing from the pain in her leg. Frank stood there feeling helpless. Finally, he slinked out, quietly, reluctantly.

He paused at the door and whispered, "I *will* stand by you, no matter what."

Loretta sat with Beverly, waiting for the nurse to bring a wheelchair. Frank was due any moment with his new van, coming directly from the funeral home with Kevin and Lizzie, Beverly's neighbor and friend from Houghton Lake.

"It's okay if you don't want to attend," Loretta told her younger sister. "Whatever you want. You need to concentrate on yourself now and get better."

"Don't tell anybody what I said," Beverly reminded her. "She doesn't want anybody to know."

"Whatever you say," Loretta agreed, patting her hand.

"I just wouldn't know how to act at the funeral—her not really being dead and all."

"It's okay," Loretta placated. "You just stay home and rest. I'll represent our family."

Beverly shrugged. "It seems like we ought to cancel it."

"No," Loretta disagreed, "you can't do that. Everyone will be there, so we need to go through with it. Later on, you'll be glad you did. For now, though, don't worry, your big sister is here to take care of everything."

The nurse came in, helped Beverly into the chair, and pushed her out toward the elevator. They rode to the ground floor and met Frank just as the doors opened to let them off. He kissed Beverly gently on the head, but said nothing.

Frank asked them to wait in the lobby while he brought the van up to the door. Once he parked, Kevin jumped out and led Lizzie inside. Frank unloaded and unfolded a new wheelchair, pushing it into the lobby while Kevin and Lizzie took turns hugging and fawning over Beverly. Frank helped transfer Beverly to the new chair, then pushed her to the van, followed by her entourage.

"This certainly is impressive," Beverly remarked as the lift hoisted her inside.

During the drive, Frank and Loretta made small talk about tomorrow's funeral, covering issues like what to do with flowers, a last-minute pall-bearer substitute, the request from Linda's friends to play a CD of her favorite song at the end of the service, and arrangements Frank had made for a platform at the cemetery to accommodate a wheelchair if Beverly changed her mind about attending—making sure they said "if she decides she feels up to it" for Lizzie's benefit.

"I don't think so," was Beverly's only reaction.

"Then while Loretta's at the funeral home," Frank offered, "I want to stay with you. Kevin can go with Lor or Henry—"

"No thank you. I prefer to be by myself."

They rode on in silence, interrupted only by Lizzie making several awkward attempts to initiate conversation. When they finally pulled up in front of the condos, Beverly seemed mildly amused by the ramp. Frank lowered her to the driveway and offered to let her try entering by herself. She had no trouble negotiating the new route.

They followed her inside, Lizzie marveling at the beautiful new home Beverly had made for herself, the portrait of Linda on the living-room wall a poignant reminder of the sad occasion. Loretta put several bottles of medication on the kitchen counter. Frank had Beverly confirm that her wheelchair would fit into the bathroom. Lizzie fussed around trying to find something helpful to do while Kevin brought everybody cold drinks.

After a few minutes, Beverly pointed out that she was tired and her leg hurt, that maybe she should rest. Frank wondered if she might want something to eat, but she politely declined. He offered to take the others out for dinner and promised to bring something back for her before heading back to the funeral home for the final visitation.

After a round of hugs and encouragement and a brief bout of tears from Lizzie, they left her alone with her grief.

Beverly wheeled into the ground-floor bedroom and climbed onto her bed. She lay there several minutes, wishing she could talk to Linda.

Finally, alone and lonely, she drifted into a fitful nap, floating through a world where up meant down and love sometimes brought with it a dull, aching pain.

Dear MoM,

How are you? I am fine. Really I am sad. In the morning we are going to Lindas funeral. I have never been to a funeral before but you know that. It is bad that she died. Sometimes I think about having fun with her and how Beverly can never have fun with her again. Frank is sad too. I don't understand why Beverly is acting so different. She thinks Lindas still alive. Frank says she is still in shock. Shes not going to the funeral. Frank got me some nice clothes to wear so I will have a tie and stuff. I'm going to be one of the pall barers. That means I get to help carry the casket. I hope its not too heavy. I wish people didn't have to die.

I hope your doing fine in there. I think about you all the time. I wish I could come see you more. I hope you have enuff money from Frank. I wanted to put in some of my money from my account but Frank said thats for college or a car when I get older and he promised that he put in enuff. I hope so. I get all your letters. It sure is good when you write me letters. Dont you worry MoM cuz that lawyer will help you get out real soon. I cant wait until that happens.

I sure am lucky that Frank takes care of me while your in there in that jail. He keeps saying that I take care of myself and he makes me do things on my own a lot but I do things for him and he does things for me too. When we was talking about how hard it is on Beverly to lose Linda he said it would be hard for him when I move back home with you but thats OK cuz thats where I belong but he sure wants to make sure I still come spend time and do things with him no matter what even if we move somewhere else. He looked sad and gave me a really big hug and I hugged him too. Hes a good guy for sure. I sure wish I could hug you. Oh well I will when you get out.

I got to sleep now cuz were getting up early for the funeral. I know I'm going to be sad. I will mail this tomorrow. Good night MoM and remember I love you very much.

Love your son,
Kevin Riner

P.S. C-ya Sunday

CHAPTER 14

The night before the funeral, Frank sat next to Kevin at the dining-room table, returning phone calls, taking messages, and watching the boy draw a picture of roses and a butterfly. Frank had encouraged him to go to bed, but the youngster insisted he wasn't tired. Frank had, at first, sat across the table, but Kevin moved around to the seat next to him. He was staying close to his protector, emotionally strung out from all the recent tragedies.

Most of the calls were questions about funeral details—times and locations, the phone number to pledge donations in Linda's memory, and expressions of sympathy for Beverly from people who couldn't attend. Many let on that Beverly had recently referred to him as her companion. Through the pain and grief, he found in this a small measure of comfort, confirmation that she really had begun to consider him an indelible part of her life.

One message had come from Eli Rumsey. He wanted to meet with Frank before leaving on a two-week business trip. He said he had an apartment at Clearwater Beach that he kept for trips south, so Frank called and caught him there.

"Yeah, I wanted to feel you out on an idea," Eli explained. "I'd rather do it in person. Can I get you to come by here tomorrow?"

"I'll be driving down to Seminole tomorrow afternoon," Frank said. Since Lizzie wanted to spend some time with Beverly, he had offered to take leftover funeral flowers to Loretta's volunteer organization for delivery to sit-ins. "I'll have the boy with me, but I could stop by for a few minutes."

"Just tell the gate-man to show you to my private space."

Frank made several other calls while watching Kevin struggle to get the petals on the roses just right. Frustrated, the youngster pulled out another sheet of tagboard, starting over for the third time. Frank took his hand in his and guided the pencil in the shape of a curled petal. He helped him through several more, then let go and watched him continue on his own. After making one last call, he sat there with him for nearly an hour, watching him add subtle shading and highlights.

Finally, Kevin whispered, "The butterfly is Linda." They discussed his feelings and what he was trying to express with the drawing. Frank wrote Kevin's phrases on a sheet of paper, even teaching him a new word—"ephemeral"—the end result a poem to go with the picture, a tribute to Linda. Frank suggested they take it to the funeral home, put it on display, and have Kevin read the poem. The youngster admitted he was nervous about performing in front of a group, but he liked the idea of contributing somehow to the service, of standing up and paying his respects, of feeling like more than a helpless waif subject to the whims of fate controlling his life.

Finally, Kevin went off to bed. Frank stole quietly next door and checked on Beverly. She slept soundly, so he kissed her gently on the forehead and went back home. Slipping into Kevin's room, he sat on the side of his bed for a moment, watching him breathe softly and twitch in that odd way he did occasionally right after falling asleep. Frank reached over and stroked his hair, whispering, "Good night, buddy," then headed for the bathroom. He got undressed and stood for a moment, looking at himself in the mirror.

You're starting to show your age, old man, he thought.

He climbed into bed and drifted off into a fitful sleep, worried about Beverly.

Discharged from the hospital, asleep next door, she still hadn't found her way home.

Frank checked in on Beverly before leaving for the funeral. She said she felt reasonably well, that she'd cut down on her pain medication, leaving her more alert and lucid than she'd been since the accident. Again declining to attend, she asked Frank to call afterward in case she was up to making an appearance later. He knelt down, put his arms around her and the wheelchair, and kissed her. She responded more than he expected, giving him another glimpse of the Beverly he remembered.

Eschewing the Corvette as too symbolic of freedom and fun, Frank opted to drive the van. When he and Kevin pulled into the parking lot at the funeral home, he was directed to park immediately behind the limousine that fronted a growing line of vehicles. A teenager in shirt and tie moved among the cars, placing little flags on them.

Inside, people surrounded them. Many were new acquaintances that Frank had met at the funeral home in the last few days, some he had contacted by telephone, still others who just arrived in town. Loretta received some attention, but not like Frank and Kevin.

Everybody wanted to meet Beverly's new companion.

Beverly looked at the clock and realized the funeral would start in fifteen minutes. Feeling a pang of grief despite knowing that Linda was still alive, she wheeled into the living room and gazed at the large, framed photo of her beautiful daughter dominating the wall. She looked up just in time to see Linda coming in the front door.

"Hey there, Mama! You didn't want to go to the funeral?"

"No, no. I just wasn't up to it. I knew it would start feeling like you're really gone, and I just couldn't face going through that."

"Well," Linda observed, "you *do* have to start learning to deal with the fact that things never will—never *can* be the same again."

She hugged her mother, then helped her onto the couch, sitting beside her. They talked and laughed and reminisced about Marshall, sharing precious moments the way only a mother and daughter can in a world that often makes little or no sense.

Strains of organ music filled the chapel, signaling for those not yet seated to enter the main room and take chairs. The funeral director gently steered Frank and Kevin toward a low couch at the front, seating them next to Loretta, alongside several couches holding Sherry and some of Linda's other friends. As he turned to sit down, Frank caught the eye of Henry, who was sitting a few rows back. Henry nodded, reminding him in one glance how important friends can be.

As the music stopped, the minister Loretta had hired for the occasion stepped up on the dais. He welcomed everyone and explained how this service would be dedicated to honoring the memory of a fine young lady, tragically lost in the prime of her life, yet having lived so fully that she left behind many fond memories and loved ones enriched by having known her. He spoke directly to Loretta, Frank, Kevin, Sherry, and several others about how much they meant to Linda. Generic sentiments, his words nevertheless resonated with an important truth, that each had lost only Linda, but the greatest grief dwelled in the understanding that Linda had lost them all.

Then he introduced Frank, who stood up on the dais while the minister waited off to one side. Frank looked across the room filled with more than a hundred faces. Feeling a lump rise in his throat, he looked at Kevin. His young friend watched expectantly, expressing confidence that Frank would always do what needed to be done.

"Linda would have been proud of what a big crowd came today," he started, a wry smile creeping into his countenance. "Virtually all the time I spent with her, she took responsibility for making sure everybody around her had fun, getting the most out of life, enjoying the blessings we so often take for granted." With a sidelong glance, he added, "I don't think she would approve of us all getting together just to cry or preach sermons, so with that in mind, I would like to share a few letters from people who cared about her."

He read more than a dozen that related personal stories, expressed profound loss, sparked knowing chuckles, and touched the hearts of everyone present.

Lizzie stepped up and said, "I've got an old hound-dog, some kind of mutt the vet can only guess at, which I got from Linda. She was about eleven years old that summer when she found him out by the visitor's center. Still a pup, he was half-starved, eaten up by fleas, and had a bad ear infection. She brought him home and nursed him back to health. Bev and Marshall sure were tolerant of her always having her animals around. Every day she came over with that puppy, showing him off to me, playing in front of my house, watching to make sure I was looking. She'd bring him in to show me new tricks she'd taught him.

"She knew better than to ask me to take him 'cause Harold and me always had a house cat, but not some dog. Anyway, she waited until I got to where I'd pick him up and pet him and play with him a little. She paid for his medication and his shots out of her own allowance, and started talking about how whoever adopted him would get a good doggie and not have to pay for nothing but food . . . *and he eats real cheap*, she used to say.

"Then one day I was sitting on the porch when I heard her talking to him. She told him Aunt Lizzie was going adopt him, that I just didn't know it yet. I went out and told her I didn't want no filthy dog getting hair all over my clean house. She held him up and, using him like a ventriloquist's doll, mouthed the words, If you'll adopt me, I promise I'll only shed outside. Well, she worked on me for weeks after that until she just plain wore me down. She was working on Harold, too, at the same time. We finally took him. Houghty, is what she called him—after the lake we lived by.

"Houghty is still with us. He's getting old and don't get around like he used to, but God never made a better companion. He's a friend and a protector. It seemed like after Harold died some five years ago, Houghty took it just as hard as I did. I give credit to all the loving he got from that little girl—from Linda. Somebody abandoned him, and she showed him not all people was bad. That's the way she was. Her friends saved their allowances up for clothes and records and movies and such, but Linda spent hers helping take care of a sick little puppy that needed somebody to love."

Lizzie misted up, her voice all choked with emotion. "The night I got the call—" She looked over toward the rose-draped casket surrounded by a sea of beautiful flowers. "That night, I just sat down and cried. Houghty sat there and cried with me. He knew. He sure did. He knew something happened to that little girl who took care of him. Yeah, she was special, and there'll never be another like her."

Lizzie sat down and dabbed her eyes with a tissue.

A young lady about Linda's and Sherry's age got up. She spoke softly, telling how she had lived in the same apartment building as Linda near the campus. She said she had a drug problem, and that Linda kept trying to get her to seek help, but then her boyfriend left her, and she made plans to commit suicide. She said Linda came over to see if she was okay, saying she sensed maybe she needed a friend.

"She stayed up all night with me and drove me the next day to get me into the drug program. Linda was not only my friend, but I owe her my life. I loved her like a sister, and I sure will miss her."

Sherry got up and told how they had been friends since Linda stepped in to mediate a dispute with the playground bully in fourth grade. "It's hard to imagine going on without her, but she would've wanted me to. I'll never forget her, though, and someday I'll get out her pictures—" She looked toward the boards on display along the wall. "I'll show 'em to my grandkids and tell them all about her. Bye, Linda. I love you."

Kevin got up and, since he couldn't see over it, stood beside the podium. Frank held the picture Kevin had drawn the night before, a brilliant butterfly fluttering amid an exquisite patch of roses. "Go ahead, buddy," Frank whispered.

Kevin spoke softly, but with feeling and conviction. He pointed to the butterfly and explained, "This is Linda." Then he read the poem, pausing for a moment between each stanza:

> "We say farewell with a drawing,
> To symbolize all of our love,
> Some stunning pink roses,
> And pretty butterfly above.
>
> "We, like these flowers,
> Are anchored to this place,
> To blossom among thorns,
> Strive for vision and grace.
>
> "But now you fly free,
> A butterfly on the breeze,
> Spreading your beauty so far,
> Floating wherever you please.
>
> "Each lifetime is ephemeral,
> But of one thing we're sure,
> Though short, yours was quite special,
> And now your love will endure.
>
> "You've left us fond memories,
> We can't be at your side,
> But we'll carry you with us,
> In our hearts, deep inside."

He walked over and placed the drawing and the poem on top of the casket and went back to his seat, looking toward Frank, his eyes glistening. Frank gave him a wan smile and nodded approval. Deeply moved, the crowd applauded, several coming forward to shake his hand or offer a hug.

The funeral director whispered something in Frank's ear.

"We'll be concluding our services," Frank announced, "with a short prayer at the cemetery. Beverly and Loretta and I want to invite all of you to join us—yes, Beverly, too—I just received word that she thinks she feels up to stopping by for a while—down at the harbor club where we've reserved a room for a luncheon."

The entourage drove to the cemetery for a brief ceremony. A few people hugged and said their good-byes there, but most left for the harbor club while Frank and Kevin drove home to pick up Beverly.

They found her waiting on the porch. She had managed to put on some nice clothes and fix up her hair.

"Wow," said Kevin.

"Yeah, wow," agreed Frank. *How did she do that by herself?*

Out at the cemetery, close to the pond with three eternally spraying fountains, surrounded by flowering trees and shrubs, a dark patch of earth marred the otherwise manicured lawn. A casket spray of 240 red and peach roses sat in the middle of a low mound, surrounded by bouquets of flowers, some in baskets, some on wire stands.

A pair of wild geese floated across the pond, then waddled over to investigate. They settled down to rest next to Linda's grave, sentries on guard in the warm sunlight, protecting their new, unseen friend.

A vivid yellow and blue butterfly fluttered by, paused on one of the flowers, then disappeared into the breeze, never to look back.

CHAPTER 15

Frank and Kevin sat with Elijah Rumsey around the dining-room table in his Clearwater Beach apartment, snacking on delicious Greek carryout. Kevin wrinkled his nose at several of the dishes, but found plenty to fill both of his hollow legs. Reminded his guests were short of time, Eli motioned Frank toward the vacant chairs on the balcony. Kevin passed time by straightening up the mess.

"Well, here's the thing," Eli explained while Frank admired the view. "I appreciate what you're doing, working on getting the valuation down on the print biz before opening it up to investment, but I'd like you to consider me—me and my brother Larry—taking an option sooner. You know, locking this thing up, maybe in the next week or two."

"What's your hurry?" Frank wondered.

"Well, see, we got other irons in the fire. We might have a real attractive opportunity coming up, but we don't have the scratch to do both, so we'd kinda like to know where we stand."

"Then you should probably jump on that one. I've got some interest from other directions."

"That's all the more reason we might think about locking this thing up. I like what you got, and I believe you can make it grow. Larry says you're top drawer."

Larry doesn't even know me, thought Frank. Out loud, he asked, "What do you have in mind?"

"Well, I would need some information. For example, you say you plan to get the value down before offering the stock."

"I have to acquire the rest of it before I can offer it," Frank interrupted.

"Yeah, well, I guess that's just a formality. You said you got a way to break the backs of your shareholders."

Frank nodded without saying anything.

"Anyway," Eli continued, "I need to know what you anticipate, you know, to see what the price would be. I also need to know more about your timetable and what you're doing to bust down its value."

"I see," Frank remarked, watching a yacht in the distance.

"We need to make sure the company really is solid, not just something you're prettying up. In other words, is it really going to be undervalued, or are you working it up to be overvalued and just giving me a line?"

"If you don't trust me—"

"Oh, don't get me wrong. I just need to show my money guy so he can make sure all the legal stuff is straight. If you give me the real skinny and we plot out some solid numbers, then I—we—just might be willing to buy in on option right away."

"What kind of option?"

"Well, straight stock option would be the simplest. For that, we'd negotiate the price, you back it up enough to sell my money guy, and then we sew it up. At that point when the stock, based on some agreeable kind of valuation scenario, hits the magic number, we can exercise the option to buy."

"That gives you an escape hatch," Frank pointed out. "What's the advantage for me?"

"You get your deal sewed up in advance, knowing the money will be there when you need it. I expect you'll have to cover your end of the acquisition—you know, buying out the rest of the stock—before you can sell it to me."

"My rate on any buyout," Frank argued, "will depend on what I can negotiate. As I see it, I could get stuck, having to agree to a higher rate just to make stock available if you exercise your option. Not only am I not getting any advantage out of this, I could get burned."

"What if we tie it to your acquisition rate?" Eli asked. "I trust you'll hammer it down as low as it can go without bleeding your shareholders too bad. We'd still have to make it an option, though, in case you scam up paying too much. That way, I don't have to play unless the numbers you get are reasonable to the value of the company."

"So let me get this straight," Frank summarized. "We set the price. You and Larry execute a joint option—"

"Or split one," Eli added.

"Or split one. The option is set at the same rate I need to acquire the stock—"

"Except that you're keeping an extra one percent to retain the majority while selling us a forty-nine percent minority stake."

"Once I make the buy, you can exercise your option if whatever valuation you use tells you my price is reasonable. If it's not, you can bow out—"

"And you can pursue your other buyers," Eli finished.

"Still no big advantage for me," Frank pointed out.

"Well . . ."

Frank leaned forward. "How about this? We set the price, execute your options, and let you decide to exercise them within a set deadline. But here's the rub: This price we set is tied to my acquisition price with a built-in profit margin for *me*."

"Hmm . . . So we mark it up a few percent and let you go out and party a little?" Eli grinned, nudging Frank in the ribs.

"No," Frank replied, dead serious, "we set it at exactly what I paid, but you walk away with twenty-five percent of the stock covering my costs for putting the rest in *my* portfolio."

"Whew!" Eli sat back and chewed on his thumbnail for a moment. "If we could negotiate exactly what that percent would be—"

"It's non-negotiable. Half of the fifty percent I'd be acquiring."

"Well, that'd be paying an awful lot for just getting half of what we paid for—"

"You've got the value escape clause. If a quarter of the stock isn't worth what it'll cost you, then you can walk."

Eli chewed his thumb until the cuticle started to bleed, wiping it on his sleeve. "Hmm . . . I see what you mean. Well, if we go for that, we'll still need to see your numbers and find out what you're planning on doing in the next month or two—"

"No, you don't. It's none of your business until it's time to exercise your option. We can build in full disclosure of current valuation information at that time. Until then, she's my baby, not yours."

"Well, yeah sure. But I couldn't recommend to Larry that we even get into this without at least knowing—"

"Yeah, you could. What it boils down to is that you're guaranteed a chance to snap up a very valuable piece of a good company only if you think it's worth what you're paying. It gives me the incentive to make sure it's worth so much that you'd be a fool not to jump on it. Everybody wins, Eli."

"Well, the only problem is, I might pass up a pretty little fish waiting for this one to swim along. That's why I need to know—"

"That's why it's a gamble," Frank concluded, heading back inside. Eli followed him to where Kevin sat patiently eavesdropping on the conversation. The dining room looked spotless, the leftovers packaged up and put in the refrigerator.

"Come on, hoodlum, we're late for Loretta," Frank told him. He turned to Eli, stuck out his hand to shake, and said, "Why don't you think about it and maybe run it by Larry? This has been a good conversation. I think I'll pass this idea by a few other people, too." They left him standing there chewing his thumb.

Once inside the fragrant, flower-filled van and on the way to Seminole, Kevin remarked, "He just wanted to find out how you're going to get the stock from the Taylors."

Frank grinned. "You noticed that, too, huh? He thought he could dangle something pretty in front of me and get me to run my mouth."

Kevin pulled a sheet of paper from his pocket, slightly torn and soiled. On it were some numbers he had written. "Frank, you remember when you were teaching me how to figure out quarterly profits and we worked on this?"

"Yeah, why? You been carrying that around to study it?"

"No. I left it with all those records that later got stolen."

"Well," Frank started, "how did you—"

"I just found it in Mr. Rumsey's kitchen trash."

Tuesday morning began with Kevin rising earlier than usual to try on numerous outfits, excited about his first day at school. He decided on surf shorts, a baggy Key Largo t-shirt, and his new basketball shoes. Because Frank needed to drop address-change papers at the school, Kevin got to be seen by his friends tooling up in a classic Corvette, dressed in new, stylish clothes, carrying an expensive book bag. As much as people decry misplaced emphases on materialism, style, and peer acceptance, Frank wouldn't trade Kevin's burgeoning confidence and pride for any kind of lesson imparted by the types who discount the challenges of being twelve and starting a new grade. Frank went inside to the office and, after some first-day crisis delays, managed to fulfill his foster-fatherly responsibilities.

He drove back to the condos and called on Beverly, finding her diligently writing thank-you notes to the many names listed by the guest register and stack of flower cards. These did not include the list she would receive from the Humane Society in a few weeks specifying who made donations in Linda's memory.

Beverly greeted him warmly, then mentioned that the doctor wanted to see her the next afternoon. Frank offered to go with her, which she graciously accepted.

"Frank," she told him, "I can't thank you enough. Everybody I met yesterday said it was the most beautiful service they had ever seen, one that Linda would have been proud of."

He nodded and took her hand in his, squeezing gently, looking into her eyes.

"You know," she added, "I never mentioned to anyone there that Linda is still alive."

"That was probably a good idea," Frank pointed out.

"Still, though, it sure seemed strange to get sympathy from all those people when I knew full well—"

"Beverly, you need to accept the fact that Linda really is gone."

"But she's not!" she protested. "She sat right here with me during the service. She helped me get dressed and fixed my make-up and even my hair!"

"But Beverly—"

"But nothing. Look, I know it doesn't seem possible, but I *know* what I'm talking about."

She sounded like she was getting angry, so Frank let it drop. "Now that things have settled down a bit," he said, "I want to finish going over your records so I can help you settle the problems with Charles's and Marshall's estates."

She agreed and told him where in the den to find all the paperwork. He went and looked, only to learn that every bit of it was missing. Frank mentioned that Kevin had seen Loretta leaving with a lot of boxes the week before, and that maybe she had them. Beverly called Loretta's apartment, but couldn't reach her. She left a message to return the call.

After helping her sort and organize thank-yous for a while, he suggested they break and go have lunch before he had to leave for a meeting.

She left a note for Linda telling her when she would return.

CHAPTER 16

Kevin enjoyed his first day back at school. He renewed acquaintances with old friends, met some new people, and found great pleasure in seeing how many girls seemed unusually friendly—some even to the point of flirting. More acutely aware of his appearance than ever before, he dared to act more gregarious than his shy self of the past.

In the last class, physical education—or "gym" as it was called—the teacher collected information on each student. They took turns being weighed and measured, then having the number of push-ups and other exercises they could do counted, but mostly they horsed around, waiting for their turns. A group of several boys isolated Kevin and began to taunt him, calling him "Jail-baby" and labeling his mother a murderer. He tried to explain that she wasn't guilty, that it was some guy she used to go out with.

"Oh yeah? Then why is she in jail?"

"She has to go to court first before she can be found innocent."

"Well, *my* mom said," challenged another, "that she already went to court. That's why she's in jail."

Before Kevin could talk, another half-dozen boys joined the group.

"You're the one whose mom's in jail?"

"Wow! Your mom's a killer?"

"She's the one that killed those guys in a big drug deal."

"His mom must be a drug dealer."

Kevin's cheeks reddened. "She is not!" he protested.

"Bam! Bam! Bam!" another shouted, pretending to shoot a gun at the other boys.

"Better stay away from Riner," someone taunted. "He'll run home crying, and his mother'll come kill you!"

"No she won't," corrected another. "She's in jail!"

"He might sneak in a file, though, and help her escape!"

"Shut up!" Kevin yelled. "You don't know what you're talkin'—"

"Watch out, he's gonna cry!"

"Oh no! He's got a gun! Help! Help! Killer Riner's gonna get me. Yaaa!"

"Shut up—"

The boy who started it all pushed him from behind. "You gonna go home and get your gun, Riner?"

The teacher interrupted the fray, ordering everybody to stand over by the wall and knock it off. Kevin kept quiet, diverting his gaze. His cheeks burned blood red.

He wanted to crawl into a hole and disappear.

"This is it?" the detective asked. "This is what you got?" He turned the stained piece of paper over in his hands, then handed it back to Frank.

"But it was found *inside* his apartment. There is no way he would have that unless it was stolen from my place."

"And we're taking the word of a kid that he found it there, huh?"

"Kevin has no reason to lie."

"I'm not saying he does. I'm just saying that it doesn't amount to much. There's no way to get a search warrant based on something this flimsy."

"Well, what more would you need?" Frank asked.

"Look," the detective explained, "your missing business records are the only thing taken. They have no intrinsic cash value, and you already replaced them."

"Well, my disks have a value."

"Yeah, what? A few bucks a piece?"

"What about corporate espionage?"

"Then get yourself a corporate attorney and look into civil action."

"But this was a breaking-and-entering," Frank protested.

"Look, guy, let's be real. We got serious crimes to solve. We've still got open murder files, operators conning widows out of their life savings, car thefts—real crimes we need to spend our time on."

Frank nodded, then reached over and took the paper Kevin had found. He carefully placed it back into a folder. "I best let you be getting to it then," he said, standing to leave.

The detective followed him to the door. "It's just that, at best, you've got a simple plea bargain for misdemeanor here. The judge would consider it a nuisance. At worst, the guy might get probation or a small fine."

Frank turned at the door and made a mock gesture of tipping his hat. "Sorry I wasted your time."

Frank called Henry from his car phone, asking if he'd be available to meet on the *Fine Print* in about ninety minutes. Henry checked his calendar and said he could leave in an hour. Frank drove on to Mr. Mogill's office, parked, and went inside.

"The prosecutor is starting to talk deal," Mogill said.

"For what?" Frank asked.

"He'll want her to testify against Sisk."

"Would she go to prison?"

"I don't know. I would make a sentence guarantee part of the deal, and we'd have to get the judge to agree."

"What if there isn't a deal?"

"We'd have to take it to trial. I'll file a motion for discovery to see what they have; then we'll have to decide what our odds are."

"What's discovery?"

"That's when the prosecution turns over access to the evidence. It gives us a chance to prepare a defense. The fact that they've not been forthcoming with it is a good sign. If they let me see how many holes they have, it puts *me* in a better bargaining position. If they had it locked up fairly tight, they'd want me to know that before talking about a deal."

"So when is he going to let you know?"

Mogill flipped open his desk calendar and scanned several pages. "He's gone the rest of this week. I'll be up in Tallahassee the first part of next week. I figure we'll get together early the following week. That gives us about a week to dicker before the pre-trial."

"What happens at that?"

"Not much. It may just take place in the judge's chambers, especially if we have a deal on the table. It's sort of a deadline for letting the judge know if there's any way to avoid tying up his docket with a trial—or at least to estimate how long a trial might last for scheduling purposes."

"It needs to be a good deal, or she *has* to go to trial. That kid can't lose his mother. He's been through too much, and she needs a chance to get her life together."

"I'll do what I can," Mogill assured him. "That's what I do—the best I can."

Frank changed the subject, explaining about his situation with the break-in and his suspicions of Eli Rumsey. Without going into all the details about how he was playing Eli and Larry against the Taylors, he asked about his options for jamming up the brothers at just the right time in order to pull the rug out from under them all.

Mogill called in one of his firm's other attorneys, one who specializes more in civil and corporate matters. They chatted for a few minutes. Frank left with several good suggestions in mind.

Their ideas were, of course, entirely off the record.

Kevin lingered out by the parking-lot entrance waiting for Frank to pick him up. Several students stood by, taunting him. Word about his mother had spread through the school like wildfire. Lonnie walked by, heading toward his bus, but he pretended not to notice.

Some friend, Kevin thought.

Several boys surrounded Kevin, attempting to pick a fight. Frank pulled into the lot with the top down on his Corvette. Because he had to drive through stop-and-go traffic, waiting for parents to pick up their children, he had time to hear some of what was going on. Instead of stopping at the curb, he pulled into one of the parking spots and walked up to the group. The boys got quiet and backed off slightly. Frank stood over them, giving them a very intimidating look.

He stared each one down individually for a second or two, then calmly offered, "You know, I've had to deal with some very intense people in my time. There's two things I've learned that you guys may want to think about. First, never stir up crap when you don't know what you're talking about—" He paused for effect, then in a slightly more sinister voice offered, "And second, *never* stir it up when you don't even know *who* you're messing with." He turned to Kevin and asked, somewhat mysteriously, "We've got business to take care of—you ready to go?"

Kevin nodded. Frank gave each boy another look. Two of them turned and walked away quickly, the others not far behind. Frank and Kevin got into the Corvette and drove off.

In the car, Frank asked, "Do you want to be dropped off at home or go with me to the boat to meet Henry and the investigator?"

"With you."

They drove on a while, not mentioning what happened at school. Kevin calmed down, feeling a lot better than he had earlier. Frank had a way of doing that for him.

Kevin watched him out of the corner of his eye, secretly amused at that flap of long hair blowing in the wind and exposing his tanned pate. To Kevin, Frank embodied strength and perseverance, intelligence and savvy, reliability and—well, friendship seemed like an awkward term, but whatever they had, it sure was great.

"By the way," Frank said, "you were right. Loretta took all of Beverly's financial papers."

"Bitch," Kevin said.

"Conniving bitch," Frank agreed.

They found Henry waiting in the parking lot at the yacht club. The two men greeted each other; then Henry turned to Kevin and said hello, shaking his hand. Kevin always liked how Henry treated him as a peer rather than with the old seen-but-not-heard attitude so many adults had about young people. Soon Rob Buchanan, private investigator, pulled up in his rental car. The four walked down and boarded the boat. Frank got a round of cold drinks while Kevin unpacked deck chairs for everybody.

Frank opened the meeting, explaining, "Henry, Mr. Buchanan here has an update on his diggings with the company. I plan to go over it in more detail tonight and get with you in the next day or two. The reason I asked you to stop by is mostly for the second part of the meeting. I want to consider some options, with Mr. Buchanan's input, and I value your opinion—not just as a business associate, but as a friend."

Henry rubbed his hands together. "Ooo! Intrigue. Count me in!"

Frank turned to Buchanan and said, "There might be something else you could do for me while you're here."

"Ooo! Intrigue! Count me in," he replied, rubbing his hands together. He grinned, pulled out a cigar and chomped down on the end.

"First, let's quickly see what you have," Frank prodded.

"Well," Buchanan began, "you got some pretty loyal people up there. That list of associates you thought you could count on panned out a hundred percent. They's *all* working with me." He pulled out a sheaf of more than a dozen files.

Frank grinned and told Kevin, "See that, hoodlum? Treat people straight and it always comes back around."

Buchanan continued, "We can go through these one at a time, but the bottom line is, it looks like you got the Taylors running scared. They've already switched some of the accounts back to the original vendors—mostly the ones where the new middleman had that Rumsey feller's name on them."

"I'm not surprised. They're trying to clean up their mess now that they know I'm on to them."

Henry added, "And you put them in a position where they might want that valuation to be high after all."

Kevin pointed out, "If the Taylors are getting rid of the contracts they had with Eli, they must not want to do business with him anymore."

"Or," Frank added, "they might just want to hide him for now."

Buchanan leafed through each folder, showing them numbers, lists of orders, and various other details provided by each vendor. While Henry took notes, Kevin watched intently, occasionally asking surprisingly astute questions. Once that was dispatched, Frank brought up the next subject.

"Let me start with the background," he began. "I first started to suspect the Rumseys might have something to do with my break-in when Eli betrayed too much knowledge during our meeting. Then Kevin found some notes . . ."

Frank finished filling in the details, then proposed a plan.

Everybody approved. There sat four conniving men, one a lot younger than the others, all toasting their anticipated victory, satisfied that anybody who tried to pull the wool over their eyes just might wind up leaving his own fanny exposed.

CHAPTER 17

Frank came back from the store with a sack of drinks and snacks. He looked around for Kevin and, not seeing him, put the munchies away. He went to the boy's bedroom, pushed the door open, and peeked in. Kevin was lying in bed, having just retired for the night, but still wide awake.

Frank whispered, "Can I come in?"

"Sure." Kevin sat up, propping his pillow behind him.

Frank pulled a chair over next to the bed, sat down, and offered, "I was hoping we could talk a few minutes before you doze off to La-La Land to zap warriors, fly through outer space, and slay mighty dragons for all the pretty girls . . ." Frank leaned forward and, quieter, finished, "And where you can flatten all the school bullies with one mighty blow."

Kevin lowered his head and started to fidget with his bedsheet.

"You had a pretty rough day, huh?"

Kevin shrugged. "It was pretty good until those dick-heads started in about my mom during gym class. Then the rumor got around and everybody started raggin' me."

"Are you worried about tomorrow?"

Kevin managed a half-shrug, but turned it into a nod.

"Well, I don't have an easy solution for you, but I *can* give you some advice."

"What?"

"Don't let 'em get to you. When they start getting on you, it's so they can get a response. They want you to get upset and cry or run off, or they want to goad you into trying to lash out or start a fight, or they want to embarrass you so much that you hide and avoid them and maybe not even come to school."

"Or all of the above," Kevin added.

"That's right. Tell me something. How do you feel about yourself?"

"What do you mean?"

"You know—are you smart? Are you good looking? Can you handle challenging situations? Are you a likable person?"

"Well, I think I'm pretty smart."

"You're *very* smart, buddy. I get more and more impressed every time we work on things together. That's one of the reasons I'm teaching you about business—you already understand more than a lot of people who go to college to learn about it. What else?"

"Well, I think I'm okay looking, but I'm too little."

"You're not even thirteen yet, and the puberty monster is just starting to chew on you. Trust me, you'll be a foot taller and a lot more filled out by the end of the school year. At your age, young guys are lots of different sizes—and when they grow up, too—but you've got a long way to go, and no matter how big you wind up, a guy is still only as big as his mind—" He touched Kevin's head. "—And his heart." He laid his hand over the boy's heart for a brief moment. "And to me, you're bigger than most of the grown-ups I know. What else?"

"I guess most people like me."

"What's not to like? So you're an obnoxious little hoodlum—but you always turn on the Riner charm and disarm them. You could be quite the salesman someday with that."

Kevin grinned, then mocked his adorable look. "I wish I was one of the cool people at school, though."

"Well, a lot of times, those people spend all their energy putting on an act. I'm always proud of how you just be yourself. Yourself is a pretty good self to be. You'll make a lot of friends, and you'll lose a lot of them over the years. Hopefully, you'll find one or a few really good ones who stick with you over time, no matter what—like me and Henry."

"Money-grubber."

"Yeah. You know, I started calling him that in eighth grade."

"You knew him in school?"

"Oh yeah. He moved around the block from me when we were thirteen. We always used to hang out, stirring up ways to make money. He was the tightwad who saved all his, opening a savings account, figuring out his interest, and so on. He always wound up being treasurer for the scout troop or the student council or what-not. We both went to college together, and he's helped me with my company through the years. When I retired and moved down here, he came down to visit and liked it, so he sold his accounting practice and moved down here, too. He wound up opening another small one down here, just so he could keep his fingers on a calculator. Anyway, the point is, most of those people won't matter in the long run. If you're lucky, one or two like Henry will really count."

"I like Henry," Kevin observed.

"At your age, it's not always easy to spot the good ones. In fact, being popular and fitting in is *very* important. I understand that—and that's okay as long as you don't try so hard that you quit being who you really are or, worse yet, do things that can get you hurt just to go along with people who don't really give a damn about you."

"Like getting drunk and stealing and stuff like that."

"Right. I have to tell you, buddy, I know the difference—I know how to spot good people, and you're one of the best. I intend to work hard at being your friend for the rest of my life. Other good people, like Beverly or Henry, can tell you're one of the good ones, too, which is why they'll do anything for you. So when the dick-heads, as you called them, start getting on your case, just remember, you're *better* than they are. You really don't have to care what they think."

"But they make it hard to get along at school," Kevin pointed out.

"Only if you let them. Just ignore them and go on about your business with full confidence. They'll go off and find somebody more fun to pick on. In the meantime, the few good ones will see that you *know* who *you* are, and they'll want to get to know you better, too."

Kevin looked relieved, maybe even enthusiastic about wearing a new attitude along with his other new outfits.

Frank grinned and tousled the boy's hair. "Then, before you know it, some little gal will be trying to get to know you, too." Frank stood up and looked down at him, softening his voice. "You feel better, buddy?"

"Yeah." He pulled his pillow down and slid back under his sheet.

"You think you can handle things at school tomorrow?"

"I'll try. To hell with the dick-heads!"

"To hell with the dick-heads!" Frank agreed, slipping out of the room so Kevin could doze off into La-La Land to zap warriors, fly through outer space, and slay mighty dragons for all the pretty girls.

Beverly awoke to the smell of fresh-brewed coffee. She struggled her braced leg and sore body into her wheelchair, then rolled out into the hallway. She could see Loretta in the kitchen making toast and setting out marmalade and jams.

"Hi, Loretta! I'll be out in a minute."

By the time she came out from the bathroom, Loretta had the table set. She wheeled over and joined her sister for a light breakfast.

After a few minutes, Loretta casually remarked, "You know, in all the commotion after the accident, not knowing how long you would be in the hospital, I cleared out some of your important records—to keep them safe."

"Keep them safe?" Beverly asked.

"Well, yeah. I know Frank—or at least that kid—has a key to this place."

"Loretta," Beverly admonished, "you don't need to protect anything from Frank or Kevin, as the kid prefers to be called."

"I just wanted to make sure everything was in order—you know, in case you were laid up for a while."

"I understand you took all of Linda's records, too."

Loretta stopped eating. "I don't have everything sorted out yet."

"I don't need them sorted, thank you."

"Well, I know it's going to be hard for you to close down Linda's accounts and take care of her affairs, so I brought something to make it easier." She retrieved a document and pen from her purse.

Beverly looked at the power-of-attorney form giving Loretta signatory authority to handle any legal or financial matters on her behalf. "No thank you, Loretta. I can take care of everything myself."

"You can't even drive, and the pain medication—"

"I'm sure I can manage."

"But you only have half a foot!" Loretta protested.

"I need all my toes to sign papers or handle a bank account?"

"Well, I think you should—"

"Loretta, just bring back all the records. I need them right away."

"Well, I'll be busy—"

"I can send a courier."

Loretta stood up, picked up her purse, and said, "Make sure you call first. I'm going to be very busy this week." She hurried out the door.

Frank walked up Beverly's ramp just as Loretta reached her car. "Hi, Loretta!" he called. She must have ignored him.

Frank knocked, then stepped inside. "Is there a foxy lady with a stiff leg in the building?"

"Hi, Frank," she said quietly, sitting at the table with mostly untouched food, obviously agitated.

He kissed her on the cheek, pulled up a chair, and asked, "Why's Loretta in a snit?"

"Because I demanded my records back, and I'm in a snit because she's stalling."

Frank tried to lighten the mood. "Does this mean I can eat her breakfast?"

"Oh yes; I'm sorry. Help yourself." She smiled, asking with a southern drawl, "Would the kind gentleman care to join a little ol' belle in some morning repast?"

"Why madam, I don't mind if I do." After they ate for several minutes, Frank pointed out, "For now you can at least start a list of what needs to be done. I'm free until your doctor's appointment after lunch. Would you like my help?"

"Oh yes, definitely."

"Do you keep records anyplace else?"

"Stockbridge has copies of just about everything, mine *and* Linda's."

"Why does he need all that?"

"For something about full disclosure."

"That sounds skanky to me," Frank said. "Let's get him on the phone and insist he express ship it all back."

"You'll do most of the talking?"

"If you want. Just make it clear these are *your* wishes."

Stockbridge proved less than friendly. "In fact, today she'll be receiving a registered letter resigning my representation," he said.

Frank asked, "Why is this?"

"She suspended me from taking any more action on her behalf, so I exercised my option to withdraw. Now, as the letter will indicate, any further advocacy would be a conflict of interest."

"How's that?" Frank asked.

"I have agreed to represent Loretta Marlowe in certain matters."

"*What* matters?"

"That's confidential."

"Yeah, well, Beverly wants every last scrap of paper in her file. You may keep only *copies* of your work notes and documents filed with the court. Have it all here tomorrow."

"We'll need more time than that—"

"The hell you will. Send a secretary with a few boxes and empty the file. Don't sort, don't censor, don't photocopy, nothing. In fact, you'll receive a fax within thirty minutes, signed by Beverly, witnessed by me, formalizing this demand and clarifying that you are expressly barred from retaining *any* copies of her personal records."

Stockbridge paused for a moment, then argued, "I'll have to review the status of her account. If she owes the firm any payment for services, I may need to hold these records until it is up to date."

"If they're not here by tomorrow morning, Beverly will call for a full ethics investigation, file complaints with every governing body, then slap you with a civil lawsuit—and heavily trump up the damages caused by your delay in furnishing critical records which you had no reason to possess. In fact, I have a private investigator up there on retainer. I wonder if he might be able to root out any other improprieties in *any* aspect of your life."

Stockbridge paused, then replied quietly, "I'll see what I can do. I really must go now; I have a meeting."

Beverly grinned at Frank as he came back into the room. "So there!" she mocked.

Frank shrugged. "He pissed me off."

"Frank, can we do one of those power-of-attorney things for you? That means I could still sign things, but you could sign for me, too, right?"

"Well, it's not really necessary."

"Frank—" She gestured toward her injured leg. "I can't get around very well. If you'll help me settle Linda's affairs and get all my finances together, I don't want you to have to run back and forth getting my signature witnessed."

He put his arms around her, hugging tightly, then called Mogill's partner, Alex Posner, the lawyer who handled civil and corporate matters, asking him to have a power-of-attorney form drawn up and faxed over as soon as possible. Posner promised it would be there within the hour. Frank also asked if he would follow up on the appellate motion in Michigan, the one originally filed by Beverly's husband Marshall challenging the lower-court ruling that allowed the bank to keep his deceased brother Charles's discretionary trust. It had been going on for years, preventing Marshall's widow, Beverly, from collecting those funds, and she no longer had an attorney to apprise her on the status of that ruling. Posner said he would put somebody on it as soon as Beverly's records arrived. He asked for the docket number, filing date, and some basic information. Frank promised to pass it along.

Frank and Beverly spent the next few hours making lists. Linda's affairs included things like getting copies of her death certificate, canceling credit cards—of which Beverly could remember three—cashing out stock and bond funds as well as money-market accounts and other capital assets that also had Beverly's name listed on them, starting the paperwork to bypass probate on the rest, paying bills and covering obligations so Sherry wouldn't be left in the lurch for things like rent and utilities, closing savings and checking accounts, cashing out retirement funds, filing insurance claims with the auto carrier and several other companies for death benefits, plus continuing her monthly Humane Society pledge.

They made a miscellaneous list for Beverly's affairs which included arranging to have Marshall moved to the cemetery where Linda was buried. As the list grew longer, Frank grew impressed by how much she really *did* remember, as well as the breadth and value of her holdings.

As they wound down their discussion, Frank answered Beverly's ringing phone, Lizzie letting them know she had arrived safely back in Michigan. "I want to come back down there," she offered, "as soon as she feels up to it, and spend some time with her."

"What a great idea," he agreed before handing Beverly the phone.

"That would be nice," he heard Beverly tell her without hesitation, her enthusiasm surprising him.

The two women chatted for a few minutes; then Beverly dropped the bombshell. "You know, I'm not supposed to tell people, but you're one of my best friends." She hesitated. "Linda really is still alive. She told me to go ahead and settle her affairs as if she were gone, but secretly she's been visiting me." She fell quiet for a minute. "I can't explain it. I don't even know where she's staying. She's being real mysterious about it, wanting me to pretend she's really gone."

Lizzie must have changed the subject, because they talked about various other things until Beverly begged off, handing the phone back to Frank. "She wants to say bye," she said, clearly pleased to include him again.

"I don't want to discuss it now," Lizzie told him, "but I'm worried about her. This nonsense about Linda isn't healthy. Please look out for her. I'll check in with you later."

"That's right, Lizzie," he replied. "It was good hearing from you. Take care now."

Frank followed Beverly into the examination room. It proved hard to watch her wince with pain, her tears welling up while her leg and foot were pulled and prodded and poked and subjected to various kinds of intrusive but necessary scrutiny. He held her hand, letting her squeeze hard, and kept eye contact so she wouldn't look too closely at the injuries. All at once, he felt indescribably helpless. All he could do was be there for her, devoting himself to making sure nobody and nothing would ever hurt her again. *Now, if only I could be sure of that—but in life there are no guarantees . . .*

While the doctor made some notes on his chart, Beverly asked, "Is everything healing okay?"

"Couldn't be better. You're right on schedule, if not ahead. I'd like to get the physical therapy started early next week. The bones should be fused enough by then to withstand some serious stretching. We can't let those muscles atrophy, and we need to limber up your joints."

"You still think I'll walk again?"

"No question—if you're willing to do the work. Stick with therapy and do your exercises. You'll probably need a simple prosthesis for that foot—mostly to help you with balance, but you should be able to get around, maybe even without a cane. You'll not be scuffing up any dance floors or running a marathon, but it won't prevent you from getting out and living it up."

"Is there anything else she should be doing?" Frank asked.

"Well, no, not for now. I want to see her every day—to check on progress and change these bandages—but by next week, she could learn to change the dressing herself." He asked Beverly, "Do you think you need some personal help in your home?"

"Well, the bird-baths are getting old fast. I'd like to prop up my leg and get into a hot tub real soon."

"Well, I can recommend some home-care attendants to help with things like that."

Beverly thought for a minute. "No, I think I can get by for now. I'd like to do as much as I can on my own. I'll try the bath routine only when Frank is around, in case I need help. My daughter Linda can help me, too, whenever she comes by."

The doctor looked puzzled, then glanced at Frank. "I'm sorry; I don't understand. I thought you lost your daughter in the accident."

"Well, if that's what you think, I won't say otherwise."

The doctor looked at Frank again, who shrugged just perceptibly. To Beverly, he offered, "You might want to talk with somebody and get some of your feelings out. You know, learn about grief and coping. I can recommend some good therapists. Plus, there are lots of support groups in this area."

"That won't be necessary. You just help me get this confounded brace off so I can relearn how to walk."

In the van, Frank tried to broach the subject again, suggesting counseling might not be a bad idea after all. Beverly argued against it, then started to grow angry. Frank slowed to a stop in yet another local traffic jam, lost in thought.

How do you help someone you love when she doesn't even think she's in trouble?

Frank pulled up to the middle school to see if Kevin wanted a ride—really to see if he was having any problems. After a few minutes, the bell rang and the building exploded with students scattering every direction. He spotted Kevin and Lonnie working their way toward the busses and shouted, "Kevin!"

They switched directions and approached the van. "Cool! The Ridemaster is here," Kevin announced. Not exactly a vintage Corvette, the van had at least achieved a modicum of cache.

"Where shall I take you, O Masters? To the mansion? To the yacht? How about a tour of your tenement properties?"

"How about to Lonnie's house to pick up his bike, then back home?" Kevin asked.

Frank chauffeured like the most dedicated of soccer moms, parking out front of the Caselow residence while Lonnie ran inside.

Ms. Caselow came out to the van, wiping her hands on a dish towel, and introduced herself to Frank. "If he's going over to your place sometimes, I want to know who you are."

A ten-minute barrage of personal questions later, she still seemed a bit reluctant.

Frank lowered his voice and confided, "Look, these are two good boys, and when they're with me I'll keep them on track for becoming two good men. In the meantime, I'll make sure they're fed and watered, too."

She told Lonnie to go get his bike. Kevin whispered in Frank's ear, asking if Lonnie could sleep over Friday night. Lonnie loaded his bike into the van, Frank agreed, and Kevin issued the invitation. Ms. Caselow gave her permission before Lonnie could even ask.

Back at the condos, the boys rode off to do whatever it is boys do when hanging out with a good friend is a higher priority than moping alone. Later, Frank ordered pizzas and took some over for Beverly. After dinner, Frank interrupted a video-game tournament and told Lonnie he should hit the dusty trail in order to be home before dark. He sent Kevin off to do his homework and said he would be at Beverly's for a while.

He kissed Beverly, then suggested it was time for her to have a good, thorough bath and, by gosh, he would be just thrilled to help. He ran some hot, sudsy water and helped her out of her clothes.

"I do believe," she remarked in a mock drawl, "that it's hard for a li'l ol' gal to have *any* kinda modesty when placed in such a *compromising* position."

"Well, madam," Frank replied, "it occurs to this gentleman that the lady will probably be splashing all over his good clothes anyway, so with your permission, I would like to *equalize* our circumstances."

She batted her eyes and declared it a grand idea. "The lady warns, though, that she may have to protest if the gentleman attempts to take liberties."

Frank helped her into the oversized sunken tub, then stripped and climbed in with her. Being careful to keep her leg propped on the side and out of the water, they played and washed and tickled and massaged sore muscles and wound up engaging in a bit of the old kissy-face.

In an awkward, in-the-water, leg-off-to-the-side sort of way, Frank *did* take liberties with the lady, but she never protested and, by all accounts, seemed rather to enjoy herself.

Frank eased Beverly into bed, kissed her goodnight, and left her to catch up on magazine reading.

After he'd gone, she read several articles, then looked up in time to see Linda coming into her bedroom. Pulling up a chair, the young woman placed a cold drink on the nightstand, then hugged her mother before sitting down.

Beverly told her about Loretta's shenanigans with the records and power-of-attorney form. Linda looked dismayed, but not overly surprised. "I think you did the right thing giving Frank signatory power. He knows what he's doing, and I *know* he'll do everything he can for you. Mama, you are *so* lucky to have him. Don't ever let him go."

"Yeah," Beverly said with a gleam in her eye. "I think he feels the same way." Then she mentioned that the doctor tried to refer her to a counselor.

"Mama, don't let me being here stop you from adjusting to the fact that I *will* be gone."

"What do you mean?"

"You have to start learning to deal with everything changing after the accident. I can't go back to that life I had before."

"But I don't understand. Why can't you just—"

"Mama, I can't explain—I'm not even sure I know how. I just want to make sure I'm here long enough to help you move on to the next stage. You have so much that can be wonderful ahead of you. Don't let losing me stop you from getting everything you can out of life."

"You're not going to leave me, are you?" She reached over to hold Linda's arm tightly.

"Not yet. Don't worry, I'll come visit you again. But there's a complicated process I don't yet understand which you're going to have to get through, learning to live with your grief and carry on for both of us. I won't abandon you, but you *must* understand that eventually you'll have to learn to let me go."

Beverly started to cry, so Linda crawled onto the bed beside her like she had so many times as a scared little girl hugging her mother. They lay there together, quietly sharing their precious time. Eventually, Beverly drifted off to sleep, into a world where Frank held her tightly and Linda would live forever, a world with no problems and no pain, a world of beauty and peace.

Amid the flowers and the sunshine and sparkling blue water, she spied a swirl of pinpoint lights in all imaginable colors, shimmering and iridescent, forming shapes, then scattering every which way, calling out how much Linda loved her, reminding her that, in time, everything would be okay.

CHAPTER 18

Frank showed up early the next morning, right after the express-delivery truck left. He and Beverly unpacked all three boxes, eventually finding files pertaining to the appellate-court appeal. Frank called Alex Posner and gave him the docket number, then retrieved his ten-key calculator, two boxes of file folders, two portable file tubs with hanging dividers, and a ledger pad. Beverly made coffee and set out some sweet rolls.

Over the next hour, Frank sorted envelopes and files and loose papers and statements and notes in Marshall's handwriting and bonds and certificates and various odds and ends into numerous piles, tallying and filing, making several lists of things that needed to be dealt with or explained. Occasionally, he opened packets, rubbed his jaw, and whistled quietly.

Once he got the last of the papers into files and ran several totals based on the stock listings from the morning's newspaper, Beverly asked, "So am I a rich old widow or a pauper?"

"I'd say rich *young* widow. Beverly, if this is handled correctly, you could top four-million dollars."

"Well, if you don't mind the trouble, I'd like to see what you can do with it. Cash it out, move it around, invest in wild schemes, buy me a silver cloud—whatever you want as long as you don't waste it too frivolously or leave me broke."

"Why, ma'am," Frank drawled, standing up to bow in a long, gracious arc, "I'd be delighted to spend your money."

Beverly laughed, then got serious for a moment. "There's one thing I want to do, Frank. That lady from the Humane Society down here was thrilled when we designated them for memorial contributions. She said they desperately needed to raise money for an animal hospital. If you think I can afford it, I would like to contribute toward one in memory of my little girl." Tears suddenly welled in her eyes. "Lord knows, I was going to leave all this to her anyway. That's what she would want me . . . to do." Beverly looked off in the distance and paused, then looked back at Frank and smiled. "I would like that very much."

Frank leaned over and kissed her on the cheek, whispering, "It will be my highest priority."

He needed to leave for his meeting with the Rumseys, so he closed up the portable files and placed a leftover stack of papers on top, most pertaining to investments

Marshall had made for Linda but for which information was missing. He quickly straightened up from their snack. Beverly followed him to the door.

He cupped her face in his hands, cocked his head, and smiled. Then he smooched her on her nose and announced, "Yer a heathen temptress who'll have me out of my knickers and missing meetings if I stay just one second more!"

Beverly watched him drive off down the road, that shock of sparse hair flapping in the open-convertible breeze as he disappeared into the hot glare of Florida morning sun.

She smiled and whispered, "You're right. I would've."

Frank parked behind the office and entered through the back way. Finding Henry at his desk, he took a seat across from him. "Are they here yet?"

Henry grinned. "Eli's been waiting out there for more than thirty minutes. I'd say he's a bit, uh, *eager.*"

"Good. Good. Let's try to reach Buchanan before we let him in."

They made several calls, but didn't manage to get hold of the private investigator. Giving up, they let Elijah Rumsey in. He was surprised to see Frank already there.

"Larry won't be joining us today?" Frank asked.

"No. He's decided to take a pass. It will be just me." Henry led them to the conference table over by the window, exchanging barely perceptible smiles with Frank behind Eli's back. Eli laid out some documents. Henry did the same.

"I had it all drawn up, just the way we discussed," Eli began.

"Good," Frank replied. "This must mean you *are* interested in negotiating a stock-purchase option in the nature of what we informally discussed."

Eli looked back and forth between Frank and Henry, then countered, "Well, I decided to accept your offer just as you made it."

"I probably would have been willing to go with that if we had done something that day. Since then, I've made *considerable* progress in my various, uh, *efforts* to accomplish certain things on the agenda I have for my company. I'm real pleased with how it's going."

Henry grinned and, for emphasis, added a nebulous, "*Real* pleased."

Eli looked frustrated. "You're making a different offer?"

"Yep," Frank remarked. "I now have things set up so I'm virtually guaranteed that my other shareholders will have to sell to me—at a very attractive price. Then I can turn those shares into gold. So, since you've been a good guy, negotiating in good faith, someone who really seems to believe in this company, I'm still willing to give you first crack at a private stock option—just as we discussed. Only . . . the percent has changed."

Eli sat back. "To what?"

"Well, I buy the other half of the company from the Taylors. You pay me exactly what I pay them, subject to verification, and receive fifteen percent of the total shares. I increase my holdings by thirty-five percent."

Eli rolled his eyes. "You're kidding, right?"

"The option still works the same. You put your own vultures on the books—no offense to you vultures, Henry—" Henry responded by tipping his non-existent hat. "And if you think it's worth it, exercise your option and you're in. If not, you walk away."

Eli looked rather unhappy, but he still needed this as a bargaining tool to use against the Taylors, proof he might get the shares even if not directly from them.

Henry passed around copies of a stock-option agreement Alex Posner had sent over. Everybody initialed the new percentages and signed.

After Eli left, Frank grinned and observed, "That went very well."

Henry agreed, then asked, "One thing I don't understand, though. If you know Eli is in the Taylors' pants, why couldn't he use this to have them match your purchase price and sell to him, instead, just to spite you—especially if he arranged some kind of kickback for them?"

"It's those pesky by-laws, Henry. When Jack and I wrote 'em, we gave each other right-of-first-refusal." Frank tipped his own imaginary hat. "I get sixty days to match any offer Eli or anybody else makes."

Linda found Beverly in the bathroom taking medication and checking her bandages.

"Linda! I'm so glad you came."

"What'cha doing there, Mama? Taking your pain pills?"

"Yeah, I'm a real druggie now. Sometimes, if I don't take 'em, my leg gets to throbbing. My foot don't hurt much, but that leg gets started and just won't quit."

They went to the den where Frank had left the financial records. "I've got questions about some of this stuff," Beverly explained. She had Linda get a pad and pen from the desk and sit with her. They looked through the pile that Frank said pertained to Linda. "Like, what is this?" she asked.

Linda smiled. "You know Daddy, always trying to anticipate. He opened these mutual funds several years before he died and told me that whenever I got ready to settle in one place for a while, use these for a down payment—if not total payment—on a nice house. He didn't believe in renting if you could own an appreciable asset."

"That's Marshall, all right," Beverly reminisced.

"I've been getting the statements every quarter. They should be at my—at Sherry's apartment."

"Loretta took all those records. Why don't you write that down and I'll have Frank contact them for current information."

Linda handed the pad and pen over to her mother. "Here, I'll explain what I know in this pile and *you* write it all down."

Together, they managed to decipher most of the items Frank didn't understand. She filled four pages with notes. Next, they moved to the living room so Beverly could sit in a comfortable recliner.

Linda sat on the couch, gazing at her mother for a minute before asking, "Mama, what is it about that bond between a mother and daughter, between any parent and child? I mean, we're two different people, but even after I'm grown up, we're—you know—*connected* in a special way."

"Well," Beverly murmured, pausing, "I guess it's because you're *my* little girl. You're a part of me."

"Yeah, I suppose you're right. So even though you might like someone like Sherry, for example, I'm always going to mean more to you—as your daughter—than any other younger woman will."

"Well, yeah. You know there's different kinds of relationships. I might have woman friends; I might have a man friend who is different than a lover or husband. I might like some or all of *your* friends—but nobody else, ever, can be my daughter."

"Well, what about all those foster kids that stayed with us through the years?"

"Those kids needed attention and protection and love. I always had enough to spread around. So did your dad. You didn't feel slighted, did you? 'Cause I sure didn't want it to take away from—"

"Oh no, Mama!" Linda interrupted. "I've just been wondering about these things." They fell quiet for a minute before she asked, "That's why you can't stand to let me go, isn't it?"

Beverly's lips trembled, and her eyes grew moist. "Oh Linda, when I thought you died, a piece of me died, too. That's why I'm so glad you're really okay. I don't know how I could stand to lose you. It seems like every minute of every day I would hurt so much I just wouldn't want to go on."

"If I had left a grandchild behind for you, would it have been easier?"

Beverly thought for a moment. "Well, I don't know. It wouldn't lessen the hurt any more, but I *would* have that little boy or little girl of yours to look after." She reached for a tissue and wiped her face.

Linda asked, "What about Kevin? Is he just another kid who needs help?"

"Oh no, he's become a lot more than that." Beverly smiled slightly. "Sometimes it seems like he's that little brother you never had. He sure does—did—adore *you*, too."

"He's a wonderful boy. Mama, do you just care for him and want to look out for him—or do you *love* him?"

"Oh, there's no doubt, I *love* the little rascal." Beverly smiled through her tears. "What's not to love? He's such a good boy—but I guess even if he turns into one of those hellion teenagers, I'm already too far gone. I'd still love him anyway—just like people still love their kids no matter how they turn out."

"He loves *you*—you know that, don't you?"

Beverly looked away. "Yeah," she said softly. "I know. I'm lucky, too, because he always makes it a point to show me."

"It's the same thing with Kevin and Frank, isn't it?"

"Oh yes. No doubt. He's been hooked on that kid since the boy was little."

"When did it turn to love?"

"Oh, there's no telling. You can't draw a line between affection and love. Sometimes you're on one side; sometimes you just know you're on the love side." Beverly thought for a minute. "Sometimes it takes something happening—something bad or challenging—to make you realize which way you feel. That's when you learn *who* really loves *you*. That's when you figure out who *you* really love."

"Did that happen with Kevin?"

"Well, yeah. Not only did Kevin need me, but Frank did, too."

Just then, the phone rang. Beverly wheeled over to the end table and answered it. "Hi, Lizzie! You just caught me sitting around talking with Linda. Yes, with Linda. She's here now. I *told* you she's still alive. No, I can't explain it, but I don't care if it don't make sense. Sure. Oh yeah, she seems fine. You want to talk to her? Hold on."

She turned to beckon Linda to the phone, but she was gone. Beverly found herself alone again, suddenly confused and sad, sitting there looking at the phone receiver in her hand, not sure what to say.

"Hello?" came Lizzie's voice. "Hello? Beverly? Are you okay?"

Frank returned with Beverly after an encouraging doctor visit. Kevin and Lonnie had been at the condo for a while, having rode home together on the bus. Lonnie brought a gym bag with clothes and such for the big Friday-night sleepover. Hearing Frank drive up, they came out to greet him and Beverly. She invited the boys in for some cold Mountain Dew. "I know you hate the stuff," she teased Kevin, "but I'm all out of whiskey."

Kevin held out his arm and insisted she twist it before he would agree. He took over wheelchair duties from Frank, and all four went inside.

Beverly listened to her phone messages, most from friends up north checking to see how she was doing. Conspicuously absent was any contact from Loretta, something that disappointed but didn't surprise her. Alex Posner had called, too, saying he had information regarding the appeal.

Frank called him, talked for several minutes, then ended by saying, "Okay, I'll let her know. Thanks, Alex." He hung up, walked over to sit next to Beverly, and announced, "It was overturned last week—and I don't mean remanded, just flat-out overturned."

"You mean—?"

"Yes! You won!"

CHAPTER 19

'Twas a warm Friday night in Tarpon Springs, and celebration electrified the air. Frank called several courier services before he found one that would bring in a fully prepared feast from his favorite Tampa restaurant. He placed the order, chilled a fine wine, stuffed Mountain Dews into the refrigerator, and set up for a festive celebration in Beverly's dining room. He took Kevin and Lonnie next door to clean up, promising to return before the food arrived.

He checked his own phone messages and took a shower in his private bath. With a fresh shave, after-shave lotion, and careful combing of his still-damp shock of pate-covering hair, he was ready to go. He could hear the boys still in the guest bathroom, apparently horse-playing, so he stood outside the door and threatened to break in and mete out severe beatings if they didn't appear, ready to go, in five minutes.

They met the deadline. Just before leaving to go back to Beverly's, he coached them by saying, "Okay, you guys, after a bad time with a lot of bad luck, Beverly has something good to celebrate for once. Let's make sure we keep the mood festive and have a good time. She *does* have this thing where sometimes she thinks Linda is still alive. If that happens, just go on about your conversation without acting like you think it, too. Don't argue with her about it, though. Tonight is just for fun."

They devoured an excellent dinner with more fancy desserts than even the four hollow legs could hold. The adults sampled a very expensive wine, getting a little tipsy and enjoying every minute while the boys told jokes and amusing stories. Kevin ran next door and came back with a tape of bloopers and funny videos. They laughed so hard they could hardly catch their breaths, with in-between giggles so infectious that all it took was for one to start and the whole group would lose it again. Frank acted out a monologue skit he *thought* he could remember from college. Beverly demonstrated an impromptu wheelchair ballet, ultimately breaking an ashtray, something that seemed a lot funnier than most people might imagine. Lonnie knew several limericks, one of which normally might not be a good idea in mixed, older company, but it caused Beverly to laugh the loudest. She surprised everybody with a few limericks of her own.

Eventually, the festivity faded down. Frank suggested it might be a good time for the boys to go back next door and find some non-combustible, non-lethal ways to occupy themselves. With a nudge-nudge and a wink-wink, off they went.

Frank poured more glasses of wine for himself and Beverly, then proposed a toast . . . to Marshall. "This is *his* victory, too," he explained. "He worked very hard at making this come together. He was in the right. He knew his brother's wishes, and he wouldn't back down from the leeches and sharks. I never had the pleasure of meeting him, but I believe I would have liked him a lot."

Beverly's eyes glistened. "Oh Frank, I know you would. He was such a *wonderful* man."

They held up their glasses while Frank concluded, "To Marshall Herndon, and to his victory." They both drank; then Frank leaned over and kissed Beverly tenderly.

They opened another bottle of wine and went out to sit on the deck, leaving the lights off so they could see stars twinkling in the crystal-clear, moonless night sky. Frank lifted Beverly into an oversized chaise-longue and crawled in beside her, careful of her leg. Lying there sipping their wine and gently caressing each other, they watched fireflies and caught glimpses of swirling, unexplainable iridescence reflecting across the springs. The sounds of Florida nightlife played them a song, the chirrups and twitters and rustles of a world always alive, no matter who might be there to drink it in.

"That was a wonderful toast," she whispered. "I don't always feel comfortable mentioning Marshall in front of you."

"I wish you would," he whispered back. "You loved him very much. Just because you and I are lucky enough to be here together now doesn't take anything away from all those wonderful years. It sounds like he always wanted you to be happy. I think he'd be glad I'm here trying to assure the same thing."

"It was so hard that first year. I just felt lost sometimes."

"Grief is a paradox. The more you love someone, the more it hurts to lose him. Over time, your perspective changes from focusing on the loss to seeing the bigger picture, the times you had together, the special moments, the good memories you carry on in your heart."

"Oh Frank," she whispered back, snuggling up very close, "this is a night I'll always remember."

Kevin and Lonnie carried a mattress from another room into Kevin's bedroom. They put it on the floor beside his bed, fetched sheets and pillows from a linen closet, and made up a makeshift pallet for Lonnie to sleep on. While they worked, Lonnie wondered aloud if Frank and Beverly were over there "doing it." Kevin surmised probably so, which led to a lot of grinning and lewd remarks.

They shed their shoes, jeans, and overshirts, then donned gym shorts. Lonnie rummaged through his gym bag and pulled out an oversized envelope.

"What's that?" Kevin asked.

"Nookie!" announced Lonnie, grinning mischievously while pulling out an adult magazine. They sat on the side of Kevin's bed and flipped through the coveted periodical Lonnie had purchased from one of the guys at school. Kevin remembered looking through one of these the year before, awkward and embarrassed, but this night he had a whole new perspective. Going through the pictures for the umpteenth time, they shared much speculation and misinformation about how exactly one would go about doing it with one of those ladies, but regardless of their convoluted conjectures, both agreed it would be a fine experience, indeed.

"I'm going to ask Frank about it," Kevin decided.

"No way! Really?"

"Oh yeah, sure. I can talk about anything with Frank. He doesn't get embarrassed. He made fun of me once when my voice was cracking. I got worried, but he just said it was normal for my age. He explained about puberty and stuff. He said if I had any questions, I should come ask him."

"Whoa. Must be nice. I sure as hell can't get my mom to tell me stuff—like I'd want to hear it from her anyway."

They eventually lost interest in the magazine and laid it aside, then went into the living room, turned on the TV, and started flipping through channels with the remote control, continuing their discussion.

"Your mom seems all right," Kevin observed.

"Yeah, well, sometimes she's a bitch. She rags on me all the time, treating me like a little kid, embarrassing me in front of people. Like coming out and getting in Frank's face that day. Lucky, he was pretty cool about it. He knew how to handle her. Frank's as cool as it gets."

"Yeah, I know," Kevin agreed.

"My mom never goes out with any guys. It would be nice if she'd get married again—to somebody like Frank."

"My mom used to go out with nothing but assholes—like that Mark. That's why she's in jail—for something *he* did."

"That guy who's been living with Doug Erwin's mom beats the hell out of him whenever he gets in trouble."

"She should kick him out. I don't know how she could let somebody stay there who hits her kid."

"Do you think Frank would ever get mad enough to hit you? You know, if you *really* screwed up?"

"Not a chance. Frank's too good a guy. I think the only way he'd ever go off on somebody would be if they were trying to hurt me or Beverly or somebody he cared about."

"What do you think he thinks of me?" Lonnie asked eagerly, leaning forward in anticipation of Kevin's assessment.

Kevin looked at him for a moment, sensing it was an important question for his friend. "When those dick-heads were raggin' me at school, he gave me a speech about how most people don't matter—just the ones who are the *good* people. He said like you."

Satisfied, Lonnie punched him on the shoulder and took away the remote control. They wrestled around on the floor until they got winded, eventually lying back against the couch and flipping channels.

"Wait! Go back!" Lonnie commanded.

Kevin flipped back to the premium movie channel. "Wow!"

"Titties! Look at 'em. Bare titties! What movie is this?"

They looked it up in the guide and decided it warranted intense budding-adolescent attention.

Their scrutiny lasted through several more movies before they finally drifted off to sleep.

Frank and Beverly started to feel chilly, so they moved back inside. Beverly skipped her pain pill, feeling better than she had since the accident. The wine helped, too.

Frank put on a CD of Chick Corea and Gary Burton duets, then moved Beverly to the couch, propping pillows behind her until she felt comfortable. He nestled up beside her, and together they drifted with the harmonies of piano and vibes, wafted to and fro, carried aloft and floating back down, only to be carried off again before they could touch the ground.

Next, Frank put on a collection of Al Jarreau standards. When the song "We Got By" started, he pulled Beverly over onto his lap. They held each other tight, swaying with the music, dancing in their minds to new heights and new places, across the horizon and into new worlds.

Despite what the boys might have surmised, Frank and Beverly did not "do it." Love can be expressed in many forms . . . and on that now-chilly Florida night, Frank and Beverly forged new ways for themselves to feel close, to be closer, to touch and become one, a whole greater than the sum.

Frank returned to his condo and spotted the boys snoozing on the floor in the living room, curled up against each other, with the flicker of television playing over their gently breathing forms.

Kevin had left him a message from Ward Bodnar, the developer who built the condo units where Frank and Beverly lived. The rest of the project had stalled when he lost his financing. Now Ward wanted to meet with him, preferably sometime the next day, Saturday, so he could make a proposal. He asked that Frank call him when he got home, no matter how late.

Frank went to his bedroom and called. Ward sounded a little bleary when he answered, but woke right up when he recognized Frank's voice. He said he had a package lined up that included some bank financing, but his investor had pulled out at the last minute, and now he had until next Friday to take a new package back to the bank or he would lose the loan. He wanted to show Frank his numbers as soon as possible to see if he might be interested. Frank offered to meet with him the next morning, then said he would call Henry bright and early and try to have him attend, too. They agreed to meet on the *Fine Print* at 9:30. Frank mentioned that he would have Kevin with him since they planned to go into Clearwater to visit his mom at 1:30.

Frank looked into Kevin's bedroom and saw they had made up a bed for Lonnie. He went back to the living room and turned off the TV, then nudged Kevin for him to get up and go to bed. Not getting much reaction, he knelt down and lifted him up into a drowsy walk. He got him down the hall and onto his bed. Half-awake, Kevin mumbled, "Hi, Frank."

"Good night, buddy," Frank replied. He pulled up the sheet and shifted the boy's body down into a sleeping position. He was surprised when Kevin hugged him tightly and for quite a bit longer than usual. Frank hugged him back.

"Thanks, Frank," Kevin whispered, then rolled over on his side and fell asleep before he could respond.

Frank went back to get Lonnie, who proved even harder to wake up. He lifted him into the same walking position, but wound up practically carrying him to the room. When he set him on the mattress, the boy started sniffling. He looked at him closely in the dim glow from Kevin's clock and saw tears on his cheeks. "Lonnie, what's wrong?"

The boy shook his head, but kept crying quietly. Frank put his arm around him and asked, "Are you okay?"

Lonnie nodded his head and wiped off his face with the back of his hand. Frank reached up and swept the boy's hair out of his eyes. Lonnie put his arms around Frank and squeezed really hard. Frank squeezed him back. Just as suddenly, Lonnie relaxed his hug and let go, then crawled under his sheet.

Frank sat on the end of Kevin's bed and watched both of them for a while. He heard their breathing slow and grow deeper. Kevin twitched a few times in his characteristic way.

Caught between being sensitive little boys and big, tough men, he thought. *They needed those hugs from some guy who truly cared about them back when they were four or seven or nine.*

He looked from one to the other.

I guess twelve and thirteen's not too late.

CHAPTER 20

Frank and Kevin relaxed in morning sunshine aboard the *Fine Print*, watching storm clouds loom on the western horizon until Ward arrived precisely on time. Henry dragged his sorry carcass aboard soon after, so they moved below deck and spent the next hour reviewing the plans—four more units of condos, a common pool area built above the water table, and a 36-unit, two-building apartment development across the road.

Predicting completion in fifteen months, Ward recommended that the two apartment buildings be built first for an earlier, more immediate revenue stream from rentals. Condos would involve the slower and less-reliable process of making sales before monies would pour in. Henry agreed whole-heartedly. Kevin suggested consolidating costs by building the condos' pool at the same time as the apartments'. Ward admitted that made sense. Frank and Henry grinned.

Ward said he had already ordered many of the materials and booked some of the crews and machinery before his two money-men backed out at the last second—and killed his bank loan in the process.

"Did something happen to scare them off?" Henry asked.

"No," Ward replied. "They just pulled out without explanation."

"Were they stringing you along?" Frank asked.

"I don't think so. They put a lot of time into this."

"Who were they?" Kevin asked.

"Two brothers, Larry and Eli Rumsey."

Everyone but Ward exchanged knowing glances, but nobody mentioned their other Rumsey travails. Frank told Ward he was confident something could be worked out, that he might be able to scrape it up himself if he cashed out some assets and got a loan, but that his friend Beverly needed something she could prorate and depreciate, and he thought she might come in, too. He promised to talk to her and give him an answer first thing the next morning.

A chill, stormy wind blew in from the gulf, steadily nudging the *Fine Print* against the pier while the four of them, sheltered from the elements, toasted their anticipated new venture.

"You look *so* handsome, and you're getting *so* big!" Ruth exclaimed into the telephone, drinking in Kevin with her eyes. He stood before the video monitor, talking into a similar phone. "And that's a *nice* outfit."

"You look pretty good, too, Mom. I sure missed you all week. I wish they had visiting at night on school days."

"That's okay, sweetie. I understand. Frank's too busy a man to be driving down here all the time anyway. I got good news, though. I talked to the lieutenant and she said maybe she'll let me into the general population."

"What's that?"

"Well," she explained, "right now I'm in the hole—in max security—for my own protection because they heard some friends of those guys that got killed might be in here. Anyway, in general population I'd be sharing a cell with other women, but I'd get to come out three times a day into the cell-block where I can make phone calls. That means I could call you sometimes!"

"Cool!"

"Remember, honey, no promises—but I sure do have my fingers crossed."

"If I'm not home—um, at Frank's place—keep trying."

"So how do you like the seventh grade?"

"We're not the littlest kids in school anymore."

"Has anybody mentioned—do any of the kids at school know about, you know, me being in here?"

"Naw," he lied. "Only my friend Lonnie, and he doesn't care. How about your cozzumtology class?"

"That's the other good news!" she practically squealed. "I got my first four lessons mailed in. The first two done come back already. I got all A's."

"All right, Mom!" Kevin thrust his fist up, an exclamation of triumph. "Have you heard anything about your court yet?"

She looked past Kevin at Frank lounging unobtrusively against the back wall. "Mr. Mogill came by here last night and said they might want to make a deal. The bad thing, though, is it would mean going off to prison for a while."

Mortified, Kevin couldn't begin to articulate his fears. "Why?"

"Don't worry, we'll get it worked out. Why don't you let me talk to Frank for a minute; then you come right back, okay?"

Kevin gestured Frank over and handed him the phone, stepping back and diverting his attention, a skill practiced all those years he and his mother shared various cramped quarters, times when a single woman and her son learn to pretend the other has even a tiny modicum of privacy.

"Frank, I don't know what to do. Mr. Mogill said I have to testify, then get sent to prison for ten to twenty years." Her eyes darted back and forth between Frank and Kevin, panic in her face.

Frank measured his words carefully. "Ms. Riner, understand—when a situation is bad, and it looks like there is too much of a chance of conviction—sometimes it's best to take a deal that guarantees less than if you were to lose at trial. Now, I can't ask you here—shouldn't talk about it here—about what really happened. All I can say is that you need to consider how guilty you are, whether it's what they say or something else—something less. Consider if you believe in your innocence strongly enough to take the risk, or if you really are guilty, or you're afraid you look too guilty—then maybe something that has you out in eight or ten years is better than not risking the rest of your life in prison—" Frank lowered his voice almost to a whisper. "—Or receiving the death penalty."

Ruth nodded; then started, "Well—"

"Now be careful what you say," Frank interrupted.

"Oh Frank," she said, her voice starting to quaver, tears welling in her eyes. "Frank, I'm *not* guilty—not of murder. I wasn't even in the house when—when those guys— I was in the car. I didn't know he was going back in for—"

Frank interrupted her. "Ms. Riner—Ruth, if you weren't involved, then we'll talk to Mogill about fighting it all the way. If you want me to know what's going on, to be able to give you advice or discuss it with him, then you need to give him permission— sign a waiver or something—so he can talk to me about this. Otherwise, it's confidential, attorney-client privileged information."

"I will! If you talk to him first, tell him I want you to—you know, be involved."

"Okay. You also have to decide how much you want said to your son. You know he'll ask me questions. If I have to tell him that I can't say, that's one thing. I'll never lie to him, though—*never*, under any circumstances. He trusts me, and I trust him, and that's a two-way street that's too important for me ever to violate."

"Oh, I worry so much about him. Is he doing okay?"

"For a boy who loves his mother *very* much and is scared about what might happen to her, he's doing fine. Even if you have to spend time in prison, I *promise* you, Kevin will be taken care of. He'll visit you, and he'll have plenty of stamps and paper and envelopes to write you *lots* of letters."

"If I can get moved to where there's a phone, is it okay if I call collect to talk to him sometimes?"

"As much as you want. Just remember, he's almost thirteen—and if a thirteen-year-old boy isn't a moving target, I don't know what is."

She wiped her eyes and whispered, "Thanks, Frank."

That left her and Kevin only three minutes to visit. It was a good three minutes, though—as good as a mother and her almost-adolescent son can have through TV screens, over a phone, with noise and distraction and a ticking clock, each putting on a brave front, both very scared deep inside.

On the way home, Frank noticed Kevin's customary after-visit melancholy. For the boy to see his mother there, in that jumpsuit, locked up, so close yet so far—it always took a lot out of him. He tried to be the trouper, only sometimes succeeding. He cried after the first visit, a bit less the next few times. Now he looked out the window, keeping his face diverted from Frank. These were awkward moments for the older man. He wanted to do or say or help or—something!

As they headed up Highway 19, he finally reached over and stroked down the back of Kevin's head, stopping with a squeeze of his shoulder. Quietly, he offered, "I'm trying not to be so macho I forget to say I love you, hoodlum."

Instantly, Kevin's tears flowed. He reached up with his right hand and squeezed the one Frank had on his shoulder, not letting go. He sniffled and cried a little before calming down, never once turning his face away from the window. Frank merged to the outside lane away from other cars during this most private moment. By the time they turned into the road that led to the condos by the springs, Kevin had regained his composure.

"Hey, Henry's already here," Frank pointed out as he pulled in and spotted his friend's conservative sedan. "He must be visiting with Beverly while he waits for us."

After they parked and stepped out of the van, Kevin tugged on his sleeve and whispered, "Frank," as if someone might hear him.

Turning toward him, Frank asked, "Yeah?"

Kevin fidgeted and diverted his gaze like children do when they're either guilty or embarrassed. "What you said in the car, you know . . . Is that okay?"

Frank cocked his head and pondered for a brief moment. Leaning down to Kevin's eye level, he asked, "You tell me. Is it?"

Kevin shrugged, then nodded, then nodded again more vigorously.

"Good," Frank responded. "I know better than to go around announcing that in front of a boy's friends—and I do try not to embarrass you—but it's *true*, and there's nothing you can do about it."

Kevin managed a half-smile. Frank poked him in the chest with his finger and turned to leave again.

"Frank?"

"Yeah?"

"You know I, well—"

"Yeah, I know. I count on it."

Kevin regaled everybody at Beverly's place with a full rundown of Ruth's progress in her cosmetology course and her pending move out of max. He even explained "the hole" to Henry with all the authority of a seasoned correctional-systems expert. Beverly made him sit next to her, grabbing him in bear hugs and tousling his hair every few minutes, finally graduating to tickling his ribs until he giggled.

Frank suggested they send out for subs and begin the meeting. With Beverly taking a serious interest in business matters for the first time in her life, all four plowed through the details of Ward's development proposal. Then Frank went next door and came back with a box of his own records. They sorted through some of those while Henry and Kevin totaled up liquid assets. The conclusion: Frank could come up with not quite $600,000 by the end of the week.

Frank asked Beverly if he could show her documents to Henry. She readily agreed and suggested that Kevin should be privy, too. Frank laid the pile atop the file boxes and went through the papers inside. It quickly became clear that Beverly could make up the rest of what Ward needed. Delighted by the idea, she placed only two conditions on her participation: first, that if Loretta wanted to rent one of the apartments, she would have to pay double—no, triple—and second, that *both* swimming pools got put in during phase one.

"Swimming would be good exercise for me without having to put weight on my bad foot," she explained, winking to Kevin in their conspiracy. "Besides, my personal advisor here—" She pulled Kevin over and put her arm around him, finishing, "He's gonna need a pool to sit beside while he manages my business empire!"

Frank put her records back in the box, then noticed extra notes in the pile he had left on top. "What's this?"

"Oh, that," she replied. "I forgot to tell you. Linda went through it and explained everything to me. I wrote it all down for you."

Frank exchanged glances with Henry, then looked through the pile with him. The more they looked, the more puzzled they became.

"You know, Beverly," Kevin added, "we might just need a go-cart track out here, too."

CHAPTER 21

Frank finally got the proper bank vice-president on the phone. "Yes. This is Frank Tanyon, personal representative for Beverly Herndon."

"Oh yes," replied Mr. Faulkner, "the discretionary trust. How are you, Mr. Tanyon?"

"I'm not sure yet. I have a lot on my agenda today, so I'd like to accomplish our business quickly and efficiently."

"I see. Well, I can't very well talk to you about private matters without some sort of—"

"It came over your fax about five minutes ago. Original notarized copies are being express delivered to you later today. I can hold for a moment if you need to call Alex Posner—you'll find an affidavit of representation from him in the package I just faxed—in case you need to confirm anything."

"If you'll hold for a moment—oh, yes, it was just handed to me." Faulkner paused, then continued, "Yes, I see you were very thorough."

"You should have everything you need there to cut a check today. The last page includes instructions where to have it expressed—"

"Mr. Tanyon, this is all a bit premature. There are still some unresolved matters—"

"Not by my estimation—not according to Ms. Herndon's attorney. What matters are you referring to?"

"Well," Faulkner continued, "we *are* aware of the recent court ruling. However, we have not yet been advised by our legal staff whether or not they intend to appeal—"

"Your organization had twenty-one days to file. That expired last night at midnight. Neither Ms. Herndon nor her representatives have received any notice, so as of today, when you received your fax, Ms. Herndon is claiming the funds she is owed."

"Well, we would need some time—"

"Of course," Frank agreed in mock conciliation. "I understand how you'll need to move a few things around, draw up a check, put an address on the envelope and all. I don't care if you delay a few hours as long as it goes out tonight."

"I'll have to consult with my legal—"

"Oh sure, I understand. I'll hold." Frank waited silently.

Faulkner paused a minute, then asked, "How can I contact you later today?"

"I'll be out most of the day. I'll tell you what; since you seem to need some time, call me at a quarter to five. I'll make it a point to be here then. Just remember, this delay doesn't change my expectation that a check for the full amount will be out before close of business today."

"Mr. Tanyon, I can't promise—"

"Then don't; just get it done."

"You're not being reasonable, Mr. Tanyon," the banker accused.

"Ah, but I am," Frank retorted. "Trust me on this, Mr. Faulkner. Your shenanigans robbed Marshall Herndon of his stamina, contributing to his premature death, and they have caused great hardship to Beverly. Now you are being considerably less than accommodating to a valued customer who recently lost her only child to a sudden, tragic death. A delay of even one day will severely hamper her investments, causing her to incur substantial, unnecessary costs. It's not your money—never was your money. Your attempts to steal it out from under a grieving widow in her golden years are reprehensible, but they do make an interesting story to tell."

Faulkner paused again. "I'll call you at a quarter to five. Good day, Mr. Tanyon."

"Yes, I do believe it is."

Frustrated in his attempts to reach Mr. Mogill, Ruth Riner's attorney, Frank finally got an assistant on the phone who scheduled him for an appointment the next afternoon. "In court" seemed to be the mantra his staff always chanted. Like every client any lawyer has ever had, Frank wanted to be first and foremost on the agenda.

He picked up Beverly, loading her carefully into his van, and headed toward New Port Richey to meet with the recommended physical therapist. They stopped for lunch, taking advantage of a new handicap sticker on the van, appreciating wheelchair access at the newly renovated restaurant. Frank wanted to make a suggestion, but decided to wait until after the appointment.

He watched her eat, so proper, so precise, so relaxed . . . He rubbed the back of his neck, feeling the knots that extended down into his shoulders. He made himself relax, too, taking several deep breaths and forcing the muscles to go limp. He must have been worked up over the conversation with the bank. Maybe . . . maybe that was a contributor, but the nagging uncertainty of Ruth's plight surely played a major role. Her son, Kevin, ever the brave soldier, depended on him to do his best—yet he sometimes felt inexplicably helpless, out of the loop, unsure. He watched Beverly, not realizing he had stopped eating. She noticed, but said nothing.

It's her, he thought. *She's not dealing with Linda's death, and I just don't know how to help her.*

Images of Linda flashed through his mind: showing off the toads, laughing on the boat, flirting with Kevin until he blushed, acting the peacemaker between her mother and Loretta, running up to hug Frank every time she saw him . . . so full of life . . . battered until even a mortician couldn't make her presentable . . . He gasped with a start, feeling his heart pound, his hands cold and clammy with sweat.

And there sat Beverly, so at peace.

Is she learning to accept it? Is she drifting further away from the harsh reality that Linda's gone? Could she go on if she truly grasped what happened to that sweet young lady who had lived every minute like life was a gift to be cherished?

His heart pounded harder. Beverly reached out and squeezed his hand. His eyes burning, he looked away so nobody would see. Beverly sought his other hand and squeezed them both, bringing them together on the table, hanging on tightly.

The sounds of the restaurant, the voices and clinks and swinging doors and ringing telephones—it all faded away. He looked up and there she was . . . Beverly . . . the only woman who mattered.

I love you, she mouthed silently.

Everything would be okay. Frank smiled and winked back at her. They finished eating without saying another word.

They drove on to the physical-therapy clinic and met a young man, Gregory Dean, not much older than twenty-five and very athletic-looking. He reviewed her file, examined her leg and foot, and explained how her recovery would have to proceed in stages. He recommended a schedule of every other day and offered to fit her into a morning routine at her own condo since he had two other patients in Tarpon Springs and one in Holiday also on a 48-hour home-visit schedule. Beverly agreed and they set 10:30 to 11:00 a.m. for her time-slot. She would be pushed and pulled and prodded and stretched—all a part of her next painful steps toward regaining mobility.

Throughout the appointment, Frank hovered as close as possible, watching her intently, trying never to stray more than arm's reach from her. His vague feeling of helpless frustration would not subside.

They went out to the parking lot where he used the lift to help her get into the van. Without saying anything, he pulled out and drove a half-mile south, then turned into a side road and drove west about a quarter mile, stopping at the gates to a memorial garden.

"Would you like to see Linda's grave?" he asked. "It's a beautiful spot."

Beverly panicked. She looked at the stone entranceway, then to Frank, then back to the beautifully landscaped opening that invited visitors for a peaceful commune with loved ones lost. "No," she whispered. "I can't."

"Okay," he said quietly, reaching over to hold her hand. "You let me know if you change your mind—anytime."

He turned around and drove back to Tarpon Springs. He couldn't think of anything to say. Beverly remained quiet.

They held hands all the way, all that needed to be said that warm September afternoon.

Frank left Beverly at her place, then went home to check on Kevin and listen to his phone messages. He found both boys there, playing video games in the living room. The housekeeper had been in, too—not that Kevin ever left messes around. *For having an almost-teenage boy in the house,* he thought, *I lucked out finding the neatest one from here to the panhandle.*

Frank had started toward his office to put away the bank file when he heard the phone ring. Kevin jumped and answered it right away.

"Hello?" he asked eagerly. Obviously disappointed, he told the caller to hold. "Frank, it's Doug Taylor."

Kevin set the phone down as Lonnie remarked, "Don't worry, she'll call as soon as she can."

"Hi, Doug. How you doin', guy?" Frank greeted him.

"I'm all right, I guess. Just tired from working my butt off."

"Yeah, I remember those days with your dad. I was proud of what we accomplished, but I sure don't miss the long hours. That's why at least one of us had to have some good kids to turn it over to."

"Yeah, he made that clear when I was *very* young. That's why by the time I was twelve, I started learning all I could about how to run things someday, wanting to make Dad—you and Dad—proud of me."

"He always was, you know. We both were. You did a fine job, and we felt good about taking it easy, trusting our baby to you and your brother," Frank assured him.

"That's why I'm calling, Frank. I want to talk to you, just between us."

"Anytime, Doug. My door is always open to you."

"Well, first I want you to know that I've been taking control again and cleaning up this, um—this mess."

"Uh huh." Frank left him hanging. It was Doug's dime; let him set the agenda.

"I want to ask several things. I want your help, um, smoothing it out. I want you to relax and not do anything that will be hard to *undo* until you give me a chance." He got quieter, finishing his list with, "—And I want you to trust me."

"I always did, Doug. I always believed your dad raised you right—that you were a good man with honor and integrity. It's only recently that I questioned that, but I've given you the benefit of the doubt. In fact, I've *counted* on you being a good man, though I *have* had my fingers crossed more than a few times these last few weeks."

"Frank, there was one thing I didn't learn from my father back then, but now I understand."

"Oh yeah?"

"He kept Mom out of his business."

Frank chuckled. "Yeah, she nosed around every now and then. He wouldn't let her get involved, though."

"Yeah, well, he knew what he was doing. Don't get me wrong. I love her and would never do anything to hurt her, but I made the mistake of letting her call the shots too much this past year."

"And now you're not?" Frank asked.

"Now I'm not," Doug confirmed. "Don't get me wrong—I've still got a *lot* to work out with her, but I want you to know I've taken control. The company is in *my* hands, and *I'm* going to dazzle you with how fast this thing gets on track."

"Glad to hear it, son."

"Frank, I know what you're up to with the vendors. Call 'em off, would you? They're making it tough—making it hard for me to get costs back under control."

"Well, I think I might be able to help with that."

"Good. Frank, you've got my word. I'm working on some solutions that will make *everybody* happy. Give me a little time, a little help, and a lot of faith."

"Okay, Doug. All you had to do was ask."

Frank went back to Beverly's ten minutes before the deadline he had given Mr. Faulkner, the bank vice-president. "Has he called yet?"

"No," she replied. "Do you think he will?"

"Oh yeah. He may be a few minutes early because he's scared. He may be right on time. He may be a few minutes late just to assert himself, but he'll call. The bigger question is, what news will he have for us?"

"You think he'll send the money?" she asked hopefully.

"Probably—but you can't be sure. He may have a few more tricks up his sleeve. But then, so do I."

Just then, the phone rang. Beverly smiled as Frank tipped his imaginary hat and answered it. "Herndon residence. How may I direct your call?" He paused for a few seconds. "Yes, this is Frank Tanyon. Ahh, Mr. Faulkner—how are you this afternoon, sir? Yes. Good. Uh huh. Yes. Okay, thank you for your assistance. I appreciate how you expedited this matter. Bye now."

He hung up the phone, looking grim. Beverly asked anxiously, "What? What? What did he say?"

"Well, I need to go into town in the morning and get to the bank before ten."

"Why?"

"To get the account set up. You don't think I would have the check sent to your condo, do you?"

CHAPTER 22

Bzzrrzzrr— Bzzrrzzrr— Bzzrrzzrr— Bzzrrzzrr— Bzzrrzzrr—

Frank raised his head, sort of opened one eye, looked at the dark window, put his head back down—

Bzzrrzzrr— Bzzrrzzrr—

By the time he got up, cleaned up, and wandered into the kitchen, Kevin had started the coffee pot and loaded breakfast into the toaster oven. Frank enjoyed starting each day with the boy, always making an effort to get up in time to eat with him and see him off to school. Of course, that perspective sometimes didn't come back to him until he gulped down at least those first swallows of coffee.

Dressed in black jeans and a fluorescent-blue jersey emblazoned with the logo of some heavy-metal group—the name of which Frank could never remember except that it had a "Z" and at least an "X" or two in it—Kevin served the food and sat down to eat, keeping uncharacteristically quiet. Usually he would chatter about all manner of things, excitedly anticipating his day, ready to take on the world.

Frank watched him for a minute. "What's on your mind, buddy?"

"You still gonna see that lawyer today?"

I'm juggling so many things, it's easy to forget how much this must weigh on him every minute. He remembered how diligent the boy had been about writing his mother every night, how he always headed for the mailbox the moment he got home from school, how he had started racing for the phone these past few days, seeming at times to anticipate the first ring. "Yes."

"You know," he continued, his eyes on his plate, "at first I wanted everyone to know that my mom didn't kill anybody—that she's not that kind of person." He looked up at Frank. "It's just, well, now I don't care what people think. I don't care about deals or trials or whatever anymore. It doesn't matter if she's in the news again. I just want her to get out."

"Yeah, me too," Frank answered quietly.

Kevin took another bite, then put his fork down. "Frank, if they put her in prison, that's gonna be a lot worse than Pinellas Jail, ain't it?"

"I honestly don't know, Kevin."

"Well, I saw this thing on TV. It didn't look very good."

"You know, buddy, all we can do is take it one step at a time. I'll go talk to Mogill today, and if I'm not satisfied he's doing his best, then I'll find someone else."

Kevin nodded, then finished his milk, cleared the mess, grabbed his book bag, and paused before heading out the door. "I'll come straight home after school—by myself—to see what you found out." Making a fist, he added, "Every time I try to worry, I just have to remember that Frank-Man is on the case." With that, he was gone.

And the Frank-Man sat there, foundering in doubt.

I should be preparing him for the worst.

Frank started next door and noticed a work truck parked across the road.

"Frank! Morning, guy!" Ward Bodnar walked up the road with two men who carried clipboards and surveying equipment. He said something to them, pointing toward the area where the apartment units were planned, then walked over to meet Frank.

"Out working, huh?" Frank asked, shaking his hand.

"Yeah, well, let's just say I have a lot of confidence. I wanted to check and see how much is still staked out—if I'll need to redo the whole survey or not—and check on the condition of the footings that were already poured—you know, in case we get something going." He looked at Frank with a half-grin, arching his eyebrows higher than most people are capable.

"Well, I've decided not to take out any loans to get involved in your project—" he started. Ward looked very disappointed. "Instead, I'm going to cash in with part of it, and my friend Beverly will cash in with the rest."

Brightening like the morning Florida sun, Ward grabbed Frank's hand and pumped it vigorously. "Excellent!"

"We need to draw it up as partnership, file as a DBA, then start the process of converting it into a corporation."

"That sounds like the way to go," Hank agreed.

"Good. Then we're not mixed in with your other projects, and you're not too wrapped up with us."

"Yeah, I prefer it that way. Hell, I shouldn't have any trouble with the loan now. Can we sweeten it by putting the corporate account in the lending bank?"

"That's smart business," Frank agreed. "Since your company will be the builder, I want it structured so that Beverly and I can call for competitive bids on any aspect of the job, and I want to hire a part-time supervisor representing all three of us. That way, we don't get into any situations with hard feelings. Lord knows, I'm tired of those."

"Good. I like that. I want this to be so smooth that you and Ms. Herndon want to keep your shares for future projects."

"That's my thinking, Ward. Let's grow this thing. Oh! I almost forgot. There's one other condition. My twelve-year-old business assistant requested it, and Beverly insisted on it: the pool for the condos goes in during phase one."

Ward grinned and pumped his hand again. "Deal!"

Frank walked back to the condos and slipped quietly inside Beverly's. Still drowsing in bed, she stirred when he crawled in beside her.

"Frank, is that you?" she teased.

"Were you expecting someone else?"

"Well, you know, I figured it had to be either you or Lance or Walter . . ." She started counting off her fingers. "—Let's see . . . Bob, William, Michael—"

Frank leaned over and kissed her passionately. Before she could make a sound, he kissed her again, a longer, more aggressive kiss. Finally, he snuggled up against her, careful of her leg, and nuzzled her neck.

"Well," she whispered, "that narrows it down to Frank or William or Seth or Todd."

"You're a tramp, Miss Beverly, an out-and-out tramp."

"You like me that way."

"Yeah," he whispered, "I guess I do . . ." He kissed her again, then pulled away and announced, "I've got to be at the bank in Tampa. Got to work on moving my money around, check on some things—hmmm . . . there must be something else . . . Oh yeah! I need to get a check for you and open an account to work out of. I guess this means you'll never see *me* again."

"I'll track down your scurvy hide!" she shouted, shaking her fist in the air as he stole out of the room.

Frank took care of his and Beverly's banking business in Tampa, then drove down to meet Rob Buchanan on the *Fine Print*. He found him sitting on the upper deck, working up a good sunburn on the end of his nose. His loose-fitting, beige-polyester Bermuda shorts accented a two-inch white stripe of pasty skin just above each knee, and patchy red areas between there and the brown socks he'd pulled well up over his calves. A bright-yellow crew shirt, sunglasses, visor cap, and the customary unlit cigar clenched between his teeth completed a rather incongruous picture of Florida leisure-living.

Frank climbed up, shook his hand, and unlocked the entrance to the galley. "What'll it be?"

"Any kinda beer so long as it's cold," the investigator replied, stabbing the air with his cigar for emphasis.

They sat in the sun while Frank asked the obvious question. "Well, did you get anything?"

Buchanan unpacked several large envelopes and an accordion file. "Everything you need." He paused and grinned. "You'll be *real* pleased."

"Good. Good. You had no problems?"

"Piece o' cake—not that I don't work my butt off for my pay—but it was like getting in some chickie's panties after she done had too much to drink."

Similes aside, Frank wanted to see what he had, so they spent about fifteen minutes looking at photos, a diagram, several lists, and the requisite invoice with itemized back-up to cover expenses. Buchanan was right; Frank was pleased. "You have the originals of these?" he asked, gesturing toward the envelopes.

"But of course," Buchanan answered, taking his cigar out to stab the air again as he finished. "Just remember what you have to say about how you got 'em."

They ended their meeting with a final draught of beer. Rob Buchanan, private investigator, headed off to have some Florida fun before returning to slog cases and earn a buck back up north.

Frank drove toward Clearwater for a fast lunch before meeting with Mr. Mogill.

"How you doin' today, Mama?"

"Linda! I'm doing much better. I'm only taking those pills three times a day—maybe just twice today. I start physical therapy tomorrow with a nice man named Gregory Dean. He's about your age and *very* handsome. You never know, he might be your type."

"Now Mama, I can't go meeting people. I'm just here for *you*—for now—and that's all."

"Linda, I need you to explain things to me. Why is it you aren't . . . ?" She had trouble focusing on the concept of death. "How are you still here when—" She gestured toward the brace on her leg. "—When all this happened to me, and everybody says you were—you know."

"Mama, I can't explain it. I don't understand it myself. I mean—well, sometimes it seems like I do, but then I don't. All I know is that I'm trying to learn about things—to understand. I want to look out for you and help you get through all this because I love you so much."

Beverly reached for Linda, wrapping her in a hug. The confused mother, talking more softly, confided, "But it's so hard, not knowing when I can see you again—if I'll *ever* see you again. I don't know where you're staying. I don't know how to get a hold of you." She got more emotional the more she talked. "I don't know if you're all right . . ."

"Mama," Linda whispered, still holding her awkwardly because of the brace, "I don't have answers to those questions, but maybe we can figure them out together. I do know I can't be here with you forever. These people are right—the ones who care about you. You need to learn how to face what really happened that day."

Beverly had to fight back tears. "Linda, if you're really . . . gone . . . I don't think I could go on. I couldn't get over it."

"Mama, you don't *have* to get over it. You just get more used to it over time. It won't mean you love me any less. From what I understand about grief, you'll learn to focus less on losing me and more on remembering the good of having had me."

Beverly's grip on Linda relaxed some. She looked away, spatters of anger welling up inside. "It's not right. It's not fair. I shouldn't *have* to learn to live without you." She turned toward Linda, asserting, "It isn't your *time* to go. *I'm* supposed to go first. That's how it's supposed to be."

"I know," Linda agreed. "People place a high value on some things. Love—of their families and friends—is one of the biggest. Yet, it's something many people have to lose. Fair or not, they have to learn to live with that heartache."

"I don't want to be one of them."

"Nobody does, Mama. Nobody does."

They talked about Beverly's recovery, about Frank and Kevin, the new condo/apartment development venture, and the victory that forced the bank to cave in and pay out the trust. Linda seemed especially delighted with the latter, pointing out how their love for Marshall made the victory particularly sweet. More than anybody, they understood how much that meant to him—especially after his first heart attack, when he started worrying about leaving it for his loved ones.

Eventually, Linda broached the subject of the cemetery. She wanted to know if it looked pretty, what kind of marker had been ordered, and so forth. Beverly admitted she'd not visited her daughter's grave, so Linda suggested the two of them drive out there to see it, and Beverly reluctantly agreed. They left in her car, the wheelchair folded in the trunk, Linda driving.

During the trip, Beverly sometimes felt heart-pounding apprehension, brief flashbacks to the moments after the accident. She kept trying to put them out of her mind, but could only replace them with frustration and anger. Linda seemed to sense these, chasing them away with new topics, shared memories of happy times.

Linda helped her mother into the wheelchair and pushed her gingerly over hard ground to the site. It upset Beverly to see the flowers all wilted and brown from the intense Florida heat, so Linda set about gathering up and carrying them away, cleaning up the area and making it more presentable. Twice she filled the trunk with debris, driving over to a trash bin to unload. Eventually, the grave looked spartan, but neat.

Linda sat on the ground next to her mother and admired the beautiful surroundings. A half-dozen geese swam across the pond, then waddled over to within a dozen yards, watching over their precious territory, yet understanding the need to share it with people of honorable purpose.

"You know, Mama, Loretta really *did* pick out a beautiful place. I like it here."

"I do, too."

"This is a lot prettier than where daddy is buried."

"Oh, yes, that reminds me. I want to make arrangements to have your father moved down here."

Linda hugged her mother, whispering, "What a wonderful idea. I think I would like that very much."

Mother and daughter stayed out there for quite a while. Several times Beverly dissolved into tears, but Linda kept trying to keep her focused on learning to envision a future in which love and memories gave her the strength to carry on.

When Beverly recited the poem Frank had helped Kevin write, admitting that she had memorized it, Linda had tears in her eyes, nodding and whispering, "Yes, I think I understand."

And Beverly really did feel better for the first time, imagining she could let go and still hold her close.

Linda gestured at the geese several times, mesmerizing them with movements of her hand, until they finally waddled over and settled down next to the women.

A single yellow and blue butterfly flitted by, hovering for a moment near a mother and daughter lost in their thoughts, while the geese swayed in a gentle rhythm, slowly closing their eyes.

"Oh look, Mama, a butterfly."

CHAPTER 23

Mr. Mogill came in through the client waiting area where Frank sat reading a *Lawyer's Weekly*. The attorney carried a briefcase, a satchel, two accordion files, and a newspaper, looking a bit harried as he hustled by. Greeting Frank, he told him he would be just a minute. "I need to talk to Ruth, anyway," he explained, "so I'll call you in shortly to go over some quick things. Then, if you have time, you could go down to the jail with me and sit in on my meeting with her."

Frank agreed and Mogill disappeared. After several minutes, the receptionist sent him into an office at the end of the hall.

"Well," Mogill started, "it's not going so good. The prosecutor is more worried about playing the media on this thing than whether or not justice is served."

"So what else is new?"

"Yeah, well, it's just that the mayor has been getting a lot of heat about Tampa's drug problems moving into this area. There's a half-dozen community-based crusader organizations keeping the pressure on."

"We're talking about a woman's life here—a mother's life," Frank asserted, "—not a cause."

"Right," Mogill responded, "but we're also talking about people who get elected. Most voters truly care little about facts or justice—even less about mercy and compassion—and right now these politicos are getting more media attention than this kind of case normally gets. In Tampa, it could be a paragraph or two in the paper. But, since it's Clearwater, it gets front page in the same Tampa paper—not to mention lots of follow-up in the local section. This got so much TV up front because the county sheriff *and* the prosecutor's office kept feeding them info, hyping it up, playing it like it might be part of a bigger pattern—a growing threat!—invading your community!—coming to take your children!" Mogill pounded the desk. "Anyway," he continued, "these guys have a big case that's buying them face time in front of the cameras. Fast deals don't drag out in the media and, worse, they look like criminal-coddling."

"So there's no plea bargain on the table?" Frank asked.

"Yeah, sure there is. But it's not a deal. They're talking guilty plea on two counts of second degree, thirty-five to life, to avoid a trial for first degree and a possible death penalty."

Frank held his breath, then let the air out all at once. He could feel his heart beating faster. "Why do you say it's not a deal?"

"Because she didn't shoot anybody, she wasn't in the building during the shooting, and they can't prove she was. It's not a deal."

"So what do we do?"

"Try to bargain some more. Go to trial."

"On second degree?"

"No," Mogill corrected, "a trial would be for all or nothing."

They drove to the county jail, submitted to being frisked and scanned by a metal detector, then settled into a cramped room. After a fifteen-minute wait, Ruth Riner appeared in the characteristic jumpsuit, carrying a pad, oversized envelope, and pen. They sat around a small table.

"Please tell Kevin," Ruth directed to Frank, "that I'm still in the hole, but Sarge *did* say I can make a call tonight between five and six."

"I'll make sure he's there," he assured her.

As quickly as Mogill explained the prosecutor's offer, she started crying.

I can't even begin to imagine how she must feel, Frank thought. *I can't ever let Kevin see her like this.*

Mogill summed up, "I don't want to tell you not to take it, but I will say there are holes in their case we can exploit if we go to trial."

She looked to Frank and asked, "What should I do?"

Frank thought for a second, then asked, "Will you tell me, briefly, what happened?"

"It'll remain confidential," Mogill told her.

"And I want you to understand," Frank added, "that I'll do everything I can to help you, no matter what the truth is. Plus you can rest assured, there is nothing—*nothing* you can say that'll affect my commitment to helping your son. Tell me the truth, and I'll tell you what *I* would do if I were in the same situation."

She wiped her eyes and looked directly into Frank's. "Well, Mark's been living—*was* living with me off and on for a while. He was no good, but I got too hung up on him. I know better now."

"When did you get into drugs with him?"

"Well, that night was the first time. He came over with some rocks and told me it was high-class, that we would have the most intense sex—" She diverted her eyes for a moment, embarrassed. "Anyway, he called it free-base. Now I know it was just street crack."

Frank asked Mogill, "Is there a difference?"

"Just purity. There's no adulterants—other drugs—and it melts cleaner without the crackling sound from bubbles and impurities. Free-basers cook up the cocaine themselves so they know what they're smoking."

"So it *is* cocaine?"

"Oh yes," Mogill confirmed. "It's just that crack is a bit of a concoction, usually."

Ruth continued, "I never done coke before, except once at a party at Sandy's house I did a few lines. I couldn't much feel it, though. Anyway, Kevin wasn't gonna be home, so I figured what-the-hell. We smoked some, and it really was intense at first. But then, instead of having sex, he kept just lighting up this coat hanger with that cotton thing he made, dipping it in rum, and trying to burn more out of that pipe. He said we didn't get enough of a buzz, and he kept bugging me for more money." She paused for a minute, embarrassed.

"Then what?" Frank asked, noticing that Mogill was taking thorough notes.

"He started tearing up Kevin's room until he found the money he was getting from you. I figured it would be easier for me just to pay Kevin back from my paychecks. He said we had to go down to Clearwater—out by the east end. He don't got no car or nothin', so he told me to drive. I was kinda scared, but that buzz was wearin' off and, I gotta admit, I really did wanna get that buzz back."

"He told you where to go?"

"Yeah. He said he knew a couple places we could do a hook-up. Anyway, he had some stash in his duffel bag, so he lit up a joint for the drive. Then we got to this one place, but nobody was home."

"How do you know?" Mogill asked.

"It was dark in there, and nobody answered. He came back to the car real pissed and told me to drive to that other house—the one where the guys got killed. When we parked in front, there was some people on the porch across the street."

Mogill nodded toward Frank, then asked her, "How many? Describe them."

"Well, there was a young black guy, and a white guy maybe a little older—more like thirty—with curly brown hair in a ponytail." She looked sheepish. "I notice hair. Anyway, there was a white woman, too, kinda fat, with black hair tied up in the back."

"Were they there when you came back out from the house?" Mogill asked.

"No, they was gone."

"Okay, go on from when you pulled up," Mogill instructed.

"Um, well, Mark gave me the money and told me to put it in my bra. He said act like *I* was the one buyin' it, and that it was for my friend who had good money and really liked to party, like this was just gonna be a sample and we'd be back later for a lot more if it was good. He wanted to get nice big rocks and a good price. I didn't wanna go in, but he started getting real mean—"

"Mean?" Frank asked.

"Yeah, he got kinda loud. He got up in my face and gives me that look. He said don't mess with me, bitch, or I'll bust your face—that and some other stuff."

"So you went in?" Mogill prodded.

"Yeah. The guys inside knew Mark. He told 'em I was cool, so we sat in the living room. That's when this woman comes in from somewhere down the hall—"

"Describe her," Mogill said.

"Real skinny, long brown hair cut straight across her mid-back, bangs in front. She wasn't wearing no make-up or nothin'. Anyway, she takes the money and leaves the room with the skinny guy—the one that died first. The fat guy—the one that died in the hospital—he stayed there with me. He didn't say nothin'—just kept staring at me."

"What happened next?" Frank asked.

"They came back out and stood there, so I got up, too. Mark asked her if we could get more that night. She said yeah, however much we needed. We went back out to the car and started to leave. Mark had me to circle the block and go down another street. Then we went back and parked a few doors down—"

"Which way? Where?" Mogill asked.

"Um, on the same side of the street, toward Tampa."

"Go on," the attorney said, taking more notes.

"Mark took something out of his duffel bag and went back in. It looked like the two guys let him in. I didn't see that girl. Anyway, he was in there about five minutes— maybe a little more. Then I heard pop-pop-pop, kinda like firecrackers."

"All right in a row?"

"Well, kinda pop-pop, then another pop a few seconds after. Then Mark come walkin' out real fast. He got in the car and said get the hell outta here. I pulled out and he got the duffel bag from the back seat and put something in it and stuffed it under the seat."

"Where?"

"Under *his* seat, but from behind. He put it in the floorboard, then pushed it up underneath. He was real nervous, though, and sweating. I noticed he wiped his face on the front of his shirt three or four times. He was kinda freakin' out a little, so *I* started freakin' out."

"How?"

"Well, I got scared. I couldn't hardly drive. I kept askin' him what was going on, but he told me to shut up. When I even pulled off and stopped by Tampa Road, he started screaming at me, calling me stupid bitch and stuff."

"Pulled over where?"

"In the parking lot of the tire store."

"Okay, what then?"

"Well, I pulled back out on Nineteen, and this police car started flashing its lights behind me. Then another one pulled up next to us and shined a spotlight on us and started flashing its lights, too. Mark told me to pull over on the left side, in the middle part between the two roads. All of a sudden there was cops everywhere. They opened our doors and had guns pointing at us."

Ruth started crying softly. After a minute, she caught her breath and added, "They put handcuffs on us and put him in one car and me in another. That was the last time I saw him. They came here and kept trying to ask me questions and get me to sign papers and stuff. I can't hardly remember what else happened. I was scared to death."

Mogill directed his comments to Frank. "There were bags of pot, apparently packaged for sale, in the car—I guess in the duffel bag, along with a couple sheets of acid—LSD or lysergic acid diethylamide—"

"Sheets?" Frank asked.

"Yeah, blotter acid—on paper with little squares. They say there was forty to fifty hits, plus enough crack to be worth probably four- to five-thousand dollars, some broken into small packets, the rest in one big package. There's serious possession charges, a strong case for trafficking, plus conspiracy stuff they'll tack on that might or might not stick. I've not seen the list, but they'll hit her with another arraignment and exam as we get closer."

"What should I do?" Ruth asked.

Mogill said it was up to her, but he couldn't recommend she take that deal.

"I don't see much choice, Ruth," Frank said softly. "You don't deserve to spend most of your life in prison."

Tears welled in her eyes and, looking at Mogill, she nodded her head.

Frank said, "It's settled then. We're going to trial."

Frank started the van's engine—he was getting in the habit of leaving his Corvette in the garage and driving "the beast," as he called it—then powered down the windows to air it out before turning on the air-conditioning. He looked at his watch and decided he had time to pick up flowers and still catch Kevin at school. He selected a vase of fresh-cut daisies, lilies, and eucalyptus stalks with a point at the bottom for sticking into the ground, plus a basket of silk blooms with colored ribbons.

He tried calling Beverly from his portable phone several times, but kept getting her answering machine. She must have been in the bath.

Kevin came out alone, immediately spotting the van. Confirming he had seen Ruth, adding that she would call Kevin that evening, Frank briefly explained that she had refused the deal. Kevin liked his suggestion that they go by the cemetery to clean up around Linda's grave, so they swung by Beverly's condo on the way, hoping she would agree to go along.

They were surprised to find her and her wheelchair gone, and no note explaining where or how. Kevin checked her garage and reported her car gone, too. She couldn't have driven herself somewhere, not wearing that cumbersome brace. Frank left her a note requesting she call his cellphone as soon as possible.

They did a quick clothes-change for grave cleaning, then loaded a rake, broom, garbage bags, and a watering can into the van.

During the drive, Kevin asked, "Will it be like on TV with a jury and everything?"

"Yeah, except it'll last longer and be a lot more boring."

Kevin rode along, saying nothing for a while. Finally he asked, "Is she gonna win?"

"Well, if the jury believes she had nothing to do with those guys getting shot— "

"She didn't!"

"I know. She just made a mistake. She shouldn't have gone with Mark that night, and she shouldn't have been messing with crack."

"She wouldn't have done that unless Mark was getting her to."

They rode along for another mile, then turned down the road leading to the cemetery. Frank said quietly, "I know you have a lot of questions, and you know I don't have all the answers, but keep asking and we'll try to learn together."

Kevin nodded, then turned away to gaze out the window. He was getting better at acting stoic about the events in his life.

Frank said, "You know, bud, doing things like getting my company straight is important, but looking out for people is the biggest thing you can do—especially when they need you most. Even though I'm filling in as a foster dad right now, I expect we'll be friends long after that foster part's over." He hesitated, then continued, "We want to solve all our friends' problems, but sometimes we can't. Like with Beverly losing Linda, I can't bring Linda back. All I can do is help Beverly face what can't be changed."

Kevin looked at his lap, a smart boy who understood what Frank was trying to say.

"I'm doing everything I can for your mother, but you have to be ready in case it doesn't turn out like you hope. I'll always help you look out for her, no matter where she is."

Kevin took a deep breath. "I know that, Frank, so I've decided to quit worrying about you."

"Worrying about *me*?"

"Yeah. I decided to stick by you, no matter what—" Trying to suppress a grin, he finished, "And you're *very* lucky to have me."

Frank reached over tenderly, then surprised him with a light smack up the back of his head.

"Ouch!"

"Oh my, if I drink any more of that iced tea, I'm gonna wet myself." Beverly chuckled.

Linda said, "Well, we need to head back. If Frank can't find you, he'll get worried."

"Yeah, it's getting hot out here."

"That sunshine sure is beautiful, though," Linda said, closing her eyes and breathing deeply. "Close your eyes, Mama, and turn your face up to the sun. Feel the warmth and see all the little sparkley colors playing across your eyelids."

Beverly sighed. "It sure is pretty. Yes, it's very . . . pretty . . ."

Frank and Kevin pulled into the cemetery and wound their way back toward Linda's grave. First, they spotted Beverly's car. Frank slowed to a crawl, not wanting to disturb what might be a personal moment. He eased over to the side and shut off the engine, suggesting Kevin keep quiet. They climbed out of the vehicle, carefully pushing the doors to, and walked silently toward the flowering bushes ringing the area. Stopping next to some shrubs, they peered through branches gobbed with brilliant magenta blossoms hanging motionless in the hot, breezeless air.

There sat Beverly beside the grave in her wheelchair, her eyes closed, face turned up toward the sun, all by herself.

CHAPTER 24

Kevin snatched the phone up on the firt ring and accepted the charges, all grins as his mother gave him the good news: she had been moved out of protective custody. She would have yard time thrice a day and start calling on a regular basis. They agreed that since they could talk more often and for longer periods of time, they wouldn't impose on Frank to drive Kevin all the way to Clearwater *every* Sunday for those frustrating visits limited to talking through a TV anyway. Once Kevin relayed the good news to Frank, he smiled, tipped his imaginary hat, and stole quietly out.

He paused and, instead of going right over to Beverly's, walked around to the back. His gnawing confusion and frustration had weighed heavily on him since he'd found her inexplicably alone in the cemetery, still insisting that Linda had brought her.

True, there *were* some odd occurrences: somehow driving the car still parked at the cemetery, having her hair done the day of the funeral, the information about Linda's assets and accounts mysteriously popping into Beverly's head—yet, none were entirely implausible. He couldn't comprehend how this woman unable to attend the funeral would suddenly appear there at graveside, serene and seemingly at peace. Frank had seen grief before, had even experienced it himself, but this seemed entirely different. Worried about her, it frustrated him that he didn't understand or know how to help.

In many respects, he and Beverly seemed to be on a fast track toward enduring friendship. They shared an occasional physical relationship, at times very passionate, intense, satisfying; and she also had the capacity to share close personal moments— wheelchair dancing, enjoying music, watching the stars, celebrating their good fortune, enjoying life to its fullest with a cherished loved one.

But has she ever told me she loves me? he wondered, realizing he had wandered down Kevin's path to the clearing. A woman still in love with her dead husband, she'd been pushed toward Frank by her daughter. Only when they had to work together to help Kevin did their relationship rise to a new, more personal level. Maybe she'd simply been impressed by his capacity for caring about this young friend, his loyalty through adversity, regardless of cost or the emotional price he might pay.

Frank had experienced only one romantic love in his lifetime, one that turned out to be a hollow sham, leaving him hurt, betrayed, untrusting, and self-protective. Sure, he really liked spending time with Beverly, the idea of developing a friendship, of finding a companion he could take out on the boat or dance with at the club.

But love? Full commitment can't-live-without-her love? My-happiness-depends-on-her love? When did that happen? Why did that happen? Did I let my guard down too much, too fast, too far?

Could this lady be worth whatever baggage she might bring? Might she be a little too far over the edge, talking to ghosts, quick to let others take advantage of her, giving her money over to strangers?

He came upon the hollow log. Kevin had told him about it many times, but somehow he had never bothered to wander back there and see for himself. It did look kind of cool—such a pretty spot, sand and exotic plants and crystal-clear springs, the setting sun refracting through leaves, sparkling pinpoint colored lights swirling off in the distance . . .

What were those lights? Had he really seen them?

There they are . . . No—over there . . .

He decided his eyes were just tired.

He climbed on top of the smooth-as-varnish log and sat. Beverly certainly proved to be an enigma. *Woman—enigma—woman—enigma . . . they're practically synonyms!* He chuckled out loud, chagrined at how the sound seemed to shatter the magic of the place. He listened as the chirrups and twitters and buzzes of a world alive gradually returned.

He felt like a boy Kevin's age struggling with his first middle-school crush. He had found Lonnie's magazine in Kevin's room that night. Another time, after working in his office until shortly after the boy's bedtime, he had quietly peeked in, noticing a little tent formed under the covers. Once, he'd gathered up laundry to put in the hamper and noticed tell-tale signs prompting a brief but very personal talk the next day. He envied Kevin so many new experiences to explore—a vista including feelings, relationships, and a world to conquer. Yet, on this warm, dusky evening, Frank felt like he knew little more than that twelve-year-old talking on the phone, his mother the most important lady in his young life. In the next few years, surely some girl would drive the boy to hidden tears, touching his heart in ways difficult to comprehend. *Will he ever understand? Will I?*

Many years ahead of Kevin, Frank had long understood how to express sexual feelings, but he wondered if there might be something about sharing unconditional love that he was still learning from the boy. He remembered all those hundreds of times over the years that the little brat showed up to hang out with him. The youngster always took whatever attention he could get, content to share time with his older buddy, even if to work, or watch, or just check in and say hi. Frank felt guilty for not taking the kid more fun places, maybe showing him more affection. It wasn't until Kevin got desperate and scared that Frank had finally crossed that bridge, demonstrating a commitment that confirmed, *Yes, I'm here for you. I do care.*

Somehow that had made it easier for Frank to take another chance, to show Beverly how much she meant to him. In some strange, convoluted way, he owed Kevin for that.

That kid spent years coming around, never asking for more than whatever I wanted to give, happy to get whatever he could. If that's what it takes for me to be close to Beverly, so be it. If her mind and spirit have been hurt by Linda's death in ways I may never understand, so be it. However much she wants to give back, however close we become, it will be worth it, because I can't imagine trying not to care about her.

With unparalleled resolve, he started back up the path toward the condos.

By the time he got back, the sun refracted shades of orange and yellow and red and blue and purple, all shimmering in the sky while back in the clearing with the smooth hollow log, millions of pinpoint lights came together to swirl and form shapes and break apart, only to come together again even more beautiful as they danced in the warm Florida night.

Frank walked up to Beverly's porch and noticed an unfamiliar car in the driveway. Sherry Lubinsky, Linda's roommate from the apartment in Tampa, let him inside. He joined the two women in the living room after helping himself to one of Kevin's Mountain Dews.

"Frank," Beverly explained, "we were just discussing what to do about Linda's things at the apartment. I gave Sherry a check to cover expenses until the end of the year, but she thinks it might be a good idea to start sorting out her personal stuff."

"Well, I can see why in some respects there's no rush, but on the other hand, it must be hard for Sherry, living there with those constant reminders every day."

Sherry appeared grateful that Frank understood. She explained, "Oh, it's no disrespect to Linda. She was my best friend—" She paused, fingering her sleeve nervously. "It's just . . . I can't pretend she's ever going to come home again—" Realizing what she said, her eyes darted to Beverly.

"She's been trying to convince me Linda didn't really take me out to the cemetery today," Beverly explained.

"Well, I'm worried—it's not, well—"

Frank wasn't sure how to defuse the topic. "Well, as far as the apartment, I think we agree Linda isn't going to stay there anymore. I know she has a lot of things that should be saved—like her photographs and personal mementos—so I think it *would* be a good idea to, um, to help Linda by taking care of things she valued so much."

Sherry nodded, wiping her eyes with a tissue from her purse.

"I guess you're right," Beverly said quietly. "Frank always seems to know best. Sherry, can we call you in the next week or so and set aside a good time to come out and maybe, all together, start sorting things out?"

Sherry got up and went over to Beverly, taking her hands, smiling sweetly. "Yes, I would like *very* much to do this together. It won't be easy, but I've been so afraid to try it alone." She hugged Beverly, then Frank, whispering in his ear, "Thank you, Mr. Tanyon."

After she left, Frank took Beverly in his arms, lifting her from the chair and moving her to the couch. He held her tightly, feeling the tension slip from her body. She started to cry softly, still saying nothing. He stroked her hair, gently drew his fingertips down the contours of her face, then looked into her eyes, searching, hers glancing back and forth before returning the gaze, both now crossing the transom, melting together as their eyes slowly closed, allowing the lights to play across their lids to form beautiful patterns.

"You *will* count on me, Beverly."

"Will I?"

"No matter what, we face it together. The good and the bad, no matter what."

"I believe you, Frank. You'll count on *me*, too."

"I already do, Beverly."

CHAPTER 25

Frank spent the next few days running errands and making financial arrangements, setting up the development business with Ward Bodnar, and catching up on some of his personal affairs like boat maintenance, condo upkeep, and a car tune-up. Having anticipated substantially less, the hefty draft Beverly received from the bank in Michigan added some unexpected investment shuffling to Frank's list of transactions. The area around the condos started to buzz with activity, too—especially across the road where workers continued preparing the apartment sites.

Ruth Riner's pre-trial didn't amount to much more than a meeting in the judge's chambers, a lot of posturing, agreement to disagree in front of a jury. Ruth called Kevin almost every night, usually after Lonnie had left to ride his bike home. Her spirits seemed good, her confidence consistent, the support of her son a lifesaver. Frank took Kevin to Clearwater to see her Sunday afternoon despite their near-daily calls, a surprise thrill for Ruth. Kevin started getting other calls, too, with increasing frequency, mostly other boys from school . . .

And someone named Cynthia.

Kevin consistently brought home class assignments to show Frank, showing off exemplary grades, occasionally asking for help, always coveting the old dude's approval and encouragement. They spent time going over business records, Kevin asking questions, making simple yet astute suggestions, and impressing Frank with his budding acumen. Kevin also started teaching Frank new ways to use his computer, honing his own software skills at the same time.

Lonnie came for another sleepover Friday night, bringing along some home-baked cookies from his mother. She called to make sure they'd been delivered, confiding to Frank how grateful she was that he tolerated her son being over there so much, gushing about how much the boy enjoyed his time with both him and Kevin. Frank spent most of that evening next door, giving them adolescent privacy while enjoying some adult behavior of his own. Later that night, he went back home to watch a late movie with the boys, eating microwave popcorn, swilling ice-cold Dew, and disregarding the anticipated smirk of housekeeper disapproval over their mess. Frank made it a point to show them both plenty of middle-school-aged guy-like affection, including lots of wrestling and punching and teasing, and some impromptu noogies.

Beverly finally selected and ordered a grave marker from the brochure Frank brought home. Sherry called one night to talk to her, not about anything in particular, but just to chat for a while. Loretta refused to return calls, but Beverly pointed out that her sister's typical snits usually lasted a few weeks or even a month before fading away as if nothing ever happened. The financial records, not yet returned by Loretta, had all been replaced anyway.

The physical therapy proceeded apace. Gregory coached and encouraged and expressed confidence, keeping Beverly's focus positive, sometimes good-naturedly flirting, always trying to keep the ordeal as upbeat as possible.

Beverly insisted that Linda had come for a visit one afternoon while Frank was out. They had compiled a list covering which of Linda's mementos she would like to have given to certain friends, then spent more time discussing grief, trying to prepare for when they would no longer be able to spend time together. She seemed to be accepting the fact that, in spite of believing these impromptu visits were real, maybe Linda really had died after swerving to avoid a raccoon in the road that awful day.

Frank spent more time reflecting on the circumstances that had brought him and Beverly together, remembering his determination never again to risk the heartache that can come from investing his feelings in others, surprised by how much his own happiness had come to depend on a woman he didn't fully understand and a boy who wasn't even his own. He did feel more confident with Beverly in the time they spent together. She proved increasingly committed, more open with her feelings, more consistent in her expressions of affection, unwavering in her resolve to make Frank a part of her life.

Their sex-life also grew from pretty gosh-darned good to—gimpy leg aside—downright fabulous.

On Monday, Ruth Riner faced arraignment on open murder and other various charges. What normally might have been news of moderate interest mushroomed into a major media story because earlier the same day Mark Sisk had pled guilty to second-degree murder as part of an agreement to testify against Ruth. The local-news lead stories, complete with footage of Ruth draped in chains and manacles and cuffs, described her as the mother of a twelve-year-old Tarpon Springs boy, now in foster care, then gave her address and showed a shot of the trailer. One local video crew even did a live remote asking neighbors in the trailer park how they felt about the alleged murderer who used to lurk in their midst.

By Tuesday morning, Kevin found himself again targeted at school by taunters and bullies. He and Lonnie wound up getting banged and bruised in an after-school fight. Since Lonnie's mother couldn't be reached, Frank picked up both boys from the school office. They went back to the condos where Beverly intercepted them from her front porch. She called them into her place and proceeded to examine both boys thoroughly, doctoring small cuts on each, alternately clucking sympathy and rage at the hooligans who would start such a thing.

The staff's version described Kevin being jumped and Lonnie wading in to defend him, but even with Frank, Kevin refused to talk about it, his anger palpable, so Lonnie followed his lead until Frank gave up. At one point, Frank climbed under the bathroom sink looking for antibiotic cream while Beverly stooped behind him, trying to remember where she had put it. They could hear Lonnie in the other room, quietly telling Kevin, "Hey, don't let 'em get you down. If they try to start anything again, we can get at least ten other people to kick their ass. You got too many friends to let those dick-heads bother you."

Frank found a measure of satisfaction in recognizing that Lonnie had grown to the next level of friendship with Kevin: commitment even in the face of adversity. The ministrations complete, Beverly hugged them enough to embarrass them before she went off to make teenage boy-sized snacks for all. Frank finally reached Ms. Caselow, explaining what had happened and assuring that her son would be okay. Relieved to see she also approved of how the boys had stuck together, Frank suggested that Lonnie sleep over, even though it was a school night, and promised he would drive them the next morning. Both boys brightened at the idea, so all three drove over for Lonnie's change-of-clothes and toiletries.

After fawning over her son for several minutes, Ms. Caselow advocated demanding that the school do something about those bullies. Frank respected Kevin's and Lonnie's assertion that it would be better for them to resolve the situation themselves.

When they arrived back at the condos, the boys headed into Frank's place to get homework out of the way—a condition for the sleepover—and Frank went next door to see why a courier had just left.

Beverly opened a letter-package and scanned its contents. Wordlessly, she handed it to Frank. After a quick perusal, he looked at Beverly with dismay.

"Is it what I think it is?" she asked.

"It's a notice of petition," he explained. "Loretta is asking the court to declare you incompetent and appoint her as guardian over you and your affairs."

Frank treated all three to dinner at a casual seafood bar, Kevin's favorite place for snacks and desserts. The adults enjoyed watching the boys eat as they wrestled their way through a basket of snow-crab legs before going off to play pinball. Beverly felt okay without pain medication, but she seemed bewildered and subdued, slowly working her way to outright anger.

"She's got a lot of gall," she snapped. "How can she do this? What could she mean by *increasingly exhibiting signs of dementia characterized by hallucinations— something something something deceased relatives*? Is she talking about Linda coming and visiting me sometimes?"

"That must be it," Frank admitted.

"Well, I'm not crazy. I know it doesn't make sense, but I can't help it if that's what's happening."

"And it strikes me as relatively harmless, too."

"Loretta just doesn't like you helping take care of my affairs. She's always tried to get her nose into my business—into my money."

"Remember, Stockbridge *did* say he was representing *her* now."

"Is that who did this?"

"Well no," he explained. "Technically, it was an attorney out of Tampa. Stockbridge probably can't practice law in Florida, but it wouldn't stop him from hiring somebody down here."

"How would she pay for this?" Beverly wondered. "She lives month-to-month. She can't afford to go hiring expensive lawyers."

"I suspect they're banking on her getting control so she can pay for their services out of your funds. I think by now Stockbridge has figured out that you don't intend to pay him for mishandling the lawsuit against the bank and filing the appeal. If Loretta was calling him for advice on how to get control of your money—or, worse yet, if she'd been in cahoots with him even when he supposedly worked for you— then he may have decided it would be smarter to throw in with her. If Loretta can write your checks, she'll probably pay that two-hundred grand Stockbridge says he's owed. In fact, if a court appointed her to handle your affairs, she would be *obligated* to pay it unless she legally challenged its validity."

"That lawyer-thief has been screwing me for years."

"Yes he has—or he's been trying to, anyway. But if he's been relying on *anything* he knows about your affairs when he deals with Loretta, then it's a breach of confidentiality. That needs to be looked into, maybe complained about, and possibly sued over." Frank's mind raced with the possibilities.

"That's why she stole all our records—mine and Linda's."

Frank ordered coffee and pondered the situation. "Well, the good news is that the attachment listing assets that are frozen pending a hearing is based on the records she stole. Nearly everything on that list has already been moved, reduced, or eliminated. You're in several stock investments, lots of mutual funds, some bonds and certificates, plus now you're a substantial owner in the development company. Loretta can't cash out or move anything unless she wins, so *nobody* can mess with your money right now. It's a good thing I got it all set up over the last few weeks. That leaves tangible assets like your condo, those cottages up north, the land you own in Houghton Lake, your car, and your personal property. That's all okay sitting where it is right now."

"What about all of Linda's finances?"

"Well, that's the thing. We should go ahead with the probate proceedings so you can be declared her heir. Loretta can't mess with that until you have control, and then only if she wins. Most of Linda's stuff is okay where it is for a while, too. I already moved things that were in both of your names—like those bonds Marshall accumulated with all three names on them."

"What else is there?"

"Well, there's your easy cash—checking account, liquid savings, income and dividend checks, your ATM card—stuff like that. You can't use any of it right now. Don't worry, though. I have more than enough cash available to support us both until we get through this."

Beverly relaxed a little, playing with the last bit of cheesecake on her plate, then sat back and sighed. She shook her head, looked at Frank, and asked point-blank, "Is there any chance she'll win?"

"She would have to prove that you're not capable of handling your affairs."

"Can she?"

"I don't see how. I will say, though, that you need to quit talking about Linda's visits to anybody except Kevin and me." He looked past her to where the boys were engrossed in a video game. Another boy stopped and talked with Kevin and Lonnie before leaving with his own parents. It seemed to be an entirely friendly encounter.

"Well, who else knows?" she wondered.

"I've heard you tell Lizzie and Sherry, and your doctor—plus Loretta. Lizzie has probably talked about it to others who know you."

"Frank . . . it *is* true."

"I believe you," he said quietly. "It's just that you're not going to convince others, and you certainly can't prove it."

"Well, I can avoid talking about it . . ." She shook her head and looked down. "But if I'm asked, I can't say Linda's dead when I know she's not."

Frank noticed the boys were heading back to the table. He whispered, "Then let's try to prevent anybody from asking."

Frank got up early the next morning and made breakfast for the boys. He sat with them while they ate, pep-talking about the situation at school. He could sense their apprehension, but if he thought they truly were in danger, he would intervene. Their now-proven willingness to fight back would likely discourage other physical confrontations. *But what people say about you is sometimes harder to deal with than what they do to you—especially when you're only twelve or thirteen.*

He drove them to school and watched them go inside without incident, then went back home and prepared a light breakfast for Beverly while she got ready to go out. He called and made an appointment with Mr. Posner before they left to visit several banks. At each place, they confirmed that neither of them had authority to transact any business. They also determined that everything Frank had recently set up was not yet frozen. Apparently Loretta didn't know where all the money had been stashed. He assumed she couldn't afford an expensive investigation to uncover the rest.

At the legal offices, Posner reviewed the petition, asked a few questions, and assured them he would do everything he could. He brought in one of the firm's young attorneys with expertise in competency hearings, putting him in charge of researching precedents and suggesting strategies. Everybody agreed to meet again in a week, fifteen days before the hearing.

Frank asked to meet briefly with Mogill. Beverly, not being cleared by Ruth in advance, had to wait in the outer office.

"Mark Sisk's plea bargain *is* a problem," Mogill confirmed.

"How so?"

"Well, he bought his way off death row by giving up Ruth. He must be telling a good story or they wouldn't have paid such a high price to get him to repeat it in court. I'm working on finding out what it is, but I don't know anything yet."

"What can I do?" Frank asked.

"Sit tight. There *is* something else you'll be interested in knowing—something you need to tell her son."

"What?"

"Well, I just heard that Sisk got beat up in the county jail this morning. That means this situation will be a news story again tonight. I've already been called for statements three times, and I don't even represent him. It also means that Ruth got moved back into protective custody. They let her call me about an hour ago before locking her down. She's *real* upset about losing access to the phone, and she wanted me to make sure her son understands."

"I'll take care of that," Frank assured him.

"Good. Until I know more, like I said, sit tight."

They stopped for a quick lunch, then picked up some fresh flowers and went out to the cemetery. They only stayed a few minutes because Beverly's leg hurt, but to Frank it represented a symbolic victory: progress in confronting her grief. He dropped her off at the condo, then went to watch for the boys. When school let out, he saw them loiter briefly with friends, then work their way over to the van before climbing in.

Both seemed very pleased. Kevin explained, "Everybody was being real cool today, trying to show how they would stand by me, saying they hope my mom gets let go."

"Yeah," Lonnie added, "those guys that were hassling him—everybody was getting on their case today."

On the way back, Frank had to pull over several times so emergency vehicles could scream by with their lights flashing. Closer to home, they noticed clouds of smoke billowing from the area by the trailer park. The boys had their faces pressed against the window, urging Frank to go that way. He drove down the side road that led toward the trailers, but got stopped by a police car blocking the lane that went down the back side of the park. From their vantage point, they could see that it was Ruth Riner's trailer—Kevin's home—engulfed in flames.

Frank ordered the boys to stay at the van, then worked his way closer to the action. He talked to a police officer idly standing by, introducing himself as the foster father of the boy who lived there.

"Yeah? Well, somebody spray-painted Murderers & Dealers Stay Out all over it, then torched it."

Frank went back to the van when a local news truck pulled in. He found Lonnie sitting there stunned.

Kevin stared straight ahead.

CHAPTER 26

The news reports proved brutal. The murder story portrayed Ruth as a "crack-addicted mother" out gunning down pushers to satisfy her habit, leaving a twelve-year-old son abandoned in a squalid trailer. Interviews with neighbors, friends, several so-called chums of the boy, and other people long on opinions but short on facts fed that image. Any interview footage that suggested otherwise never made it out of the TV-station edit suites.

The trailer arson got packaged as fed-up citizens out to protect their communities. An outraged, righteous woman heading up some kind of grass-roots organization commanded several minutes on each station to comment on the social significance of people protecting themselves and their children from the "plague" festering in their neighborhoods, resorting to means that police were incapable or unwilling to use. The interviews that survived those edits showed people who canonized the arsonist. Several local politicians called for increasing the power of police—and themselves—all in the name of "taking back our streets." Mug-shot photos of Kevin's mother played prominently in promos and over-the-shoulder news shots, usually followed by footage of her in court.

Kevin spent the evening in his bedroom, avoiding TV and radio altogether. Frank felt he needed to monitor it so he might, if nothing else, anticipate any new problems. Beverly begged off spending time together so she could rest her leg and go to sleep early.

After the evening news ended, Frank took some cookies and Mountain Dew to Kevin's door, asking permission to enter. Peeking in, he saw the boy nod. Kevin still had said nothing since the fire. He lay there, staring at the ceiling.

Frank sat on the side of the bed while they shared the snacks. Then he lay back beside him. Kevin moved over slightly to make room.

They lay there for a full ten minutes, neither saying anything. Eventually, Frank reached over with his hand, putting it gently on the boy's chest, rubbing softly back and forth. After a minute or so of that, a single tear formed at the side of Kevin's eye, then trickled down sideways toward his ear. Frank stopped massaging, but left the hand on his chest. Kevin reached up with his own hand and tentatively put in on top of Frank's, hesitating, then wrapping his fingers around it. Frank curled his own fingers around the boy's and squeezed. Kevin squeezed back, still holding on.

After several more minutes like that, Kevin shifted slightly closer to Frank, putting his head against his shoulder. Softly, he said, "Dick-heads."

Frank quietly confirmed, "Yeah, dick-heads."

Kevin breathed deeply, then seemed to release some of his tension, finally closing his eyes, still holding on to Frank's hand. They lay that way for about ten or fifteen minutes more; then Frank felt the grip relax. Kevin's breathing slowed and his body twitched slightly, his eyelids fluttering. Getting up gingerly, Frank went out to the linen closet and came back with a sheet. He carefully covered the boy, then stood there looking at him.

He turned off the lamp, leaving the door ajar as he slipped out.

Frank decided it would be a good idea to drive Kevin to school again. He called Henry and moved their meeting up an hour, then went next door to check on Beverly. While he was gone, Kevin called Lonnie to see if he wanted a ride, too. Lonnie declined, acting uncomfortable and very mysterious. With lots of "ums," he refused to make any commitments for after school or even the next few days. Kevin heard Ms. Caselow in the background rushing him off the phone. Lonnie begged off and hung up, leaving Kevin feeling even more unsettled.

Frank slipped quietly into Beverly's place and looked in on her. Not wanting to disturb her sleep, he stood there for a minute and watched her gentle breathing. Her bottle of pain pills sat open on the night stand beside a half-full glass of water. He reached out to touch her face, to stroke her hair, but he stopped short, afraid he might wake her. He'd kept her too busy the day before, but at least the trip to the cemetery had proved worth it. He leaned over and kissed her lightly on top of her head and eased just as quietly back out.

As they pulled out in the van, Frank asked Kevin about picking up Lonnie. His demeanor subdued again, Kevin simply said, "No." Frank dropped the subject.

Outside the school, he saw Kevin head over and position himself to await the busses. Several students spoke to him as they walked by, but there didn't seem to be any problems. Curious, Frank pulled out and drove around the block, then drove by the school again. He saw Lonnie talking to Kevin and decided everything looked okay.

He hesitated, watching for a moment, then reluctantly drove away.

"My mom freaked," Lonnie explained. "She thinks somebody's gonna burn our house down or try to kill me."

"That's crazy," Kevin responded.

"Yeah, well, she don't want me over where you live anymore—or, uh, hanging out with you."

"Are you gonna listen to her?"

"Well, I don't have a choice—for now. Don't worry, things'll change."

"But—"

"Um, I gotta go." With that, Lonnie disappeared into the crowd.

In the hallways, several students made wisecracks to Kevin. A few told him to hang in there. Most stared or pointed at him as he walked alone to his locker, then to class.

Halfway through the second period, he got summoned to the office and told without explanation to sit off to the side and wait.

After a few nervous minutes, he saw Lonnie come out from the conference room in back, his face flushed like he was embarrassed or mad or in trouble or—or what? He noticed Kevin, then diverted his eyes and picked up a pass from the secretary before exiting, never acknowledging the presence of his friend.

The principal came out and summoned Kevin, then took him into the conference room where two men in suits, a well-dressed woman, and a uniformed sheriff's deputy waited. A tape recorder, some files, and several notepads sat on the table.

They needed to talk to him, they said. It seemed cold—very cold in the room. He felt vulnerable and alone—possibly even in danger.

"What about Frank? Where is he?"

One of the men in suits asked, "Frank?"

The woman asked, "Frank Tanyon?"

"Yeah," Kevin responded. "Where's Frank?"

The first suited man said, "That won't be necessary."

The other explained, "That's all covered." He gestured to some papers before him. "We just need to ask you some questions—to cover some things with you."

"I wanna talk to Frank about it," Kevin insisted. "Can I call him?"

The other suited man started to act angry. "Look—we can do this here or we can take you down to Clearwater and do this the hard way—"

"Hey," the woman interrupted, shooting a harsh glance at the threatening man. "It's okay, Kevin. We just need to talk, is all."

The first suited man started the tape recorder, reciting, "Interview with Kevin Riner . . ." He added the date, the names of those in the room, where they were located, and the time.

The first suited man asked, "First, tell us what your full name is."

"I wanna talk to Frank," Kevin asserted, now fighting back the urge to jump up and flee.

He sat in that room for nearly an hour, a bad memory, a blur. They asked too many questions about his mother and Mark and how they lived and his friends and what he likes to do and his experiences with drugs and sex and what about Frank and what about Beverly and where does he sleep and has anybody ever done anything to him and are you sure you're telling us the truth and tell us again what you said and oh come on you don't really expect us to believe that and are you sure it wasn't really . . . ?

Kevin begged them to let him go to the bathroom. They shut off the recorder and ushered him to the principal's private rest room. He went inside and unzipped his pants, but then dropped to his knees and bent over the toilet.

He tried hard not to vomit, but he just couldn't help himself.

Frank and Henry waded through piles of financial documents, signing, adding, discussing, adding some more, consulting records, calling and checking on things, then adding some more, occasionally scratching their proverbial heads. Finally, Henry sat back and said, "We need to ask Doug about this."

"I'd like to stroke him a little for making such progress cleaning up the mess. Let's call him with our questions, and I'll take the opportunity to encourage him more."

They set up a speaker-phone call and got Doug on the line. He answered all but one of their questions, sending an assistant off to dig up the elusive information.

"Doug," Frank offered, "I want you to know I'm proud of how you've been hustling all this together. It does me well to know I can count on you."

"Well, thanks, Frank. It's not been easy on this end. Everything is smooth with Junior and the outlets and all, but it's not too smooth with Mom."

"She's not pleased with you jumping ship, so to speak?"

"Well, is it okay to talk?"

"I can leave," Henry offered.

Frank stopped him with a wave of the hand. "Yes, Henry is privy to everything that's going on."

"Well, I'm sure you figured out that Mom wanted to try to pressure you to sell out—even squeeze down the value so it would be a good price."

"Yeah, it was kind of obvious."

"Now she's livid. We're not getting along very well, which I don't like, but dammit I have to take care of business."

"When business comes between family or friends," Frank observed, "then they shouldn't be in business together."

"Yeah, well, I wish Mom *wasn't* in our business."

"How were you going to buy me out?"

"Well, I think you can guess. She had investors lined up, but apparently you got wind of that."

Henry grinned. Frank smiled back, then kept his voice serious, asking, "Did I mess something up?"

"Not entirely, but you put her at a disadvantage. Look, Frank, she would be *real* upset if she knew I was talking about her business, but you know about Rumsey. He's been waving around some kind of agreement to buy our shares when and if you acquire them. He was already planning on financing our acquisition of your stock. Now he's telling Mom he can get those shares of yours anyway, and he's using it as leverage to change Mom's deal."

"What was their agreement, Doug?"

"I don't really know all the details."

"That's all right, Doug. I don't need to know your mother's business."

"Well, anyway, she doesn't want you to walk away with her deal."

"Doug, somebody needs to get control of the company—to get a majority of the shares. Either your mom gets some or all of mine—and controls yours and your brother's—or I get some or all from one of the three of you."

"Neither me nor Junior," Doug explained, "would want to sell out. We really want to keep making the company grow and be successful—" He paused for a second, adding sheepishly, "and have jobs."

"I'd like to see you keep at it, too," Frank confirmed.

"That just leaves you or Mom."

"And I don't want to sell."

"Well, Mom's pretty adamant, too. She's got too much time invested in her, uh, plan."

"Listen, Doug, if your mother's plan falls apart and she winds up back where she started, convince her to sell her shares to me at fair market value and walk away. She'll have a nice retirement, better than having it tied up in a company. You guys will still have your investments *and* your jobs. I'll have control of the company and make sure I look out for you."

"Well," Doug started, "that's a pretty big if."

"Ask her if she's sure she saw the entire agreement Rumsey supposedly has with me. Tell her to check the page numbers and demand to see the original copy. It's seven pages long."

"Um, okay. I haven't talked to you then, right?"

"Right. To her, you're just curious about this so-called agreement."

"Okay then."

"Doug, keep me informed. I want to make this work for everybody—your mom included."

"Sure, Frank, and thanks."

After they disconnected, Henry said, "You know Eli won't show it to her because he can't admit it's at her expense."

"Yeah, but if he does, she won't trust him anymore. If he doesn't, she'll wonder what he's hiding and still won't trust him anymore."

Henry gathered up his papers, still wearing a satisfied smile. "Aren't *you* the sneak?"

"I think it's time to kick in the next phase."

"You're going through with it, huh?"

Frank arched his eyebrows while gathering up his own papers. "Who—*me?*"

"Well, aren't you the sleepy-head?"

Beverly felt drowsy from a late-night dose of pain pills. "Huh? What?"

"Aren't *you* the sleepy-head?"

"Linda? Is that you?"

"Do you need to rest some more?"

"What time is it? Oh me, it's almost nine o'clock. I went to bed last night at seven."

"Do you need some help?"

Beverly managed to slide into the wheelchair parked at the side of her bed. "Just give me some time in the bathroom and we'll get something to eat."

"I'll root around and find something in the kitchen."

By the time Beverly came out, Linda had laid out a light breakfast for her mother, explaining that she had already eaten.

"You know what's happened? Loretta's trying to take your money *and* mine, then put me away in a home or something."

"But Mama, she's your *sister*. I thought sisters were family, and family took care of each other."

"Well, most families work that way. Apparently not Loretta."

Linda looked confused, shaking her head. "I thought two sisters were linked together stronger than other people."

"She's always been jealous of me and of Marshall, of our success, of my having a little girl . . . Now I think she's jealous of Frank. She wants money, too."

"Why does money matter?"

"Honey, money corrupts absolutely. It can tear apart friends, and it can tear apart family."

"Even a bond that has lasted a whole lifetime?"

"Oh yeah, it happens all the time."

"Why?"

Beverly thought for a minute, taking several bites from a sweet roll. "I don't know, sweetie. I'm not like that, so I've never understood it, either."

"Mama, how come you haven't cleaned out my stuff from the apartment?"

Beverly looked at her, searching for some kind of answer. Softly, almost whispering, she asked, "Linda, are you dead?"

Linda looked chagrined, thinking for a minute. "You do need to get used to that idea. What about the apartment?" she asked again, quickly changing the subject back.

"That's gonna be hard to do," Beverly responded quietly. "I'm supposed to get with Sherry, but I still haven't called her."

"Why is that hard?"

"Well, it's a reminder that you're, um—passed away. It's like intruding into your personal life."

"The part about me that's separate from being your daughter?"

"Well, the part of you that's a grown woman with a life—" Beverly used a finger to wipe the side of her eye. "A grown woman who *had* a life of her own. You know how it is. When kids grow up, they become more and more independent until they go off and live their own lives."

"But they can still be the son or daughter anyway, right?"

"Yeah, in most cases—but not everybody."

"How were we, Mama? Did we still have a good mother-and-daughter, uh, relationship?"

Beverly tugged tentatively on her daughter's arm, then pulled her into a hug. "Oh Linda, the best. The very best."

They chatted while Beverly finished eating. "Mama, I think I would rather show you some things at my place, just between us, before you and Sherry start sorting the rest. Did Frank help you get your car back here yet?"

Beverly smiled. "Yeah. He never did figure out how it got all the way out there to the cemetery."

With Linda behind the wheel, they drove into Tampa. Beverly brought her spare apartment key, knowing that Sherry was at work and they would have several hours alone. Linda wheeled her on and off the elevator and into the apartment. They went to the bedroom where Linda helped her mother onto the bed and made her comfortable.

Beverly looked around at all those pictures, and tears filled her eyes. Nearly every shot was of somebody Linda loved, yet so few of them actually included her. *Always behind the camera, that was my little shutterbug.*

Linda dug a small jewelry box from the bottom of a drawer where it had been hidden under some clothing. She sat on the bed next to Beverly and opened it. It revealed a strange collection of things that didn't appear to be of value.

First, a Cracker Jack finger ring with a purple-plastic shiny stone. "I was in kindergarten when you went to stay with Loretta for a few weeks—remember, after her operation?"

"Oh yes, that's right. I wound up staying with her for three weeks," Beverly recalled.

"I told Daddy I was gonna marry him and be his wife if you didn't come back home. That night, we were eating some Cracker Jack, and he had this ring in his box. He put it on my finger and said we were engaged, but don't tell you 'cause we didn't want to make you jealous." Linda smiled, gazing off into some far-off place from the past. "I knew I couldn't ever marry him, but that ring always reminded me I was Daddy's other girl. I've had it all this time. I remember the night Daddy died—"

Beverly put her hand to her mouth. "That was a terrible night," she whispered.

"I sat there in my bedroom in Ann Arbor and cried. I got out this ring and put it on my pinkie finger and remembered how I would always be Daddy's other girl."

Tears crept down Beverly's cheeks. "He sure did love you," she whispered.

"Yeah, and he never let me forget it, either."

They sat there quietly for a minute before Linda dug out a fourth-grade report card. "The only D I ever got," she explained.

"I remember that."

"That was the day you sat me down and spent an hour giving me that speech about how I was smarter than that. I didn't care about arithmetic, but you wouldn't hear of it. You kept telling me I should always learn everything I can in life, even if I don't think it matters much right then, because someday I might need to know it and, if not, it never hurts to learn anyway."

Beverly turned the card over gingerly, recalling that day so long ago.

They continued to go through the box, Linda explaining why so many silly things evoked such special memories—sentimental, humorous, loving—the symbols of a lifetime, the reminders of a daughter both loving and loved.

A dog collar, a blue ribbon, a broken thimble, a torn-up and taped-together photo of a teenage boy, a bent penny, the clasp from a training bra, a subway token, an empty ball-point pen, a lens cap . . .

Sherry came home and found Beverly, all by herself, sitting on Linda's bed and holding a box full of knickknacks, tears in her eyes, the hint of a smile from deep inside her heart.

CHAPTER 27

Frank paced around Mr. Mogill's office, too furious to sit down, too upset to lower his voice.

"They had Lonnie's mother's permission, but they lied to the administrators about having mine!"

"That was illegal, Frank," Mogill said, "but suing for damages is a tough row to hoe."

"And then those bastards tried to send him back to class! He couldn't go in. He took off and ran to a pay phone, calling and leaving messages on my machine, begging me to come pick him up. I found him huddled behind the brick wall where they put the trash bins, practically in shock."

Mogill shook his head, looking alternately mad and sympathetic. "That wasn't right—"

"You're damn right, it wasn't right! Since when are police allowed to question minors without a parent *present?*"

"Well, they're not supposed to—"

"Then where the hell was I? I'm the foster father here. Nobody tried to contact *me*. There was no reason they needed to talk to him right away."

"No, there wasn't—"

"And what about Lonnie? Why did they need to talk to him?"

"Well, I don't know—"

"Kevin said most of it had to do with his mother. Why couldn't they wait for me?"

"Well, they didn't want you to have a chance to influence him—"

"So they scare the hell out of him? He said they kept getting mad when they didn't like his answers—trying to convince him things he was saying weren't true, or that he didn't remember them right—trying to get him to turn against his mother. They even told him she must not be much of a mom if she had that kind of stuff going on in the house, putting his life in danger." Frank picked up a statue, looked dangerously like he might throw it, then put it back down to resume his pacing.

Mogill asked, "Does he remember what else they asked?"

"I tried to find out. I was even going to take notes for you, but he can't think about it without freaking out. He was shaking like a leaf. Last night, he kept waking up scared. I had to sit with him just to calm him down. Soon as I'd get him to sleep, he'd jump up again!"

"Do you think he needs professional—?"

"He *needs* to be left-the-hell alone. What can we do about this? I want their asses fired. This ain't right, and I'll be *damned* if they're gonna mess with him anymore."

"Where is he now? Is he in school?"

"No, he doesn't ever want to go back. He said he doesn't have any friends left any-way, and that everybody at school knows about him. Dammit, he's nearly thirteen years old. You remember what it's like—your whole world revolves around your friends and how popular you are and what the girls think of you. He feels like he's ruined there—and he's terrified the police will come get him. He thinks they got his mother—now they're gonna get *him*."

"Well, he's in no danger of being arrest—"

"Yeah, tell *him* that. Convince *him* he's safe. Go ahead, tell him they play by the rules, and they won't do what they're not supposed to, and that an innocent woman doesn't get her life destroyed, and they won't take him away without calling me first— go ahead, convince *him* of that—then convince *me*."

"Where did you say he is?"

"He's at Beverly's. She's the only person I'll leave him with right now. She's the only other person he feels safe with." Frank had spent enough of his anger to sit down and remain seated for the first time. "God knows, Beverly's dealing with more than she can handle now, too. Dammit, I'm fed up with *my family* having to suffer. I'm not going to take it anymore. I'm telling you, they better stop messing with us."

Kevin moved the box over by the other three they'd already sorted, closing the lid with masking tape, then using a thick black marker to write *CD's & Cassettes* on the side. He brought another one over to where Beverly sat on the couch, put it on the table in front of her, and carefully unsealed it. Peering inside, they could see it con-tained a lot of small items wrapped in cloth, packed with towels.

"Is that the butterflies?" she asked.

Kevin gingerly unwrapped one to reveal a small ceramic butterfly, painted blue with streaks of various colors, and mounted on a piece of driftwood. "Ooo. This is pretty. Is this *all* butterflies?"

Beverly smiled. "Yeah, she collected them ever since she was a girl. Some of them are quite valuable—especially the one that's cut crystal, but most are gifts from people she cared about. She got started by making one in art class in sixth grade."

"Wow, cool. How many are there?" he wondered.

"Oh, there's probably forty at least. One of these other boxes is full of them, too." She looked around the room. "You know," she announced, "I think I'll have a nice cabinet built over there—maybe in oak with some glass doors to keep off the dust—then I'll put all of her butterflies on display."

Kevin smiled. "Cool. Since she collected them so long, she'd probably like you keeping 'em for her." He carefully wrapped the butterfly and put it back in the box.

Beverly motioned him closer, guiding him onto the couch beside her. She put her arms around him and hugged. He melted into her. *He's so easy to hug,* she thought. "And you gave her one, too," she said.

"I did?" he asked, pulling back slightly to look at her.

"Yeah. I'm going to have that picture and the poem about the roses and the butterfly framed together, then put them right in the cabinet."

He looked pleased, though somewhat sad, reminded of his heartfelt expression of grief at the funeral. Without saying anything, he hugged her again, then got up to move the box over to the sorted pile, taping the lid and marking it *Linda's Butterflies.* He brought another box from the first pile to the table and opened it carefully. Inside were various garments.

"More clothes," she pronounced. "Seal it and mark it—that's another one for charity." Following her instructions, he finished labeling it. She suggested, "Why don't we take a break now and get us a snack?"

"I can get a tray and bring it in here."

"Oh, yes. That would be very nice."

He headed for the kitchen, calling out, "What do you want?"

"How about some cheese and crackers?"

"Sure!"

"The crackers are—"

"Got 'em," he said, pulling two kinds from a lower cabinet.

"The cheese is in—"

"Yuck! This stuff smells weird!" he exclaimed, wrinkling his nose at the small block of white Gouda he pulled from the refrigerator. He set up a tray with small plates, napkins, a cheese slicer, and a glass of soda, calling out, "What do you want to drink?"

"How about a small glass of that Chardonnay?"

He poured it from the open bottle in the refrigerator, then carried it all very carefully to the living room. He put the tray on the table and spread some cheese on several crackers for her, putting them and the wine within her reach. He opened several napkins and spread them around, explaining, "Got to protect the nice couch—you're a cripple and I'm a sloppy kid."

She laughed. "We *do* make quite the pair, don't we?"

He sniffed the cheese again, then with the trepidation of a youngster about to take some bitter medicine, tasted it. Surprised, he liked it enough to eat several more.

"You know, just in the time I've known you, you've really started to shoot up."

"I'm four-foot ten now."

"Yeah, well, I keep expecting that next time I see you, you'll have grown another foot."

"Oh no! Then I'll have three feet! Yaah!"

They both laughed until she tweaked his nose. Looking down at the bandaged stub at the end of her injured leg, she added, "I sure wish *I* could grow another foot."

"Well, you'll just have to buy one."

They ate more crackers and sipped their drinks. Beverly put hers down and looked at Kevin, tilting her head and pouting her lips. "Thanks for helping me with Linda's things," she said softly.

"You don't have to thank me. You do a lot more for me than I do for you. Besides, I like just being with you. Any time you want some help, you just let me know— even if I'm married and have kids and a job and live in another state—I'll just get on a plane and come right over."

She smiled, her eyes sparkling. *Such a charmer, he's going to break hearts someday.* "You're starting to feel better, aren't you?"

He shrugged awkwardly, then nodded.

"Will you be ready to go back to school tomorrow?"

He shrugged again, avoiding eye contact. "I don't want to."

"Well, I don't think Frank will *make* you go if you're not ready, but you can't miss for long, you know."

"Yeah, I know." He looked up and into her eyes. "Beverly, why does things have to be so hard sometimes?"

Looking over at the boxes that represented the loss of her daughter, she shook her head and admitted, "It sure don't seem fair, does it?"

"No."

They sat there a moment; then Beverly continued, "But if you have to go back to school eventually, you might as well go soon so you can get on with doing everything else that needs to be done."

"Yeah, I guess."

"Like me cleaning out Linda's stuff. I can't pretend the accident didn't happen, but I can't change it. It's not doing her any good leaving everything sit like nothing happened. I need to get on with remembering her and enjoying the rest of my life just like she'd want me to."

Kevin reached his hand over and took Beverly's into his own. They both squeezed for a moment before she pulled him into another hug, whispering, "You're a pretty good guy to have around."

She held him tighter, rocking gently back and forth.

Henry waved Frank to a chair across from his desk, handing him a fat envelope to peruse until he could wrap up his phone call. Frank looked at the collection of photographs, layout drawings, and typed pages of background information. There were two sets of everything.

Henry hung up the phone and greeted Frank, accepting a different envelope from him. Looking through the multiple sets of legal papers and press releases, he found several pages covered with lists particularly interesting.

"Wow," Henry exclaimed. "He's wrapped up in ventures in four different states, several that look fairly high-profile."

"Yeah," Frank agreed, grinning. "Look at the two listed for Atlanta."

"Hoo boy—teen dance clubs and a business-security service. Yowzer. Those little enterprises wouldn't cotton to some bad PR now, would they?"

"I'd say not at all."

"You still want to call Doug first?" Henry asked.

"Yeah, he's expecting us."

They got Doug Taylor on the speaker phone. "Mom's pretty pissed," Doug related. "She's feuding with her money-man, but they still have a tentative set-up. She swore that she'll give her shares to Junior and me—or charity for that matter—before she'll sell 'em to you."

"Why?" Frank asked.

"She wants him to give up the idea he can exercise that option he has with you. She wants him to focus on financing *your* shares for her to control. She's been making some generous concessions to him. I don't know the details, but it sounds like she's trying to beat your offer."

"Okay, Doug, thanks for letting us know. It's time for us to yank her investor out from under her. When she starts to freak, tell her I'll buy her out at fair market value and let her walk away to live the good life. You convince her that if she doesn't play, my next move might jeopardize you and your brother. She's a good mom—she'll listen."

"Sure. I'll let you know how it goes, Frank. What are you planning to do?"

"Can't say."

"Hmm. I guess I understand. Okay, Uncle Frank. Good luck."

After they hung up, Henry offered Frank some coffee. "We got a half-hour to kill before Rumsey gets here—though I'm guessing he'll probably show up early. I thought you were going to file it first. You decided not to?"

"Posner said, Why bother? He said it would cost more, take more time, maybe stir things up more than necessary for it to work like we expect. In fact, these documents are sort of just mocked up. They'd need to be beefed up before it could really be filed."

Henry grinned. Changing the subject, he asked about Kevin.

"Well . . . Beverly seems to have brought him out of it okay. He spent most of the day yesterday with her, helping her sort out Linda's things, organizing her closet, rearranging her kitchen to make it more wheelchair-reachable."

"Oh good. Good."

"He's not over it, though. He's jumpy as a toad in snake country. Every time the phone rings or there's a knock on the door, he gets skittish."

"Did he go back to school today?"

"Yep. I told him he didn't have to, but apparently he and Beverly worked that out. He's being the brave trouper."

"I try to remember how it felt at that age," Henry commented, shaking his head. "I don't know how he handles all the pressure."

"You and me both," Frank agreed. "I didn't know if I *should* let him go back to school, or protect him even more, or just try to toughen him up. I'm lost, Grubber. I've never been a dad, and I sure as hell don't know how to be a youngster's friend. Sometimes it scares me just thinking about it." Frank propped his face in his hands, resting his elbows on the table. "That kid is depending on me so much, I just have to make sure I don't let him down."

Henry walked over and put his arm around Frank's shoulders. "You're doing more than anybody could expect. He's lucky to have you."

"God I hope so—"

A buzz signaled a visitor in the lobby.

Everybody exchanged friendly greetings, Eli assuming Frank was ready to make a move. Henry brought in another mug of coffee for Eli, and all three sat around the conference table.

"Eli," Frank began, "I'm suing you."

"Huh? For what?"

"For stealing business records, conspiracy, corporate something or other, and violation of federal so-and-so's. I don't remember it all; I've got a pocketful of lawyers handling the details."

"This is pretty serious, Mr. Tanyon. You're saying things that can come back and bite you in the ass. Lucky I don't have a temper—"

Frank started laying out photos taken *inside* Rumsey's apartment, some shot with a telephoto lens, others wide-angle. Then he laid out shots of fingerprints and comparison charts. Henry picked up Eli's mug, holding it gingerly with a napkin, then walked over to a cabinet and placed it inside, locking it away.

"What *is* this shit?" Eli demanded.

"Relax, Eli, there's more." Henry laid out a series of press releases, specifically addressed to the newspapers and TV-station news operations in all of the towns Eli and his brother owned businesses. Scanning the top release, then shuffling through others, Eli argued, "You can't say this stuff—it's slander! It's libel! It's—"

"It's the grounds on which the lawsuit is based. Those releases only announce the civil suit and describe what you're being sued for. Whether or not you win and clear yourself doesn't matter, because doubts will remain—*your* reputation will be shot. A company that provides after-hours security for businesses owned by a guy being sued for stealing corporate secrets? Somebody operating teen dance clubs accused of B & E?"

"I'll find some way to bring you down," Eli raged, pacing around the office.

"Oh calm down, Eli," Henry admonished.

"Hey, everybody here's pals," Frank added. "Just to show you what a nice guy I am, I haven't filed this yet. I wanted to give you a chance to work this out."

"I'm not paying extortion—"

"I don't want your money. I just want *you* to go away."

"Go away?"

"Yeah, call Marta Taylor right here from this office and tell her all bets are off; she's on her own. We'll sign a neat little form voiding your stock option. You fade into the sunset. Get out of my face, and I won't ever file this suit or send out press releases—unless you come back and get in my way."

Eli looked at Frank, then Henry, then back to Frank again, finally ending up glaring at the stack of photos and documents on the table.

"If Marta comes up with *any* financing," Henry explained, "I'll trace it back to the day every dollar was printed, so Frank means *no* involvement—not direct, not indirect—nothing."

Eli sat back, flustered and mad. "Call her *right* now?"

Frank listened on an extension while Eli gave her the bad news. She demanded explanations, but Eli simply told her never to contact him again.

Eli signed the option-void, then gathered up his materials and headed toward the door.

"One last condition, Mr. Rumsey," Frank added. "Mail my *Sailing The High Seas* disk back to me. I miss it."

CHAPTER 28

Cheese omelets had fast become Kevin's favorite cook-it-himself breakfast. Although Frank sometimes got up first and made something for the two of them, Kevin prepared the morning meal more often than not.

Frank sauntered in and sat down, giving Kevin a noogie as he passed.

"Hey! I get my hair all combed up the way Cynthia likes it; then *you* come along and mess it up!"

"When do I get to see what your little girlfriend looks like?" Frank asked, hesitating with the salt-shaker until finally deciding it might be smarter to pass up such an egregious dose of sodium.

"She's *not* my girlfriend," Kevin corrected, "but you can see what she looks like when I get some pictures developed."

"You've been taking pictures?" Frank asked.

Kevin picked up an automatic 35mm camera from the counter, framed Frank, and snapped a picture of the disheveled foster-dude hovering over his plateful of eggs.

"Where'd you get that—from Beverly?"

"Yep. It was Linda's. She's got a bunch of cameras in a box over there—a bunch of parts and lenses and stuff, too—and this was the easiest one to use." He set the camera down on the table and poured eggs for his own omelet.

"You thinking about getting into photography?" Frank asked.

"Sure. Beverly said if I get serious about it and learn how to use the complicated cameras, maybe she'll let me use Linda's—or give me one. But *this* one's mine, and I'm gonna take pictures of everybody, and cool things, too."

"Good for you." Frank picked up the camera and examined it.

"Man, this one is gooey," Kevin remarked, folding the omelet. Scooping up the awkward, oversized concoction onto the spatula, he turned toward the table, holding the skillet with his hot-mitted hand.

Click. Portrait of a boy on the threshold of becoming a man, master chef cooking up a hearty breakfast for himself and his guardian-protector-friend.

Oh my! Beverly thought, a mischievous twinkle in her eye. *Waltzing around the room in the arms of two handsome men!*

"Now turn this way just slightly and help her shift her weight forward," Gregory

Dean explained.

Frank carried her like a delicate China doll, afraid he might somehow hurt her, but he proved determined to learn how to help. "Why, madam," he drawled, "you are light as a feather. You must float like an angel!"

Gregory smiled as Beverly batted her eyelashes and affected a look of mock modesty. "That's right," he said, "keep a positive attitude. I'd like to see you up and around on these crutches at least twice a day—even three or four, if you're up to it. Start out at a few minutes, but don't be afraid to work up to a half-hour or more—there, see that? Frank, did you feel how she started to lose her balance when she shifted her weight?"

"You're saying *let* her?"

"Yes, but that's why the first few days it's better if you keep your arms around her. You want to let her struggle some—she's got to work on her balance and strengthen up those muscles again—but don't let her fall or stumble so much she aggravates her injuries."

"What if it starts hurting?" Beverly asked.

"Well, keep Dr. Rumschaak informed, but you have to learn to judge this for yourself. It *is* going to hurt—there's no way around that. Besides, we don't want you so doped up on the painkillers that you'll lose your balance or not be able to monitor the nature of the pain.

"Other than that," he continued, "you know what the injury pain feels like, so watch out for that. Expect the muscles and joints to be tender. Expect the forward part of your foot, the area that was amputated, to be aggravated when you fall into the old habit of trying to shift your weight forward onto it. Expect to feel tightening and fatigue all back through here—" He rubbed along the muscle in the back of her thigh. "But if the pain in this area feels like it's in the bone, or if it's in this part of your foot, particularly if it feels like it's throbbing, then back off. Take a rest. Report it to the doc. More so, if it persists after you've rested ten or fifteen minutes, then don't try walking again until you've been checked out."

"You're not prepping her so she can get up and run away on me, are you?" Frank asked. "She's hard to keep under control."

Gregory smiled. "That's the goal, Frank—that's the goal." Then to Beverly he added, "And don't be afraid to give in and let him take your weight. Don't be like the guy who swam halfway across the lake, decided he might not be able to make it, then turned around and swam back. If you walk across the room and feel like you're losing it—then you've done enough. Let Frank catch you, even if he has to lower you to the floor and go get the wheelchair."

"Gee, I hope I don't forget what I was going for and leave her there all day," Frank mocked, scratching his head with a confused look on his face. "This ol' brain's not what it used to be."

Gregory let go as Frank lowered her onto the couch. "Let's see you do one more before I leave." He watched while Frank helped her up into the walking position. She positioned her crutches and, with Frank gingerly holding on, moved a step at a time across the room, then turned and worked her way back. Frank helped lower her to the couch again.

Gregory shook Frank's hand, then leaned over and kissed Beverly on top of her head. "You look out for our girl, Frank," he said before slipping out the door.

Frank went over and put on Al Jarreau's "We Got By," then held out his hand in a gallant sweep. "Would the lady care to stumble around the dance floor with a forgetful feller?"

Beverly wound up not moving very much; Frank did all the work, supporting her and dancing around her. It was awkward, a jumble of bandages and brace and crutches, but the soft melody filled the room, flowing around her, lifting her weight and taking away the pain.

Frank felt so strong. Where he touched her, she tingled—a gentle ripple that sparked and spread, transporting the two of them until it seemed they would be swept beyond the horizon to dance in the clouds.

Lonnie hurried to the front of the school-cafeteria line. Kevin rushed past everybody so he could be right behind him. Lonnie took his tray to a far table and sat down. Kevin followed, taking the chair across from him. Lonnie looked embarrassed. Kevin casually opened his milk and took a drink, watching his friend carefully. Lonnie started eating the red and brown medley on his plate, keeping his eyes diverted.

Kevin asked, "What is it about Frank you like?"

"Huh?"

"Frank—what do like about him?"

Lonnie shrugged. "I don't know. He's pretty cool."

"There's a lot of people who are cool. Frank's better than just cool. What is it?"

"Hmm . . . Well, he treats us better than most grown-ups—like we're one of his friends instead of just kids."

"Yeah, that's one thing," Kevin observed. "How about compared to your dad—or those guys your mom goes out with?"

"None of those guys are around anymore."

"No they're not, are they? How about: one of the cool things about Frank is that he sticks by his friends, no matter what?"

"Yeah, I guess."

"You have any idea how much crap he's gone through for me?"

Lonnie shrugged. "Well, yeah."

"That's the kind of friends *I* want—the kind that stick with you, especially when you need 'em—not just 'cause you wanna hang around and have fun." He stopped eating and held up his hand, counting off one finger. "So far, Frank's one—" He paused, looking directly at his friend.

Lonnie appeared even more embarrassed. He leaned forward and spoke quietly so the growing number of students taking seats around them wouldn't hear. "I've done nothing but fight with my mother these last few nights," he explained. "I'm wearing her down."

Kevin, also keeping his voice down, responded, "Don't let me get in the way of you and your mom. It's not worth it."

Indignant, Lonnie asserted, "Yeah, it is. I just don't know how to get her to let up."

"Ignoring me at school ain't helping."

"I didn't know what to say. I thought you would get on my case about it."

"I know how it is trying to work on a mom. I'm not gonna get on your case for that. I just can't tell if you're working on *her* or blowing *me* off." He added the afterthought, "—Or both."

Lonnie whispered, "Sorry."

Kevin nodded, then resumed eating.

"How about coming home with me after school?" Lonnie asked. "We'll *both* work on my mom."

"What if she don't want me there?"

"Then you won't have a ride. You'll have to call Frank." Lonnie grinned. "Then *he* can come work on her, too."

Kevin paused again. "You really want to?"

"What? You think I'd rather be—" He swept his arm in a gesture encompassing the cafeteria. "—Best friends with one of *these* dick-heads?"

Mr. Posner opened the file on his desk, talking to Frank and Beverly as he sorted through papers. The young attorney he had introduced as Mr. Maier looked on.

"It all boils down to two things," Posner began. "First, the argument is that you—" He looked carefully at Beverly. "—That you are delusional and hallucinatory, probably stemming from the tragic loss of your daughter and severe injury to yourself. Furthermore, that the hallucinations are not waning but, rather, getting more severe."

Beverly shook her head, "But—"

Frank interrupted, putting a hand on her arm and saying softly, "Let him finish." Then to Posner he asked, "What's the other thing?"

"That while in a state of delusion, you recklessly and against your best self-interest signed over control of your entire estate to a stranger—" He nodded toward Frank, continuing, "—Who immediately cashed out or hid all of your assets in questionable ventures." He looked at Frank, adding, "There is even some speculation about your print company being in dire straights—apparently somebody looked into your tax filings for the last few quarters—which supports the argument that control needs to be taken back before you use her life savings in a misguided attempt to bail out your sinking empire."

Frank simmered, but said nothing for a moment. Beverly vacillated between hurt and angry, but looked toward Frank for reassurance rather than speak. He stroked her arm.

Posner continued, "This is one of the few kinds of proceedings where speculation and pre-emptive legal actions are usually allowed—even encouraged."

"I can justify the soundness of all my investment decisions," Frank offered.

"You shouldn't have to. What matters is if any have been put into your name or turned into disappearing cash. If they're all legitimate investments—not like a company planning to tow icebergs to the Sahara dessert so it can sell farmland—then that's not a big problem."

"It's all straight—even impressive," Frank assured.

"Good. Then the bigger problem is their delusion and hallucination argument." He spread out several sheets of paper. "Loretta has statements from a Sherry Lubinsky, Loretta Marlowe—that's her, I guess—Elizabeth Brannigan, and Dr. Rumshaak—the latter clearly violating patient privilege. They say variously that you have claimed on numerous occasions that your daughter is still alive, and that you've spent time with her—even going places together. Sherry apparently found you in your daughter's bedroom claiming that Linda had been there, too, and that you were confused about how she suddenly disappeared. Loretta is also asking the court to subpoena Kevin Riner about what he may know, but there is no statement from him here."

"Kevin would never turn on me," Beverly said, having decided to be more hurt than angry.

"When he's brought in and put under oath, he'll have to answer the questions. If he's an honest boy, those answers won't mean he's turning on you—but they might be used against you anyway, depending on what they are."

"What's the quickest, simplest, least damaging way to win this?" Frank asked, ever the pragmatist.

"Well, we need three things," Posner explained. "Third-most, you need to bring financial records to show the legitimacy of what you've been doing, just in case it gets that far."

"Okay," Frank agreed. "That's *third?*"

"Yeah. Second-most, we should have a professional evaluation by a qualified psychologist or—better yet—a psychiatrist."

Mr. Maier interjected for the first time. "I have several I've worked with before." He passed a sheet of names over to Beverly. "Any of these people are easy to work with," he added. He shot a knowing glance at the senior attorney.

Posner continued, "And first, what matters most—what might make it so we don't even have to look at the finances—is how you . . ." He directed his comments to Beverly again. "Answer the magistrate's questions."

"She can't say Linda is still alive, can she?" Frank asked.

"Well," Posner replied, "I can't tell you to lie. I *will* say that the ideal situation for me to do *my* job would be if you said that you were misunderstood—they only have statements from a few people and those are weak—and that you understand that your daughter *has* passed away. Saying that Linda came to visit you could be explained that it just seemed like you could feel her presence. You felt like she guided you when you sorted out her things. You know—it was thinking about her that gave you the strength to climb into your car and drive it all the way to Tampa."

Beverly appeared flustered. Frank reached over and held her hand. She looked down at her injured leg. Speaking very softly, she explained, "I'm trying to get used to the idea that Linda is no longer part of this world. But I can't pretend she doesn't come visit me sometimes—I don't mean in my thoughts, I mean that she really comes and visits me. She drove that car. How could I drive? She may be gone from *this* life, but I can't pretend she's gone from *my* life forever."

Frank stood up behind her, bending over and wrapping his arms around her in a hug.

She whispered, "I can't imagine thinking that she won't come see me again."

Ms. Caselow acted very nice toward Kevin, explaining how she was only scared of what *other* people might do—not of Kevin or Frank. She still wanted to talk to Frank anyway, but when Kevin called the condo, he got no answer. He tried Frank's cellphone, catching him and Beverly in the van. Feeling good, Bev wanted to meet Ms. Caselow, so she and Frank stopped by Lonnie's house together.

Ms. Caselow welcomed her guests graciously, clucking over Beverly as Frank helped her struggle up the two steps to the stoop, then into the dilapidated, two-bedroom bungalow. Lonnie's mother clung to her son protectively, apologizing for the misunderstanding and explaining she didn't fully understand what was going on. Frank reviewed the nature of recent events, assuring her that at no time was her son ever in danger. Beverly clung to Kevin nearly as much as Ms. Caselow did to Lonnie. Both women seemed to recognize and respect that about each other.

Kevin realized how much easier it must be for a scared mother to avoid things she doesn't understand than it is to confront them, easier to banish unseen faces than to dismiss them in person, easier to console her own fears than to consider the needs of others.

What most won over Mrs. Caselow was Frank pointing out how much Kevin needed a friend during these difficult times, and how equally valuable it would be for Lonnie to practice the kind of unselfish loyalty that fosters enduring relationships throughout life. "When a boy's not able to see this in his father, it's all the more important he learn it where he can."

Because it was Friday afternoon, everybody agreed an immediate overnighter for the boys would be a very fine way to cement this new level of understanding. Lonnie packed a gym bag, loaded his bike into the van, and rode with them back to the condos.

Preparing to head back into the springs so he could hang out with Lonnie and seek out potential photo subjects, Kevin packed his camera, some after-school snacks, and two sodas into a sack. Lonnie told him to hold on, then took the sack to the bedroom for a minute. As they headed down the path, he explained he had stashed two magazines in it. With a grin and a leer, the boys went off to their private sanctuary in the sandy clearing with open springs, a big hollow log, and more than a creature or two.

Sprawled out with their backs against the log, they munched their snacks, then broke out the magazines. They spent time first scrutinizing the new one, then reviewing the old one, and finally re-examining the new one again. The conversation, when there was any, consisted mainly of misinformation about sexual techniques and considerable speculation about which model's attributes Cynthia and several other girls from school would most likely someday resemble.

Assuming they had complete privacy, and with intense attention to the subject matter, they grew oblivious to anything going on in the surrounding area. Their interest in matters libidinal eventually exhausted, they stashed the magazines in their envelope and wandered off to search for photo subjects.

Kevin got a shot of Lonnie sitting on the giant log, plus several more of him exploring and climbing in the area. He took another of his friend holding up a large toad, then noticed swirling pinpoints of colored light in the background. Motioning for Lonnie to stand still and be quiet, he waited patiently for several minutes before snapping a shot of a small whorl, capturing them just before they disappeared, apparently into the water.

"What were you doing?" Lonnie wondered.

"Trying to get a shot of those colored lights."

"What lights?" he asked, gazing around.

"I don't know. I don't see 'em anymore."

They explored a while longer before heading back to the log, then pulled the magazines out for another perusal before packing up and heading back to the condos. Inside Frank's place, they found the older fellow marinating steaks for the barbecue while talking with Beverly, who sat on the living-room couch.

"*There's* those monsters!" she called out.

Both boys went over and gave her a hug. "Frank's the monster," Kevin corrected. "We're just innocent little boys—the kind *that* monster likes to eat."

"I'd have to marinate you first," Frank answered from the kitchen.

"Did you guys get some good shots out there?" she asked.

"Naw," Kevin replied as he headed toward the bedroom to stash the contraband sack. "Just Lonnie goofing around."

Lonnie followed him toward the bedroom, adding, "Oh, and a big old warty toad."

Beverly remarked to Frank, "Those boys seem to be good for each other."

Kevin and Lonnie shouted with delight, each simultaneously reeling in triggerfish. Unable to get a captain for such last-minute plans, Frank had to leave the boys to their own devices while he piloted the *Fine Print* himself, trolling for a school of suitable fish. The flip-floppy comical pan-fryers seemed to be ideal—fun to catch but not too big for boys under five-feet tall to wrestle in by themselves. Beverly, dressed in beach shorts, blouse, and straw hat, watched from her vantage point on the upper sundeck, no longer self-conscious about exposing her injured leg and foot.

The boys joshed each other with some good-natured mine-is-bigger-than-yours competition before dissolving into giggles over some private joke, then managed to reel in several more before losing the school. After going for a stretch with no bites, they lost interest in fishing and went up front to help Frank pilot. Thoroughly delighted, they took turns actually handling the controls under the older fellow's watchful eye.

Beverly reclined her chair and closed her eyes. After a moment, she heard a soft voice.

"You doing okay, Mama?"

"Linda!" she exclaimed, catching herself and lowering her voice. "I knew I'd see you again."

As they hugged each other tightly, Beverly noted that her daughter looked just too real to be an illusion. Linda pulled a chair over and sat beside her mother. "It appears you're healing."

"Frank's been helping me practice getting around with crutches. I'm like a toddler learning to walk all over again."

"Well, it's what you need to do, so don't let up. You're lucky, you know. It could have been a lot worse—you could be hurt even more."

"Frank helps me so much," Beverly added, "—*that's* where I'm really lucky."

They sat for a moment before Linda changed the subject. "Mama, how else can I help you learn about trying to get along without me?"

"But sweetie, I don't want to."

"Mama, you're going to have to accept what happened that day. Being able to spend time with me is a bonus; I don't want my coming to see you to make it harder."

"You know what Loretta's using to have me declared incompetent?"

"What?"

"The fact that I've told people about our visits."

"Mama, I *told* you you can't tell anybody."

"I only told a few."

"You can't anymore. Mama, this is important. If you let Loretta take away everything, or if you can't learn how to deal with the fact that I, um, *passed away* that day, then I shouldn't visit you anymore."

"Linda—no!" Beverly hissed, still trying to keep quiet. The roar of the twin inboard diesels blanketed their voices.

"Maybe it would be better for you just to move on with your life."

"Please don't stop coming to see me," Beverly said, tears starting down her cheeks.

"Mama, you've got to say whatever it takes to stop Loretta. Don't talk about our visits with people who won't understand. Maybe Frank can, maybe Kevin can—I don't know, maybe nobody can—but you've got to protect yourself."

"I will, Linda, whatever it takes."

"As long as my visits don't hurt you, then I'll come sometimes. It won't be a lot, but every now and then might be good for both of us."

As the yacht slowed, a disc of sun shimmered across the indigo surface, refracting into sparkles of color. Frank climbed to the sundeck to check on Beverly. He found her reclined in the deck chair, eyes closed, tears on her cheeks.

He got on his knees and put his arms around her, nuzzling her gently with his face, whispering, "Linda was the lucky one, having the best mom in the world."

CHAPTER 29

"Motion denied! Now, were there any other matters today, or did that dispose of them all?" the judge asked, a hint of annoyance in his voice.

"Your honor," Mr. Mogill addressed the bench, "I would like some clarification on your ruling. Are you saying the arresting officer can testify to statements the defendant allegedly made prior to being read her Miranda rights?"

"No, I have simply denied your motion to suppress *all* testimony from the arresting officer. As to the nature of that testimony, that will have to be clarified during the trial."

"But your honor," Mogill continued, "that puts my client in the position of having to object to certain questions or their answers in front of the jury. That creates prejudice—"

"Mr. Mogill," the judge admonished, "if the state's attorney crosses any lines, I will instruct the jury to disregard."

"But your honor—"

"If you have no other motions today," the judge asserted, glaring his impatience, "then we will move on."

Mogill stepped away from the podium just as the court clerk called the next case. He gathered up his briefcase and walked out to the hallway, motioning for Frank to follow.

"That didn't go well, did it?" Frank asked once they were out of earshot of the crowd holding various private conferences outside the courtroom.

"No," Mogill responded, shaking his head. "This judge doesn't like to let law or procedure get in the way of a good prosecution. Most of the people who come through here have public defenders who they've just met five minutes before their appearance—lawyers who aren't even familiar with the facts of the case, let alone prepared. When private attorneys like me come through with lots of pre-trial motions and meticulous attention to detail, it annoys him. He gets zinged by the appellate court often enough, but he never loses sleep over it."

"What's the problem with the arresting officer?"

"He's claiming Ruth apologized and said she didn't mean to do it. She told me she did say something sort of like that, but didn't know until later at the jail that two guys had been shot. She thought it was just about drugs. The cop claims he told her she was being arrested for murder before she said it."

"Maybe he did tell her," Frank hypothesized. "Maybe she didn't hear him, or she got confused owing to all the stress."

"I doubt it," Mogill countered. "But it shouldn't matter who said what. It was all done before anybody read her rights and gave her the opportunity to ask for an attorney. Even if he disallows that testimony during the trial—as he should—the jury won't disregard what they've heard just because they've been told to—and they can't disregard how it's made them feel."

"What if he *does* allow it during the trial?" Frank asked.

"Well, it would make a strong appeal issue, but it could also cost her a conviction and put her in prison for years before her appeal is ruled on."

Frank sighed, mentally calculating Kevin's age, wondering if the boy would have any childhood left when finally reunited with his mother. "What was the motion that he granted?"

"That was simple discovery. He *had* to grant that one. The prosecution is required to turn over all evidence to me—not just what they plan to use, but what I might be able to use to help her defense."

"But if they have to anyway—"

"Supposed to—that's part of how this works. The prosecutor withholds every possible detail, and delays the rest until the last minute—especially if there's a trump card they plan to play. Better for them to let me chase wild geese and have to shift gears with no time left."

Frank rubbed his jaw. "That's not how it's supposed to work."

"No, but remember, it's *my* job to work it."

Sh-wu-sh-wu-sh-wu-shsh . . . The stream of wet concrete snaked down the chute and into the hole. *Clunk.* Sweep sweep. *Oooooommmmmmmmmmm—clunk!*

Kevin watched, enthralled. There is something about big machines and boys, and on this sunny afternoon, young Mr. Riner found himself caught up in it.

"You didn't want a swimming pool, did you?" Ward Bodnar asked, interrupting Kevin's reverie. The developer walked up behind the boy, dressed like a cross between site foreman and businessman.

"Naw! We've got enough water around here anyway—what with all those springs and all," Kevin joked.

"Ooosh. I don't think I could stand more than a minute in those springs without a wetsuit—too cold for me."

"Frank says the manatees will come through back there in a few months *because* they look for warm water in the winter," Kevin added, displaying all the erudition of a well-informed middle-schooler. "I'm gonna swim with 'em when they do."

"I went swimming with the manatees at Crystal River a few years ago. Damn near froze my pecker off."

"Ouch," Kevin said. Then he asked, "All this stuff you're doing isn't going to hurt the springs is it?"

"Oh no," Hank replied more seriously, "not at all. They wouldn't give me permits for that, not that I would anyway. This development is soft-impact, meaning having humans here won't change the natural balance of wildlife that's all back in there. That's why we've got the dozer building up the ground where we erect, keeping the foundations above the water table, and sloping the area to drain away runoff."

"Good. This place is too cool to wreck."

"Have you noticed how there are slopes and wide openings underneath the road every fifty feet?" Ward asked.

"Yeah," Kevin answered, turning and looking along the street.

"Those are for animals to get across—especially the hermit crabs, frogs, toads, and the fiddler crabs that migrate to the springs. You'll also find box turtles all through this area."

Kevin had seen them all, even recently snapping photos of some fine specimens. "How do you drive one of those bulldozers?" he asked, changing the subject.

Ward rubbed his jaw, turned to scan the progress of his crew, and finally answered, "Wanna take her out for a spin?"

With eyes bigger than his head, Kevin climbed into the operator's seat. Hank put a leg over the seat and slid in behind the boy, pushing him forward so his feet could reach the pedals. Holding the boy's hands in his own, he guided them over the hand controls, whispering instructions for his feet, making the blade go up and down, the dozer move forward and back, the diesel engine roar and belch a foul smell.

There were no friends visiting this afternoon, no criminal trials, no business records or homework, no funerals, nothing to fear. Instead, Tarpon Springs hosted a giant of a man, all of four-feet ten, pushing a pile of sand back and forth, forming a mountain higher than any on Earth, preparing to build a dam or superhighway or great skyscraper that would pierce the sky, a testament to his mighty power, standing against the wind so clouds must dance circles in the air, a whole world pausing to admire this monument to Kevin Riner, the invincible.

"Ms. Herndon, I would like to ask *you* some questions now," the magistrate explained.

She turned and looked to Mr. Maier. He nodded assent, offering a hint of smiled assurance, telegraphing confidence.

"Um, okay," she replied.

"Now, do you understand what's been going on here today?"

"Yes, I believe I do."

"Will you tell me, briefly, in your own words, what has happened so far?" he requested, sitting back in his chair and setting his pen to the side.

"Well, first you read the petition as it was filed by my sister, Loretta," she responded. "It sounded like it was prepared by a lawyer with all the proper language and legalese." She looked over to Frank, catching his faint nod and reassuring smile.

"You read the attachments," she continued, "which were basically four letters from people who expressed concern about how I was dealing with my daughter's death. That, by the way, seemed to be the only thing they could come up with to suggest I'm going loony—"

"We're not here to say anybody is loony, Ms. Herndon," the magistrate corrected.

"Well, Loretta is," Beverly rejoined, glancing at her sister, who fidgeted awkwardly at the other side of the room. "Anyway," she continued, "then you read some highfalutin' opinion from an expert-for-hire talking gibberish about delusions and hallucinations being an occasional extension of personality disorders when people are forced to react to untenable situations, vis-a-vis the death of a loved one. I don't recall anything in there that described me or the kind of person I am—it all appeared to be based on nothing more than what my sister told that so-called expert," Beverly added.

"What happened next?" the magistrate asked, shooting a glance at Loretta.

"Well, then Mr. Maier, here to represent me and *my* best interests, asked you to dismiss the petition because it didn't meet certain statutory criteria. You blew him off—rather rudely, I might add—and asked us to respond to the petition. You read the report from the psychiatrist stating there were no biochemical problems, no recognizable disorders like epilepsy or schizophrenia or drug addiction, no observable behavioral defects, no problems with learning or comprehension or cognitive processing, and that—" She paused, remembering how carefully she had worked this part of the evaluation out with her doctor. "—That I am dealing with the death of my daughter in ways that, though not typical, are well within the realm of normative, meaning not debilitating or interfering with my everyday functioning." She directed a glance toward Loretta. "—Certainly meaning I'm capable of taking care of myself and making decisions about how I want to live."

"Please direct your comments to me," the magistrate instructed.

"Then my friend Frank Tanyon made an elegant statement on my behalf. He verified that his assistance helped settle a lawsuit that had gone on for years before my husband died, and he explained how all of my investments since I've moved to Florida have remained firmly in my own name. Finally, you heard from Kevin Riner." She looked over toward Kevin and smiled. "He explained how much I've done to help him as a foster mother and good friend." The magistrate nodded and sat forward again. Beverly finished, "Then you asked me to recount what has happened."

"Ms. Herndon," the magistrate asked, "does your daughter come visit you?"

"No. Sometimes I like to think about her and imagine what she might say or how she would want me to handle her affairs, but she cannot come visit me."

"What about the day you were found in her apartment, the one she shared with—" He shuffled the papers in search of the name. "—With Sherry Lubinsky?"

"Thinking about Linda, imagining that she was urging me to gather up her things and give them to her friends, that was what gave me the strength to make that trip."

"Is there anything else you would like to say on the record?"

"Yes," Beverly replied, exuding confidence. "Please dismiss this petition. Regardless of however good-intentioned it might be, it is misguided and based on erroneous assumptions." She looked toward Frank again and nodded her head, satisfied.

"Is there anything more from counsel?"

"Yes sir, the defendant in this civil action requests summary dismissal."

The magistrate sat back in his chair for a moment, then sat forward again, picking up his pen and writing on a form. "I will delay issuing a ruling for thirty days. We will meet again on, um—we'll determine the date with the clerk—to see if there is any new information the plaintiff can present that might influence the opinion of this court."

Out in the hallway, Loretta approached Beverly. "I hope you know I just want what's best for you, little sis—"

"Then try asking what *I* want," Beverly replied, turning her back and walking away, flanked by Frank and Kevin.

Loretta stood there and watched them go. They paused at the door, Beverly turning and burying her face in Frank's chest. He put his arms around her and held tightly. Kevin watched for a moment, then tentatively moved in and put his arms around them both. The adults opened their hug just enough to admit the boy.

They lingered for a moment, holding each other tightly, the bright glare filtering through glass doors forming a glow, silhouetting an image of unselfish love.

"Oh, it's okay, honey. Don't worry," Ruth assured Kevin. "Those motions would've helped, but the trial is what really counts."

Kevin nodded sadly. "I know, Mom. I just wish something would go right for a change."

"Well then, you'll like my good news!" She brightened at the change of subject. She wanted desperately to hang on to these precious moments with her son. Seeing him through that monitor, noticing that he looked a little taller, a little more filled out, hearing his little-boy voice crack and reveal brief hints of the young man he was trying to become—with or without her . . . A dozen years trying to take care of him, and now he'd become *her* life-preserver, the one keeping her head above the surface long enough to work toward a better life. "I did it!" she announced.

"Did what?"

"Got my certificate. I passed the last written test a few days ago. All I have to do is pass the demonstration test when I get out, and I'll graduate. Then I can get my license!"

"All right, Mom! Totally stellar! I knew you could do it."

"It was a lot of work, but I did it for *both* of us. Oh, Kevin, I wanted you to be proud of me."

"I *am*, Mom. Real proud."

Mother and son beamed, a bright spot in a dark place. For a moment, they forgot the phones, saying nothing. She could tell he was searching for the mother he remembered. He looked again into her eyes, this time at her tears—maybe a release from fear and pain, maybe expressions of joy, even *she* couldn't be sure.

And they recognized their familiar selves once again.

"I love you, Mom," he whispered.

Tears ran down her cheeks. She tried to say "I love you too, son," but got too choked up to make a sound.

She knew he could hear her, though . . . loud and clear.

"Good for you, Mama! I knew you could say what needed to be said." Linda poured more mango nectar for Beverly, then reclined in the chaise-longue, admiring the view across the backyard and into the undergrowth crisscrossed by crystal-clear springs. A light breeze and darkening sky suggested a brief shower might soon chase them back indoors.

"But I didn't win yet," Beverly pointed out.

"But you didn't lose, either. It sounds like that judge as good as told Aunt Loretta she better have a lot more reasons to prove you incompetent, or she might as well give up."

"Well, I hope so," Beverly begrudged before taking a long sip from the nectar.

"You know," Linda mused, "it seems like I'll never understand how brothers and sisters can so willingly give up everything—even their lives—for one another, yet somehow turn against each other so easily. If Loretta loves you—is connected to you like sisters should be—how can she try to hurt you this way?"

"I don't know, honey. Sometimes I think she really does mean well, but just doesn't understand. Other times I think she's nothing more than a lowdown thief who'll walk on her own family to get control of a good sum of money. It breaks my heart to think about it."

Sensing the hurt in her mother, Linda changed the subject. Speaking softly, she pointed out, "I always marvel, too, at how death for some is separation, but for others, that connectedness between them stays very strong."

"Well, yes, I guess so," Beverly commented, somewhat confused.

"Like, just because you're fond of Frank *now* doesn't mean you have to stop loving Daddy, does it?"

"Oh heavens no. I'll love your daddy as long as I live." Beverly struggled into an upright position, gingerly swinging her leg around to the deck, then reached out and took Linda by the hand. "I'll always love your father," she whispered.

"Are you still going to have him moved down here and buried beside, um, me?" Linda asked.

"Yes, in fact, it's time to get that done. I'll ask Frank to help me make the arrangements tomorrow when the offices are open."

"Will you feel better with him down here?"

"Oh yes, then I can visit *his* grave, too, and fix it up and feel like somehow I'm still looking after him." Beverly gazed off into the springs, growing even quieter. "Then I'll feel like you two are together again . . . Oh, I know it doesn't make much sense, but it's how I feel."

"Feelings are all that count, Mama. Feelings are all that count."

"Oh come on, Beverly, you don't hug a Klingon!" Kevin admonished, pretending to resist, but bending down to accommodate her. She sat on the edge of his bed, helping him adjust his costume for the big Halloween dance at school.

"Well," she laughed, "when he's *my* Klingon you do. Now turn around and let me fix the back."

She swept his cape aside and pulled the bunched up tunic out of the waistband of his leotard. She lifted the tunic up, tugging down on the black undershirt, smoothing it across the bottom. She pulled the waistband of the pants down three or four inches— "Quit peekin' at my drawers!" he joked—then flattened the undershirt, pulled the leotard back up over it, smoothed the tunic down over the top of both, and adjusted his weapon belt to cover it all.

"You hush!" she told him. "You're not too big a Klingon to turn over my good knee, you know." She pulled the cape back down, turned him around, and adjusted the crossband draped from his shoulder, then inspected him from head to toe. "I'll bet that wrinkly thing on your forehead is gonna get hot," she predicted.

"Beverly, I'm *already* hot," he bragged. "When Cynthia gets one look at me," he added, alternating between an innocent grin and a leer, "she's just gonna lose *all* control."

"Well don't you be gettin' too big for your britches," she warned, poking him in the belly.

"*Hey*, lady, you should *never* poke a Klingon."

"Did you get the kids dropped off okay?" Beverly called from Frank's bedroom.

He wandered in to find her lying on his bed. She sat up and moved to the edge. "Yeah, they made quite a picture." He sat down beside her.

"What were they dressed up as?"

"Well, Lonnie was a dead guy, slashed up and covered with blood. Cynthia was dressed as a punk rocker—lots of leather, green and pink hair tied up in a weird shape, huge safety pins hanging from her ears, tattoos, garish make-up—not *too* different from how kids really dress these days. As weird as the eighties turned out, I'm not looking forward to whatever the nineties will bring."

Beverly laughed. "So what about the girl Lonnie took?"

"Her name was Darla. A full head taller than the boys, she was painted all green, wearing green stretch clothes, and had leaves hanging all over her. She said people call her Beanstalk anyway, so she decided to dress like one." They both chuckled at the image.

"Did you meet their parents?"

"I met Cynthia's mother. She didn't want to be bothered, too busy watching TV and chain-smoking cigarettes. Darla was already waiting at Cynthia's house. I don't know, maybe it's just me, but if I was sending my daughter off with some strange man to go out with a boy I didn't know, I'd want to meet everybody first."

"Well, people are usually different parents from what they *would be* than when they *actually are*."

"Yeah, I guess. I'm still getting used to the idea of acting like one for Kevin's sake."

"Well, Mr. Tanyon, *I* think you're doing a fine job. There's no complaints from the brat, either." She leaned back and looked behind him, asking, "What was that on your back pocket?"

He stood up and twisted, trying to look behind himself. Beverly reached over and tugged down on his elastic-banded shorts, exposing his white briefs. "Hey! Quit peekin' at my drawers!"

"Fine then. It's not your drawers I was peekin' at," she added, feigning indignation. Then in one quick motion she snatched his briefs down and pinched him in the butt.

"Yow! You're a *she*-devil!" Then, making no move to retrieve his wayward undies, he changed to a southern drawl, adding, "I believe, madam, you have me at a disadvantage. I'd snatch *your* panties right offen ya if it weren't for that leg brace."

She reached down and carefully unfastened the brace, first the two snaps, then the Velcro straps. "What excuse do you have now?"

Frank laid the brace on the floor, then tugged her shorts and panties off in one swoop, twirling them around over his head in mock victory. Then he climbed onto the bed and got on his knees between her legs, unbuttoning her blouse. He paused long enough to kiss her briefly, whispering, "This isn't exactly storybook romantic, you know."

She growled, biting playfully at his chin, answering, "I'm a Klingon wench. We *like* it coarse and rough."

Coarse and rough it was, at least for an older guy whose back sometimes bothers him, and for a lady with a bad leg. Worried about hurting her, he limited "rough" to making occasional animal noises. She eventually forgot she was a Klingon wench, thinking only how much she truly wanted to be close to this guy with the balding head and bad back and spindly legs and that magnificent heart of gold.

"Grrrrrrr . . ."

"Cool costume, Kevin," Cynthia volunteered. Only about two inches taller than her date—a better height match than most seventh-grade couples—she had the lithe body of a gymnast who practiced every day after school as a member of the school's club. She boasted light brown hair—when it wasn't painted green and pink—a softly-tanned complexion, and deep emerald eyes with just a hint of almond shape. Although she'd only just begun to develop her feminine contours, Kevin nevertheless found her more appealing than anything Lonnie could point to in a magazine.

"You're a hot-lookin' babe, Cynth—but why didn't you wear a costume?"

Feigning a pout, she snuggled up close to him and ran a finger down the center of his chest. By the time it reached his navel, showing no sign of stopping its descent, she admonished, "You be nice to me or I'll grab your phaser!" She tickled just below his navel and quickly pulled away, giggling.

Man, this thing on my forehead sure gets hot, he thought.

"Hey, Caselow, you a murder victim or what?" Three eighth-grade boys loosely dressed as hobos stopped in front of Kevin, Lonnie, and their dates in the back of the semi-dark school gymnasium. Orange and black crepe-paper streamers hung in-differ-ently from the ceiling while cutouts of ghosts and skulls watched from deco-rated walls.

"He musta been over at Riner's mom's house!" another remarked for the benefit of his cohorts.

"Naw, this guy got killed with a knife. Mama Riner likes to use a gun," corrected the third, breaking into laughter at his own remark.

"Just shut up," Lonnie ordered.

"That's right," taunted the first. "It couldn't have been Riner's ol' lady. *She's in jail!*" All three chuckled.

The two girls sat mortified. Kevin's heart pounded. "Get outta here," he told them.

"Why? You gonna send your mother after us?" mocked the third hobo, adding a mean edge to his voice.

"Watch out, Chuck, he may be a killer, too!"

"You gonna shoot us, Riner?"

"Ahhh! Oh no!" number one exaggerated like some actor in a Grade-B movie. "Look out! He's got a gun! His mom taught him how to use it! He's gonna get us. Ahhhh!"

All three broke into peals of laughter. More than a dozen other students started to form an audience. Kevin tried to ignore them, but they wouldn't let up.

"You gonna send your mom to shoot us, Riner?"

"Hey, Cynthia! Lose this criminal or *you're* pond scum, too!"

Suddenly furious, Kevin stood up.

"Hey, get off his ass," one of the larger boys in the gathering crowd ordered.

"Yeah, his mom didn't shoot no one," a girl added. "Just wait till the trial. My dad says she's gonna be found innocent."

"Yeah, leave him alone," another boy ordered. "He don't need your shit."

The murmuring in the group echoed the same sentiments. All three bullies backed off, one offering, "We're just jokin' with him."

"Yeah, well, it ain't funny," the largest boy asserted, getting up in the face of number one.

"Geez, it's no big deal," number three mumbled as he and his hobo friends wandered off in search of a kitten to kick or an insect to step on.

The biggest boy reached out and gave Kevin a fist-style handshake, offering, "Hey, don't let 'em bug ya, man. They're just dick-heads."

Kevin nodded, trying to look unfazed. The group faded away to resume their socializing and dancing.

The chaperone watching from over by the refreshment table looked satisfied they'd handled it themselves.

"Dick-heads," Lonnie pronounced.

Cynthia put her head on Kevin's shoulder, her hand on his chest. "You okay, Kevin?" she whispered.

"Yeah, I guess," he answered quietly, putting his arm around behind her back and squeezing her gently.

"Don't worry, it'll all turn out okay," she added. "Just give it some time . . . and remember, you can be sad with me; I'm your friend."

Kevin put his other arm around her and hugged tentatively at first, then with more resolve. A slow song started playing in the background.

"You wanna dance?" she asked.

"Um, okay. I've never danced before," he warned, whispering in her ear.

"That's okay, it's easy."

They walked out to the middle of the dance floor with Lonnie and Darla not far behind. It seemed like too many elbows, feet pointing the wrong direction, bony knees protruding well beyond the safety zone, centers of balance all wrong, but when Kevin put his arms around Cynthia, she melted into him.

They swayed gently with the rhythm, first at cross-purposes, then finally in sync. She felt soft, her breath on his face warm. He shifted his weapon belt to the side, pressing closer and feeling her petite but very real bosom against his chest. Their feet and elbows and knees and all their parts finally seemed to fit together very well indeed. He forgot about the dance and the music, holding her more tightly, his heart pounding, his breaths deepening, his skin tingling. He closed his eyes, shutting out the crepe-paper streamers and ghosts and skulls and all those people in the crowd, both bullies *and* friends.

A single pinpoint of magenta light swirled around the two of them, unobserved by others, unnoticed by Kevin and Cynthia. She nuzzled him gently, resting her head on his shoulder and kissing him lightly on the neck.

He held her even tighter, now leading the steps, this Klingon warrior and his punk-rock princess, dancing across the warm Florida sky, radiating magical lights all their own.

CHAPTER 30

"I don't know how, but apparently you scuttled her whole deal," Doug Taylor observed, his voice over the speaker phone in Henry Wanamaker's office. Frank and Money-grubber sat on opposite sides of the desk, grinning, making sure they sounded serious when they spoke.

Frank responded, "Well, I'm not going to reveal what I did—probably never will—but I hope you understand that I *needed* to do it."

"Oh, I can't blame you. Ma tried to play hardball against a major-leaguer."

"So is she ready to sell me her shares?" Frank asked.

"Um, no. She's not. She *is* fed up and wants to walk away from the company, but she wants Junior and me to get some of it. She needs money to retire on, so she was hoping to *give* each son a fourth of her stock, then *sell* us each the other fourths. That way, she would have money to live on and still be doing something for us."

"That's a good gesture on her part," Frank commented, looking to Henry with a grimace and shaking his head no. He didn't want the Taylor boys to acquire *all* of her stock because it would leave Frank without a clear majority.

"Yeah, the problem is, though," Doug continued, "that Junior and I don't have the money to pay her outright. Oh, we could probably put up everything as collateral and finance it—maybe—but neither of us wants to go into debt like that. We have a pretty good standard of living, but that would have us spending everything we make on loan payments for however many years."

"I've got an idea for you, Doug. It's one that requires all four of us to cooperate."

"I'm ready for a solution, Frank."

"Doug, here's what everybody wants. First, *I* want a majority of shares. Trust me, I still want Junior running the print-shop operations and I want *you* running the company. You said you planned to retire in about ten more years, and I have confidence you'll earn the right to stay on until then. Second, your mom wants to increase the ownership percentage for you and your brother. Third, your mom wants to cash out half the value of her stock and retire. Fourth, you and your brother want a fair deal for her—for everybody. Am I right?"

"Um, yeah. You got a plan that does all that?"

Frank looked at Henry. They nodded to each other.

"Henry Wanamaker and I have done an exhaustive analysis of the company's assets, cash reserves, tax projections and so forth. I want to have *the company* buy out your mother's stock—*all* of her stock. It'll slow down expansion and make us run lean for the next year or two, but I have faith you can make that work.   That's why I need somebody like *you* at the helm."

"I think that could work!" Doug agreed, excitement growing in his voice.

Frank continued, "If the company absorbs the shares, then I'll own sixty percent of the voting stock; you and your brother will each own twenty—that's more than the seventeen percent each of you now owns. I'll have my majority, you guys will gain half of your mother's voting power, you won't have to finance any of this yourselves, and your mom can cash out *all* of her shares on day one—just in time to start one helluva retirement." Frank paused, then added the kicker. "I think your dad would have been pleased with this kind of deal."

Doug paused for a minute, then said, "I like it, Frank. It's a good idea. I think Junior would go along, too. I'll talk to Mom about it—strongly recommend it, in fact—and get back to you as soon as—"

"You got a deal," Marta casually interjected, revealing that she'd been listening in on the call.

"You sure, Mom?"

"Yes, son. Everybody gets what they want and, most importantly, we can all start getting along again. He's right, you know; your dad would have liked it."

"Sounds like you've got a deal, Frank," Doug added.

"Good then," Frank agreed. "Call Junior to make sure he likes it—"

"I do, Uncle Frank," Junior interrupted.

Frank smiled at Henry. "Well okay then. Doug, write it up that we held a board meeting today and voted unanimously on the motion to buy back all stock from shareholder Marta Taylor. Make it effective Friday at noon; that should give you enough time to move the money around. Henry will fax you a breakdown of the best way to do it—" To Henry he asked, "How long do you need, Hen—?"

"Done. It's ready to go."

"Then he'll fax it as soon as we hang up."

"Frank?" Marta asked. "What *did* you do to the Rumseys?"

"Marta," Frank replied. "All that's in the past. Let's start fresh again. Your sons and I have a company to grow, and it's a whole lot more fun to be in business with friends."

"You're not going to tell me, are you?"

"I haven't the *slightest* idea what you're talking about."

Stretch a little farther . . . a little farther . . . just a little more—relax. Stretch the other way . . . a little farther . . . a little farther . . . relax. Beverly lay panting on Frank's bed, tears in her eyes. Frank fought the lump in his throat. Gregory Dean had taught him how to help with her therapy exercises, recommending they get into a routine of two or three times per day. He would monitor their progress during her every-other-day sessions with him.

It required a tremendous leap of faith for Frank to *hurt* her for her own good, hoping it really would help. Sometimes, when he heard her cry out during the stretches, he would have to imagine her throwing aside that crutch and walking with ease.

Stretch . . . stretch a little more . . . just a little bit more . . . stretch—relax. "You sure you don't want to stop?" he asked, almost pleading.

"No, huh huh, no, not yet," she voiced, slow and panting from the exertion. "Not yet, huh huh, a little more."

Pull . . . pull harder . . . a little harder . . . "Farther!" she ordered. Pull just slightly more . . . more . . . more . . . "Ahhh!" she cried out.

"What? Are you okay?" he worried, gently releasing the pressure. *Never release all at once—always gently* . . . always gently.

Beverly wiped away tears spilling over onto the pillow, tugging down the t-shirt which, along with exercise shorts, were all she wore. Frank hovered over her on his knees, dressed only in shorts and socks, cupping her face in his hands, searching her eyes.

"I'm okay Frank, huh, huh. I know this is hard on you—"

"Naw, it's you it's hard on. I'm just afraid of hurting you."

"You won't hurt *this* spring chicken, huh huh, you ol' rooster."

"Yeah, well, as long as Gregory says this is good for you, I wanna help—whatever it takes."

Beverly's breathing slowed. She pulled him down against her, resting his weight on his hip, pressed against her side. "You just want to get these damned exercises out of the way so you can get in my drawers," she accused, smiling up at him, a twinkle reflected in her tear-wet eyes.

"Why, madam," he drawled, "purty as you are when yer panties is hangin' on the lamp, that's not the *only* thang I like to do with ya."

"Nor you, ya big galoot."

They held each other tightly, nuzzling and whispering wonderful words back and forth. In spite of her earlier assertion, just being there with her, holding her close, making her comfortable so the stretching and pain and injuries could fade away, a moment to float off together—that was all he really wanted.

He hoped that was what she really needed.

Kevin came home alone from school to a quiet condo. Thinking Frank might be taking one of his occasional afternoon naps, he crept back to the bedroom and peered through his door.

There, in a jumble of arms and legs, sound asleep, he found his old friend, dressed only in undies and socks, holding Beverly. In spite of feeling like an intruder, he watched for a moment, flashing back to the time Mark Sisk had grabbed his mother and kissed her forcefully against her struggles; and that Bob guy who used to walk around the trailer clad only in underpants, uncaring of the ten-year-old boy who understood only that guzzling beer and rubbing a too-obvious erection meant that soon Mom would be chased into the bedroom; and the time that guy with the butch haircut—what was his name?—wrestled his mother on the living room floor, pulling off her panties, telling the scared six-year-old who cried, "Don't hurt my mom!" to shut up and go to bed. There lay Frank holding on to the woman he loved, tenderly, gently, protectively . . .

Kevin remembered how being taunted at the school dance seemed not that hard to take, but when something was said to Cynthia . . . He flashed on the photos in Lonnie's magazines, feeling the puberty confusion that stalks boys his age, but understanding that sex is more than a hand under the covers, tingles in the body, acrobatics with just any woman who's willing. It is one very special, very lucky way to express feelings, to demonstrate love, bathed in the glow of *being* loved.

Commenting on Frank and Beverly, Lonnie sometimes joked, "Geez, can you imagine those two actually *doing* it?" There they were, cuddled together, in love even in their sleep. Yes, he could imagine Frank holding Beverly very close and whispering, "I love you," because that's the kind of man Frank was.

He closed the door quietly, feeling like he had already intruded too much on their privacy. He walked to the kitchen, lost in his thoughts, glad that all these things they did for him were not out of pity, not because they felt sorry for him, not because it was the right or admirable or charitable thing to do. He believed as much as any boy can believe that Frank and Beverly both genuinely loved him—loved him for who he was, recognized that there truly was something special about this boy that made him worth loving. He couldn't imagine those two without each other, and he knew Frank had found something that had been missing from the old guy's life too long.

In all, he felt pretty good inside.

Drinking some Mountain Dew, he thought about his mother. *Why does she always fall for those trashy guys?* he wondered. *The ones who treat her bad? The ones who just want a place to stay or a woman to climb on top of? Maybe she doesn't know what to look for.*

He put his glass in the dishwasher and went back to his bedroom, then changed out of his jeans, put on some loose-fitting shorts, and lay on his back on the bed, resting his hand on his lap. He closed his eyes and thought about the women in those magazines, but that couldn't hold his interest for long. He thought about Cynthia, remembering her smile, her pout, that teasing look, her expressions of curiosity and wonder. He remembered how it felt to dance with her, to hold her so close, to feel her body against his own. He could feel her hair in his face, her aroma, that tentative kiss on her front porch.

He rolled over onto his stomach, gathering his pillow and putting his arms around it, holding on to Cynthia, satisfied just to snuggle.

"Aww, he's asleep," Beverly whispered.

"Yeah," Frank whispered back. "He always twitches like that for a while after he falls off."

They stood in his doorway, peeking in, feeling a little bit like they were intruding on a boy's privacy.

"He's so precious, so adorable," she whispered.

"Yeah, he still looks like a boy, but the way he's just started shooting up, I'd say he'll be a big gangly-looking teenager in no time."

"He'll still look adorable even then," Beverly said, her eyes sparkling like a new mother gazing at her baby's face. "He's so innocent with his little-boy hopes and dreams."

Frank countered, still keeping his voice down, "Oh, I don't know, Beverly. Sometimes he comes to me with some big questions, not afraid to have some earnest talks. He thinks about some pretty grown-up stuff. He's got a lot to learn, and it means a lot to me that he lets me help, but I think he's on the right track."

"Bless his heart."

They closed the door quietly, not wanting to disturb the dreams of that little guy of theirs, only a whisker and an octave away from becoming a man.

"You should turn on the radio," Beverly teased. "We don't want to disturb Kevin when you let out that Tarzan whoop of yours."

"Well, you're the one who squeals like a chimp," Frank countered.

"I swear I'm gonna get you a zebra-striped loincloth for Christmas, you hairy ape!"

"All right," he agreed, finally giving in, "I'll get up and turn the radio on—but only because I need to get your panties off the lamp. Pretty as they are hanging there like that, they *are* a fire hazard, you know."

The sound of a car pulling into Beverly's driveway distracted them from the massage

Frank was giving.

"Who is it?" Beverly asked as he peeked through the curtains.

"It looks like Loretta."

Beverly sat up, put her leg brace on, and struggled off the couch with the aid of her crutch. "What's she doing? With the hearing tomorrow, she's probably coming by to find something to use against me."

"Oh, Beverly. Give her the benefit of the doubt. Maybe she wants to make up."

"Yeah, *that'll* be the day."

As Loretta walked up the wheelchair ramp, Frank asked, "Do you want me to leave?"

"No, please stay."

Frank let Loretta in, then scampered off to get cold drinks for everybody. Beverly sat on the couch, Loretta in a chair across from her.

"I hope I didn't come by at a bad time," Loretta offered, surprisingly demure. "I wanted to call first, but, well . . . I wasn't sure how you would feel."

"You're always welcome at my house, Loretta. You should know that."

Frank came back with the drinks, serving everybody and sitting beside Beverly.

"Bev, I made a mistake." Loretta wrung her hands, looking away, somewhat distraught.

She looks somehow suddenly older, Beverly thought.

"Bev," Loretta continued, "please believe me. I was worried about you."

"Loretta," Beverly pointed out, "Linda hadn't been dead a day before you were cleaning out *her* records *and* mine. You had no right. Your priorities were misplaced. Plus, you've had a hundred chances to undo that ever since. What did you do? You got lawyers involved, took me to court, humiliated me, made me waste good money on legal advice, got people like Lizzie and Sherry involved—"

"But I just wanted—"

"You hurt me," Beverly cut back in. "You hurt me a lot—and tomorrow you'll hurt me even more."

"I went down and withdrew the petition today, Bev. I know I was wrong, and I wanted to fix what I could before I made it even worse."

Beverly looked to Frank, registering mild surprise. Frank offered the slightest hint of a smile, raising his eyebrows just a little. "Well good then," Beverly responded.

After an awkward silence, tears started to well in Loretta's eyes. She looked at her lap, explaining, "Look, I know it's too much to ask for you to forgive me right now. I just hope that, well, um—"

Beverly's expression softened, too. "You surprised me, Lor. I didn't know what to think—"

"Surprised you! Surprised you?" Loretta asked, looking up, tears fighting their way through a thicket of make-up. "Heavens, little sister. Why should you be surprised? I've meddled in your life since you were big enough to call me Letta." She smiled through the tears. "Lord knows I've been wrong more than right, but I've *never* stopped meddling."

Beverly's eyes glistened, too. "That sure is the truth, Letta. Long as I can remember, you've been trying to run things for me."

"There's been lots of times I regretted all these things I tried to do for you. But there's been lots of times I believed in my heart you were lucky I did."

"Well, sure," Beverly conceded. "You *have* helped me out of a few jams."

"But even the ones I messed up—why do you think I always tried? When Mama carried you inside her, I used to ask so many questions about you. She always told me you was gonna be my little sister—somehow she seemed to know that—and she used to say it was gonna be *my* job to look out for you. She said someday her and Daddy would be gone, but you and me would be sisters for life . . ." Loretta looked off toward the kitchen. She dug in her purse for a tissue and dabbed her eyes. "She said we was always gonna have each other, and I would always be the big sister."

A lone tear spilled onto Beverly's face. "Mama used to tell me I had to look out for you, too," she reminisced.

"Problem was, she didn't teach me *how* to look out for you." Loretta added. "I tried so hard for so long, I always overdid it. I know I hurt you sometimes, but I always believed in my heart I was doing something good for you."

"Yeah," Beverly admitted, "I guess I've always known that. It just didn't always seem that way at the time."

"At least I tried," Loretta said. "I never let up, no matter what."

Everybody looked at each other for a moment, then Beverly asked, "Why did you do this—this competency thing?"

Loretta looked at Frank, embarrassed. "I was afraid of Frank," she admitted. "I'd been hearing all these horror stories from the ladies I work with, especially how some of the older widows who just moved down here got taken advantage of. I was already worried, but then when the accident happened, I thought, well, I knew you were vulnerable." She looked away, then continued, "I called Stockbridge to see if there was anything I could do to freeze things or protect them or whatever. He advised me to get all the records right away—to make it difficult for somebody else to make use of them. In further conversations, I mentioned how vulnerable you seemed, how worried I was about you seeing Linda even though she was—" She wiped the tears from her face, digging for another tissue.

"He suggested the competency challenge?" Frank asked.

"Suggested it? He wrote it and sent me to see that local lawyer—his brother-in-law—and called me a bunch of times telling me how to do it."

"How did you pay him?" Beverly asked, barely containing her anger over Stockbridge.

"He did it all for free. He reminded me that you had an outstanding balance with him. He said if I could get him paid right away, then everything he did to help me— um, to help me *look out for your interests* would be at no charge." Loretta paused, adding, "He took advantage of me. Can you imagine that? I asked for help protecting you and he took advantage of *me?*"

"Yeah, I guess I can," Beverly said softly. "You still should have known better, though," she admonished.

"Yes, I should have. That's why I'm trying to fix what I can, and hoping you'll give me a chance to win back your trust—" She managed a smile. "—At least as much trust as you ever had in me."

They had a very nice visit for the next hour. It almost seemed like old times, whatever old times used to be. Frank and Loretta warmed up to each other considerably. The two sisters hugged a number of times. Beverly bragged about Kevin's accomplishments like a proud mother and praised Frank like a smitten teen. Using her crutch and occasional assistance from Frank, Beverly guided her on a tour of the ongoing construction project.

Later, when Loretta had gone, Frank remarked, "I told you she might be here to make up. You said that'll be the day, as I recall."

"Did I?" she asked. "Are you sure? I thought I said *this'll* be the day."

It looked somehow sad, broken down, beaten into submission, vulnerable to the elements. Wood blocked its windows; a chain and padlock sealed the boarded-up door. Covered with smoke and soot and rust and burns, outwardly it looked injured, plywood bandages covering the harshest wounds. As the boys moved closer, the smells of smoke and fire and lost childhood all mingled to assault Kevin, forcing him to face the fact that the house he had known all his life would never be there for him again. No matter what happened with his mother, she could never come home. *They* could never come home.

Click. Kevin got a wide shot of the whole trailer, Lonnie pausing curiously on the stoop. Click. A close-up of the area around the door. Click. Click. The pile of burnt, water-logged furniture dragged out to sit forlornly by its shed. Click. The shed, long since vandalized, picked over for junk not worth anything in the first place.

The boys tried to get inside, prying the windows, tugging against the door. They wanted at least to peek, to make sure this hadn't been some giant joke, that everything really was normal after all.

Kevin thought about his bedroom at Frank's place—well, at *home.* That made him feel better—until he thought again about his mother. She had no place to go.

"Come on, man, let's get out of here," he told Lonnie, getting on his bike and turning his back on the desolate hulk. He pedaled away, making Lonnie work hard to catch up. They had made plans to hang out at Lonnie's house this Saturday. Frank would be away, going over stock papers with Henry. Beverly was home resting after a grueling session of physical therapy.

They stopped by the store for snacks where Kevin bought them both candy bars and sodas because Lonnie never had very much money. After standing in an unusually long line of customers, Kevin found Lonnie already waiting for him outside. They pedaled down the road to Highway 19 and stopped in front of a closed lounge that had benches out front. Kevin offered a soda and some candy to his friend. Lonnie lifted his shirt, revealing four comic books tucked into the front of his pants.

"Where'd you get those?"

"Five-finger discount," Lonnie boasted. "They were too busy to watch me."

"You ripped 'em off?"

"Helped myself," he corrected.

"You dick-head! Why'd you do that?"

"Why not?"

"Because it's stealing, you dick-head. And you coulda got caught, too, and got us *both* in trouble."

"I ain't gonna get caught. You're just a wuss."

"Yeah, that's what Brad used to say. He lived in the trailer park. He got busted a bunch of times, and they sent him to the youth ranch until he turns eighteen."

"He was stupid then. You gotta be smart about it."

Kevin grew increasingly angrier. "You mean you might steal from Frank if you stay at *my* house?"

"Not people, stupid, just stores."

"You done this before?"

"What do *you* care?"

"It's dumb, dick-head. It ain't cool."

The disagreement persisted, growing more and more heated until Lonnie got on his bike and pedaled off toward his house, instructing Kevin not to come over until he was ready to quit being such a dick-head.

Kevin sat there and simmered for a while, then felt sad, then suddenly vulnerable. He didn't want Frank or Beverly to know that Lonnie was a thief. He felt ashamed that his best friend thought something like that could ever be okay. He remembered the time he stole a candy bar when he was eight years old, only to get caught and sent home with his mother. She was furious. Never as long as he could remember had she ever hit him, but that day she got so enraged that she bent him across her lap to spank him. He started crying, more ashamed that he had driven her to this point than afraid of the swats.

But no spanking ever came. After a minute, he climbed off to stand crying in front of her, surprised and confused to see that she was crying, too. Yes, stealing was wrong—and it was something he would never do again.

He looked toward the direction Lonnie had gone, not sure if he should follow, then decided not to, preferring instead to be alone. He thought of his hollow log in the clearing and, carefully putting the snacks back in the sack and holding them under one arm, pedaled off to his private sanctuary.

He climbed inside the log, drank a soda, and ate some candy. He lay there for a few minutes, then climbed out and went over by the spring to urinate. He unzipped his pants and—there they were! Those lights were dancing down by the other end of the canal, near the bend. Quietly rezipping, he sneaked back to the log and retrieved his camera. Crouching behind some bushes, he took two shots before the lights disappeared into the water.

Click. Swirling and dancing.

Click. Forming the hint of an image.

Then they were gone.

He watched for hours, but the lights never came back.

Walking his bike through the sand, Kevin headed back toward the condos. He stopped just before the path opened into the yard area, snapping two photos of a spectacular butterfly. It flew to another flower at the edge of the clearing. Wanting an even tighter close-up, he quietly crept toward it. As he approached, camera poised, it suddenly flew away. He tilted the camera up, and its auto-zoom feature adjusted for the condos some forty yards away. Through the lens, he saw Beverly sitting on her deck, talking to another lady . . . Linda!

There was Linda, big as life, sitting right there on the deck. With the camera auto-zoomed and auto-focused, he snapped the picture. He tried to take another, but that had been the last shot of film, and he had no other rolls with him.

He grabbed his bike from where he had quietly laid it minutes before, picked up the food sack, and walked toward the opening, excited about greeting Linda, yet also confused and, somehow, a little scared. His heart racing, he jumped on the bike as soon as the sand gave way to grassy ground. Expecting to ride over to the deck and surprise the women, he was disappointed to find Beverly alone. Linda must have stepped inside. He raced to the deck anyway, dropped his bike in a heap, and leaped over the steps.

Panting more from excitement than exertion, he practically shouted, "Linda! Beverly, where did she go?"

Beverly sat stone-faced, looking first at him, then away as if deep in thought. Kevin rushed to the doorwall, peering inside to see where she had gone. "Linda?"

"Kevin," Beverly said quietly, patting the open spot beside her on the chaise-longue.

Peering about again to no avail, he sat down beside her. She put her arms around him, hugging him firmly. He hugged back tentatively at first, then succumbed and held on to her tightly. Finally, she relaxed the hold, but pulled him against herself, resting his head on her shoulder, stroking his hair gently. He pulled his feet over and lay very still.

After another minute, he rolled over, still leaving his head above her bosom, nuzzling a little, but facing toward her rather than away. He looked up into her eyes and whispered, "She was here, wasn't she?"

Beverly sort of shrugged, sort of cocked her head like she wasn't sure how to answer, then sort of nodded assent. She started to rock gently back and forth, the boy still enfolded in her arms. He rocked with her, closing his eyes, floating off into the warm afternoon sky.

Maybe five, maybe ten or even fifteen minutes went by before Beverly spoke. She kissed Kevin gently on top of his head and whispered, "Please don't tell anybody what you saw today."

Turning his face up to hers, he whispered back, "It was Linda, wasn't it?"

Beverly nodded, adding, "But please don't mention it to anybody. It's private; Linda wants it that way. It *needs* to be that way."

He nodded back, lost in thought. "Um, I thought she was, you know . . ."

"She *is* gone, sweetheart. She just comes to see me sometimes is all."

"But how?"

"Shhh," she whispered, still stroking his hair. "I don't know. But when I told people before, it caused problems, and she almost wouldn't come back. She doesn't want anyone to find out. But she knows I can count on you; I know *I* can count on you, too."

"Don't even tell Frank?"

"No. Never *lie* to him—he's always honest with *you*, ya know—but unless he asks, please don't mention what you saw."

Kevin thought a few seconds, then whispered, "Okay."

He wasn't sure how much longer they lay there together. He raised his head and rubbed his itchy nose, noticing Beverly's eyes closed. He laid his head back and closed his eyes again. Then he heard a car in Frank's driveway. The slam of a door without the familiar sound of the power garage-door going up alerted him to somebody other than Frank. He gently got up, trying not to disturb Beverly, and ran around the exterior of the condos to investigate. When he returned several minutes later, Beverly was awake.

"Who was that?" she asked.

Kevin walked up, puzzling over a paper and envelope in his hand. "It was for *me*," he replied. "Some guy." He stopped in front of her, still studying the documents in his hand. "Beverly, what's a sub-po-inna?"

"A what? A subpoena?"

"Um, yeah, I *guess* that's what it says."

CHAPTER 31

Warm and quiet, darkness filled the room, providing the backdrop for a slash of moonlight filtering through the window. A digital alarm on the nightstand cast a soft glow on Linda's face. She lay back against propped-up pillows beside Beverly. Both wore light nightgowns—like a couple of middle-school girls having a sleepover and talking about boys.

"I'm telling you, Mama, if you look at him in the right light, you can see he's just starting to grow a mustache."

"Well, you must have *special* lights, dear," Beverly jibed, "because he's still a long way from shaving."

"I do have special lights, you know."

"Yeah, well, I guess you do—though I still don't understand."

"Now Mama—"

"I know, I know. But there *is* something I need to tell you. He saw you, ya know."

"Did he?"

"Uh huh. He told me he watched for a while from over by the woods."

"Hmmm . . . He definitely recognized me?"

"No question. It really rattled him—I mean, you being passed away and all. He had to sit with me a while and calm down. I gave him such a long hug that we both fell asleep out there on the deck."

"Yeah, I wondered why you two decided to nap all of a sudden."

"I told him it had to be a secret."

"He agreed?" Then, catching herself before her mother could answer, she added, "Of course he did."

"He didn't want to be put in a position of lying about it, though—especially to Frank. He tries *so* hard to be like Frank—to be the kind of person Frank would respect."

"Then he'll tell the truth if Frank ever asks."

"Yes, but there's another problem, too."

Linda cocked her head, looking over at her mother.

"He took a picture of you."

Linda caught her breath, not saying anything at first. Finally, she relaxed and whispered, "Have you seen it?"

"No. He's going to ride his bike up and get them developed today or tomorrow.

He wanted to wait and do it without Frank's involvement so he wouldn't get put on the spot to show off his pictures."

"Smart boy. It shows he's serious about the promise, too."

"You know, he made some reference to other pictures he's taken, too—something about colored lights."

Linda looked dashed. "Wow." She shook her head. "When did he take those? Where? What do they show?"

"I don't know. Does *that* have something to do with you?"

"What did he describe?"

"Zillions of eensy-weensy lights in a whole bunch of colors all swirling around—to use his words. He said he saw them once by the lake and several times back there in the woods. He said some came out of the water the same day he managed to get a shot of you visiting me."

"And the pictures?"

"He said he just barely caught them a few times. The times he could see them most, he didn't manage to get pictures."

Linda climbed off the bed and picked up a tiny jewelry box from the nightstand, the one her father had given her when she was ten years old. She opened and closed it a few times, distracted. Finally, she looked over toward Beverly and remarked, "I need to talk to him."

Beverly scooted over to the edge of the bed anxiously. "Talk to *me* first, sweetie. Why don't you explain things to *me* before you talk to him?"

Linda sat on the edge of the bed and hugged her mother. "Mama, I can't. I don't think I could answer your questions if I wanted to. I don't think I *know* the answers."

"You *are* dead, aren't you?" Beverly asked, emotion catching in her throat.

Squeezing harder, Linda whispered, "I've tried to get you to understand that all along; you know that. What happened that day can't be changed. What is special now is that the Linda you lost, her hopes and dreams and memories, can visit you sometimes—but will never get older. She only exists while spending this time with you."

"Why are you here? What is this for?"

"You help me learn and understand you and people like you. I help ease your grief, and I give another chance to embrace what you've lost—as long as it doesn't hurt you in any way."

"*I'm* okay, baby," Beverly whispered. "People like Loretta are the ones who created problems—"

"Which is why it's critical that my visits remain a secret."

"What about Kevin?"

"He'll have to be in on our secret, too."

"And Frank?"

"No, Mama, never Frank. He can't know. Even though you've told him many times about our visits—even though he doesn't understand, he cares about you so much that his, um, *connection* to you is unbreakable. He may worry. He may disagree. But he's yours and, lucky you, you're stuck with him."

"Will you keep visiting me always, then?"

Linda fell quiet, picking up the little jewelry box and fingering it again. She looked into Beverly's eyes and squeezed her lips together tightly. Already knowing the answer, Beverly started to cry. It started with tears; then she wept openly, finally burying her face in her hands.

Linda put her arms around her and whispered, "It's okay, Mama, you don't have to give up yet. I'll see you again . . ."

The bedroom filled with zillions of eensy-weensy lights in a whole bunch of colors all swirling around. Beverly lifted her head and looked at the smiling picture of her daughter, framed and sitting on her dresser.

"Oh Linda," she cried quietly. "I miss you so much. Sometimes I just don't know how I could go on without you."

"I just got the witness list," Mogill told Frank and Kevin, pausing to munch a baked potato skin dripping with melted cheese and fresh-chopped chives.

Frank bit into a jumbo garlic shrimp, obviously pleased with the flavor. He leaned over to Kevin, warning, "Don't get between me and that platter, shrimp. I'm liable to snatch you up and bite your leg off before realizing it's you."

Kevin grabbed a steamed clam, holding it like a puppet to make it talk. Pitching his notoriously cracking voice to sound like a cartoon character, he acted out, "Oh no! Don't me mixed up with Frank—" He placed a piece of parsley on top of its "head," then added, "—just because I comb my hair so I don't look like a clamshell!"

Mogill laughed, nearly choking on a mouthful of fried calamari.

"That's all right," retorted Frank, feigning insult. "You gotta go to sleep sometime."

Frank decided that Mogill had been right. Getting together for a hearty dinner down at the sponge docks *was* a much more comfortable way to talk about the trial and the police questioning that had both scared Kevin and left him sick.

"Yeah, you're on the list, Kevin," Mogill said. "You're a prosecution witness."

Trying unsuccessfully to peel the breading off a piece of deep-fried mozzarella, Kevin asked, "That means they want me to testify *against* my mom?"

"Well, it means they want you to testify. Apparently, they think something you say can be used against her."

"Like what?"

"Well, that's the thing. I don't know."

Frank snatched the piece of cheese from Kevin and took a bite from it. Kevin picked up a baby squid, inspecting it and wrinkling his nose.

"I tried to get a transcript of the tape," Mogill continued, "—the one they made during your interview at school. They told me there was no tape made."

Holding the tiny squid up under his nose, Kevin was pretending a huge snot hung from his nostril, but he suddenly stopped playing, looking first at Mogill, then at Frank. "Liars," he pronounced.

"Kevin," Frank asked, "you're *sure* they taped that interview?"

"I'm not *stupid*. I saw the tape recorder. I saw 'em start it. That dick-head cop was talking into it. I could see the cassette turning. I heard it click when the tape ran out. They turned it over and started it again. If they say there's no tape, they're liars."

"What can we do about that?" Frank asked Mogill.

"Nothing really. If they were planning on using the tape as evidence, I'd be entitled to hear it—even obtain a copy. But if it's part of the investigation—even though I'm *supposed* to have access to those things—all they have to do is say it doesn't exist. They don't want me to hear it—or read a transcript—probably at least because they don't want to reveal what they were trying to elicit from him. Worse, they may have been planting ideas or bullying him into bending the truth or twisting his statements and feeding them back to him so he would use *their* words rather than his own." Mogill bit into a shrimp, continuing, "It's sickening what they do to kids they want to put on the stand. They take advantage of them, trying to get them—not to tell lies—but to believe a new truth. What is a kid surrounded by his parents and all the authority figures in his life going to do? Go along with them. What choice does he have?"

Frank snatched a shrimp from Kevin's plate. "That's why they bamboozled him, questioning him without me."

"Yep," Mogill agreed. "You're sympathetic to the defendant. You're also too smart for them—not intimidated by their authority like most citizens are—so you'd have seen what they were doing and put a stop to it."

"What do you think they were doing, Kevin?" Frank asked, just missing grabbing the boy's marauding hand as it snatched a peppered scallop from his plate.

"Um, well, they kept trying to find out about drugs around my house. They kept acting like they knew all about my mom being a dealer and stuff. I kept telling 'em she never does drugs—except she smokes cigarettes and drinks too much, which *is* drugs—but they kept wanting to know about cocaine and marijuana and ecstasy and stuff. I said she never tried that stuff before that night, at least not that I know of. I can always tell what's going on with my mom. Even with, you know, like sex and stuff."

"Are you *sure* she was never involved in anything like that?" Mogill asked.

"Oh yeah. They kept telling me that Mark was a dealer, working out of our house selling drugs and stuff. They said my mom was helping him."

"Based on what?" Frank asked.

"They said people were coming there buyin' drugs—even from my mom when Mark wasn't there. I tried to tell 'em that isn't true 'cause Mom never had nobody there except her friend Audrey and that lady who works in the beauty place. If Mark had people over, it was only when he was there. They wouldn't listen, though. They just kept saying they knew what was really going on."

"What made them think you might go along with their story?" Mogill asked.

"Um, when I started getting bummed out, they kept being all friendly and telling me they were gonna help my mom, but I had to help them first. Then when I'd get mad, they'd start acting like *I* was gonna get in all kinds of trouble for not cooperating. Once, I kinda started just a little like I was gonna cry, they kept saying I'd feel better if I'd just tell 'em what was really going on."

Kevin looked increasingly angry. Remembering that he and Mogill had agreed to keep this conversation light, Frank snatched the boy's nose, mocking, "*Don't be so nosy!* is what you could've told 'em."

They spent the next few minutes eating; then Mogill asked, "What other kinds of stuff were they interested in, Kevin?"

"This woman was all hung up on that good-touch/bad-touch crap. She kept wanting to know if my mom ever touched me or if Mark did, and when was the last time I slept in my mom's bed, and have I ever seen her naked, or Mark naked, or anybody else, and did people try to get me to take off my clothes, and stuff like that. No matter what I said, she just kept going on and on about it."

"Was there anything in particular that she seemed more interested in?"

"Yeah, like when me and my mom fell asleep on the couch together, and about the times Mark saw me naked."

"Like when?"

"Well, I told about a few times, but she kept asking about the one when I was taking a shower and Mark came in and sat on the toilet, takin' a crap. He kept opening the curtain and teasing me about how little my, um, you know—still being kid-sized and stuff."

Frank didn't like hearing about that. His protective feelings toward Kevin kicked in, imagining the boy in so vulnerable a position, being teased by the kind of sicko who would kill people. His face tensed up, so he stared off into the distance.

Mogill waved a hand in front of his face, breaking his thoughts. "See how easy it is to rouse up protective instincts, rage, or hatred when you put a cute kid on the stand?"

"I was just, um—"

"You were just imagining, is what you were doing. I wouldn't want you on the jury."

"But this isn't about—"

"Frank, it's about painting a picture of Ruth. The jury doesn't know her, but they get fed little bits of information from which they have to decide if she's a cold-blooded killer or not. You see why they were fishing for ways to make her look bad?"

"But what does that have to do with the facts of what happened that night?"

"That's just it, they don't *have* a whole lot of facts, so they have to layer on impressions."

Kevin quietly followed the conversation, studying each man carefully. When they paused, he asked, "So they're gonna ask me a bunch of questions that make my mom look bad, right?"

Mogill nodded, answering, "That's our best guess."

Kevin looked thoughtful for a minute, then chewed absently on a now-cold piece of mozzarella. Finally, he asked, "Can I say anything I want?"

"No, all you can do is answer questions—and you *have* to tell the truth when you answer."

Kevin looked indignant, glancing at Frank before announcing to Mogill, "I'm *not* a liar."

"I'm sorry," Mogill offered. "I just wanted to remind you. The good thing, though, is that *I* get to ask you a bunch of questions after the prosecutor does. So I'll try to give you a chance to say things that tell the real story instead of what they want it to look like."

"Good."

Mogill twirled a celery stalk in his hand for a second, casually asking, "What were you thinking when you asked if you could say whatever you want?"

"I dunno. Just stuff about what kind of person my mom is. She's really a good lady—she just had a couple of bad habits, but that doesn't make her a bad person." Lowering his voice, he added, "And she's not a murderer."

Frank reached over and put arm around Kevin's neck, gently squeezing his shoulder, massaging the knots in his muscles for a moment or two. Mogill suggested he eat more of his food, munching a few pieces himself. Frank waved off a waitress who hovered a bit too much.

Mogill suggested, "Kevin, what do you think of this? How about if you and me—and sometimes Frank might be there, too—we get together three or four times in the next month before the trial starts? We'll talk about you and your mom and what kind of person she is, and I'll just get to know you. Then during the trial, I'll take notes on what the prosecution does, decide what needs to be said to overcome the bad impression they create, and I'll ask you questions that give you a chance to tell about the kinds of things we talk about."

"Excellent! That'll work."

"Then we can practice how to act so the jury likes you, too."

"Practice? Hey," Kevin said, turning on an overstated look of adorability while reaching over to pat Frank on the back, "I practice that on Frank all the time."

Mr. Mogill sat with Kevin Riner on a bench by the sponge docks, Frank hovering nearby. Assured that Kevin felt comfortable alone with the attorney to talk personal talk, Frank drew Mogill a map to the condos, then left for home.

Pulling into his driveway, he noticed Lonnie's bicycle next to the garage. He went over to Beverly's and quickly determined that she was asleep, then walked around back and found the boy sitting on the deck. Clearly disappointed that Kevin was not with Frank, Lonnie nevertheless followed him inside. Frank checked his messages and opened some mail, then settled on the couch, inviting the boy to have a seat. He turned on a football game and asked, "So, how ya been?"

Lonnie acted unusually awkward, even uncomfortable. He shrugged. "All right, I guess."

Frank went to the kitchen and brought back a beer for himself, a soda for Lonnie. They watched in silence for a few minutes. During the next commercial break, Frank casually remarked, "So, Kevin's pretty mad at you, huh?" He avoided looking toward Lonnie, appearing instead to watch television.

Lonnie looked stricken. "Um, yeah. I guess."

Frank nodded, saying nothing.

The awkward silence closing in on him, Lonnie added, "It was *my* fault."

"Oh?"

"Um, did he tell you about it?"

Frank looked over toward the boy, studying him for a moment, then replied, "No." He looked back at the television.

After another few minutes, Lonnie got up and went over to study the controls on the stereo equipment. Frank watched him finger the dials, pick up and set down several knickknacks, even tug at his own shirt a few times. *He doesn't want to face me*, he thought. *He's ashamed of something.*

Without turning to face Frank, Lonnie asked, "Was he *real* mad? I mean, did he say—what did he do?"

"Lonnie, he didn't discuss it with me. I know him pretty well, though, and I got the impression his feelings were very hurt—like he was disappointed."

Lonnie said nothing at first, then finally asked, "Do you wanna know?"

It was Frank's turn to pause. "Did you do something to hurt Kevin?"

"No, it was just me."

"Then only if you want to tell me."

Lonnie considered this for a moment, then said, "I don't want you to get mad at me."

Frank had to weigh how much Lonnie looked up to him, remembering how in Kevin's bedroom that night, his guard completely down, he had hugged Frank unabashedly. More than just a role model, what this fatherless boy desperately needed was his approval, even his affection.

Okay, Frank thought, *I'm the one with all the power here. Let's put it to work.* Then aloud, adding a harsh gruffness to his voice, he intoned, "Well, if all you're going to do is turn your back on me and play riddles—" He started to walk toward the front door. Lonnie quickly turned toward him, a worried expression on his face. Frank stopped, then sat on the arm of the nearest chair, staring the boy down. "Come here," he ordered.

It must have been one of the longest walks of Lonnie's life. He wound up standing directly in front of Frank, both at each other's eye level. Lonnie squirmed, fidgeted with his clothes, and looked everywhere but at Frank's face.

Quietly, the older man said, "I decided a while back that you were a pretty good guy—a good one to be friends with, maybe even after you grow up—" Lonnie glanced at him, then cast his eyes downward. Frank continued, "But now I feel like I don't really know you. I mean, you can't even look at me, the one guy you can talk to about anything, the guy who only asks that you be honest with him."

Lonnie's lower lip quivered, his eyes filling with tears. "Kevin got mad . . ." He looked away, then with new resolve, looked back at Frank again. "Because I was shoplifting."

Frank had expected, well, he wasn't sure what he expected, but he'd worried it might be something worse. Not betraying his relief, though, he registered disappointment, even disgust, then stood up and backed away just enough for symbolic distance, announcing, "So you're a *thief,* huh?"

Lonnie's tears spilled out, but he stood there stock-still, looking directly at Frank, determined. "No sir. I only did it three times. Today, before I came here, I took the stuff back. That's what I came here to tell Kevin."

Frank studied him, softening his expression. "You mean, then, that you're *not* a thief—just a young guy who made mistakes he's never going to repeat?"

"Never."

"Oh, good then. Boy, what a relief. I really liked you, but then I was afraid I'd been wrong about you, that you'd turned out to be a *bad* guy."

"I'm *not* a bad guy."

"Thanks for proving me right. My judgment in people lately has been pretty good." He pulled out a handkerchief, reaching with it as if to wipe off the boy's tear-soaked face. Catching him off-guard, he instead grabbed his nose, got him in a headlock, and gave him a vicious noogie. They wound up in a wrestling match, then collapsed on the couch and sort of watched the ball game.

Frank asked, "You think you can fix things with Kevin?"

"Yeah, he's a good guy."

"And very loyal, too," Frank added.

After a pause, Lonnie pointed out, "You know, I wasn't gonna tell *you* about it."

"Why did you?"

Lonnie shrugged.

Frank answered his own question, "It's because it matters to you what I think. That's why."

Lonnie looked slightly embarrassed. "But I thought you would get mad if you found out."

"I would've been mad if I found out from somewhere else—even more so if you denied it—if you didn't have enough respect for me to be honest."

Lonnie nodded.

Frank added one last request. "Will you do something for me? It would mean a lot."

"Sure. What?"

"Every now and then, whenever it's a good time, give me a call or come by here without Kevin—just you—and tell me something that'll make me proud of you."

Lonnie grinned. "Sure."

"See, it took a real man to admit what you did. Now make sure you tell me the good things you do, too."

"Even little things?"

"Listen, son, it's the little things that add up."

Kevin tilted his chest of drawers forward several inches and, holding it with one hand, reached underneath from behind, extracting an oversized manilla envelope. Even though he thought Frank would understand about his young friend having some girlie pix, he still felt he should keep them private.

He took the envelope to his desk and laid it aside. He extracted four prints from one of the processing packets in his backpack, then examined them one by one for the umpteenth time.

Click. Lonnie mugging for the camera with a hint of colored lights over his shoulder. Click. Lonnie cut in half, out of focus, with a small swirl of colored lights in the lower corner of the shot, partially obscured by a shrub. Click. Streaks of magenta and vivid blues painting lines down into and under the water of a spring. Click. Beverly, sitting on her deck; beside her, bathed in a multi-colored corona, one hand touching her mother's arm . . . Linda Herndon.

He carefully placed the photos in his private envelope, then put it back under the chest. He gathered up the rest of his photos and turned to leave.

Very softly, barely audible, he heard a woman's voice. "Please keep those photos private, Kevin. I'm counting on you . . ."

He whirled, looking in every direction, but nobody appeared. He walked to the door, paused in the hallway, then poked his head warily back into his bedroom.

Still, nobody in sight.

He whispered, "Okay, Linda."

CHAPTER 32

As Frank walked back to the van, Kevin and Cynthia stole a quick, gentle kiss there on her front porch. He squeezed her hand, promising to see her in school, then trotted out and climbed into the waiting van.

They drove toward Henry Wanamaker's office, time to review the latest financial and management reports from Doug Taylor, a process in which Kevin always participated.

"Did you have a nice visit?" Frank asked.

With a hint of smile, Kevin replied, "Yep." Usually the non-stop talker—especially with Frank—he offered nothing else.

"What did you do?"

"Just hung out."

"Well, if it was hanging out, I hope you zipped it back up."

"Funny, Frank. Actually, I thought her mom was gonna try to pull *yours* out."

"Yeah, well, she *was* a bit friendly, wasn't she?"

"Friendly? She was comin' on to you since you walked in the door. I thought she was gonna jump your bones."

"She'd have been out of luck; I'm a one-woman guy."

"Yeah, well, me too. I *do* hope her daughter turns out as friendly as the mom."

They arrived at the office, greeted Henry, and set right to work. During the next ninety minutes, Frank and Henry exchanged glances and raised eyebrows numerous times, impressed by the boy's insight into how the numbers could be broken down and looked at from different perspectives.

At one point, Henry quietly asked, "You know where this is going, don't you?"

Frank smiled proudly and nodded. "I can only hope."

When they finished, Henry said he had one more thing they needed to go over. Since he would be out of town all week, this might be his best chance to do it. He went out to the refreshment area, rummaged in the refrigerator and cabinets, then came back with a box, paper plates, knife, and forks. He pulled an ice-cream cake out of the box, revealing an oval decorated with eyes and mouth, a bunch of squiggles at the top, "H B Kevin" written across the face, and red dots all over the rest.

Recognizing a birthday cake, one week early, Kevin beamed. "What are all these?"

he asked.

"You're gonna be a teenager," Henry replied. "That's an outrageous hairstyle, and it's covered with pimples."

Kevin and Frank both mock-grimaced. Henry added, "Yeah, well, the lady at the cake place thought I was weird, too. Cut us some slabs Kevin, while I take out the trash."

Kevin started serving while Henry rooted around behind his desk. He came out with a large box, wrapped in ledger sheets and topped with a bow made from shredded financial documents.

Kevin grinned like a hyena. Ripping into it with all the decorum of a vulture on a fresh carcass, he revealed a most excellent assortment of office accoutrements, decorated in modern colors and bright symbols for today's cool student. In addition to a complete desk set, paper weight, paper baskets, electric sharpener, pencil holder with enough pens and pencils to fill it, art set, colored markers, reams of various papers including ledgers, desk lamp, magnet clip holder, various glues, ruler, calculator, and calendar. A smaller box wrapped in the same ledger paper concealed another surprise.

"You can't open that one yet—not till *after* your birthday," Henry intoned.

It turned out to be a fine little party, indeed. Kevin must have pumped Henry's hand a dozen times. He examined every item over and over, beaming with pride.

Kevin already had access to many of these things from Frank's office anyway—but these were *his*. He would set up his *own* office. He would arrange everything just the way he wanted.

He'd become one of the big guys, and it felt pretty good.

The wind died down some, but it still whipped up occasionally, blowing some of the loose sand into little spirals that would dance across the cemetery and disappear. The minister moved around among the mourners, grasping hands, wishing the best.

"Nice service," Sherry Lubinsky told him.

"Thank you for coming," Loretta offered.

"That was very nice," Henry added.

"He was a wonderful man," Lizzie pointed out, dabbing her eyes. She had flown down for the reburial ceremony. Marshall Herndon would rest beside the daughter he loved so much.

"I'm glad you could work things out to be here for us today, Reverend," Frank told him with a hand on the shoulder and a firm handshake.

The only one still seated, Beverly reached out and took the minister's hands, nodding her agreement through tearful eyes.

The minister walked to his car and drove away. Kevin whispered something to

Frank, who nodded and gave him a squeeze on the shoulder. The rest of the very small group walked back toward their cars while Kevin and Lonnie folded up the card-table chairs, careful not to soil their new neckties, and carried them to the van. Frank sat down beside Beverly, putting his arm around her, holding her close. Beverly stared ahead at the vault, which rested on straps ready to be lowered into the open grave. The wind ruffled and tugged at the gorgeous flower arrangements arrayed all around them.

Once everything was loaded, Kevin went over and whispered to Frank, "Loretta said she'll give us a ride back if you wanna stay here for a while."

Frank nodded, putting his free arm around the boy in a quick hug. He turned and nodded toward where Loretta stood by her car.

When the others had left, Frank gently stroked Beverly's back, softly asking, "Did you like how it went?" He offered her a tissue.

She accepted it, wiping her eyes, and answered, "It was beautiful, Frank, just beautiful." She looked longingly at the vault, slowly shaking her head from side to side. "He used to say he didn't want to retire and move to Florida. He loved Michigan. Now, here, I've moved him to Florida." She looked at Frank and smiled at the irony, another tear trickling down her cheek.

"You've brought him here to be close to you," Frank assured her. "I think he loved *you* even more than Michigan."

Beverly put her head against Frank, wiping her cheeks, crying more now than she did during the ceremony. "Sometimes I don't feel right talking about him with you. I want to say, Oh, Marshall used to like those, or That's what Marshall used to say, or things like that, but I don't."

"Beverly, I wish you would. He's so much a part of you—and always will be—that he deserves to be remembered, not brushed aside."

"Yeah, I guess. But now I have you—"

"Now you have both of us. You have way too big a heart just for little ol' me."

She looked up at him. "You *do* have my heart, you know. It's been hurt so much these last few years, you *better* take good care of it," she teased.

He hugged her tightly.

She looked again at the vault, then down at the sparsely grassed patch just this side of it . . . Linda's grave. She shook her head again. It seemed as if each gust of wind that played through her beautiful blond hair brought with it a shroud of memories, engulfing her and leaving her sad and vulnerable. Frank still held her, held her against the wind, against the flood of memories threatening to wash her away, against all that is bad and scary and hurtful in this wonderful but all-too-often harsh world.

She labored to stand, Frank helping with her cane, a protective caress. He wrapped his arms around her, embracing her for a long time. She trembled for a moment, then melted into him. Opening her eyes, just able to see over his shoulder, she noticed Linda standing off in the distance, watching her mother, tears in her eyes, too, nodding her approval.

"I'm ready to go now," she whispered to Frank.

He helped her over the uneven ground and up into the van, returning to retrieve the two remaining chairs. Another gust of wind twirled up little swirls of dust and sand and memories and loss, the pall of grief lit briefly, just in the twinkling of an eye, by a whorl of colored sparkles carried off toward the open sea.

As the van drove away, a pair of sentries waddled over to settle down at their outpost, facing into the wind, closing their eyes, waiting for the future to become the past.

Kevin's birthday weekend began with some great presents: his own laptop computer from Frank, a laser printer from Beverly, the mysterious box from Henry which turned out to be a case of burnable CD's—"Oh! I had to wait 'cause he didn't want me to figure out the computer!"—a bike lock from Lonnie, video game from Darla, friendship bracelet from Cynthia, and a hand-drawn card from his mother . . . soon to be framed for his bedroom wall.

Friday after school, a van full of revelers—Kevin, Lonnie, Cynthia, Darla, Beverly, and Frank at the wheel—all headed toward Orlando for a day of Disney. They planned to enjoy a nice dinner—yes, he got embarrassed by singing waiters serving up cake with a sparkler—then some fun time at the hotel pool or game room before turning in early. Saturday would be an all-out hit-every-attraction affair to be followed by a night of exhaustion in the hotel, then a leisurely breakfast before heading back toward Tampa in time for Kevin to see his mother Sunday afternoon, his first visit as an actual teenager.

They'd reserved a gals' room and a guys' room, but while the youngsters played in the pool, Frank sneaked over next door for some impromptu snuggling and nuzzling with *his* favorite gal. After a while, he helped her change into her swimsuit, stepped into his own, and escorted her down to the pool area. The brats had already staked out some territory in the elders' intended destination, the Jacuzzi. The youngsters engaged in some innocent snuggling of their own, an activity also favored by a newlywed couple from Tennessee. Frank helped Beverly into the steamy, churning water, then cozied up and put his arm around her, forming a pillow with his chest to keep her head up out of the water.

It was wonderful! She said it felt good on her leg and foot—all over her body—and that she understood why Frank had added a spa to the plans for the condo pool area, a luxury scheduled to be in operation within a week or two.

Stars twinkled in the ebony sky as shadows cast by concealed lights played across them, silhouettes of palm trees and exotic plants swaying gently in the warm breezes that made the rising steam swirl and dance away.

They closed their eyes and floated off with the mists for a while. Cynthia and Kevin looked on, then settled into a similar position, closing their eyes, with Cynthia's head resting on the front of his shoulder. Because Darla had grown so much taller than Lonnie, those two chose to lie close together and hold hands underwater, their heads resting on the edge. Eventually, Frank interrupted the reverie to accuse them all of looking like prunes, reminding them it wasn't good to spend too much time in the heated water.

Everybody headed up to change into dry clothes, then met downstairs for dessert in one of the rooms that featured comedy skits performed by cartoon characters. Frank enjoyed watching how the girls fussed over Beverly, looking out for her, hovering protectively. *They've adopted her*, he thought, smiling to himself. *The foster mother's come full circle.*

Afterwards, they headed back up to the rooms. Each guy gave his gal an innocent peck in the hallway before everybody retired for the night.

Frank stripped down to his briefs and flopped onto his bed. The boys, expected to sleep together in the other king-size bed, stripped down to their undies and, rather than crawl in like good little boys, pounced on Frank, attacking him with pillows. Eventually they jumped into their own bed, determined to keep the old guy awake just a little while longer with some guy-talk conversation.

"Frank's the babemeister," Lonnie observed.

"He knows how to make 'em fall in love," Kevin agreed.

"How do guys get girls to like 'em, Frank?" Lonnie asked.

Frank thought for a minute before replying. "Well, first off, I'm *not* the babemeister. I had a couple of girlfriends when I was a teenager; then I met my wife and wound up married for many years. Since my divorce, I've only dated a few times, not finding anybody interesting enough—until I met Beverly. A lot of guys are very aggressive—going out looking for women, hitting bars, joining organizations, whatever. I was never much in for any of that."

"What happened with your divorce?" Kevin asked.

Frank's face tightened. He reached over and shut off the lamp, leaving the room in soft darkness, a glow from exterior lights drawing faint patterns across the room. "The marriage was a mistake," he said quietly.

"I didn't think you made mistakes, Frank," Lonnie said, also softening his voice.

"We all make mistakes, Lonnie. We all do."

"What did you do wrong?" Kevin asked.

"I fell in love with the wrong person. Oh, sometimes you don't have any say in who you fall in love with, but you *do* have to live in the real world. Sometimes there's no way it can work out. Sometimes she won't be in love with you. Sometimes she may love you, but not be the kind of person who can share your life with you." He paused, trying to find the words. "I fell in love with her, but didn't see that she wasn't really in love with me."

"Why did she marry you then?" Lonnie wondered.

"I think she was in love with the *idea* of me. I was on my way to being successful; I fit her concept of what a husband ought to be. But then when we got together, she wanted me only to be *her husband*, not to be myself—somebody she just plain loved. After so many years, she grew less and less satisfied, even to the point of looking elsewhere, trying to find something she wouldn't even know how to recognize if she found it."

The boys said nothing, waiting for him to go on.

Frank added, "And I made the mistake of still trying because I thought I loved her. It's only now that I can see I was in love with who I thought she was, not who she really was."

"How do we figure out if our girlfriends are really the right ones?" Kevin asked.

"Well, I guess you don't worry about that yet. Young guys need to have a few relationships, fall in love, even get hurt a few times. From those experiences, you learn what makes you feel good and what makes you feel bad. Later on, when you think you may have the person who is the only one for you, then you need to be careful it's not for the wrong reasons. Decide if you're just in love with the kind of person she is, or the idea of being married, or you're hooked on the sex part, or whatever. Maybe you just have a good friend and it should stay that way rather than trying to make it something that it's not."

"But how will we know?" they both asked simultaneously, giggling at the coincidence.

"I wish I knew. I guess this old geezer—far from being the babemeister—is still learning."

The boys thought for a minute. Finally Kevin asked, "Frank, say we really *are* in love . . . and she loves us, too . . . how do we make sure it stays good—not like all those people we know who get divorced."

"Yeah," Lonnie added, "like *my* mom and dad."

"Well, the people *I* know who stayed together and stayed happy—and I think this is really important—they seemed to understand that both have to keep a part of themselves separate."

"Separate?"

"Well, everybody has interests—hobbies, friends, things they like to do, stuff like that. That's true at your age just like it is at my age. When you get with a lady, it's good to have things that you both like together. But when one of you has to give up everything you like in order to spend every minute doing what the other one wants, then somebody isn't going to be happy. For example, I know a couple that loves to travel.

They go out on the boat most weekends; plus they take two vacations a year together to places they both like. But they also do a trip each with their own friends. He goes hunting with his old college buddies—I even went one year—and while he's gone, she does a New York museum trip with two ladies she knows. She doesn't want to hunt, and he hates museums, so even though they enjoy their time together, they still leave room for each other to do their own thing."

"So you should take your own trips?" Lonnie asked.

"Well, no, not necessarily," Frank corrected. "That's just one example. It could be little things like what you have for dinner, or which friends you visit, or what to watch on TV, or maybe one likes to go to bed early and one likes to stay up late, or maybe she wants to have a cat and you tolerate it even though you don't like cats, or you want to have a workshop and she knows not to clean it up because, out of the whole house, that's *your* little space that you want to keep *your* way . . . Or it could be your sex life. Sometimes, you have to make sure you have the kind of fun *you* prefer; other times maybe you think more about what *she* likes." Frank knew that last comment would open up new realms of conjecture for later adolescent discussion, but for now the mysteries of love and successful relationships loomed foremost in the boys' minds.

"What should we do with Cynthia and Darla?" Kevin asked.

"Be yourselves, guys. If you want 'em to fall in love with you, give 'em the *real* you to fall in love with. Don't play games. Show a lot of respect for their feelings and who they are. Listen to what they say—and what they mean if they're not being very clear with their words."

They fell quiet for a minute. Then Frank added, "And when you're thirteen or fourteen, don't try to act older than just thirteen or fourteen."

"What do you mean?"

"You don't have to pretend you're engaged, or show off playing kissy in front of other people, or try to make it more serious than just a special friendship . . . and you don't need to have sex yet."

"Why not?"

"Because you still have too much to learn about yourselves before you're ready to share something so personal with others—because it comes with a lot of responsibility that you need maturity to handle—because another person's feelings are involved and it's too easy to leave somebody feeling hurt as it is to leave her feeling good. There are stages to go through—and trust me, you will—so you shouldn't be trying something just to see what it is, or because your friends say you should, or because you think you're supposed to. Wait until you're sure in your heart that it's the right time."

"We already know a lot," Lonnie pointed out.

"Naw you don't. I know you guys are old enough to get ga-ga over those magazines Lonnie sneaks around in that gym bag—"

"See," Kevin hissed in Lonnie's ear, "I told you he knew."

"—And you've probably discovered some neat little tricks you can do by yourselves, but even though all those techniques your supposedly experienced friends have told you about sound pretty good, trust me, there is so much more to learn. Just don't be in a hurry."

"How can we learn?" Lonnie asked.

"That's like asking me how to learn to laugh. You can't *make* yourself laugh, but as you go through life you find people or ideas that *do* make you laugh. And as you get older, you discover more sophisticated things that make you laugh. Eventually, you even learn to appreciate humor that doesn't *have* to make you laugh. Potty jokes you thought were funny in first grade seem childish to you now. Sex is like that. What a couple of teenagers explore is different than what two newlyweds who are in love enjoy which is different than after they've been married for many years and have a family. Then, when they get older, some parts of sex are less important while other parts—maybe just the closeness of holding each other—maybe those are the best parts. The happiest people learn and grow and change all their lives."

"Like you and Beverly," Kevin whispered.

"Yeah," Frank agreed. "I'm pretty lucky there."

"So what if Darla wants to have sex?" Lonnie asked.

"At her age, it would probably be for the wrong reasons. And it's okay for the boy to be the one who reminds her that maybe *he* isn't ready."

"So it's lots of stages," Kevin concluded.

"Yeah, which is why I don't worry when I catch on to what you guys are up to. That's the stage you're in."

For an instant, they both looked sheepish. That faded quickly, though. In fact, the more they thought about it, the more they seemed relieved. Frank knew their secret and as good as said that it was—that *they* were okay.

After a moment, Kevin said, "Thanks, Frank."

"What? Who was that?" Frank joked. "Was it that kid Kevin? No, it couldn't have been. The only Kevin here is a teenager!"

"Huh?"

"It's 12:03—happy birthday, buddy."

"Birthday noogie!" Lonnie announced, pouncing.

"Get on your own side of the bed, dick-head!"

"Well, I guess I would say it's communication," Beverly answered. Like young teens at a slumber party, Cynthia and Darla gathered around Beverly, big questions on their curious minds. Beverly propped herself up in bed while the girls helped wrap her injured leg.

"Make sure they understand your needs," Beverly explained, straightening her nightgown, "and make sure you understand theirs. And for heaven's sake, don't expect for both to be the same. Don't try to make your boyfriend into a girlfriend. Guys have a lot of guy interests, and Lord knows they won't all appeal to you, so give 'em some space."

"Kevin likes to go to the arcade with Lonnie," Cynthia pointed out. "It doesn't do much for me."

Beverly smiled. "Get used to it, hon. My Marshall used to have a poker night—smelly cigars, cussing and acting like idiots, getting all bothered about piddly amounts of money none of 'em would bother to bend over and pick up if it were in the street—and they always had a ball. So, I made them sandwiches and snacks, then cleared out for the evening. I'll tell a little secret: usually after getting all that out of his system, later that night he'd be ready to get *real* close with me again." Beverly laughed. "Heck, I looked forward to his poker nights."

The girls smiled. "Are you ready to turn out the light?" Darla asked.

"Yeah, this ol' lady's pretty tired—and you girls got a big day ahead of you tomorrow."

Cynthia turned off the lamp. Both girls kissed Beverly on the cheek, then climbed into the other king-size bed.

"Beverly?" Cynthia asked.

"Yes, hon?"

"Are you and Frank gonna get married?"

Beverly smiled to herself and, rather than answering, broke into a cartoon-character snore.

The girls giggled.

All agreed they'd enjoyed a fine birthday weekend.

The youngsters managed to do all sixteen hours of park-time, laughing and having fun, sometimes holding hands, once or twice stealing a brief, affectionate kiss. None of them worried about being boyfriends and girlfriends; they just tried to squeeze every bit of magic out of every minute they had.

Frank and Beverly spent some time with them, once with Beverly on crutches, several more hours with her in the wheelchair. They spent most of their day back at the hotel, though, trusting Kevin and his friends to make their own fun. Frank and Beverly really enjoyed the Jacuzzi, and they really enjoyed each other. At one point, they related their conversations from the night before, amused at the wonder of youth. They liked how both had touched on the theme of allowing one's partner space for his own interests. *There's something about helping young people learn that winds up teaching the teachers*, Frank thought.

By late afternoon, after a cool drink in the warm sun, a bit of relaxation in the swirling bubbles, and a gentle caress under the swaying palms, they went up to Frank's room, put out the *Do Not Disturb* sign, and explored one of their favorite mutual interests together.

CHAPTER 33

Linda and Beverly pulled into the driveway at close to three o'clock. Beverly knew Frank would be meeting with Mr. Mogill that afternoon, so she wasn't concerned about him discovering Linda. They walked over and inspected the newly-opened Jacuzzi beside the almost-finished pool. They went inside and changed into swimsuits, Linda wearing one of her mother's. Beverly removed the prosthesis she'd been using for a two-week comfort trial, opting for now to rely on her cane. They made their way back to the Jacuzzi, slipped into the warm, swirling water, and lay their heads back to relax.

"You know Kevin'll be home soon, don't you?" Beverly asked.

Swishing the water around, holding her hands in the air and letting it drip through her fingers to catch sparkles from the sun, Linda laughed and replied, "Oh yes—any time now."

"What if he has Lonnie with him?"

"He won't. I heard them discuss Lonnie having a dental appointment this afternoon. His mother will pick him up directly from school, go to the dentist, then from there to a doctor's appointment for his baby sister."

"How did you—?" Beverly started to ask, but she thought better of it.

"You're gonna like having this here, aren't you, Mama?" she asked, waving her body around under the water, feeling the rising bubbles, seeking out the hot streams of water gurgling from jet nozzles.

"Mmmm," Beverly affirmed. "Linda, how about if tomorrow you and me go down to that flea market and bazaar where the old drive-in used to be? I'd like to look for some figurines."

"I don't think so, Mama. Why don't you call Loretta and invite her? You know she likes to collect little clowns and knickknacks."

"Yeah, I guess you're right. I'll call her soon as we go in."

Kevin walked up the road from where the bus dropped him off. When he spotted the two women in the steaming water, he froze.

"It's okay, Kevin," Beverly called out.

He hesitated, then gradually moved toward the newly constructed pool area. He stopped for a moment about twenty feet from the women, then relaxed and walked over beside the Jacuzzi, greeting them both.

"Boy, look at you!" Linda gushed. "You're getting so *big!* Happy birthday, by the way."

Kevin managed a hint of a smile, then quietly offered, "I really missed you."

"You, too, my fave teen guy. I can't stay long, so unless you wanna skinny-dip, why don't you run get your suit on?"

A quick dash to Frank's place, and he climbed into the Jacuzzi. Linda pulled him over and gave him a big hug. She asked lots of questions about Beverly's therapy, Kevin's Disney weekend, her mom's new prosthesis, Cynthia and Lonnie, Frank . . . Kevin tried several times to get Linda to explain her circumstances, but she always avoided the issue, winking at him knowingly after he finally gave up.

After a while, they helped Beverly walk back to her condo. She invited Kevin to come for an after-school snack when he changed into something dry. By the time he ran next door, put on shorts, t-shirt, and moccasins, then returned to Beverly's, Linda had already gone, but they enjoyed a very nice afternoon without her, listening to music and, at one point, even dancing a little dance together.

Eventually, Frank showed up with Henry and two large sacks of carry-out . . . and a new haircut. Cropped even shorter around the sides, feathered toward the ever-lengthening tail in back, it sported one big difference: the shock he always combed over the top . . . was gone! There, for all the world to see, shone the fully tanned pate of Tarpon Springs's renaissance man—thinker, lover, guardian, and downright cool dude.

"Bitchin'," Henry concluded.

"Groovy," Beverly agreed.

"Kickin'," Kevin corrected, rolling his eyes. These geezers were something else.

Everyone at the middle school knew why Kevin was absent; his mother's trial had begun. Kevin wanted to be in the courtroom as observer and supporter, a familiar face his mother could focus on from the defense table, but instead they kept him in a sterile room adjacent to the proceedings. Witnesses weren't allowed to watch. Either way, Ruth Riner stood trial for murder, two counts, plus drug and weapons charges while a conspicuously empty seat sat in each of Kevin's seventh-grade classes.

Known throughout the school as Kevin's best friend, Lonnie found himself besieged every day—not with derision, but with messages of support and solidarity for the state's star witness. Kevin had become a celebrity of sorts, and most believed by now that his mother would be found innocent. Even those with doubts still understood—or tried to understand—how it must feel for him to be under such pressure with the stakes so high. Though legions of young teens argued with their mothers on a regular basis, this week many took a moment to imagine this happening to his or her own family.

Regardless of the trial's outcome, Kevin would have friends. He would have Lonnie and Cynthia. He would have Beverly. And, reminded late the night before when he stood trembling in his bedroom, when the only man who had ever loved him put his arms around him and held him tight, he would always have Frank.

Now to save his mom . . .

TV cameras, newspaper reporters, a packed courtroom, lots of people wearing suits, and all the resources and financial support of the state raged against this lone woman. Exhausted, scared, she needed to use a rest room, but she sat timidly, trying to understand everything happening, kneading her hands, hiding her manacled and chained legs underneath the defense table.

Any career-minded, politically-savvy state's attorney knows that two-for-two murder convictions are always better than one, so Mark Sisk, with shaky odds of going down for first degree, discovered the prudence of copping pleas to sure second-degrees with a sentence understanding that gave him odds of walking free someday, all in exchange for putting away Ruth Riner.

The prosecution theory sounded straightforward: Ruth Riner initiated the bungled robbery attempt; Ruth Riner pulled the trigger, killing in cold blood. She would be getting off easy with second-degrees, probably owing to some nuisance "technicalities" in the law, and would be spared undeservedly from execution.

Not wanting to waste media opportunities on a mere assistant, the state's attorney himself took the lead. He explained to the jury that Ruth Riner had proven herself a sick woman. With no education and very little personal responsibility, she slept around, eventually winding up with a bastard son whose father she couldn't name. She neglected the boy, and she or any of the endless string of low-lifes that passed through her twisted world may even have abused him.

She couldn't support herself adequately; foremost came financing her addictions—first cigarettes and alcohol, then eventually graduating to various hard drugs, including crack cocaine. As hard as it would be for a jury of such fine, upstanding citizens to understand how a mother could forsake her son for the evils of drugs, they nevertheless would have to confront a lifestyle that included strange men sleeping over, adults engaging in sexual relations while her scared and crying little boy was forced to watch, a mother sponging drugs and trading favors to support her habit, eventually scheming to sell drugs from the very trailer where she and that vulnerable young child lived.

Mark Sisk entered her life as a dream come true. With his connections and credit, he could set up the deals that generated profit—payable in the drugs she craved. Far from moving him in full-time as a lover, she encouraged him instead to drift among other people's homes so he could drum up business, staying with her only as much as needed, making her son's home freely available for the trafficking of drugs. Her addiction graduated to smoking crack right there in the trailer, ultimately driving her so deep into debt that she masterminded the robbery of a cocaine supplier in Clearwater.

It was a robbery that turned into double murder.

Maybe she went there intending to kill her victims; maybe she only expected to scare them with a loaded gun, but fired after something went wrong. It might not be possible to prove pre-meditation, but this trial *would* show that she was, indeed, a cold-blooded, drug-crazed killer.

On that fateful night, she and Mr. Sisk drove to the victims' home and initiated a small drug purchase—a ploy to determine if sufficient quantity would be available to rob, and so they could case the situation. They went back and, using a gun that Mr. Sisk had purchased from a common burglar—now turned state's evidence—they went inside to commit the robbery. Mr. Sisk waited in the front room while she went to a back room and forced the victims to reveal their cache, then shot them at point-blank range. Surprised and scared by the sound of shots, Mr. Sisk tried to leave.

She came out with a small sack containing drugs, then ordered him into the car. As they drove away, she gave him the gun, telling him to stash it and the drugs in his duffel bag. She removed the rubber gloves she was wearing and threw them out the window somewhere along Highway 19. They were captured by police based on a description of the car, its license plate, and the two occupants identified by the victims' neighbors. Ruth Riner showed no remorse for the killings, and she has not cooperated in the investigation.

Here sat a woman who cared more about her drugs than the safety of her twelve-year-old son. Here sat a woman who needed to feed her addiction so much she would gladly murder in cold blood. Here sat a woman who would risk everything, not caring that her little boy would be left alone without the protection a mother should provide in this often harsh and cruel world.

The jury grew incensed; it showed in their faces, in the surreptitious glares they shot toward the defense table. This woman obviously embodied not only all that could be wrong in the world, but she represented a threat to their very way of life, to society as a whole, and to the safety of their own children.

Of course, most of these "facts" would be established through the testimony of a man who preferred decades of confinement over the death chamber. But enough circumstantial bricks would be piled to lay a foundation of suspicion and innuendo, enough to erase any lingering doubts these fine citizens—though ignorant of the law and how the system works—might have.

Sad and heart-wrenching as it may be, her poor son, victim of an uncaring mother, would have to testify to these facts—a calculated attempt to stir rage against the scared, manacled woman sitting at the defense table, trying desperately to understand why all these people were destroying her life.

Yes, the state's attorney intended to put Ruth Riner away—because she deserved it . . . to protect the decent citizens of Clearwater . . . to send a message.

Lots of messages would be sent during the trial of Ruth Riner, duly recorded and printed and transmitted by the media messengers. She would be held up as an example to us all, scorned, then forgotten by a society of victims eagerly awaiting its next villain.

Ruth found a small measure of solace in knowing she would be one of the lucky ones, though.

She had an expensive lawyer who actually *worked* on her case.

In a moonless sky, clouds obscured most of the stars. With the lights in the new pool area turned off, darkness made it difficult for Beverly to see wisps of steam curling skyward from the Jacuzzi. Frank rocked gently back and forth, riding the spray from a hot jet. Holding his hand, she staked out her own jet not more than a foot away. Both lounged completely nude—the only other resident of the area, Kevin, was in bed asleep—but neither felt very sexy that night. It seemed more important just to be together, to feel free of worries, to float and let the steam carry away some of the stress that weighed so heavily on them. A subdued Thanksgiving holiday had just come and gone, a brief respite, but even the few happy moments they enjoyed had been overshadowed by the intensity of Ruth's trial.

Kevin had missed too much school, had sat too many hours in that sterile room loaded with homework and comics and games and puzzles and books and every possible thing Frank or Beverly could think of to keep the boy's mind occupied, somehow distracted if only a little from the drama unfolding on the other side of that wall. He had been sleeping better the last two nights—probably a result of sheer exhaustion and the holiday break—but the adults hadn't. Beverly had obsessed with checking on him every so often, even staying at Frank's place each night so, during the darkest hours lit only by the glow of a clock, she could reach for her cane and see for herself that he was there, resting, not being chased by the unseen demons who invaded his fitful dreams. The longer she lay awake each night, the more she needed to check. Hearing her stir, Frank would offer to go check on the boy himself, but that was never enough. One quick look is all she would need.

One quick look.

That night, even in the Jacuzzi, she felt uneasy, even though at last check he lay there breathing softly, twitching occasionally, gathering his strength for the next day—the day he would finally be put on the witness stand.

"Frank," she whispered.

He squeezed her hand, floating away from his jet to press his body against hers.

"Frank," she said softly, "I don't know if you've thought much about it, but if Ruth gets put away for a long time, some decisions will have to be made about Kevin."

"Yeah, I know," he said quietly.

"Listen, Frank," she continued. "Don't feel pressured. I want you to know that you have a choice. Maybe you *do* want to take on long-term responsibility for a teenager; maybe you don't. But don't worry about Kevin because, well, I'm ready to take him, too. If you want to be his foster dad until he grows up and goes off on his own, that would be wonderful. But if not, don't feel like you would be abandoning him. We could say we both wanted him, but that with your business and your trips up to Cheboygan, it would be better for him to stay at my place. That way, we could say he's helping look out for a recovering lady who needs a little help in case she falls or whatever. Kevin *will* be cared for, so don't feel trapped." With that, she fell quiet.

After a minute, Frank pulled her close, whispering just loud enough for her to hear. "Beverly, I'm a worrier. The older I get, the more I worry. The more I get hurt—or see people I love get hurt—the more I worry."

Some kind of small animal scurried across the open field, pausing near the pool, then running off toward the woods.

Now accustomed to the bubbling of the Jacuzzi, the sound faded in Beverly's mind, allowing the buzzes and chirrups and noises in the night to seem louder, even overwhelming.

Frank continued, "You know, I worry about what would happen if I, well, you know—if something happened to me. I feel better knowing Kevin won't be left alone—that you'll take care of whatever he needs. I worry about leaving *you* alone, too, but I know Kevin won't ever let *you* go, either. I want to see him back with his mother, but that won't stop me from looking out for him even after they're reunited. She may get married and present him with a ready-made dad, but I won't stop checking up on him. As long as he needs a place to live, I'll make sure he has one. If for some reason I can't, I expect you to. As far as I'm concerned, that wonderful offer you just made is your promise to do just that."

"It is, Frank. It is."

"Good. But if you think you can take him away from me—you'll have to get past me, kicking and screaming." Beverly laughed with him as he drawled, "And *you*, madam, have a bum leg, so you are *no* match for me!"

Their amusement faded as they relaxed in the swirling bubbles, their good feelings again replaced by the gravity of all they faced.

After a few minutes, Beverly whispered, "I *need* you, Frank."

"Yeah," he whispered back, nuzzling her with his face, "but not like I need you."

CHAPTER 34

People stood around the back, behind the last row. Space on a bench there in the courtroom usually got claimed at least an hour before the proceedings began each day. Frank had established a routine of paying Audrey, Ruth's friend who clerked at the local store, her boyfriend, and his friend to show up before dawn, wait in line, stake out some territory on the bench, then vacate it for him, Beverly, and Loretta to arrive at the last minute. The stress, the emotional toll, the evenings spent keeping Kevin and sometimes his young friends occupied and upbeat and focused on something other than the trial—all of this made for long days even without having to queue up so early for seats.

Mogill reminded Frank that, for Ruth Riner, the routine had grown even more arduous. Roused at 3:00 a.m. every day, she had to spend time sitting in a drunk tank before being chained and transported, only to spend more hours staring at the graffiti-scrawled wall in the cage behind the courtroom.

Frank noticed that those two television cameras evident during the first days of trial had been joined by three more, presumably in anticipation of interesting testimony once Mark Sisk and Kevin Riner took the stand. The prosecutor, whenever he had a soapbox in the media, played up the image of a criminal "mother" who victimized her own son. This whet appetites for lurid revelations beyond even the story of the murders.

During the short week before Thanksgiving, after the jury *voir dire* and final selection, he had paraded an impressive array of witnesses before the court. These included ballistics and forensics experts establishing that the gun in evidence was indeed the one that inflicted the fatal injuries. The medical examiner brought gasps from the audience with graphic descriptions and photographs of the fatal injuries. The detective-in-charge detailed the results of the trailer search, dwelling more on the "squalor" of the situation than Mogill's overruled objections could prevent. One of the search officers testified about finding what appeared to be a new three-pack of rubber gloves, one pair of which was missing and never found. He also testified that the residue another expert identified as cocaine had been found on Ruth's bedroom dresser.

By the time the experts and officers had disgorged their information, an impressive array of facts had been laid before the jury. They'd been subjected to charts and graphs, layouts of the crime scene, photographs, distance to the parked vehicle, the route taken toward Tarpon Springs, location of sighting, signal, pull-over, and arrest.

While very little of it was relevant to the issue of who pulled the trigger and the killer's intent, it nevertheless served to create an image of thoroughness, expertise, and the obvious expectation that these professional criminologists' conclusions should be assumed to be accurate unless proven otherwise. "Innocent until proven guilty" had been convoluted to "looks pretty guilty unless proven innocent."

During cross-examinations, Mogill established that the cocaine paraphernalia found smashed inside a bag in one of the trailer-park trash bins contained fingerprints of only two people: Mark Sisk and Kevin Riner. He also established that, even though the only prints on the gun were Sisk's, other things besides a rubber glove could have caused the smears. The gun had been removed from the duffel bag by a patrol officer using a plastic bag. It had been handled with plastic by no less than four other officers, and it had taken a circuitous route through the system being handled through the plastic bag in which it was ultimately sealed. One of the prosecution's experts finally admitted that the suggestive smears could just as likely have occurred through police handling.

One of the crime-scene forensics experts admitted Ruth Riner's fingerprints were found only in the *front* room of the house. Three people on the porch across the street identified Mark Sisk and Ruth Riner as the couple they saw come and go on the day of the crime. They also recognized the duffel bag alleged to have held the gun, the drugs, and some personal clothing and effects of Mark Sisk's. During cross-examination, Mogill established that all three had seen only one entry and exit, hadn't heard any shots fired, and had left the area before Sisk and the defendant returned.

Mark Sisk detailed the story he'd concocted as part of his bargain, emphasizing that because he was between jobs and in need of assistance—especially a place to stay—he'd been particularly vulnerable to her pressure to line up customers and suppliers so she could support her appetite for illegal drugs. Asked why he didn't leave the situation, he explained how much he cared for Ruth, how much he wanted to help her straighten out her life, and foremost, the concern he'd developed for the young boy to whom he'd taken a liking. Worried about the abuse he suspected various men had inflicted on Kevin, he was concerned that something untoward might be going on between mother and son. The latter was supported by hearsay claims that she had told him she enjoyed having the boy sometimes sleep with her, and by once seeing them sleep together in a highly suggestive position on the living room couch. Mogill objected vigorously to this topic, but the judge allowed the questions as a way to establish the character of the defendant. Mogill made sure his arguments were on the record for appellate review.

Two witnesses, officers who had questioned Kevin Riner at school, described him as a scared boy, traumatized by his mother's behavior. They related his stories of abuse, explaining that he'd been reluctant to talk about what happened to him after being caught stealing, that he was evasive about sleeping with his mother, and that he was embarrassed to talk about incidents of molestation that had occurred with various live-in men. He had, however, described at least one occasion in which he'd stood in the shower and posed naked for a man, only to be humiliated when the guy teased him about the size of his genitals and scarcity of pubic hair for a twelve-year-old. The officers testified that Kevin became upset and cried when describing to them how he had witnessed his mother having sex or possibly being raped on the living room floor one night. The jury blustered visibly at that revelation.

The same witnesses said Kevin also admitted that he thought his mother had drug problems, that he admitted concern about the detrimental effect of her relationships with Sisk and other men, that she had a poor record of work attendance, and that she had failed to follow through with her much-talked-about educational plans. They described how he told them about coming home the day of the murders, discovering cocaine paraphernalia, and attempting to dispose of it himself.

Mogill's cross-examination centered largely on the lack of a transcript or tape-recording from this interview. Both witnesses asserted that no recording was made, simply that a machine was there in case they needed it. They also denied that Kevin requested repeatedly to have Frank present during questioning, or pressuring the boy to go along with their theory of his mother as a drug-dealer. When questioned in detail, both remembered Kevin telling them about discovering his bedroom disheveled, which prompted him to check and notice his money was missing.

Cross-examination of Sisk had been postponed until after the holiday break, the same day the only unquestioned witness on the prosecutor's list, Kevin Riner, would likely take the stand. Mogill treated Sisk, in particular for the benefit of the jury, with mild contempt and mock amusement. He put a lot of emphasis, over the objections of the prosecutor, on the deal that was cut to save him from first-degree charges, a possible death penalty, and the likelihood of life in prison that would have come with second-degree convictions had a sentencing agreement not been included.

Sisk got caught off guard when Mogill read him a list of people's names, put together through a lot of legwork by Private Investigator Rob Buchanan, which detailed other women and several men the witness had stayed with besides Ruth and Kevin during the six months prior to the murders. Confronted with names and details, he had to admit that he had slept at the Riner's not more than a few days per week and was having sexual relations with at least one other woman. As Mogill hammered him with questions about his other relationships, Sisk retreated so much from his depiction of a caring man looking out for a drug-addicted mother and helpless son that his credibility started to crumble. Mogill carefully maneuvered him into looking like a predator taking advantage of as many people and situations as he could juggle. Buchanan's list gave the attorney a lot to work with; Ruth was lucky that somebody had paid for an investigator on her behalf.

When Mogill asked Sisk about Ruth's use of rubber gloves, the prosecutor's explanation for his prints being the only ones on the gun, he explained how she'd brought them along, used them during the shooting, and discarded them out the window during the drive. He couldn't explain why a woman who so carefully contrived the use of rubber gloves would deign to toss them out a car window—an obviously reckless method of disposal. In answer to more questions, Sisk asserted that she had donned the gloves in the car before going into the house. Mogill asked why somebody wearing something unusual, for example those blue rubber gloves, wouldn't cause suspicion in the home's occupants. Sisk explained that Ruth's gloved hands were in her pockets as she walked into the drug house.

Later, when asked to describe the gloves, he mentioned that they were blue. Mogill showed him the three-pack of yellow-colored gloves, now missing one pair, which had been recovered from the defendant's cabinet, then asked if they were the same style, except for color, that she had worn that night. Stuck with his description that the gloves were blue, a suggestion intentionally planted by Mogill, Sisk had to admit that the gloves "didn't look the same." Mogill also wondered why, if the shooter took such precautions to wear gloves, Sisk had never bothered to clean his own prints off the gun. His assertion of being dazed by the events that day was the best he could muster, something that obviously didn't impress the jury.

Further questioning established that Sisk couldn't or wouldn't provide the names of dealers who had accepted money from Ruth in exchange for drugs. The prosecutor objected, but Mogill prevailed because Sisk's earlier assertion that Ruth had generated drug-sale profits and spent the proceeds on her own habit allowed the attorney a chance to discredit this information. Ultimately, if he or Ruth had purchased drugs—ever—the jury would have to take Sisk's word for it. No corroboration or supporting evidence would be forthcoming.

Mogill also played around with the issue of Kevin's missing money several times, bringing it up, dropping it, then casually coming back to it. It was Sisk's claim that Ruth knew Kevin had money stashed in the bedroom, and that she was the one who took it for drugs. He explained that her expectation was to "borrow" the money for the initial buy with the intention of replacing it before the boy discovered it missing. He couldn't explain how she intended to replace it since the quantity of drugs purchased was insufficient to resell for that kind of profit. Sisk surmised that she must have known then of her intention to commit the robbery that resulted in murders.

Later, Mogill asked him about this issue again, wondering if Ruth had ever told him where Kevin's money was hidden. He said she hadn't. Asked who messed up the boy's room with what appeared to be a search, he guessed it must have been Ruth. Sisk stammered a lot, having no good answer as to why Ruth would plan to sneak the money, intending to replace it before its absence was discovered, yet leave the room obviously torn up from the search.

Overall, Mogill had managed to punch enough holes in the various testimonies to cast doubts on the prosecutor's theories. Still, though, too much hung on Mark Sisk's statements which, though roughed up in places, nonetheless still stood fairly solidly against Ruth Riner. Much would depend on using Kevin to help break down the image that had been painted of her thus far. The state would use him against her; Mogill would use him to help her.

Ruth's attorney told Frank he hoped this thirteen-year-old was up to the task. He said he didn't want to put the already-traumatized teen through one more harrowing experience, but knew he had to—for his own good, to help his mother.

It was time to hear the prosecutor's last witness.

"What does that mean?" Beverly asked Frank as they and Loretta followed the crowd into the hallway.

"It means Kevin can't go out to lunch with us. The prosecutor wants him kept in that room with something to eat so nobody can fill him in on Sisk's testimony."

"But he will be next, right after lunch?"

"Yeah, he's the next witness," Frank explained. "Wait here. I'll go tell him why he has to stay, then offer to bring some food back."

Frank went down the side hallway to the room where Kevin had been sequestered. He opened the door and startled his young friend. Kevin practically jumped, his big hazel eyes wide with apprehension.

"Whoa, buddy, it's just me. I'm here to tell you they're taking an early lunch break today, but you have to stay here. You can't go with us—"

Kevin looked stricken. It was obvious the stress and fear and waiting were keeping him pushed to his limits.

"Why can't I go with you?"

A woman pushed her way into the room, casting a disdainful glare at Frank. "Excuse me, this witness is sequestered," she told Frank. Then to the boy, she turned saccharin, asking, "Hi, Kevin, remember me?"

Kevin's expression hardened. "Yeah."

"Well, you and I are going to have lunch together before you go into court."

"Frank," Kevin asked, "can't I go with *you?*"

"No, son. They don't want you discussing what happened in the courtroom with anybody."

"Not even her?"

"No, nobody at all."

"Then," Kevin offered, "check back with me after lunch and I'll tell you if she tried to talk about the case or not." He gestured toward the woman.

"Oh, she won't—" Frank started.

"You can't trust her, Frank. She's a sneak and a liar."

"But Kevin—" she started.

Frank's expression hardened. "Why do you say that?"

"She's the one who came to my school, the one who's lying about there not being a tape. She's the one who wouldn't let me have *you* there."

Frank eyed the woman for a moment. She stammered words to put a happy face on a very awkward situation.

"You don't feel safe being left alone with her, Kevin?" Frank asked.

"No, I don't want to be near her."

Frank pushed the door back and opened his arm in a gesture to the boy. "Come with me, Kevin."

"But you can't—" she protested. Frank simply shot her the meanest glare he could muster, cutting her off mid-sentence. She followed the two of them down the hallway where they caught up with Mogill.

"Hello, Kevin," Mogill exclaimed. "Frank, he can't—"

"I know, I know. But they sent this woman." He gestured behind himself without turning to acknowledge her presence. "She's the one who questioned him at school. It's a dirty trick, intimidating him just before he testifies by putting him with the one who already terrified and manipulated him in the past."

Mogill shot the woman a glare of his own. She squirmed uncomfortably, but wouldn't retreat. "We better go see the judge," Mogill explained, leading Frank, the woman, and Kevin toward the chambers. The judge answered the door wearing street clothes and his hat, obviously ready to go out. Mogill explained the situation. The judge also glared at the woman for a moment, then told her to go get the prosecutor. She brought him back right away.

"What's happening?" Kevin asked.

"Your name is Kevin Riner?" the judge asked.

"Yes, sir."

"Kevin, you need to understand that I granted the prosecutor's request to keep you sequestered until you testify this afternoon so nobody would have the chance to tell you what happened in court today." Then to the group he said, "Well, this is an awkward situation. We don't have time to call in somebody from Children's Services who—" He glared at the woman. "—Who he's comfortable with." Then to Mogill and the prosecutor, he asked. "Do either of you have lunch plans you can't change?"

"I can be available," the prosecutor replied.

"However you would like to work it, judge," Mogill responded.

"Good, then you both agree—and we'll mention it on the record when we reconvene—that all three of us will take the witness out to lunch. First one to mention *anything* about the case picks up the tab. The second mention gets somebody a contempt citation. Is everybody agreed?"

Both attorneys nodded. The judge looked at the boy, eyebrows raised.

Kevin's face brightened. "Sure! Um, yes sir," he replied.

"Good then." He turned to the others. "My wife will be joining us today. Since we have no grandkids of our own, we can't let her get too attached to our young Mr. Riner—she may not let us bring him back," he joked, grinning and tousling the boy's hair. Kevin smiled back, moving closer to the judge as if slipping under his protective wing.

"Their plan backfired," Mogill explained to Frank after lunch. "The judge really liked Kevin. He's not going to let them make this hard on him."

Kevin Riner had always been a smallish boy, not skinny so much as appearing to be sized a year or two younger than his age peers. Frank remembered him as far back as the age of eight when the little guy started pestering to let him help move into the condo. Working for him ever since, the youngster made up for his size limitations with an inexhaustible supply of energy and undaunting determination. Now at thirteen, he'd barely reached five feet tall, but he was starting to assume a gangly shape, filling out somewhat in the process. His cracking voice hovered more often than not in a lower register. His boyish language and demeanor gave way to a more mature presence. Frank started to think of him as a big guy—a teenager, at least—and not so much a kid anymore. When the door opened and a court officer led Kevin—wide-eyed, nervous, eyes darting back and forth between his mother and Frank, desperately seeking reassurance—into the courtroom, never did he look smaller to Frank than he did at that moment.

Led to the witness box, Kevin managed a weak smile. He glanced at the judge, who smiled and nodded back. The bailiff came forward to take Kevin's oath, but the judge interrupted him and, with a protective air, took a moment to explain to the boy what he could expect.

"Listen, son, some people will ask you questions, and we need you to tell the truth—which I'm sure you will—so you just relax and don't worry about a thing. You're not in trouble here. You just pay attention and answer the questions. If you need to take a break or it gets too hard on you, you just tell *me*, and I'll see to it."

"Yes, sir," Kevin said meekly, sitting forward, closer to the microphone. The bailiff adjusted it so Kevin could sit back in a more relaxed position. Looking over at his mother, he smiled and nodded, mouthing the words *I love you* to her. With moist eyes, Ruth smiled back, nodding her head. Frank appreciated how good it must feel for her to be in the same room with her boy—no phones, no video screens, together.

Kevin looked to Frank while the bailiff finished the oath. Frank smiled and made a fist, holding it to his chest. Kevin nodded back, then smiled meekly at Beverly and Loretta. It seemed like all three adults had to struggle against urges to rush forward, scoop him up protectively, and whisk him away to some happy place.

Frank noticed how much Kevin's presence moved the jury. Several of the women, in particular, looked as though they, too, wanted to put their arms around the boy and protect him from these harsh proceedings. Mogill looked confident. Kevin and the judge had a strong rapport; sending in the woman who had caused him so much pain at school served to focus the boy's energy and give him a healthy sense of rage and injustice.

Before the prosecutor could begin questioning, Rob Buchanan came in, dressed better than usual, and passed a note to Mr. Mogill. The attorney looked very pleased, nodding to Buchanan and winking at Frank. Frank got up, followed Buchanan out to the hallway for a minute, then returned looking very pleased himself.

The prosecutor raced quickly through a series of questions. He had to rely too much on cutting Kevin off after simple "yes" or "no" responses, not allowing the boy to explain himself. Kevin grew obviously frustrated with this treatment, and so did the jury. One lady on the panel even mumbled, "Let the boy *talk*" under her breath at one point, earning a sharp look from the judge.

"Do you remember telling the officers who talked to you at school that your mother had a drug problem?" the prosecutor asked.

"Yes, um—"

"And that you worried about her a lot?"

"Well," Kevin said, "I guess—"

"Is that 'yes' then?"

"Um, yeah."

"And you told them that your mother never had enough money, and that sometimes you even gave her your own money, which you earned working for Frank Tanyon?"

"Yeah, but—"

"And that you gave her money on a regular basis?"

"Yeah—"

"And that you took care of family finances more than she did?"

"Yeah, but—"

"Did you tell them that if she spent money on illegal drugs, you had no idea where it could have come from?"

"Yeah."

"Did she ever get an extra job or do other things to earn money?"

"She did people's hair sometimes. Um, ladies she knew."

"But nothing other than that?"

"No."

"You told the officers at school that your mother did drugs every day?"

"Yeah, but—"

"That *is* what you told them?"

"Yeah, but—"

"And that you found cocaine paraphernalia in her bedroom?"

"Yeah." Kevin looked down, fidgeting nervously.

"You remember discussing with the officers that the stuff you found in her bedroom was for her to smoke crack?"

"Well yeah, but—"

"And this was the same day she got arrested?"

Kevin looked down again, picking at something imaginary on his pantleg. "Yeah," he said quietly.

"You need to speak up."

"Yeah," he said louder.

"You watched your mother having sex with strange men at your house?" the prosecutor stabbed.

"Object, your honor." Mogill jumped to his feet. "The prosecutor is trying to malign the defendant. This is not relevant to the events of the night in question."

"Your honor," the prosecutor rebutted, "it goes to the character of the defendant. The defense, through cross-examination, has tried to malign the character of witness Mark Sisk, implying that Ruth Riner is not the type of person he described. If the jury must weigh the credibility of witnesses, then I need to support Mr. Sisk's characterizations of her."

The judge pondered this for a moment, looking at Kevin almost apologetically before announcing, "I'll allow it."

The prosecutor repeated, "You saw your mother having sex?"

"Um, yeah, but—"

"Where?"

"In the living room, but that was—that was—" Kevin stammered. He wiped his eyes, fighting to retain his composure. The jury looked at him piteously, then glared at Ruth sitting at the defense table.

"The man she was having sex with finally told you to go to bed, is that right?"

"Yeah, but—"

"How old were you?"

Kevin didn't reply. He kept his head down, picking at his pants, wiping his eyes, and starting to sniffle.

"How old were you?" the prosecutor demanded, showing no compassion for the now-tearful boy.

"Um . . . about ten, I guess," he said meekly.

"You slept with your mom sometimes?"

"Only sometimes—"

"Were you uncomfortable about sleeping with her?"

"Well, no. It wasn't—"

"Do you remember telling the officers about posing naked for one of your mother's lovers?"

"Not posing—"

"You were standing in the shower and he was looking at you naked?"

"Well, yeah, but—"

"He was looking at your genitals and commenting on them?"

"Yeah, but—"

"What was he saying?"

Kevin kept his face down, blushing, embarrassed. "He was teasing me, saying I had a little penis." He paused and wiped tears from his eyes again. "And that I didn't have no hair down there yet."

"How old were you then?"

"Um, that was before I got puberty—when I was twelve."

"You were embarrassed, weren't you?"

Kevin nodded.

"Yes or no?"

"Yeah."

"You went to your bedroom and cried, didn't you?"

"Yeah."

"Where was your mother?"

"Asleep."

"Passed out from drinking too much?"

He nodded.

"Yes or no?"

"Yes."

"Mark Sisk had been staying at your house occasionally for at least six months, is that correct?"

"Um, yeah, I think so."

"And people he knew came over sometimes, right?"

"Yeah."

"And sometimes people your mother knew came over when he was there, right?"

"Yeah."

"A lot of these times, your mother used to send you outside or over to Frank's to play, is that right?"

"Well, yeah, but—"

"Mark Sisk carried this duffel bag in and out with him usually, is that true?"

"Yeah."

"Did your mom ever try to get you to use some of her drugs?"

"No! Never. She used to tell me never to start—"

"How about her friends? Did any of them ever try to get you to take drugs?"

"Um, no—"

"Didn't you tell the officers that you smoked marijuana once?"

"Oh, yeah."

"Who gave that to you?"

"It was this guy that stayed with us once. His name was Todd. When my mom was at work and he woke up, he lit a joint and tried to get me to smoke some. I pretended to but didn't really inhale. I was scared."

"How old were you then?"

"Um, eleven I guess."

The prosecutor paused, then leaned on the front of the witness box. Speaking more softly, he asked, "Kevin, did you ever plead with your mother to quit drugs?"

Kevin's jaw trembled, fresh tears welling up. He nodded.

"Kevin, yes or no, did you plead with her for many years to stop?"

"Yes."

The prosecutor turned toward the jury, a satisfied expression across his face, announcing, "No further questions, your honor."

"We'll take a fifteen-minute recess," the judge decided. Then, more quietly to Kevin, he offered, "Why don't you come with me, son? You can wait in my conference room. You can relax a little and use the bathroom if you like."

Everybody stood. Kevin dutifully followed the judge out, hiding his face, not even glancing toward Frank or his mother.

"Mr. Tanyon! You're the boy's foster parent—did you know he'd been molested?" A print reporter accosted Frank. Several more crowded around him in the packed hallway outside the courtroom. Beverly and Loretta stood by awkwardly. A man with television camera on his shoulder bustled over, turning on a bright light. A well-coiffed woman held a microphone out for his response. He motioned for the women to move away, so Loretta helped Beverly—still using her cane and prosthesis—and they found seats on a bench.

"He was never molested," Frank explained to the gathering horde of media.

"But he said—"

"He said somebody teased him once in the bathroom. That's all he said. If somebody was hurting him, he would've told me, and I would've done something about it."

"What about his mother giving him drugs?"

"He never said that. You need to pay better attention—"

"Mr. Tanyon, did you know that his mother was having sex in front of him?"

"All he described was one incident, which was against her will, I believe, and yes he told me about it, and I helped him and gave him information for his mother in case she wanted to follow up with charges—"

"Mr. Tanyon, if Ms. Riner goes to prison, will you try to adopt her son?"

"I don't expect to see his mother get convicted. After all, she's innocent." Frank saw Mogill nodding and smiling at the besieged media target.

"Won't you be worried about the boy if he goes back to his mother?"

"Not in the least. That's all the questions for now."

Mogill waved the media away, promising he'd comment after the verdicts, then escorted Frank and the women down to the basement snack shop for a cold drink before returning to the courtroom.

Frank asked Mogill, "How's he doing?"

"Couldn't be better."

"You take care of my boy," Frank said.

Beverly took Mogill's hand into her own, squeezing gently. "Please try to make it easy for him. He's so young."

Mogill nodded, whispering back, "I'll do the best I can, Ms. Herndon. But remember, he's not a little boy right now. This afternoon, standing up for his mom, he's the biggest man in that room."

CHAPTER 35

Kevin had regained his composure during the break. He retook his position on the witness stand, looked with confidence toward Frank and Beverly, then gazed at his mother. He mouthed *I love you* to her, looked up to the judge, then steeled himself for more questions.

Mr. Mogill walked over in front of him, smiling at him briefly, but maintaining an overall grave demeanor. "Hello, Kevin. Are you holding up okay?"

"Yeah, I guess—for a guy whose mother's locked up."

"Kevin, I'm going to give you a chance to explain some of the answers to your questions."

"Good," Kevin observed, shooting a poisonous look toward the prosecution's table.

"Let's start with some of the facts you gave. When you say your mother *used* to take drugs and that you worried about her, what were you talking about?"

"Cigarettes mostly, and she used to drink beer too much, too."

"So by 'drugs' you mean cigarettes and alcohol?"

"Well, yeah, they're drugs. Frank explained that to me when I was in the fifth grade. They're just legal drugs, is all. They're both more additic—*addictive*," he pronounced carefully, his voice cracking, "—they're more addictive than most drugs, and both of them cause a lot more getting sick and dying than most of the illegal ones."

"So you were worried about your mom's use of tobacco and alcohol?"

"Yeah. She's been trying to quit cigarettes ever since I talked to her about it a couple years ago. She really tried hard and did pretty good a couple times, but she always started again. She never gave up, though." He looked over toward his mother, set his jaw, and offered her a tight smile. "She quit in jail. She's gone seven months without a cigarette and says she don't have urges anymore. She quit for good."

"And the alcohol?"

"Um, when I was little, she used to drink vodka and stuff, but she knew it wasn't good for her, so she mostly quit all that and just drank beer ever since. She used to drink a couple usually, but she was making it less and less. She was working on stopping that completely, too."

"So you had no other drug worries about your mom?"

"Just those. I love my mom and want her to be around for me and my kids and my grandkids for a long long time."

Mogill looked disdainfully at the prosecutor for a moment. Then to Kevin, he asked, "Did you ever see illegal drugs in your house?"

"Just that time Todd smoked that joint. Later when I told my mom, she kicked him out for good. I never saw him again."

"What about cocaine the night of the murders?"

"All I saw was that pipe and stuff. I knew what it was from TV, but I never saw no actual drugs. What those police—what that lady said—" He gestured toward the woman seated in the courtroom. "—She kept telling me my mom had drugs there, so when they asked me later, that's when I told 'em that. I believed what they said. Good thing I know better now."

"Were you aware of any drug-selling going on in your house?"

Kevin looked thoughtful for a minute. "Um, no. I don't think so. I know my mom couldn't have 'cause I was around too much. I wondered what was going on with Mark one time when he had two guys over. My mom got mad at him. Later, when I was in bed, I heard 'em fighting. She kept telling him *not in my house*, so I knew he done something that wasn't cool. She kicked him out that night. He didn't come back around for a couple of weeks. I heard her tell him when he came back that he could only stay if he was straight. He was bein' a lot cooler. I heard him say, 'Yeah, I know takin' care of the kid is the most important thing to you'."

"What do you think they were talking about?"

"Object, your honor," the prosecutor protested. "Calls for conjecture."

"Your honor, the prosecution asked the witness to draw conclusions. To clarify this, the jury needs to ascertain how he arrived at those."

The judge allowed it, so Mogill asked the question again.

"I don't know. It didn't seem to matter 'cause when I told Frank, he said it sounded like Mom was taking care of it and that I should let him know if I hear anything else or get worried about anything."

"Frank's been a pretty good guy to have around, huh?"

Kevin looked at Frank, his hardened features softening. "Yeah," he said.

"What happened with your mom's money?"

"When I was little and she gave me an allowance, she used to let me help pay the bills and figure out the checkbook and stuff. Frank always taught me about math and money, too, and I'm pretty good—I even help Frank run his company—" he added with pride, "but anyway, up until she got arrested, Mom always brought home her paychecks and I helped her when we paid the bills. I always knew how much we had and where it got spent. She might save up money for a jacket or shoes and stuff for herself, but she usually spent anything extra on me."

"Where did you get your own money?"

"Um, from Frank mostly. I also did yard work and stuff for other people, but mostly Frank. I been workin' for him since I was little. I know he could get bigger guys to do stuff and maybe even not pay as much, but he always gave me jobs and helped me out 'cause he, um, you know."

"Because he loves you?"

Kevin blushed slightly. "Yeah."

"He's loved you for a long time?"

"Well, um, he didn't actually say it until this year, but I knew before that." He looked apologetically toward Frank, like he had revealed something personal.

"And what did you do with that money?"

"Mostly bought things for myself, like some video games. And I used to help out my mom when we had unespected—unexpected—" He struggled with the word, squeaking and looking chagrined. "—When something came up like having to fix the car or pay the dentist when she broke her tooth. She wrote it down and paid back as much as she could when she got her check." He looked thoughtful. "I guess the rest was—I used to buy her presents, plus I was savin' up for something."

"For what?" Mogill wondered.

"I was gonna surprise her when I had enough for her cozzumtology school. It's eight-hundred dollars, but that don't matter now 'cause Linda got her the stuff and she finished it while she was in jail."

"Linda?"

"Yeah," he replied, looking down at his lap and appearing very sad. "She was my friend—Beverly's daughter—but she got killed in an accident."

"Beverly—your foster mother before Frank got approved to be your foster father?"

"Yeah," he answered, looking out to Beverly as if sorry for reminding her—for reminding everybody that Linda was gone.

"Did you ever see your mother have or spend money you couldn't explain?"

"Oh, no. Never."

"What about this duffel bag?" Mogill asked, walking over and pointing to the bag on the exhibit table. "Whose was this?"

"That was Mark's."

"Mark Sisk?"

"Yeah."

"Did you ever see your mother go into it, take anything out, take it anywhere, or have anything to do with it?"

"No."

"Did Mark ever leave it at your house when he wasn't there?"

"Um, no. He always took it with him."

"Do you know what was in it?"

"I peeked once when he was asleep. It was a bunch of clothes and toothbrush and some pictures of people and 'lectric razor and nail clippers and a lighter and, um—" He thought for a minute. "I think that's all."

"Did Mark Sisk know about you working for Frank?"

"Um yeah, he was always askin' how much I got paid and trying to get me to show him my money when I got home. I didn't trust him. That's the main reason my money was hidden—'cause of him and burglars and stuff."

"Your mom didn't know where it was hidden?"

"No. I didn't want her to see how much it was 'cause I wanted to surprise her when I had enough for the class."

Changing the line of questioning, Mogill explained, "Kevin, we heard from other witnesses about what you told the officers who questioned you at school." Kevin glanced at the woman again. Mogill continued, "Tell us what happened that day."

"Your honor," the prosecutor interrupted, "I must object."

"The defense is entitled to examine the circumstances and methods used when collecting evidence," Mogill countered. The judge allowed him to continue.

Kevin answered, "Those police showed up and took me out of class to ask me a bunch of questions. I didn't want to, not without Frank being there. I kept askin' for Frank, but they wouldn't let me."

"They didn't explain that you didn't have to talk to them, and that you had the right to have your guardian present?"

"No, they was threatening me, saying I'd have to go to the boys' ranch if I didn't cooperate."

Mogill looked out at the officers, a disgusted expression painted across his face. He shook his head, glanced helplessly at the jury, then continued. "What were they asking you about?"

"Mostly they kept tellin' me stuff. They told me my mom was dealin' drugs, and that she was smokin' cocaine, and that she had a problem and needed me to help. They kept trying to get me to say things. When I didn't want to, they kept promising that if I helped 'em they'd get my mom some help—but if I *didn't* help them, then she'd be in bad trouble and I might get taken away and sent somewhere I could never see her—" His face clouded up. He looked over to his mother for reassurance. "—That I would never see her again," he whispered. He wiped his eyes, but kept his composure.

"Kevin, even if it brings back bad feelings—"

"Object—"

"—No matter how you feel," Mogill rephrased, "what happened to you that day?"

"They kept scaring me. I was *real* scared. I needed to go to the bathroom real bad, and I was feeling sick, and I just wanted Frank to be there 'cause I'm never scared when I know he's there . . ." He paused, breathed hard several times, then continued more quietly. "I went to the principal's bathroom and started throwin' up. That's when they finally quit and left me alone."

Mogill shook his head. So did several jurors. A current of pity for the child and disdain for such hardball police tactics swept through and continued to permeate the courtroom.

"Do you remember telling the police about somebody looking at you naked?"

"Yeah," he said meekly, his eyes cast down toward his lap.

"Did you tell them who it was?"

"No."

"Who was it?"

"Mark. Mark Sisk."

"What happened that day?"

"He was sitting on the toilet when I finished my shower. Mom was running the washing machine so the shower was kinda cold, and when I was standing there getting ready to get my towel, he teased me saying cold water makes guys get little. Then he was sayin' I was so little anyway that my, you know, might disappear and I'd be a girl. I told him I wasn't no girl, and he said if I didn't start growin' hair down there pretty soon I wouldn't be no man, either. I told him to leave me alone."

"Did he touch you?"

"No."

"Was that the only time he saw you naked?"

"No, he used to come in and pee or whatever sometimes when I was in the shower. I didn't care. He's just a guy."

"Did your mom do that, too?"

"No! Not since I was little. She's a girl."

"Did anybody every try to touch you in ways that weren't okay?"

"No," he answered, looking directly at Mogill. "I thought so after those police talked to me. They kept saying I was molested when Mark was teasin' me."

"Why did you cry that day Mark teased you?"

"Um, well," he started, casting his eyes down again, "he kinda scared me, I guess. I wanted to get puberty, and I got worried maybe I wouldn't when he said that."

"Did you tell your mom about this?"

"No."

"Did you tell anybody?"

"Not really. I asked Frank about it—I didn't tell him Mark was teasin' me—but I asked Frank if sometimes boys don't get puberty and stuff. He explained the whole thing and told me don't worry about it, that some boys might be older than others, but everybody gets it and there was nothing to worry about. A couple of days later he had a book and we looked up stuff together. It had drawings of boys and girls and how they change and told the ages and stuff. He showed me how I was normal for my age and said it was a good question and don't ever be afraid to ask." He raised his eyes to look at Frank. "I been lucky he was willing to keep puttin' up with me." He smiled weakly.

Frank returned the smile, clenching his fist in front of his chest again, reassurance that Kevin was doing fine.

"Your honor," the prosecutor interrupted, "this is not relevant."

"Your honor," Mogill countered, "the prosecutor already opened this door by portraying Ruth Riner as a woman more interested in drugs—even to the point of murdering for them—than in providing a good life for her son. She is entitled to defend herself, to shed light on a situation distorted by investigators who would threaten a boy with losing his mother forever if he didn't go along with their twisted stories."

"Overruled. Mr. Mogill, keep it to the point."

"Thank you," Mogill replied, bristling at the prosecutor, then shaking his head just slightly and glancing at the jury.

"Kevin, did your mom ever steal?"

"No! Never. She was really against that stuff. She got real mad at me one time when I was little 'cause I stole some candy. She almost spanked me, but she started cryin'. She kept telling me for weeks that if I was gonna be a thief, then she couldn't trust me anymore. I felt so bad I decided I wouldn't ever do that again, no matter if it was right or wrong, but just 'cause I didn't want her to think I was bad." He looked thoughtful for a moment, then added, "Now I know it's wrong, but she wanted to really teach me a lesson. She sure did."

"You never saw her lose her temper?"

"No, just get mad sometimes."

"Did she ever hit you?"

"When I was real little I remember she slapped my hand when I was turning on the stove, but that's the only one I 'member."

"Did you sleep in her bed?"

"With my mom?"

"With your mother."

"Um no, not usually. I did a few times—once when I was sick and once when we thought somebody tried to break in the trailer and I got all scared. When I was little, I did sometimes when there was loud thunder and stuff. A couple times we both fell asleep on the couch. I 'member waking up on the couch once and she had her arm around me—" He grinned. "—She was *really* snoozin'. I went and got a blanket and put over us and went back to sleep. When I woke up, she was making breakfast." He looked over toward the police, adding, "That guy kept telling me my mom was bad-touching me. That's when I kinda cried and started feeling sick, but he wouldn't stop saying it." Kevin looked away, seemingly lost inside himself. Then he relaxed a little and looked back to Mogill.

"Kevin—" Mogill started softly, appearing embarrassed, like he felt uncomfortable with the next question. He looked apologetically toward the jury, then asked, "Did you ever see your mother have sex with someone?"

Kevin looked down, saying nothing. He started picking at his pantleg again, fidgeting.

"Kevin?" Mogill asked.

Kevin nodded, then closed his eyes tightly as tears squeezed out and crept down each cheek. He made no sound.

"Kevin, I know it's hard, but we need to know what happened."

"That Todd guy. He was drunk, and he—he held her down on the floor, and—and he pulled her pants down—" Kevin put an elbow on his lap, resting his forehead on one hand, covering his face with his other hand. "She was beggin' him to stop, but he pulled his pants down and he started to put his—his—" He rubbed his face. "She kept sayin' please don't, and she saw me and said I should go to bed, so I went in my bed and started crying."

"What happened after that?" Mogill asked, looking like he was on the verge of losing his own composure.

"Are you okay, son?" the judge asked. Kevin nodded his head.

"He left after that, and she came in and hugged me a long time and told me that was wrong and he was gone now and he would never come back and I shouldn't be—shouldn't be scared." He took a deep breath. "After that, Audrey came over and stayed all night. I heard them talking about calling the police or something, but Mom said she didn't want to put me through what would happen."

"Was that the end of it?"

"Um, no. I told Frank. He got real mad. *Real* mad. I 'member he hugged me and he was shaking. He offered to talk to my mom or do something about it, but I begged him not to. She didn't want nobody to know. That afternoon me and him didn't do any work. We just talked about things. It was the first time we talked about sex. He was explaining how good it can be when it's love, and don't let that bad example scare me from feelings I was gonna have and stuff. He kept sayin' that sex is only good when both people wanna have fun, but not if somebody doesn't want to or if somebody gets hurt."

"Did your mom do anything wrong that night?"

"It wasn't *her* fault," he answered indignantly. He wiped his eyes again. Mogill handed him some tissues from the box on the defense table. Kevin blew his nose loudly, causing a couple of people to chuckle. Frank noticed that some of the ladies and one of the men on the jury had red eyes, too, some dabbing them with tissues.

"Kevin, I think you've been through enough today. I think you've been through enough for your whole life, so let's wrap this up. Do you think your mother was involved in illegal drugs?"

"No," he answered confidently.

"Do you think she would steal from or rob someone?"

"No way."

"Do you think she could hurt or kill someone?"

"No."

"Do you think she's a good mother."

"Definitely."

"What makes you think she's a good mom?"

He looked pensive for a moment, then drew himself up proudly, looking at the jury, then the prosecutor, then toward Frank.

Finally, looking right at Mogill, he announced, "Because I'm her son, and *I* turned out pretty good."

"But she's not on the witness list!" protested the prosecutor, pacing around the judge's office.

"She was just found today," explained Mr. Mogill.

The judge sat behind his desk. The only other person in the room, a court reporter with audio recorder, sat in a chair off to the side. At the moment, the conversation was off the record. "How did you find her?" he asked Mogill.

"The private investigator that Frank Tanyon hired," explained Mogill, "got some leads on her when he was compiling the list of Sisk's other associates. He didn't make contact until this morning. I learned about her when he passed me a note during exams."

The judge admitted noticing that Mogill had been passed a note earlier in the day. Directing his comments to the prosecutor, he intoned, "I can't disallow a material witness simply because *your* investigation failed to locate her. I'll tell you what: I'll allow the witness to be presented as part of the defense, then if you need a recess to prepare your cross, I'll grant that. Depending on what she has to say, I may give you overnight." Then to Mogill, he asked, "Is she ready to go?"

"Well, no, your honor. She's not. I need to offer her immunity for her testimony."

"No way!" the prosecutor disagreed.

Mogill snapped back, "Oh sure, *you* can hand out immunity to buy all the witnesses you want—even letting Sisk off from what he *should* be tried for, just so you can cut deals. This woman has a legitimate concern, and I can't assure her memory will be accurate if she's compelled to testify as a hostile witness."

"I can't force the prosecutor to cut deals on your behalf," the judge said. "What *does* she have to say?"

Mogill laid out what he expected from the new witness's testimony. The judge listened attentively, nodding several times. When Mogill finished, the judge looked at the prosecutor with raised eyebrows.

"I'm not giving her immunity," he persisted.

The judge put his fingertips together, lost in thought for a moment. Finally, without looking at either man, he explained. "It is a reasonable request, in my unofficial opinion, for her to ask for immunity from any *drug* charges. It sounds like her testimony could fill an important hole in this case. If she's not allowed to speak, it seems to me that there will be a strong element of reasonable doubt. I might look very favorably on a defense motion to direct verdict of acquittal on the murder charges."

"But your honor," the prosecutor protested, "we've not heard if she's really going to testify what he says."

"Then if you want to find out, ante up. Give her the drug immunity and let's hear what she has to say."

The prosecutor squirmed for a moment, then reluctantly agreed.

"Good," the judge concluded. "Let's put this on the record."

With court proceedings recessed for the day, Frank joined the ladies in praising Kevin's performance before heading off to meet with Mogill for some last-minute, late-night planning. He also had to go out to Henry's condo later to review and sign papers he'd been putting off, so Kevin left with Loretta and Beverly.

They drove out to Tarpon Springs, stopped at the condos, and changed into comfortable clothes. After some bathroom time and a bit of primping, they went down to the sponge docks for a casual dinner. Despite Beverly's record for grabbing Kevin in the most impromptu hugs, Loretta surpassed her younger sister for a change. Young Mr. Riner was clearly the most-squeezed thirteen-year-old in all of Tarpon Springs that night. He started to feel pretty good about how things were going. The time he'd spent with the judge made him feel more confident with the system, and the faceless people trying to hurt his mother finally had a persona that didn't seem so all-powerful when pitted against Mogill.

Kevin caught Loretta off guard when he used a miniature octopus to fake some hanging snot. Beverly's cackling convinced her that it was indeed funny in a juvenile sort of way. She lightened up and, having fashioned two clam shells into a makeshift bra for herself, got into the spirit of childish fun.

Loretta remarked how much Kevin could eat, too, readily accepting her sister's explanation about hollow legs. "Oh! Well, that explains it then."

Rather than taking him home to call his friend, they stopped by Lonnie's house.

Kevin went off and regaled his buddy with courtroom accounts while the sisters chatted with Lonnie's mother. Kevin liked how Beverly was getting along with Ms. Caselow. She even invited her for dinner the following week, Lonnie included, and suggested they might like to rent a pontoon boat for an afternoon on Lake Tarpon sometime soon.

On the way back, Loretta suggested they stop for ice cream. They bought hot fudge sundaes in oversized cups at a stand along Highway 19, then decided it was too chilly outside, so they drove back to the condos and finished their treats around Beverly's dining-room table.

"You know, Kevin," Loretta pointed out, "your mom's pretty lucky."

"How?"

"She's got a good son. She must be so proud of you. I know *I* would be—even though you have that problem with things hanging out your nose."

They horsed around a little, laughed a lot, reminded each other several times how they were three of the best darn people in all of Florida, then finally started to peter out, taking turns catching the yawns.

Loretta begged off and drove back to Seminole. Beverly invited Kevin to stay, but he preferred his own room at Frank's this time, so she walked him next door, fussed over him a minute, and left him to get ready for bed.

Trying to listen for Frank, Kevin drifted off, then suddenly awoke with a start. Somebody was sitting on the side of his bed.

"Linda?"

"Hi, sleepy head. I just wanted to tell you how proud I am. You did a fine job in a very scary situation today," she whispered.

"You were there?"

"Let's just say I keep an eye on Mom."

"Linda, I wanna understand how you can appear like this."

She leaned over and kissed him gently on top of his head. "I'll come see you soon, and we'll discuss it," she promised. "I have to know I can count on you to keep whatever we talk about to yourself, though. It's important."

"Linda, you *know* you can trust me."

"Yeah," she whispered, "I know. Now you get some rest."

With that, she was gone, dissolving into a swirl of colored lights, every imaginable color dancing around the room before disappearing through the walls.

Kevin heard the garage door open and close. A minute later, Frank peeked in and, seeing Kevin's eyes open, came in and sat on the side of his bed. "Did Beverly tell you how proud of you we are?" he asked quietly.

"Yeah."

"Then I have only two things to say. The second one is good night."

"What's the first one?" Kevin asked.

Frank leaned closer, somewhat awkwardly at first. Kevin sat up and melted into him. Frank held the boy tightly for a minute, then whispered, "I've been wishing I'd said it more often, so I was glad to hear you say you've known for a long time. Now get some sleep. I'll see you in the morning."

He hurried from the room, closing the door behind him. Feeling pretty good right then, Kevin snuggled down under his bedsheet and curled up with his pillow.

Just as he was closing his eyes, he saw one last pinpoint of light, a sort of fuchsia color, very fluorescent, dancing around in the air over his bed before disappearing into the darkness.

Linda propped up a pillow and sat in bed with Beverly for a while. They talked quietly before settling into comfortable silence. They held hands, squeezing occasionally. Finally, Beverly drifted to sleep, catching only a glimpse of swirling colored lights that reflected in the shiny chrome wheelchair sitting forlornly in the corner.

The trial resumed early the next morning. Mr. Mogill kept his opening remarks brief so he could present his surprise witness early.

Rica Garza explained how she came to be in the house the day of the murders. The petite nineteen-year-old had dark skin, long dark hair, and big brown eyes that somehow seemed to look scared even when she relaxed a little. She'd come from the Miami area after a customer murdered her hooker mother. Having resisted a life of prostitution herself, she moved in with her only brother, staying in an apartment at the east end of Clearwater.

She had started to date Raul, one of the murder victims. Raul worked for the other murder victim, helping him traffic small and medium quantities of drugs—mostly cocaine and marijuana, but occasionally pills when available. On the day of the murders, she was in the house watching television with her boyfriend.

"Yes," she answered, her Hispanic accent fairly thick, "I met Mark Sisk and Ruth when they came for some rock. I went in the bedroom and waited while they was takin' care of bi'ness."

"Who made the purchase?" Mogill asked.

"The man. He the only one who go back where Raul been keeping it. She stayed in the front room. From the bedroom, I hear them argue over how big the rocks was. When they was done, they went back to the front room, and he and that woman both left."

"Was that the only time either of them were in the house?" asked the attorney.

"No, the man came back. We didn't see no car this time. When he came up the front walk carryin' that zoot-bag, Raul told me go wait in the hole.''

"The hole?"

"It was a hidin' place between the bedroom closets. The wall pulled back and two people could hide in there. It's upstairs.''

"Why send you there?"

"He said somethin' not right. Maybe somethin' goin' down.''

"What happened next?"

"I peeked out the bedroom window and seen his car parked down the street. Somebody—I think it was that woman—was sittin' in it. He was standin' on the porch, knockin' on the door.''

"Then what happened?"

"They let him in. They was in the front room, and I heard him say he needed some big ones. Raul wanted to see his money and he said not here. They went in the other room and I heard Mark say, Where's the girl? he said. Where did Rica go? he asked. They said I was gone to the store. They started arguin' about how much dope could they get and kept wantin' to see his money. Then I heard Mark tell 'em this was all the money he needs.''

"What happened next?"

"I was scared. It di'nt sound right. Then I heard a gun go off three times, and somebody started pullin' out drawers and movin' stuff, and I pulled the wall closed over me so he cou'nt find me. Then I heard him leave, and I came out and looked out the window and saw him walkin' fast up to the car. He opened the car's back door, and then he threw in that zoot-bag and got in the front seat. The woman was still in the driver seat, and they drove away.''

"What did you do next?"

"I ran down and found them both on the floor bleedin'. Raul was dead, but the other one was movin' a little, and he was bleedin' real bad.''

"Did you stay with them?"

She looked embarrassed. "No. I was real scared. I went out the back door and walked all the way back to my brother's apartment.''

"Did you tell your brother what happened?"

"He wasn't home right then. But later, when he came home, I told him, and he told me shut up and not tell no one. He's mad about me sayin' I would come here today.''

"Are you sure you heard the shots *after* you talked to the men and *before* you found them injured?"

"Yes.''

"And those were the only three shots you heard?"

"Yeah.''

"And at no time after Mark Sisk returned did you see or hear Ruth Riner come into the house?"

"Never."

"And you did *not* hear anybody else come or go—never heard the door open?"

"Nobody else was there except Mark."

"And you are sure it was him?"

"I saw him walk up—saw him on the porch. I recognized his voice from him just bein' there before that. I saw him leave and go back to the car."

"Thank you, Miss Garza. Your witness."

The judge granted the motion for directed verdicts, acquitting Ruth Riner of both murder charges. He let the weapons and drug charges go to the jury, giving instructions for several lesser-included verdicts, thus giving the panel the option of finding her guilty on those or lesser charges.

Ruth nearly fainted when the murder charges got dismissed. Frank and Beverly went down the hall to give Kevin the news. Expecting to see the boy happy, Frank was surprised to see him take a deep breath, his eyes welling up, a single tear crawling down each cheek.

"I thought he'd look pleased," Frank whispered to Beverly.

"He is," she said, putting her arms around the boy and rocking him gently. "Can't you tell?"

CHAPTER 36

The court recessed for the weekend without verdicts on the remaining charges. Lonnie pulled the now-traditional overnighter with Kevin Friday night. They watched the news reports with Frank—including shots of Kevin on the witness stand—then spent a good bit of their time on the phone with school friends who called to express congratulations on the dismissal of the murder counts.

Frank asked the boys if they would arrange with Ms. Caselow for Kevin to sleep over at Lonnie's house Saturday night. She agreed, so he convinced Beverly to set aside the evening for just the two of them, promising to take her someplace for dinner and entertainment.

Frank roused the boys early Saturday morning, hired them as laborers for the day, and put them to work. By late afternoon, he dropped them at Lonnie's, checked in with Beverly, and went home to fancy himself up for the lady of his life. He selected his favorite sweater because, as he had warned her, they might have to wait outside.

As six o'clock approached, Beverly answered a call from Frank. Checking to see how soon she would be ready, he said he had to run out one more time for about fifteen minutes, then would swing by to pick her up. At more like twenty minutes, he called from his cellphone, asking her to come out on her front porch. She smiled, caught up in the mystery, amused by how seriously he was treating their first evening out in more than a month. With Kevin tucked away at his friend's house, no place to be early the next morning, her leg and foot feeling so much better the past few days, she felt a giddy-schoolgirl pre-prom excitement.

Silly me, she thought. Far from fading over time, Frank's attentions had a way of making her feel more excited, more alive . . . yes, more content than she had in a long time.

She stepped out onto the porch and looked up in time to see a shiny white limousine gliding down the private road. It circled officiously, coming to a stop adjacent to her walkway. A long-coated chauffeur stepped out, then opened a passenger door so Frank could emerge. Carrying a small box in one hand, he approached the porch deferentially, bowing graciously and drawling, "If it please the lady, a delicate corsage, though it pales to thine own beauty."

She giggled, then drawled back with an uneducated affectation, "Okey dokey, young feller, but if'n you don't feed me good, then I may be havin' to eat these here purty flowers."

He stepped up, opened the box, and removed the arrangement, placing it gently on her wrist. She caught her breath, looking from him to the corsage and back again.

Forgetting her character, she whispered, "Oh Frank, it's beautiful." Holding it up to the sunlight, she admired the arrangement of Australian pansy orchids and several exotic flowers she couldn't name, arranged in the shape of a butterfly with jeweled eyes, set on a latching bracelet of white gold. On closer inspection, she could see the bracelet was engraved with a parade of swirling butterflies.

Stepping beside her, he crooked his arm. She placed her hand inside his elbow and walked with him, her limp only barely noticeable, until he handed her inside the elegant chariot. She had chosen to leave the cane at home. Tonight, if she needed support, Frank would be there for her.

A chilled bottle of her favorite wine, a cabernet souvignon, waited for them. He poured each a glass, offering the toast, "Here's to me, the luckiest man alive!"

She giggled, took a long sip, and countered, "And to the gimpy harlot he's chosen to indulge his basest pleasures for the evening."

As the car drove toward Tampa, they finished their glasses and set them aside. She cuddled up next to him, carefully placing her butterflied wrist in his lap. He picked up a remote control and filled their private world with the symphonic movement "Venus: The Bringer of Peace" from Gustav Holst's suite *The Planets*. He stroked her hair gently and apologized.

"What could you possibly feel sorry for, Frank?"

"For not giving you the attention you deserve, fair lady. I have been too busy to attend to your every desire."

"Oh don't be silly," she said, resting her head against his arm.

"But really . . . I'm an old fellow and, Lord knows, you're a *really* old lady—ouch!" She got him with a well-targeted pinch. "I thrust you into my business and legal problems, I got you in the middle of playing mom—especially at a time when you were so awfully hurt . . ." He paused for a moment, feeling a sting of pain over the loss of Linda. "I've given so much attention to Kevin—"

"Frank, you just hush. I wasn't looking to find another man. I liked you and thought you might be a good friend, somebody to spend time with, maybe look out for each other as we grow old—especially with you aging so much faster than me, by the way—" Before he could protest, she put a finger to his lips and continued, "Frank, you didn't hesitate to help me get my affairs in order, and all of what you did to help me with—um, with Linda." Her voice cracked, but she continued, speaking more softly. "It's just, well, anybody who'll forget about his own problems long enough to take care of a boy who needs him and an old lady who needs him—well, he's a *very* special man. And if that kinda guy says he likes little ol' me, well, then *I'm* the lucky one. So pour me another glass, gramps, and let's toast *me* this time."

They drank some more, Beverly feeling a warm glow, igniting a tentative fire that spread tingles whenever they touched. After they finished the second glass, he turned her face up gently and tentatively—as if holding back a torrent that might sweep them both away—then kissed her lightly. They held each other and rode on in bliss.

The car pulled into a turnoff on the causeway so they could watch the sunset. The exquisite panorama left them mesmerized. Eventually, the car started again, heading into Tampa. After a while, the driver announced, "We are arriving, sir."

The limousine stopped at the top of the winding drive that led down to the yacht club. Frank picked up his phone, pressed a button and, speaking into the receiver, said "I'm in love—you better hold my calls."

The car moved slowly down the drive, stopping at the far end of the marina lot, adjacent to the waterfront boardwalk leading to the gazebo where they sat the first night they spent together. The driver asked, "Would you like to go for a walk?"

"Wouldst thou accompany me?" Frank asked Beverly.

"Just don't break into a sprint."

The chauffeur let them out, then got back in the front, shutting off the engine and extinguishing the lights. It was very dark out there, but with Frank holding her corsaged hand, his other arm around her for extra support, she felt safe. What a beautiful night, warm with only a slight breeze drifting across the water. The lights reflecting from the club's main building rippled gently across the surface. He led her to the gazebo from an odd angle, stopping below three steps, turned her toward the tree-lined greens, then stepped behind her and encircled her with both arms. She melted into him and then, to her amazement, watched as each of the trees, one at a time, came alive with what seemed like millions of twinkling white pinpoints of light.

There! There! Over there!

The trees kept lighting until, except for the rippling water at their backs, the entire world ceased to exist, lost somewhere in the distance beyond an endless horizon of sparkles. Beverly felt a lump in her throat while her eyes fluttered and grew moist.

Then! The gazebo lit up with a million more sparkles, this time in every color imaginable, twinkling slightly at first, then faster and faster as the endless strings of Christmas bulbs warmed up. Amid the sea of light she could see a tuxedoed waiter standing beside an elegantly set table—fine china, silver service, sterling candle holders, a beautiful centerpiece of cut flowers. With a flourish, the waiter lit each of the six candles, turned the wine bottle chilling in its silver stand, and stood at attention, ready to serve.

Overcome, Beverly started to cry softly. Frank stood solid, holding her tightly, gently yet firm, tenderly yet supportive. He produced a handkerchief from somewhere, and after she dabbed her eyes, he handed her up onto the gazebo. The waiter held their chairs while they took their seats.

Rising softly, growing stronger and louder, then flowing all around them, the pi-ano stylings of Chick Corea wafted from unseen stereo speakers hidden among the trees. The melody flowed beautifully, the trees sparkled, the gazebo twinkled, the can-dles flickered, and Frank's eyes shined as he gazed lovingly into hers.

The waiter opened the wine, pouring each a glass, waiting for Frank's approval. With a sip, he nodded, then held his glass up in front of the dancing fires. With one sip, Beverly felt a warm glow spread from the flames to every part of her body.

Frank leaned across the table, whispering, "Are ya ready to tie on the feedbag?"

She giggled again, feeling silly, and nodded. He made a simple gesture to the waiter, who then reached into his pocket, pressing an unseen button, announcing, "We shall begin with an appetizer."

Two tuxedoed men emerged from a van that had mysteriously parked next to the limousine, carrying covered silver platters down the boardwalk. They served stone crab claws topped with a bearnaise sauce and sprinkled with crushed herbs. The first waiter placed hors d'oeuvre forks in front of them. The courses kept coming, each more fabulous than the last. The entrée, in honor of their day fishing—the last time they, Linda, and Kevin had all four spent time together—boasted Beverly's new fa-vorite: sautéed mahi mahi with a hint of fresh garlic.

The Chick Corea music gave way to the lilting rhythmic strains of Jean Luc Ponty. The dishes cleared away, the table and accoutrements carried off, the waiter asked, "Will that be all, sir?"

"Good night, sir," Frank bid. "Oh, and tell Henry I said thanks."

"Very good, sir," he replied, strolling briskly down the boardwalk and into the night, lost in a sea of sparkling lights.

Frank took Beverly by the hand and asked, "May I have this dance?"

"If you'll make allowances for my leg," she answered, standing up.

He reached under the bench and touched a button. The Ponty music faded, re-placed by Pat Metheny's "Last Train Home." He put his arms around her, supporting her weight, gently rocking her back and forth. He caressed her in rhythm with the song. Beverly boarded that train, Frank at her side, riding off into the sky, wafted about on the cascades of guitar riffs that layered each melody into a bridge joining them both in new and exciting ways.

As the song faded off into the winking trees, Frank gently lowered her to the bench. The sounds of night came to life around them, the chirrups and crickets and strum of gently blowing breeze filling the quiet.

Frank took out another handkerchief, placed it on the floor of the gazebo, and knelt in front of her. Reaching into his pocket, he removed a small box. Beverly held her breath, fighting down a tide of emotion threatening to sweep her away.

He removed a breathtaking ring, a single diamond oval, cut with 128 facets, set in platinum and white gold, sparkling with the reflection of all those twinkling lights.

Tears streamed down her cheeks as she watched him remove her old wedding ring, placing it on the fourth finger of her right hand, then replacing it with the new engagement ring.

"Will you marry me?" he whispered.

"Oh Frank, yes, but why would you want to marry me?" she breathed back.

"To get you to quit sleeping around."

The next thing she could remember, she was dancing in the soft grass under a twinkling willow tree, a firefly in the night who'd found the one spark that would carry her home.

During the limousine drive back to Tarpon Springs, before an evening with just the two of them in Frank's condo, before she removed the flowered bracelet and wrapped her arms around the man she loved, holding tightly, tighter, never wanting to let go—before they got back to the condo, Frank interrupted her reverie, turning on the light in the back of the car.

He pulled a poster tube from a compartment, then removed a set of blueprint-style drawings. "I need you to approve a few design changes before Ward starts building the next phase," he explained.

"Oh, Frank. Nobody takes care of business like you."

He held open a floor plan, spreading out a smaller layout showing the location of buildings. "This one here will be farther behind where we live now, closest to the springs." Indicating the floor plan, he showed how all four intended units had been merged into one, including a huge sunken living room—ramps all around—master suite, offices, guest bedrooms, game room, indoor Jacuzzi opening into a patio with power roof that retracts to expose the sun or stars, and a huge open veranda overlooking the springs. "If you'll approve the plans tonight, it'll be ready for us within four months. You can decorate all but my office—and I'll want to see lots of Linda's photos on display," he explained.

She started crying softly again. "Oh Frank, it's beautiful. I'll approve if you promise one of these bedrooms is for our boy, whether he's living with his mother or us, because I want him always to have a place in my home as well as my heart."

Frank smiled, asking, "Notice the smaller office adjacent to my own? Who do you think *that's* for?"

She wiped her eyes and smiled back. "Feather our nest, you ol' bird, then climb in with me and make this spring chicken sing."

She found good reason to sing that very evening, well into the night, to the sounds of beautiful music, to the aroma of flowers, to the musky scent of the man who held her and wouldn't let go—would never let go . . .

Whatever came their way.

Dropped off by Ms. Caselow at Frank's place late Sunday morning, Kevin eased inside and found Frank whipping up omelets, Beverly sitting at the breakfast nook literally, he thought, glowing. One glance at the ring on her finger confirmed his suspicions why Frank had hired him, Lonnie, and several yacht club employees to spend the day stringing Christmas lights and wiring the area for music.

Hugging the daylights out of each other, Kevin and Beverly both squealed with glee, admiring her new ring, making fun of Frank, joking about having her hooks into the geezer at last. Before Frank could make him some breakfast, the phone rang. Kevin's eyes widened when he heard the computer-voiced instructions for accepting a jail collect call.

"Hi, Mom! We're comin' to see ya today. How did you get to call?"

"They took me out of max! I'm back in the general population again."

"Cool! Are ya happy about how court went?"

"Oh, sweetie, I was up all night—even though I was exhausted. I felt *so* bad about you having to testify and all. I wouldn't have let 'em put you through that if I had a choice."

"It's okay, Mom. I'm glad I had a way to help."

"Oh honey, you sure did. Finding that witness helped, too, but when the jury got to hear you tell what kind of person your old mom is, it even convinced the judge. Mr. Mogill said I was real lucky—and that *you* were what made the difference."

"What else did Mr. Mogill say?" Kevin wondered.

"Well, I wanna tell Frank about it, too. Is he there right now?"

"Yeah."

"Can he get on another phone?"

Frank went to another phone and greeted Ruth.

"Mr. Mogill," she began, "said I'm probably gonna get found guilty on those other charges."

Kevin's face fell, his happy demeanor suddenly replaced by that haunting sadness and fear that had marked him too much during the past seven months. "What's that mean?" he interrupted.

"Well, he said there's not much I can do—I *did* go out with Mark on a drug buy. But there's good news. He said he talked to the prosecutor after court, and they agreed that he was only gonna ask for a year plus probation."

"I never thought that would sound good," Frank said, "but it sure does."

"Yeah," Ruth agreed, "and it's county time—not penitentiary—so with good time, that would go down to ten months. If I make trustee, it could take off two or three more weeks. So it would get down to a little more than nine months, and I already did a little more than seven."

Kevin brightened some. "So you mean even if they say you're guilty, you could come—" He started to say "home" but thought better of it, the image of the burned and boarded trailer looming in his mind. "You could get out in two months?"

"Could be! He also said we could have a bond hearing and probably get me bail since it's smaller charges now, but he thinks I shouldn't do that."

"Why not?" Frank asked.

"Well, a motion would just delay the sentencing and, if I have to do that minimum anyway, I would just wind up coming back to jail after getting out. He thinks it's better to get it over with all at once, then start getting my life back together. It's not easy to start again, finding a job and getting a place to live and all—then having to give it all up to go right back to jail."

"That's probably smart," Frank observed.

"Yeah," she agreed. "And he said it would complicate things with Kevin, too. If I get him back and then go back to jail again, there's no guarantee you would get to be his foster dad the second time. Something could go wrong. That's what decided it for me—my little guy is safe right now, and I don't wanna mess nothin' up until this is all over with."

"Don't worry about me, Mom," Kevin intoned. "Frank forces me to eat dirt and makes me sleep out in the cold and stuff, but at least he quit pushing me out of moving cars."

Ruth laughed. "Anyway, Frank, I wanted you to know this, and since I can make phone calls again, if ya don't mind, I'd rather have a good long talk with my favorite boy now than have you drive all the way up here this afternoon."

"You talk as long as you want, Ruth, and keep your spirits up. We'll put all this behind us someday soon."

Kevin chattered with her for another ninety minutes, his hottest topic being how thrilled he was with the new engagement between Beverly and the geezer.

It was easier to think about than a burned-up trailer and no place to go . . .

Frank led Beverly out onto the deck. They sat in the morning sunshine, some early-December nip in the air, sharing a chaise-longue while he massaged her leg. All that dancing the night before—not to mention some bedroom acrobatics—had left her cramped and aching. He felt bad about straining her so much, caught between wanting to baby her and knowing that her recovery depended on pushing the limits.

"Frank," she started, "I've been thinking."

"Yeah, well, cut it out."

"No, really. Kevin's mother—and Kevin for that matter—they have no place to go when she gets out."

"Yeah, I've been thinking about it, too."

"Then you've probably thought of the same thing *I* have."

"Yeah, probably."

"Ward said the first apartments will be open in eight to ten weeks. That's pretty close to when she'll probably get out. Let's get her a year lease, and I'll pay for the first six months while she gets on her feet."

"That's very generous of you."

"Baloney! It's selfish. Sure, it would help her out—but it would keep Kevin right here where he could still be around all the time. I don't want 'em moving farther than he can ride his bike or, worse yet, to some other town."

"Yeah, he's like having a big ol' mole on your face. You get so used to seeing it every day that you miss it when you have it removed."

She smiled wistfully. "Yeah, except we both like him a lot more than a mole."

"Wait till he's sixteen."

"I've been thinking something else," she interrupted. "You know how Ward said he wants our next project to be the other wing on that strip mall at the end of the road?"

"Yeah."

"Well, if we financed it right away, I'll bet he could have it ready within six months."

"Yeah, I guess," Frank agreed, not sure where she was going with this.

"Well, I was thinking. Now that I'm learning so much about business management, it occurred to me that maybe I'd like to be the owner of a small beauty shop."

Frank pulled her close and kissed her. "Lady, you're something else."

"Frank, let's use Ruth's visiting time today and go see her ourselves. If she likes the apartment idea, we'll go ahead and get it set up before those units get taken. Ward's already hired a manager to start filling the vacancies."

Frank returned to his condo to find Kevin still on the phone, this time with Cynthia. He gave the okay for him to go meet her, seeing as how they'd already contrived plans for an afternoon of movies at Tarpon Mall. Frank couldn't resist pointing out that Kevin had only an hour to prep—barely enough time to comb his hair the two-hundred times he would spend trying to get it to look just right.

When Kevin finally got ready, Frank insisted on throwing his bike in the back of the van and dropping him off. "I wouldn't want that hair of yours to get messed up in the wind," he teased.

Frank deposited him in front of the theater, then started to drive out of the parking lot. He remembered he wanted to tell him that he and Beverly would be out for the afternoon, so he circled back to catch him. He spotted him on the sidewalk, hugging Cynthia, standing between their his-and-hers bicycles. Waiting for an old lady trying to maneuver a four-wheeled barge out of his way, he watched as the youngsters talked for a moment. They hugged shyly, then tentatively kissed—just briefly—before Kevin glanced around self-consciously. They walked their bikes over to the rack, hooking them together with Kevin's chain-lock.

Feeling like an intruder, Frank decided to leave a note at home instead.

Beverly took charge of the jail-visiting phone, talking quite seriously about a mother's responsibilities both to herself and her son, adamant about alcohol no longer being a part of Ruth's life. "You have people who'll give you support and friendship—and be *fiercely* protective of your son—so you must work very hard at making sure *nothing* stops you from accomplishing what you need for the both of you."

"Now after seven months," Ruth said, "I don't wanna go back—and I *know* the best way is to never touch a drop. Ever! I'm gonna get my cosmetology license and get a job in a beauty shop. Audrey visited me a couple of weeks ago and said I can work there at the store nights so I can save up to get a place for me and Kevin to live. I'm gonna start saving so he can go to college, too. That boy's smart as a snake, and I want him to have a chance to be successful like Frank someday."

"You know Kevin is gonna be vulnerable for a while," Beverly pointed out. "You'll be on probation, an ex-con with a drug record, drinking problems, and allegations of abuse in the file, plus a history of him being in foster care. Loretta tells me it's not automatic that you'll even get him back, but if you *do* and mess up in *any* way—getting in trouble, violating your probation, not keeping a job, losing your place to live, having boyfriends who mistreat him—*anything*, and you might lose him. What's worse, if they *do* take him, there's no guarantee Frank or I can get him back, either. He could be put in one of the youth ranches, assigned to other foster parents, shipped off somewhere else—it scares me just to think about it. You've got a responsibility to yourself, to your son, and to Frank and me not to let that happen."

Ruth's voice cracked, tears welling in her eyes. "Whatever it takes, Ms. Herndon."

"Good. Have you thought about where you're going to live?"

Ruth looked worried, possibly even distraught. "When I get out, I'll be walking away with no money and nothing left except my beat-up old car. I didn't have no insurance on the trailer—well, except for what was part of the lot rent that only pays to haul it to the junk yard. Everything I owned was in there—my clothes, even. Audrey said she could lend me a little money, and she's lookin' for a cheap place. She said I could stay with her for a few weeks, but her mom said no to Kevin, so if I can't find nothin' else, I may need to ask Frank if *he* can keep him a little longer."

"Ruth, apart from just loving that boy and liking to have him around, Frank's been teaching him about running his business. Plus, they have a routine of Frank checking his homework every day. Kevin tries so hard to live up to what Frank expects of him—and that's good for the boy, not to mention Frank," Beverly added wryly, peering around to see if Frank heard, "—so I want a chance for that to continue. I have an offer that helps everybody—something that's good for your son *and* you, that gives you a chance to make something of yourself, helps Kevin stay on the right track, and gets you two together again . . ."

Thrilled with the proposal, Ruth even suggested that, instead of working with Audrey at night, maybe she could apply for the janitorial job at the apartments to be closer to her son.

Beverly thought she just might have some influence on the building manager.

Kevin and Cynthia rode their bikes to the condos after the movie. He read the note, curious about why they went to see his mother without him.

He gave Cynthia a tour of the place, then continued outside, looking at the deck, the springs, and checking out the ongoing construction. Ward came over to greet them, treating Kevin like the big-shot boss, making the boy look good in front of his girl.

Her eyes widened at the Jacuzzi and pool, the latter only a grout-job away from being ready to fill. They went back inside and rooted around through his clothes until she found a pair of his shorts and a t-shirt that looked satisfactory. She changed in the bathroom while he donned his swimsuit, then joined him in the Jacuzzi where they held hands underwater.

They giggled at how her t-shirt and his shorts kept filling with bubbles.

"Frank," Beverly said during the drive from jail, "I want to spend even more time learning about our finances and the business."

"That's a good idea," he agreed.

"You know, it's not the kind of thing I used to think about—Marshall always took care of everything—but it's time I learned." She looked wistful, almost sad for a minute, then continued, "If you outlive me, I know you'll be able to take care of things. But, if I outlive you, or something happens where you can't, you know—well, I don't ever want to be taken advantage of again. I won't have Linda to help . . ."

Frank interrupted, reaching over and taking her hand, "Don't worry, Bevvy, we'll go over everything together, plus make sure Henry is up to speed, and I'd like Kevin to be involved, too. You know he'll be there for us as we get older, so I want to take care of him, um, when the time comes."

She squeezed his hand harder. "I'm glad you understand, Frank. We need to think about these things."

They arrived at the condo and found the bikes parked in front. They went inside and found a note that said only, "Jacuzzi." Frank walked out to find the gigglers flicking water at each other.

"Why don't you and Beverly climb in, too?" Kevin invited.

A fine idea, indeed!

CHAPTER 37

As Frank expected, the jury found Ruth guilty on two of three remaining charges, sentencing set for two weeks later. A very favorable pre-sentence report, the fact that she had housing and jobs already lined up, letters of support from friends, Ruth's emotional yet strong verbal statement before the judge, and agreement on a minimum sentence from the prosecution—now being handled by an under-underling—all worked together successfully. She received one year with no max to cause parole complications, plus two years' probation requiring her to be employed and stay away from illegal drugs and alcohol. Out of jail in seven weeks, she stayed in Beverly's spare bedroom for two weeks until her apartment was ready.

Those first few weeks after the verdict, Kevin worked hard at getting caught up on his missed school lessons. In order to help, Frank had to relearn some of the things he had forgotten so long ago, but he worked with the boy every step of the way. Already a fast learner, Kevin embraced his education—both school as well as business—using his time and attention from Frank to practice an efficient, productive approach that would help carry him all through life.

Frank and Beverly started planning a spring wedding, choosing a date in March, intending to make it a small affair for just a few friends. As word spread from Florida to Michigan, so many people called wanting to attend, to come south and see her again, that they reserved the ballroom at the yacht club and invited close to a hundred people. Dozens of family vacations were planned for Florida that spring.

Frank kept an active interest in Ruth's progress. She proved true to her word, passing her cosmetology test and earning her license, then holding a hairdressing job during the day and working part-time for the apartment-building manager four evenings per week. She stayed away from alcohol *and* cigarettes. Once she settled into her new place just across the road from Frank and Beverly, Kevin moved in with her. It turned into a tearful day—you would think he was relocating halfway around the world, the way Beverly carried on. Frank kept better composure, but he didn't feel it any less inside. Kevin kept his bedroom at Frank's place—even left some of his things there—and used it as his office, the place where he did his homework every day and worked on business documents with his old buddy. Frank often planned his day around when the kid would be coming over.

Ruth became good friends with Cheryl, a gum-smacking hairdresser who worked with her in the parlor near Countryside Mall. Then with no help from Frank, though it *was* under his watchful eye, Beverly and Kevin put together a complete package—including a two-year business plan—for opening a beauty parlor. Beverly provided the financing, setting it up so Ruth could earn shares in the company through profit-sharing. She also hired Kevin to help with the bookkeeping and business management, putting shares into a trust for him and giving him a personal allowance out of her own pocket.

"Cynthia's a young woman," she used to say, "so being her boyfriend is gonna *cost* you."

Frank, with help from Kevin, kept up with the printing company. He made numerous trips to Cheboygan, once taking Beverly, half a dozen times taking Kevin for the weekend, working with Doug and Junior on the expansion. Not only did the business explode with success, but it afforded opportunities for Frank to spend time with the Taylors—especially Doug's three youngsters, who called him "Unca Frank"—and for them to get to know Kevin.

"Hang on until Kevin can get out of college, Doug," Frank used to tell him. "Then you might be able to talk him into assuming some of your responsibilities before you get too old to enjoy some time for yourself." Doug really took to Kevin, amazed by his natural business acumen, and embraced the idea of grooming him to "keep it in the family." Doug often reminded Frank that, if anybody needed help learning how to enjoy life after retirement, then Uncle Frank would be the one to call.

All the business and wedding planning proved good for Beverly, positive ways to avoid dwelling on Linda's death. She had mostly good days, a few bad ones every now and then, but she seemed to be getting used to Linda not coming around anymore. Sometimes she talked about wanting very much to see her, but she was learning to accept the loss, remembering all the wonderful years, and vowing that her little girl would be part of the wedding at least in spirit, in her heart, if that was how it had to be.

Much to everybody's surprise, Henry started spending time with Loretta. She had mellowed quite a bit after the falling-out with her sister, but Frank liked to espouse the theory—in private, mind you—that most of the attitude change happened when Henry started getting into her bloomers.

Sherry got engaged to the young man she had been dating since she moved to Florida. They decided to move in together, so Frank and Beverly cleaned out the last of Linda's things from the apartment. Ruth made good use of the big items, especially the furniture. The rest they donated to charity.

One afternoon at Frank's place, Kevin was working on a science project with Cynthia when he got the call that Lonnie had been hit by a car. Unashamed in front of his girlfriend, he sat and cried while Cynthia wept with him. Frank called Beverly, who rushed right over so the four of them could cry together. The injuries turned out to be some major bruising and a broken arm, but Kevin made it his personal mission to show his support, bringing him surprises every day and collecting seventy-four signatures on a giant get-well card from their friends at school. Frank noticed that Kevin became a lot more concerned about safety after that, a trait he was not unhappy to see.

Beverly's physical therapy tapered down to bi-weekly sessions. Her newest prosthesis seemed to work perfectly. She only used the cane during spells when her leg bothered her, or for longer walks. Otherwise, she grew reasonably mobile, her gait betraying only a mild limp. Driving her car even proved relatively easy.

Together she and Frank supervised every detail during the construction of their luxurious super-condo. Beverly took to heart Frank's promise to let her decorate, threatening to bankrupt first him, then her—"the kid's college fund goes last," she often joked—spending many of her days shopping for home furnishings.

Walking around the construction site one day, Frank thought he saw the glint of colored lights out the corner of his eye. Following their direction back toward Kevin's clearing, he paused, looked around, then decided the bright sunlight must have been playing tricks on his eyes. He saw a slight movement at the edge of the brush. Reaching down, he picked up what had to be the biggest toad he'd ever seen.

"Well, aren't you a monster," he announced, holding it up for a better look.

It peed all over his new pants.

Two police cars and an ambulance parked outside the small three-bedroom bungalow in Countryside. Several grim-faced people came out first, then a stretcher holding a small, still form, covered with a sheet and strapped down. They loaded it into the back of the ambulance, closed the doors, and drove away. The small crowd along the sidewalk buzzed with whispers, shaking heads, sad faces.

Inside, a helpless man tried to comfort his wife. She sobbed, "My baby. Oh God, my baby." Two policemen sat helplessly by. A county coroner's assistant filled out paperwork. A small brownish dog lay on the floor whimpering.

A tiny pinpoint of amber light floated down the hallway and into the parents' bedroom. It moved around slowly, hovering near each photograph on the dresser and walls—a little blond-haired baby propped up with a teddy bear, a toddler holding on to the end table and peering up tentatively for approval, a little girl laughing hysterically as her proud daddy gave her a horsey ride, now curled up asleep beside her sleeping mommy, a kindergartner who was shy but proud of her pretty dress, the first-grader more sure of herself, her golden tresses cut short, brazen and ready to take on the world.

The light hovered for a while at each photo, moved around the room some more, then drifted in and out of drawers, occasionally swirling and dancing in the air, sometimes changing color, usually twinkling amber, so tiny it might not even be noticed.

The light moved into a little girl's room and seemed to watch from the corner while a man took several more photos of the tipped over chest, the broken step-up ladder, a drawing of a mommy and daddy and little girl taped to the wall too high for a tiny body to reach without precariously stacking a tower to climb higher than would be safe.

The man left, and the light continued its tour. Once it had circumnavigated the room several more times, it paused in the air, then swirled and danced faster and faster. Joined by more and more points of light, more colors, some brighter, some flickering, all dancing and spinning, shapes started to form in the air—vague images of faces, animals, a gorgeous young photographer, then a six-year-old girl with beautiful locks cut short. The images shimmered and faded, formed and dissolved, moved and swirled. The little girl with the golden hair looked scared, then sad, then content. Finally, she smiled and looked satisfied before swirling away into nothing.

A lone point of amber light remained, hovering tentatively, dropping to the floor to float through the fibers of the carpet, back out to the living room to see what was happening, to understand the overwhelming grief of young parents who had heard a crash, then run desperately to the bedroom only to find their little golden-haired girl lying hopelessly still.

Kevin really knew how to throw a business meeting. Owing to a gloriously sunny day out in the gulf, he'd suggested they hold it while cruising on the *Fine Print*. The breeze wafted cool but comfortable as they trolled about looking for schools of anything that might bite.

Kevin really took to little Jared—Jared Taylor—President Doug's oldest. The precocious nine-year-old, though not very successful with his school studies, showed a remarkable flair for creativity, and could already draw like a professional. Since Doug had planned to travel down for the weekend, and his wife already had her hands full trying to throw a baby shower for a friend, they had sent their two young daughters to Junior's house and let Jared come down to play with the big guys. Kevin let the youngster use one of Linda's cameras. The two of them roamed the boat taking candid shots of the festivities.

Click. Henry with his arms around Loretta, she struggling to haul in a small but feisty triggerfish. Click. Sherry and her new fiancé, sitting quietly on the foredeck, gazing across the water and into their future. Click. Doug shaking hands with Uncle Frank. Click. Kevin and Cynthia and Lonnie and Darla mugging for the camera. Click. Darla trying to put squid-bait down Lonnie's shirt, his thoroughly signed arm cast waving frantically in the sunlight. Click. The captain at the helm, shot through the glass, showing the reflection of a very young boy aiming a camera, his teenage mentor holding him around the waist to keep him steady. Click. Ward Bodnar, drinking another beer, grinning like a goof, not aware that Rob Buchanan was about to douse him. Click. Ruth Riner, sipping a soda, caught watching her son steal a clandestine kiss with his girlfriend.

Kevin called the meeting to order on the upper deck. Frank, Beverly, Henry, and Ruth attended. The others continued to party below while he read a report on the first week of business for Tarpon Springs's newest beauty parlor. The business had proved a smashing success. Ruth's and Cheryl's previous boss lost her lease on the shop she operated for years, so she'd retired and moved to Arizona to help care for her ailing sister. That meant a small horde of clients followed the area's two best hairdressers to the new parlor called *The Rinery*.

Kevin explained the financial breakdowns as he handed them around. Under Frank's watchful but non-interfering eye, the boy had sat up late the night before putting the finishing touches on his report, then reviewed it all with Beverly in advance of the meeting. Henry looked impressed, then *very* impressed when Kevin followed up with quarterly projections, anticipated growth rates, expected tax liabilities, break-even predictions, and a chart showing possible revenue increases if a third hairdresser could be added. The final portion of the meeting was a presentation of various advertising and promotion ideas Kevin wanted the principals to consider.

Click. Kevin the businessman conducting his first meeting. Click. Beverly and Loretta hugging, the latter trying to keep her slimy fish-hands from messing up her younger sister's clothes. Click. Cynthia whispering a secret into Beverly's ear, both giggling at their private little joke. Click—this time a shot taken by Beverly of little Jared as he gave a really big hug to Kevin, his new buddy beaming with pride. Click. Lonnie with his arm around his best friend, Kevin pointing at the cast and making an *oh no!* face.

Click. A shot from behind, Frank sitting in a chair at the rail, Beverly on his lap, resting her head on his shoulder as he held her protectively, the spray from waves sparkling in the sunlight and framing them with a shining glow, the perfect picture of geezer love.

CHAPTER 38

Three days before the wedding, Beverly grew restless. With everything already thoroughly planned and organized, people would be arriving in town over the next few days. There was nothing more to do.

It turned into one of those difficult "Linda days" for her. The closer she got to the big ceremony, the more she wished her daughter could be there—at least to give her blessing and assuage any last-minute doubts with that ever-positive outlook of hers. Frank was out dealing with Henry on business matters for the afternoon, trying to get things buttoned up before the two-week honeymoon hopping the A B C's— Aruba, Bonaire, and Curaçao—three island paradises near the coast of Venezuela. Kevin was at school, Loretta working, a lonely day for the sad mother who wanted her little girl back, if only for a while.

She thought the ringing phone would be another guest confirming plans, but it turned out to be the cemetery director. The marker for Linda's grave had been installed that morning. She thanked him, hung up, then sat down to steady herself as a wave of grief swept over her, an elevator-drop sinking deep inside her. Wanting to see it, she decided not to wait for Frank. Besides, maybe this first time it would be best to go by herself. After all, nobody would ever understand—nobody *could* understand exactly how she felt.

She left a note for Frank, took her cane for good measure, and drove toward New Port Richey, stopping at a florist's shop along the way to buy a beautiful silk bouquet. At the cemetery she parked as close as the winding road would allow, then picked her way gingerly over uneven ground, balancing the flowers and lightweight folding chair in one hand while using the cane with her other. The feathered sentries casually moved out of her way as if to offer her a modicum of privacy.

One glance at the marker took her breath away. Sure, it looked beautiful—a plaque of sculpted bronze set in a base of polished marble, carved with a delicate spray of roses at the bottom and a beautiful butterfly above, her full name, dates of birth and death, and Kevin's poem in flowing script outlined to suggest scrolled parchment.

Seeing her daughter's name chiseled so indelibly brought the harsh reality of her loss to the surface where it spilled in tears and washed over her body with waves that left her trembling. She clutched her cane for support, feeling all at once too heavy, yet so light the breeze could sweep her away to float in the sky. She set up the chair, then leaned over and put the flowers in the new bronze vase adjacent to the inscription. She sat and tried to make herself relax. Catching her breath again, she closed her eyes and felt the warmth of the afternoon sun.

You know, Linda, that guy you thought might be a pretty good feller? Well, it turns out you were right. In fact, I'm gonna marry him in a few days. Oh, I know, it feels sometimes a little like I'm abandoning your father, but I'm not. Like Frank says, what your dad and me had was great, but finding somebody else to love now doesn't take anything away from that. She sighed. *I just wish you could be at my wedding.*

She felt Linda's arms wrap around her from behind. "What'cha thinkin' about, Mama?" the beautiful young photographer asked.

"I'm thinking about my wedding," she answered, keeping her eyes closed, but moving her hands up to embrace her daughter's arms. "I'm wishing you could be there."

"Ooo! So you're *finally* makin' a respectable man of him, eh?"

"Yeah, he said he wanted to get me to quit sleeping around."

"But you *weren't* sleeping around, were you?"

"Oh, don't be silly, girl."

"Mama, you know I can't appear at your wedding."

Beverly breathed deeply, then released the air and said softly, "Yeah, I know."

"Are you starting to adjust to losing your daughter?" Linda asked.

"No! Well . . . a little I guess. I used to think—used to wonder how I could ever get over not having you anymore. I've figured out that you *don't* ever get over it. It's just, as time passes by, you somehow get more used to it."

They fell quiet for a moment. Then Linda commented, "Mothers always love their daughters, no matter what, but what we had was better than most, wasn't it?"

"The very best," Beverly pronounced.

"Now you're marrying Frank because you love him, and because you want to be connected to him always. The person you have become now includes being a partner with him, is that right?"

"Yeah, I guess. I've only known him for not quite ten months, yet I can't imagine being apart from him."

"Mama, you're a wonderful woman. But whatever you make of your life, you and Frank are both better *together* than you are apart, aren't you?"

"That's why we're to be married," Beverly agreed, picturing that silly man with his pony tail who slept in the craziest positions and could dissect a business with his eyes closed but couldn't iron a shirt to save his life. Then she imagined him hovering over Kevin, helping him learn, guiding him gently, full of pride but careful not to show too much. She pictured him sitting beside her on the deck of the boat, holding her tenderly, sharing a gaze across the vast expanse, content to know that whatever's out there is not as important as what is right here beside you now, close and safe and warm. No, she couldn't imagine living without him. Yes, she believed with all her heart *he* could never be complete without *her*.

"Life is what you make it," Linda whispered, "so together you make it wonderful for yourselves."

Beverly remained quiet. Finally she opened her eyes and turned to see Linda crying, too, gazing off into the wind like she wanted to float free, to follow the butterfly.

"You know I can't visit like this anymore, don't you, Mama?"

Beverly started trembling. She cried softly, trying to catch her voice. "I know," was all she could say.

"Mama, you marry that man and you enjoy your life. Your little girl would *want* to know you're happy."

Beverly felt Linda's grip loosen. "It's so hard—" she started, barely able to talk through her tears. "It's so hard . . . to let go—"

"Don't," Linda whispered back, gently pulling her arms away. "Don't let go, Mama. Hold on tighter. Take me with you always."

Beverly turned, reaching, crying out, "But I don't know how!"

"You'll learn. It'll take some time . . ."

Linda's image faded, growing blurry through tears. Beverly wiped her eyes, desperately trying to see her.

"I love you, Mama . . ." was the last thing she whispered before dissolving into swirling pinpoints of light, glowing every possible color, shimmering and sparkling, each glimmer fading off in every direction. Then, a final swirl left only one beautiful velvet yellow-and-blue butterfly fluttering in the air, hovering for a moment before floating off with the wind.

"I love you, too," Beverly whispered, closing her eyes, feeling the warm sun on her wet face.

Frank parked behind Beverly's car and carried another folding chair to the gravesite. He set it up next to Beverly, then took her hands in his, leaned over, and kissed her lightly on the forehead. He offered his handkerchief and sat next to her, still holding one of her hands. Neither spoke. He studied the marker and nodded his approval.

Finally, he whispered, "It sure is pretty."

Beverly nodded several times, wiping her face with the cloth. They sat there in silence for a full ten minutes, Frank gently massaging her hand, wanting to be as close as he could, wary of intruding too much during this personal moment.

Looking to Frank, then back to the marker, Beverly finally spoke. "She's gone, Frank. My little girl's gone."

He put his arm around her, pulling her closer, lightly touching her chest. "Not from your heart."

"That's what *she* said," Beverly agreed. "Frank, she was here today, but she said she can't come see me anymore."

"Hmm . . . I'm sorry."

"She *was* here, Frank. I know it's hard to believe, but she *was* here."

"I believe you, Beverly. I believe she was here."

She closed her eyes and cried softly. "I'm gonna miss her," she sighed.

Frank stroked her hair. "We're gonna miss her together."

Kevin had never attended a wedding before. His first proved absolutely spectacular. The weather was perfect, the yacht-club chapel festooned with beautiful flowers and filled with excited and happy friends.

As people arrived, they were greeted by usher Lonnie Caselow, handsome in his new suit minus the arm cast that had come off only days before, and usherette Darla Picant, sweetly beautiful in her pale yellow-colored taffeta dress with matching hair ribbons. Even with her elegant coif, courtesy of Ruth Riner, she didn't stand much taller than Lonnie anymore. They guided people to the few remaining seats, reminding them a reception would follow in the grand ballroom immediately after the ceremony. Eventually, the pair of fourteen-year-olds took their seats in the front row and a hush fell over the crowd. Two men in back began playing soft jazz music on electric piano and amplified acoustic guitar.

As the melodic strains grew more dramatic, Henry and Loretta, linked arm-in-arm, entered from the rear and walked slowly down the center aisle, separating at the front to take positions on either side. Henry had lost some of his extra weight, looking tall and handsome in his light-gray tuxedo with cream-colored cummerbund. Loretta seemed to glow in flowing peach-colored gown, her hair highlighted and worn over-the-shoulder for the first time ever. She held Henry's arm, her attention more on him than the people around her.

Next, Kevin and Cynthia started down the aisle. Kevin looked very handsome, his hair cut short, obviously taller than when the same crowd had seen him read his poem at the funeral, stepping gallantly in his tailored tuxedo, holding Cynthia's hand protectively inside the crook of his arm. Her outfit matched Loretta's, except that her long hair was curled and swept up in a dramatic yet delicate statement that seemed to highlight the sparkle in her emerald eyes. She looked like a girl in love; he looked ready to burst with exuberance. They took their positions up front, posing between Loretta and Henry.

Next came Frank by himself, dapper and proud, a smug look on his face, a mischievous twinkle in his eye. He strolled, stepping with a formal cane boasting a carved silver handle, pausing here and there to bow and acknowledge the guests. He tipped his top hat, at one point twirling it in his hand and placing it firmly back on his well-tanned pate. He stepped confidently to the front, pausing to hug Loretta and Cynthia, shaking Henry's and Kevin's hands. Then, with an air of what-the-hell, he grabbed Henry in a bear hug. He poked Kevin in the ribs several times to get a giggle before grabbing him with both arms and literally lifting him off the ground. Kevin grinned and straightened his tux.

Next came Doug Taylor's son, Jared, carrying a velvet pillow with two rings. He marched quickly and determinedly to the front where his buddy Kevin helped him find his position, keeping a reassuring hand on his shoulder. Then followed Doug's little girls tossing rose and lilac petals here and there with such enthusiasm that some of the guests got showered by the fragrant potpourri.

The music faded, then transformed into a beautiful, acoustic rendition of the bridal march. Everybody stood as Beverly appeared in the doorway. She looked stunning in her full-length cream-colored gown, trimmed with delicate hand-woven lace and accented by a sparkling jeweled-butterfly brooch. On her wrist she wore the butterfly bracelet from the night Frank proposed, adorned with orchids and exotic flowers as an elegant alternative to the traditional bouquet. As she started down the aisle unassisted, her limp barely noticeable, everyone joined in for an impromptu round of applause.

Stepping down from the dais, Frank took her by the hand and guided her up to the front. They kept the service informal, simple and brief, including vows they had written themselves.

"Frank," Beverly said, facing him and holding his hands in hers, "I love you with all my heart, and I always will. I promise to share my life with you, the happiness and sorrow, successes and failures, sickness and health, good leg and bad, no matter what, because it's a whole lot better *with* than without you. I'll love, honor, and—just to humor you if you behave yourself—maybe obey every now and then. Here to beyond the sunset, you're mine."

"Beverly, you showed me how to be in love. You reminded me how to pay attention to my feelings, and gave me the reason to express them. I will always strive to find new and better ways to deserve your love. My devotion will dazzle you, dear lady. I will earn your trust, merit your tolerance, and turn out to be a better catch than the *biggest* mahi mahi in the gulf—so we can be together, against or with the grain."

The audience found this both amusing and moving, delighted these old coots could find whimsy in themselves on so solemn an occasion. Kevin rolled his eyes several times during the vows, adding to the effect.

Finally pronounced married, they sneaked in a thorough kiss, then walked carefully down the aisle, leading the applauding entourage to the grand ballroom.

The great doors opened to reveal a darkened interior glowing with a million twink-ling white lights. Tiny mirror balls hidden here and there added swirling pin-points to the effect.

They had hired an official photographer, but little Jared moved around the room with one of Linda's cameras, preserving his own vision of every magical moment. He caught Ruth dancing with her new boyfriend, a shy and gentle young man who worked for Ward; Marta Taylor with her new husband, Larry Rumsey, the latter sober and sipping a soda; and Lonnie leading Darla around the dance floor with more determination than style, more feeling than grace, making up with sincerity what he lacked in technique.

Junior sat at the center of a small crowd, regaling Beverly's friends with best-of-Frank stories from the old days, each funnier than the last. Doug and his wife chased two little girls around until the young ones wore out, then found some quiet time to themselves, captured on film during a tender moment by their oldest son, the camera freak. Loretta broke a heel, so Henry picked her up in his arms and twirled her around the dance floor, making her smile, and—truth be told—making her tingle more than a little bit. Click. Click. Click.

Kevin danced with Cynthia, remembering how he felt the first time he held her at the school dance. It seemed wondrous to him how each time always felt better than the last. He led her gently around the field of sparkling lights until both felt sure they had left the planet, then—never missing a step—he winked over his shoulder at his little buddy just as the picture was snapped. Click. Click.

The bandleader announced time for the bridal dance. Frank stepped up to the microphone and explained that he had a toast to offer first. The room grew quiet, everybody picking up a glass and watching with rapt attention.

"I want to toast the people in my life—my new bride, the best damned little gal in the world, my friend Henry for being there for me through thick and thin, and my buddy Kevin who, ever since he was a little hoodlum, has been reminding me to be the kind of friend he could look up to. I want to toast Loretta and Cynthia and all of *you* for *your* love and support, for being here to share this special day with us. Most of all, I want to remember somebody who could *not* be here in person. She *is* here, though, in our memories, in spirit, in our hearts, still a part of us all. This is for you, Linda, with my pledge that I'll be what you wanted for your mama."

Frank stepped down and took Beverly by the hand, leading her onto the dance floor. He gently wiped a tear from each of her cheeks with his handkerchief, then held her very close, whispering, "You just relax and let me do the work."

Everybody gathered around, concerned about the brides's leg. As the music started, Beverly melted into Frank, both becoming as one, floating with the rhythm among twinkling lights. There was no limp, no hesitation, only a pair of strong arms, a woman in love, a man living up to his vows.

After the first verse, Kevin and Cynthia joined them on the floor. Beverly started to falter slightly, so Frank moved closer to the teens and, with open arms, gathered them in to form a foursome. With Kevin and Frank on each side of Beverly, they supported her weight enough that she could relax her leg. They continued to sway, hugging tighter and tighter, wanting never to let go.

By the time Henry and Loretta joined them, then the Doug Taylors and little Jared, and Ruth and Lonnie and Darla and oh-what-the-hell Marta, too, and Junior and Lizzie and then others and then more, they all formed a rather strange-looking mass of people, joined as one, swaying into the night, happy and content, celebrating each other.

The professional photographer shot a whole roll of that unusual group dance. They turned out to be some of the favorite shots of the evening. That's what it was all about—a group of people, a common bond, connected with love and friendship, devotion and family, coming together to share a moment . . . to cherish each other.

This must be what Linda had seen every time she looked through the lens.

CHAPTER 39

The steamy hot water felt wonderful! It started with a warm feeling at the top of the head and cascaded down all sides, enveloping him in a wet cocoon; a nice Saturday-morning shower with no reason to hurry was, to Kevin, one of the great luxuries of life. He stepped out and dried off, pausing several times in front of the mirror to admire his burgeoning physique.

He tried to imagine how they would both look if Cynthia stood there beside him, also wearing nothing more than her sparkling eyes and pretty smile. He'd wanted to invite her to come over and go skinny-dipping—at least in the pool if not the Jacuzzi. With Frank and Beverly on their honeymoon, the construction workers off for the weekend, and his mother already gone to the beauty shop for the day, a few people in the apartment building were the only ones around. That meant complete privacy for the condo pool area.

Alas, the image of Cynthia faded, leaving only a young teenage boy staring at himself in the mirror. Embarrassed at his nakedness—like he had just noticed some-body spying on him—he filed his fantasy adventure away, preserved for maybe the next time Frank and Beverly left town.

His mind still on Cynthia, he wished he could at least see her. She was gone with her mother and aunt for the day to see some kind of doll show in Ocala. The women in her family had been collecting them for several generations, so this was the big event. They invited Kevin to come along, but it seemed like one of those things Frank was talking about when he said people in love need to give each other time for their own interests. If going to Ocala meant trotting around, exclaiming, "Oooo" and "Ahhh" over a bunch of dolls, well, then this was a good time to give his girlfriend some space. Besides, they were just being polite when they invited him; it was obvi-ously a girl outing.

As he got dressed, he thought about Lonnie and Darla's offer to hang out with them at the carnival. He declined, sensing that his friends would prefer to have some private time with each other. He suspected the pair of fourteen-year-olds wouldn't stay there all day anyway—regardless of what they told their parents—opting instead to slip off somewhere and escape from the prying eyes that seem always to be on couples who are so young.

Somehow, it felt lonely being the only one around. He decided to stick with his original plan: move the rest of his things that he kept in Frank's condo to the new bigger one just built for the newlyweds. Completed the week of the wedding, it had been fully furnished during the honeymoon, courtesy of three movers, several friends including Kevin, and the copious direction and watchful eye of Loretta. Kevin felt sure he heard the workers utter the word "bitch" at least several times during the move.

He liked the idea of having *his* stuff in the new place by the time they got back, too. Frank had hemmed and hawed about the area labeled in the blueprint as Kevin's bedroom with adjacent office. At the last minute, he admitted feeling overly presumptuous about setting aside the space without checking to see if Kevin really wanted it. Sensing this, Kevin had taken him aside and asked him if he could set up an area for himself, not only for work, but so he could sleep over on "visits" and maybe even have Lonnie stay over sometimes. Both relieved and obviously pleased, Frank shook Kevin's hand and told him that was the plan all along. Yes, getting everything all moved in right away would reassure his older friend how important it was to Kevin that he carve some occasionally practical but always symbolic space for himself in Frank's and Beverly's new home and new life.

Walking toward the original condo, he passed the pool area. He stopped and imagined Cynthia there, *au naturel*, standing at water's edge, ready to dive in. Then he imagined her lying in the chaise-longue, her soft tan skin slathered in oil and glistening in the warm sun. He tugged at his shorts and, distracted from his reverie by a bird landing nearby, went inside the condo, letting himself in with his own key.

He paused inside his bedroom, then went straight to the dresser, pulling it forward and tilting it slightly so he could reach behind and underneath to retrieve his secret envelope. Pulling out his newest girlie magazine, he hurriedly looked for page 27. Page 27 . . . that was the photo he had decided must be how Cynthia would look. He propped up the pillows on his bed, then went over and closed the bedroom door, feeling momentarily silly; there was nobody home, nobody in the whole building, nobody in the whole compound.

He stretched out on the bed and carefully studied page 27. Then he closed his eyes and remembered how Cynthia felt in his arms that first night at the dance, the warm air, the smell of her hair . . . He opened his eyes and checked the door, reassured that it was still closed; there was nobody around to intrude on a boy's most powerful gift . . . his very own imagination.

"Hey, pay attention to the leg! You can be replaced, you know!" Beverly admonished. Frank took his time applying suntan lotion, turning the process into an excuse to massage her ever-sore leg and foot. The problem was, he kept getting distracted by all those young female vacationers from Europe who frolicked topless on the Bonaire beach. Three little boys ran by, naked with sunburns on their cherub behinds, heading for the crystal-clear water washing gently up onto the sand. Beverly hadn't quite had the nerve to go topless yet, but she fully intended to try within another day or two. It wasn't like this in Houghton Lake, but the more she got used to the ways of the islands, the more she liked them.

"She's *half* your age, old man. Quit lookin' and pay attention to your wench's bum leg."

"You hush!" he retorted, grinning like a mischievous imp. "If you won't take *yours* off and give me some bodacious ta-tas to look at, then, well, you can't blame me for admiring the local sights."

With that, she reached behind, unclasped the top on her swimsuit, and pulled it off—then put it on Frank's head like a little hat, tying it under his chin. He liked what he saw.

As morning turned to afternoon, the day grew even more glorious. Birds circled in the sky, following the scuba boat back to the pier. Little crabs skittered across the beach, running from playful children and defending their territories from tiny marauders. The waves kept lapping up, pulling back gently, then washing up again and again. A little girl picked her way gingerly through the hot sand, finally deciding it was too hot to walk, then sitting down and deciding it was *way* too hot to sit. The loving arms of her father swept her up and carried her off to the sea to laugh and play and splash and laugh some more. Palm trees swayed gently in the breeze. An exotic bird sang for its mate. The newlyweds from Tarpon Springs were nowhere in sight.

"Heeeere, Bev Bev Bev Bev Bev Bev-er-leeee!" Frank called out, imitating the sound of those exotic birds. She could hear him in there adjusting the temperature of the shower, preparing to help his new wife rinse off all that suntan lotion. With no grip-bars in the shower/tub, he preferred to be available to help her climb in and out.

"Wrong animal," she teased from the next room while she tuned in a spicy island rhythm on the radio. She strolled completely naked into the bathroom before finishing her thought, "From *you*, I expect to hear the call of the old horny toad."

He embraced her, hugging longer than she expected. "I gotta hold extra tight when you're *this* lubed up," he growled in her ear.

"Well, if you're gonna get randy on me—in the middle of the day!—then you better let me get all this goo and sand rinsed off."

He helped her into the tub, then peeled off his shorts and climbed in with her. They shampooed and soaped and rinsed and massaged and hugged and kissed and massaged some more, feeling the heat of the water streaming over their bodies, the steam billowing up to swaddle them in a misty hot cloud. The music from the next room changed to a slow song. They faced together, wrapping their arms around each other, swaying gently with the sound. Their hands played sensitively over each other's bodies, pausing momentarily here and there, chasing electric tingles, causing fast goose bumps before quickly moving on, exploring once-familiar territory as if each touch delved into an exciting new frontier. They danced the dance of rapture—awkward, uncomfortable, with no place to move except closer and closer to each other.

Eventually, the water started getting cold. Remembering the time Kevin had said, Hey Frank, didja know cold water makes guys' thingies get real little? he extinguished the shower and helped Beverly—danced her really—out of the tub. They dried each other, at one point getting carried away, snatching towels off the shelf to twist and snap. After Frank scrambled for a dropped towel and Beverly caught him with a red-welter across the fanny, he picked her up and carried her to the bed, laying her down gently and crawling in beside her. He jumped up to put the chain on the door, closed the window and turned on the air-conditioning, then crawled back in.

After caressing each other and indulging in some playful nuzzling and kissing, she remarked, "You just *never* let me get any rest, do you?"

"If the lady *insists* on displaying her delicate fruits for all to see," he started, referring to her topless episode just a few hours before, "then natives can't be held accountable when they have a sudden hunger for ripe cantaloupes."

"Now don't start comparing people to food," she tut-tutted him. "You ever seen a Vienna sausage?"

"Lady, *my* attributes are sufficient to keep *me* pleased. If *you* can get in on the fun, then more power to ya."

Before she could speak, he kissed her again, then again and again. He kept moving his fingers gently around her body, playfully teasing, leaving excitement everywhere he ventured, never quite focusing too much on the same place for too long. With open hands, he continued stroking and caressing, touching and holding, getting close, then moving on, coming back before each sensation could escape.

She played with the hair on his chest, lightly brushed his nipples, moved her hands up and down, just touching but never lingering in any particular place. They paused long enough for an intense hug, then pulled back and touched more, feeling and exploring, then moving on yet again before the sensations could surge and overwhelm them.

He flowed down her body with his tongue, leaving a moist trail of goose bumps here, then there, then back and forth, and finally all the way down and back up again. She tried to do the same, but her leg was in an awkward position and she winced. He gently pulled her back up and reached down to massage the areas he had long ago learned usually hurt her the worst. They paused and hugged intensely again, then resumed petting and probing and teasing. Swept with waves of tingles, they kept pausing for longer and longer hugs, deeper and more passionate kisses.

It was during one of those long hugs that both refused to let go, holding tighter, moving closer, converging as one—no more teasing, no more tickling, just an incredible lightness as they swept into the air, out and over the balcony, floating across the sand and the water, dancing together under the warm sun in an endless blue sky.

Kevin got up and straightened his clothes, then tried to stuff the magazine back into its envelope, but it got hung up on loose photographs in the bottom. He reached in and pulled out the pictures he had hidden away—the colored lights! He sat on the corner of his bed and studied them. Eventually, he laid them aside and went into Frank's office to pull the files on the condo and apartment project. Retrieving a series of plats, he located one that covered the area of the springs. He took it back to the bedroom and examined it carefully, referring several times to the pictures. Finally, he put his shoes on, gathered up the plat and photos, then stopped in the office for a pad and pen before locking up and heading for his sanctuary with the big hollow log by a sandy clearing near the water.

He spent the next two hours exploring the area, carefully examining the places he'd seen lights, marking them on the plat he'd copied onto his pad. Frustrated and hot from the sun rising high in the sky, he climbed into his familiar log, turned sideways, and lay back with his feet up against the inside. He used to fit better when he was twelve, but he still found it a comforting, familiar place.

He arrayed the photos on his lap and studied them for some missed clue, some hint—anything that would help him understand.

The mystery of the lights would, apparently, remain just that.

Beverly liked how this shallow area had been set up at one end of the pool. No more than five inches deep, it proved perfect for propping their heads on a towel at the edge and letting their bodies rest—almost floating but not quite—in the cool water washing from an adjacent waterfall. Neither Frank nor Beverly had much energy left; they had shared a rather intense afternoon up in the room.

Beverly fell quiet, apparently lost in thought. Frank glanced at her every now and then, but she didn't seem to notice. Finally, she slid over a few inches to fit right against him, resting her head on his shoulder, holding on to his arm, looking somewhat sad.

"Sometimes, no matter how good things are, it's hard to be, you know, to feel good about just enjoying it all," she whispered.

Frank started to reply, but couldn't come up with the right thing to say. Finally, he just put his hand over hers, holding her reassuringly.

Speaking very softly, she said, "I'm worried about Kevin."

"Kevin?" Frank asked quietly, his cheek against hers. "Why are you worried about him?"

"Frank, he's *so* little, but he acts *so* big. He roams around and explores and rides that bike across Nineteen, and with Ruth working so much he's there alone and he's— oh Frank, I used to worry after Linda like this—even when she was all grown up and off at college or moving to another state—I never stopped." She wiped tears from her eyes, peering around to be sure no other vacationers could hear. "Frank, it didn't take long for me to start worrying about that boy. But that part of me that's always worried about Linda, it's still there, too. Only, when it reminds me it's time to think about where she is or who she's with or what might not be right, then I remember, and it—then it feels like she's hurt and there's nothing I can do."

"You *will* feel good about your happiness again."

She put her arm across his stomach, her head on his shoulder. "You're the one who makes me happy, Frank. If I could only stop the ache that comes from that missing piece."

"You'll never stop it, Beverly. You don't want to—that would mean forgetting her. You just need to find ways to feel *good* when you remember her."

"How can I do that?"

"You spent her whole life doing things for her. How about if you just keep on doing things for her anyway?"

"How?"

"Well, you talked about helping the Humane Society raise money for that animal hospital."

Her face brightened, then betrayed sad disappointment once again. She had lost interest in the hospital after finding out she couldn't designate how or where the money would be spent. "But they didn't—"

"Beverly, you don't need them. Let's build our own. We can afford it; we can set up the construction through Ward. Let's make it a non-profit animal hospital."

Beverly sat up, buoyed by the idea. "We could still take referrals from the Humane Society anyway! We could also help animals from the public, even strays and wild animals that have been hurt."

Frank sat up, too, then slid around facing her, taking both of her hands in his. "It would be a lot of work," he pointed out.

"That's all right. I'll hire Kevin to help with the administration—long as it doesn't cut into his schoolwork."

"That boy's so fast he could work a full-time job and never miss a beat at school."

"We'll do publicity and seek volunteers and hire some help if we have to. Oh Frank, we could get a van and go around to the shut-ins and elderly people who can't afford vet care for their little companions and—and—" She grew increasingly animated with each new possibility. "We could do things in the low-income neighborhoods, put out brochures on how to care for pets, have an injured-animal pick-up service. Frank! We could do *all* kinds of things that Linda would have been *so* proud of!"

"Anything I can do to help," Frank assured, hugging her tightly.

"This is perfect. *Every* day we'd be doing something Linda would have wanted—something that honors her memory. Then when I miss her—especially when I have bad days—then I'll help a little animal and yet another part of Linda will live on."

Her cheeks glistened with tears, but she was smiling, hugging Frank, overwhelmed with the possibilities, her thoughts drifting across the Caribbean to a shiny new building somewhere along Florida's gulf coast, comforting a scared little girl who needed to be reassured her puppy would be just fine don't you worry he'll be okay we'll take very good care of him.

They came from every direction. Out of the clear waters, up through the hot sand among the trees and shrubs and tropical plants, from Clearwater and Countryside and New Port Richey and Brooksville they came. They glowed brighter than the blinding sun, so intense, so small they could be specks of dust, yet they sparkled, alive with the fires of time shifting from one color to another—a polychromasia of fluorescence in every hue imaginable.

They came together in the little sandy clearing by the springs, greeting like excited puppy-dogs chasing each other in circles. They whirled around, joined by more, then still more pinpoints of light, growing brighter, shifting from infra to ultra then becoming all colors at once.

They swirled into images, the faces of people young and old, animals, sad doleful eyes, happy laughing smiles, the tear-stained cheeks of a child, the wrinkled visage of a sage looking right at you, through you, far past you, seeing truth hiding behind you, always moving when you turn to peek. A comical armadillo strutted out, swaying on its hind legs, joined by his friend the fat old toad who, to all outward appearances, looked simply bored by the proceedings. The lights danced, so many images coming and going too quickly to comprehend.

And they listened. They listened to the rivet of a frog, the chirrup of a bird, the soft breathing of a thirteen-year-old boy sleeping quietly in a giant hollow log, a pad and pen beside him, photos of dancing lights on his lap.

Linda knelt at the log's open end. She reached in and, using the backs of her fingers, lightly stroked Kevin on his cheek. Still asleep, he brushed his face to ward off some intrusive Florida insect. She touched him again, whispering, "Kevin . . . Kevin . . ."

He stretched, knocking the pictures off his lap, and opened his eyes. "Linda," he whispered, looking past her to make sure nobody else could see.

"Oh Kevin, you're getting so big!—and even more handsome every day."

He blushed; Linda always had a way of doing that to him. He felt a wave of fear and pain and sorrow sweep over him, a lump in his throat. He looked at her, his body twitching from a battle waged deep inside, tears forming at the corners of his eyes to prove he was losing. He tried to speak, but could only manage a small sound before he started to tremble. All of his emotions spilled out for Linda to see, for himself to feel. "I missed you," was all he could say.

"I've been with you the whole time," she cooed, looking concerned.

"Yeah, I know," he returned with an edge of anger, "—in my memories and all that."

Linda lowered her head, reaching for his hand. When she touched it, he started to pull away. Then, tentatively, he allowed her to take it, holding tighter as the distance between their worlds slowly dissolved.

"In your memories, yes," she said, her head still bowed, "but I've been with you other ways, other times—your school dance, afternoons on the boat, your A-plus oral report in science class, the wedding . . ." She trailed off, growing quiet.

"You said you would come talk to me and help me understand. I kept *my* promise, you know."

She squeezed his hand, then looked into his eyes and whispered, "I'm here to keep *my* promise, too."

Kevin picked up the photos. He studied them for a moment, then asked, "Is this you?"

Linda sat in the sand, gently tugging the boy until he turned and pressed his back against her, his head touching her shoulder. She stretched one leg out on one side of him, keeping the other crooked on his other side, pulling him in closer and wrapping her arms around him. She relaxed her hug and started gently stroking his hair with one hand. His tension slowly ebbed until he took several deep breaths and sighed, snuggling in as close as he could, reaching up with his hands to hold hers, clasped across his chest.

She leaned her head forward and lightly touched his cheek with hers, nuzzling, breathing deeply, simply content to hold the little guy with the big heart that had come to be so important to Linda in such a short time. "Yes, I guess these lights are me," she finally answered. "Kevin, we waited so long because we didn't *know* the answers to your questions."

He thought for a moment, never loosening his grip. "Is Linda dead?"

Not saying anything at first, she finally sighed. "Hmmm . . . she must be, or there wouldn't be so complete a memory."

She felt him tremble, then heard him sniffle softly under his breath. "You're a *memory*?" he asked, barely able to speak.

"Linda is a memory to you, to the people who knew and loved her, and to us."

"Who is *us?*"

"Linda would have described us as dancing lights. Is that how you see us?"

He nodded without speaking. She released one of her hands, holding it out in front of his face. She pointed her index finger toward the sky. It started to shimmer and dissolve, swirling around as pinpoints of colored light. They swirled back into her finger, the lights gone. She moved her hand back to his. He touched it gingerly, then gripped it tightly.

"Kevin, we remember Linda—just like you do. The only difference is, when we saw she wouldn't survive the accident, we passed through her and learned all her memories, her fears and regrets, her dreams and desires, what she's been and all that she might be. We remember how she appeared; we remember how she thought." Hugging him tightly again, she added, "And we remember how much she loved you. Sometimes she wished you were her own little brother; other times she wanted you to be ten years older so she could marry you and take you home and pamper you forever. She loved you *very* much."

After a moment, he asked, "So the *real* Linda doesn't know what happened ever since—ever since she, um—"

"We don't know, Kevin. She's not here anymore. Maybe she's just gone; maybe she's gone away. We have so many things to understand. Linda believed in memories, though, and so do we."

"So do I," he whispered. They sat in silence for a minute. Finally, Kevin asked, "So are you aliens or what?"

She smiled. "We don't know, Kevin."

"Whatta you mean you don't know?"

"We've been here a long time—a *very* long time to you. This is all we know."

"Is Linda the only person you look like?"

"No."

"Why do you pretend to be people?"

"Mostly to learn. Sometimes so we can communicate. It might be because we think we can help the survivors when a loved one has been lost."

"Communicate?"

"Talk to people—like you—like we're doing right now. A bunch of colored lights can't talk."

"Do other people know about you?"

"Only you."

"Why me?"

"Well, you discovered us—even got photographs—and . . . well, Linda would've thought you deserved the truth. We trust Linda's judgment; we trust you."

"Why do you wanna know people so much?"

"We have a lot to teach; we have a lot to learn." She shifted her weight, pulling one leg back to rest on her thigh, gently turning Kevin sideways so they could see each other.

"What can you teach us?" he wondered.

"We don't know how people would say those things."

"Huh?"

"You have no words for them. We hope to find ways to say them."

"What's something you've learned from us?"

"Together."

"Together? What do you mean?"

"People are—they go through life together. We didn't used to. Now, we've learned to be together." With that, pinpoints of light danced in the air before them, moving this way and that, up and down, around and around. Then, all at once, they came together swirling faster and faster, shimmering all colors combined, forming images, glowing brighter and brighter. "See? We are more when we come together."

"You learned that from us?"

"Yes, and we still don't understand it all. People are connected so many ways. There are bonds of family, friendship, lovers. They are parents, relatives, school chums, musicians who play together, artists, teammates . . . All that you do is somehow connected. A common interest, an obligation, compassion from your heart, love where it's *expected* to be; love for *no* reason except that it *is*. You always seek *more* connections; you hurt deeply when they're broken. People fade away; people die. Some find new connections; some are consumed by their loss."

"Like how I love Linda?"

"And like Linda loved you."

"But I didn't know her very long."

"It was long enough, wasn't it?"

He looked into her eyes and managed a weak smile. "Long enough," he said softly.

"Your friend Lonnie, you knew him before, right?"

"Um, yeah."

"Yet you became *real* friends when you needed one and made the effort."

Kevin looked thoughtful, then seemed to understand. "What are you gonna do now?" he asked.

"Keep learning until we connect with more people, then all keep learning together."

"Have you ever connected with people before?"

"You are the—our—you are our first."

Kevin brightened a little, liking the sound of that. "Is Linda gonna keep coming back—I mean your memory of her?"

"Do you want her to?"

He pondered that for a moment. Then, his decision made, he said, "No, I don't need *your* memory; I have *my* memory of her. That's what I'll remember."

Linda suddenly dissolved, catching Kevin by surprise. He reached for her, but his hand slipped through a swirl of colored lights. "Wait! What can you teach *me?*"

As the lights started to spin, the face of a little blond-haired girl formed, mouthing the words, "Only what you've been teaching us . . ."

Then, all at once, a billion trillion zillion lights engulfed Kevin, passing around and through him, floating him in a cloud of euphoria, each part of him swirling with the colors, dancing in the sky.

Just as suddenly, the lights raced off in every direction, leaving Kevin lying in the sand, drenched in sweat, panting. He struggled to sit up, then crawled over to retrieve his photos and pad from the log. Yes, the lights still appeared there in the prints. They were real. He sat quietly, looking off into the distance.

"Bye, Linda," he whispered.

Then, still trying to catch his breath, he opened his pad and wrote the words:

> Individually, we exist
> Sharing, we become

Briefly puzzled by these lines, finally he decided he liked them—a lot. He picked up the photos and stuffed them in the back of the pad, then started toward the path that led to the condos. He paused at the edge of the clearing and looked back, scanning the area for any sign of colored lights.

There were none.

He walked to the new condo, let himself in, and went to his combination bedroom/office. The furniture had been positioned, but none of his personal things were there. He decided that he definitely needed to get moved in right away. This was Frank and Beverly's new home. They had offered him a place in it, and now he wanted more than ever to be part of it.

He sat on the unmade bed, opened his pad, and added the words:

> Alone, we believe
> Joined, we understand

He read the four lines over and over again, then closed the pad, satisfied.

He went to Frank's office, gingerly opened the door, and peered inside. The room looked and felt and smelled and seemed so much like his older friend. Frank's things were there, his desk and desk set, knickknacks, the pencil holder Kevin had made him in art class, the framed photos here and there. Kevin sat at the side desk and turned on the computer. Booting up a graphics program, he selected a large font and format-ted for making a small poster. He typed in the four lines, studied them, then decided he must be a very lucky guy.

He thought about Cynthia and Lonnie and his other friends, images in his mind, good feelings, building a foundation of memories. He thought of his mom hugging him—so many hugs through the years—pushed to her limits while her whole life crumbled around her, yet worrying through it all about her boy. He knew he had helped keep her going, had helped keep her . . . connected.

He thought of Beverly and that unconditional love of hers, how she had accepted him from the very beginning, even trying to win him over so he would like her and not be afraid of sharing Frank. Part granny and part friend, she was always there for him, no matter what, even with so many challenges of her own. All she seemed to expect of him was that he be himself. She liked him that way, and he liked that, too.

He thought of Linda. He had learned a lot from her in their short time together, some already taken to heart, more probably not yet realized. From Linda, he decided, he had mostly learned how to enjoy a true zest for life. There is a way to enjoy every-thing you do, and Linda always found that way. Kevin would, too. He would never forget her. He would tell all the people in his future about her.

He would remember.

He looked up at the photo Frank kept prominently over his desk. It was the shot Linda took that day on the boat. She had caught Kevin at the helm, Frank behind him with his arms wrapped around his young friend—partly guiding, mostly protecting, always loving. Kevin, feeling proud of "piloting the yacht," had laughed. Frank smiled. Kevin turned his face toward Frank's, seeking his approval. There they were, their faces close together—the homeless waif who finally had a true friend, the weathered visage of a foster dad cherishing every moment with his boy. They were connected in a way that could never be broken.

Kevin took the picture down and set it beside the keyboard. He gently touched the faces for a moment, then typed in a final two lines. He sat back, picking up the photo for another look, and smiled.

Click . . . the picture of contentment.

This is what Linda saw when she looked through that lens, he thought.

He turned on the laser printer and gave the print command, then headed toward the old condo to collect his things and move in. It was time to stake out some new territory in the lives of the people that mattered so much to him.

It took a long, hot, sticky afternoon, but Kevin got it all in place. Once he had his knickknacks all arranged, he went back to Frank's office to retrieve his poster. Reading it again, he decided he liked it a lot. He went back to his office and tacked it up on his bulletin board, then went to call Cynthia to see if she was home yet, to call his mom and just say hello, to think of a wonderful something he could do to surprise

Frank and Beverly when they returned.

That poster hung there for many years . . . the thoughts of a young teenager and his dancing lights—a boy connected in many extraordinary ways:

Individually, we exist
Sharing, we become

Alone, we believe
Joined, we understand

Apart, we wonder
Together, we know

CHAPTER 40

It happened in a small cluster of condos, across from a few low apartment buildings, at the end of a private road, near a series of canals and deep-water springs surrounded by tropical trees and shrubs and flowers and more big toads and lizards and scurriers and critters than you could shake a stick at. A small group of people, connected by friendship, linked through family and bound by commitment, lived out their everyday lives in some of the most unremarkable ways, yet they cherished every moment, even when they seemed to take it all for granted.

The four condo buildings filled mostly with retirees. Of Beverly's and Frank's original condos, they sold hers long ago, keeping his for renting out seasonally. They had lavishly furnished their new custom-designed building—the one closest to the springs—and spent a lot of time enjoying their screened deck with private Jacuzzi. The apartment buildings teemed with young singles and couples, a few retirees, several families, and of course Ruth Riner and, until he got married, her son Kevin.

As a teenager, Kevin tended to sleep at home during the week, but he kept his combination office and bedroom at Frank and Beverly's for school and business work. He slept there for occasional weekend "visits," sometimes bringing along Lonnie—if only to keep things interesting for "the old folks." Those nights were usually reserved for renting a movie everybody would enjoy, or playing games out on the screened deck.

Beverly and Ruth both tended to sleep late, so Kevin—all through middle and high school—kept up his routine of waking early and going over to share breakfast with Frank. They enjoyed some mean omelets during those years.

There weren't many kids in the "neighborhood"—certainly none Kevin's age—but when he turned fifteen, a young single mother hired him to watch her ten-year-old son four days a week after school. Lucas tended to be shy, a blond-haired moppet rather small for his age with big blue eyes that missed little going on around him. He clung to Kevin a lot at first, just happy for the attention, then eventually settled into a friendship that would long outlast those "babysitting" years.

Since Kevin liked to do his homework and keep up on his business responsibilities after school each day, the younger boy got into a routine of working at Kevin's office, too. He did his homework whenever he had some, then spent his extra time writing little stories—usually about bugs with personalities. Kevin's patient tutelage kept the boy on track at school; his friendship kept him in line during those tenuous early-teen years when peers with poor judgment can be such a strong influence. Lucas took to calling Frank "Geezer," something the older fellow bristled at but, Kevin could tell, secretly enjoyed. More than a few times Kevin and Lucas accidentally discovered each other down the secret path through the springs, pausing to ruminate in the small clearing with the big hollow log where there always seemed to be more and more toads every year.

The beauty salon really took off. The company opened a second shop in New Port Richey and established a clientele somewhat older than those who frequented the Tarpon Springs location. They added a large panel truck—a mobile beauty parlor—to serve shut-ins who lived in the condo and apartment complexes. Ultimately, the business grew until three trucks, each with two beauticians, kept busy full time.

Kevin continued as a paid employee of The Rinery Company, handling the financial administration. His salary and stock bonuses—increased ownership in the company—accumulated in a trust controlled by Frank until he reached age twenty-one. Once a month, Kevin met with Beverly to report on the status of the operation. She would don her new reading glasses, sit at her massive cherrywood desk, and be very serious about examining all the numbers and information.

Ruth flourished, supervising and training all the beauty-salon employees, rotating among the stores and mobile vans, a company fixture respected by an always-growing base of clients. She enjoyed a wonderful personal relationship with one of her cutters, a man named Balon, but they maintained separate residences all through Kevin's teen years because she felt uncomfortable allowing a man to move in while she shared a home with her son. After Kevin moved out, they bought one of the condos together and settled into loving domesticity.

The non-profit animal hospital also proved a hit. Beverly implemented all the programs she dreamed of, then thought up and tried even more new ideas. Most met with enormous success, owing mostly to Beverly's dogged perseverance. Kevin supervised the administration, but he had a full-time bookkeeper/office manager to handle the routine work. Beverly tried to spend at least several hours each day down there volunteering, working as much with people as animals. She once confided to Kevin that every day she felt like something was making Linda proud. He hugged her and agreed, adding that he was proud, too.

The printing company, as Henry always used to say, "kicked ass." Junior came up with a lot of good ideas for expanding and modernizing the services offered at the consumer locations, always keeping them at least several leaps ahead of the competition. He never married, several times hinting that his personal preferences might be a bit different. This upset Marta at first—until her husband, Larry Rumsey, reminded her that there are more important things to care about in a family.

Henry came out of retirement to work full-time as chief financial officer for the printing operation. He converted his old office into the "Florida headquarters"—a good excuse for Doug to fly south for meetings and bring along one or more of his children to see Kevin and Uncle Frank and, of course, Aunt Bevvy.

Doug expanded the corporate sales staff and substantially increased the number and value of their contracts, keeping the plants operating at full capacity. He continued to groom Kevin to take over his job someday, especially since none of his own three kids had shown any interest in the business. His little girls wanted to be singing fashion designers—or fashion-designing singers—and little Jared kept up his passion for art and photography.

Frank stayed involved enough to mentor Kevin, even though he spent most of his time with Beverly either at the animal hospital or boating on the *Fine Print* or lounging on the deck by the springs. He transferred a sizable portion of his personal stock every year to a discretionary trust in Kevin's name, staying just within IRS guidelines and retaining control of the board votes until an unspecified date in the future.

Lonnie and Darla drifted apart by the time they reached ninth grade. He tended, after that, to have a new girlfriend every year until he met the lady of his dreams in college. They married and moved into Ruth's old apartment when she and Balon got the condo. The friendship between the boys—the young men, Kevin and Lonnie—remained strong, just as it always would.

The real-estate development company did very well, its biggest project being a small subdivision out Highway 50, west of Brooksville. Lonnie really took an interest in construction, so Ward took him under his wing and taught him the ropes. It started as a part-time job during high school; then Ward let him work full-time after graduation under the condition he attend the local community college and work toward a degree.

Loretta moved into Henry's house, taking a job at a local senior center that promised a lighter work schedule and less time on her feet. They decided to become foster parents, using that as an excuse to get married. After a beautiful private ceremony with friends and family, they wound up canceling their honeymoon because a little girl with learning disabilities suddenly needed a home after her alcoholic mother committed suicide. More than a year later, the adoption became official on the little girl's twelfth birthday. Loretta and Henry's love seemed to grow stronger with each passing year. She wound up quitting her job to stay home with him after his prostate surgery. Then, when he recovered, she started volunteering a few hours each day at the learning center their daughter attended.

Kevin and Cynthia achieved one of those rare loves that starts very young but flourishes with maturity. They stayed together in spite of drifting apart for most of their eleventh-grade year. Only after dating other people did they learn that each other was who they most wanted. She worked afternoons for Ruth during high school, earning her credentials and going full-time after graduation.

Kevin attended the University of South Florida at Tampa for two years, commuting to classes three days a week. Another year and half at the University of Florida at Gainesville, commuting twice a week for long days on campus, earned him a double bachelor's degree in business administration and psychology.

It was during the summer before starting at Gainesville that he proposed to Cynthia. Married that August, they moved into the wedding present Frank and Beverly gave them—Frank's original condo there by the springs where a lonely little boy used to pester the old fellow to let him help work in the flowers.

Kevin still liked to putter in the flower beds when he had time. Frank would often hang out, too, dragging a chair over, complaining how his bad knees prevented him from helping. His knees really weren't *that* bad, but it made a good story. Lucas often joined them, bringing along his pad to take notes for stories, or to record his observations on life, capturing the human condition, exploring the wonder that is friendship and family and the everyday miracles so many take for granted.

Linda's mysterious image no longer visited Beverly. She was remembered often by her mother and all those who loved her. Her and Marshall's graves never wanted for flowers, meticulously cared for and visited often. Beverly set up a scholarship in Linda's name for the Tampa School of Veterinary Medicine and used the non-profit animal hospital to offer internships. Beverly had those occasional bad days, but she always felt good about the ways she found to honor the memory of her little girl.

Beverly's foot and leg healed as well as could be expected. She only wore the prosthesis when she planned to be on her feet for a while. Only rarely did it hurt enough to warrant using her cane. Like learning to live with the loss of her daughter, her injuries left her with both good days and bad.

Frank and Beverly embodied the very picture of devotion. They'd made room in their hearts for each other, and they'd found their place together . . . there in a fancy condo with a nifty deck overlooking the water near so many of the people they loved in a town called Tarpon Springs.

Kevin sat in his office with Lucas, helping his young friend plan a college-application strategy. The mid-afternoon sunshine streamed through the open window, spotlighting dust particles hovering curiously in the air. Twenty-two-year-old Kevin—recent college grad, printing company vice-president being groomed to ascend, and full-time manager of numerous other business enterprises—sat back in his chair and stroked his bushy brown mustache. Lucas, a month shy of seventeen, watched him curiously. The sunlight highlighted the teenager's long silky-blond hair.

"This isn't right, Luke," Kevin said, contorting his mouth thoughtfully, then stroking his mustache several more times.

"What do you mean?" Lucas asked. "I thought you'd—"

"That's just it," Kevin interrupted. "You're trying to please *me*. You're looking at all these bachelor's programs, knowing what an advocate I am of education, and trying to do what you think *I* want you to do."

Lucas looked down at the moccasins on his feet. "Well, what do you think I should do?"

Kevin got up and started toward the hallway, motioning Lucas to follow. "Come on, let's go to the bathroom."

"Huh?" Lucas followed his older friend down the hallway.

They stood in front of the large mirror, Lucas in front, Kevin right behind him. At nearly six-feet tall, Kevin could look across the top of the teenager's head. Kevin stepped to the side and implored, "Look at yourself."

Lucas studied the reflection carefully, obviously not understanding. "Um, what am I looking at?"

"You're looking at my friend Lucas. What do you see?"

Lucas described himself: small thin body, big elbows and Adam's apple, blue eyes, long blond hair, downy-soft mustache—though you had to look for it to notice. Then Kevin asked him to describe the man inside. Lucas wasn't sure what to say.

Kevin mused, "You know who *I* see? I'm looking at a guy who, after two hundred people have walked by and ignored it, is the only one to stop and look at a fat toad beside the path. I see a guy who hurries to finish his homework *only* because it's required, then spends most of his time working on a nice story. It's a guy who'll sit out in the dirty sand by the springs near the big hollow log with a pad to work out every possible detail of that story before he *has* to come inside and sit at the computer in a dark dungeon to preserve his thoughts. I see a guy who likes people—old people, young people, challenged people—and who especially loves watching children play, rarely able to resist the urge to join in with them. I also see a loyal friend who wants to please all the people he loves."

Lucas grinned. "You can see all that, huh?"

"Yeah," Kevin said, "I do. Now I want to see my favorite yellow-haired pest understand what I learned from Frank a long time ago."

"Frank's pretty smart."

"Yeah. I remember once when he got mad at me for trying to please him all the time. He told me to go away and don't come back until I was ready to be Kevin. I think I was about fourteen then—before I knew you. I got all mad, then bummed, and finally just had my feelings hurt. I sat out by the springs for a while, then came back practically in tears, still not understanding what he meant, but wanting desperately to figure it out. He made me stand here in front of the mirror and talk about who I really was. We went at it a lot longer than I just did to you, but by the time we were done, I could see a lot of things about myself from the way he saw me. Then he said he loved me." Kevin looked away, a little embarrassed at the personal recollection.

"That's it?" Lucas asked, maybe starting to understand.

"Finally, I asked what this was about. He said he'd been a lucky guy from the day I started hanging around his condo, and that through the years I had become as good a friend as anybody could ever have. The thing was, it was Kevin he liked so much, not some guy who was trying to be someone else."

"Okay, Rinestoner, maybe you noticed some things I haven't really been thinking about."

"Yes, I've been noticing Lucas, the guy who likes to experience nature and people and quiet moments to himself, then wants to make up characters and give personalities to bugs. That's my friend Lucas. Now, let's try to find out what Lucas would like to do after he graduates."

They went back to the office and sat, pondering, laughing, contemplating, discussing a trek through Europe, considering a creative-studies program or taking a year off to write or getting a job in publishing or working with children . . . By the time Lucas left for dinner with his mother, his head brimmed with new ideas and new possibilities.

Kevin settled in by himself to proofread a series of silverprints for a brochure on pet care. He heard Frank and Beverly come home, assuming she—if not both—would come to offer him the customary snack always followed with a hug. By the time he was finished, he noticed that neither had appeared. He walked down the hallway and entered the living area. Still not finding them, he called out and got no response. Ultimately, he located them out on the deck, sitting together on a stand-up swing, bathed in the warm late-afternoon sunshine. Feeling like an intruder, he greeted them and tried to duck back inside.

"Kevin!" Beverly called. He stepped back out. "Would you like to sit with us, sweetie?" He pulled a lawn chair over. "Cynthia's still at work?" she asked.

"Oh yeah, this is her late night. She won't be home till after nine."

Beverly nodded. Frank looked at him, then looked away, obviously distracted. Beverly shifted in her seat, wincing slightly, something Kevin had first noticed a few weeks before.

He felt a sense of panic rising inside. Something was wrong, and she was trying to bring herself to say it. Kevin noticed Frank's hands holding Beverly's; what at first glance looked like a casual caress was actually a very strong grip. Frank wanted to protect her, a posture he remembered from so many years before. Kevin tried to search Beverly's eyes, noticing they glistened from newly formed tears, but she looked down at the deck.

She normally looks me in the eye.

"Kevin, I've been having problems lately. I've been going for tests. I've been so sore because a couple of weeks ago they put big needles in me to draw out some cells."

Kevin searched Frank's face, but his friend wouldn't look up, either. Beverly kept glancing at him, but invariably ducked her head. He felt like a scared little boy running through the woods looking for Frank to help—except that Frank was here and maybe this time Kevin would have to be the strong one.

"—Malignant," he heard her say. "—Operation . . . —Radiation . . . —Chemotherapy . . ." The words kept coming, like she could finally tell him, like he deserved to know. Kevin felt sick, but remembered to be strong. He vaguely recalled hugging her, assuring he would be there for her every step of the way.

It'll be okay . . . it'll be all right.

They sat for a while, all three of them, not saying much, feeling safer there together than if they tried to face their fears alone. They spied a young boy, not much older than five or six, creeping along the edge of the woods, peering into the spring, looking for fish, prowling among the bushes, excited by the lizards and intrigued by the toads, enjoying the wonder of his tiny world. Kevin noticed the deep grooves in Frank's face, the white hair rimming his bald pate, the gaunt lines in his stiff, tense body.

Finally, Frank said, "It's scheduled for three weeks from Tuesday. If you want to be there with me in the waiting room—"

"I'll be there."

"Kevin," Beverly interrupted. "Please, I don't want any fuss. It's okay to let your wife and your mom know, but please don't let them make a fuss. I guess you can tell Lonnie, too. I'll call Lor and Henry tonight, but I'd like to keep it just among us for as long as we can."

Kevin nodded, reaching over to squeeze their hands. He wanted to run, cry, panic, wave a magic wand. He wanted for Lucas to write a story where it all goes away . . . But all he could do was, well, be strong. His friends needed his support.

"I'll look out for the animals and the businesses," he assured them, "and you concentrate on getting healthy." He tried to be upbeat *and* look confident. "It's not going to be easy, you know, but it *will* be okay in the long run."

Beverly smiled, her wet eyes gleaming, her face aglow with that same proud look she had given him so many times since he was twelve. "You're always such a sweetheart," she said, repeating it again softer, almost in a whisper.

"Hey," he added, "I'm on my own tonight. How about if I go get us some grub and invite myself over for dinner?"

He called in an order to their favorite place on Highway 19, then drove out and picked it up. They ate on the deck, finally relaxing a little, not speaking very much. Once Frank seemed to snap out of his stupor, he put all his energy into hovering protectively around Beverly.

Later, Kevin left them to themselves and walked over to his condo. While he waited for Cynthia to get home, he called Lonnie and gave him the news. Lonnie's reaction was to get angry. He was tired of good people having to suffer. It wasn't right; it wasn't fair. Not Beverly . . . Not Frank . . .

Cynthia burst into tears. Ruth came and cried with her for a while. Kevin repeatedly talked them out of rushing over to commiserate with Beverly. "She doesn't want the fuss," he kept reminding them.

Late that night, after Ruth had gone, long after Cynthia had fallen asleep, Kevin sat and stared at his softly breathing wife. He loved her with all his heart; watching her sleep was something he found himself doing often. He tried to imagine her facing cancer, surgery, treatments, and possibly worse . . . He snapped out of his trance, breathing hard, sweating, his heart pounding. It was too hot, too stuffy. He needed to get outside.

He pulled on shorts, t-shirt, and sandals before heading out into the warm night. Far too late to be bothered by insects, he stood around and stared at the sky. Finally, he walked around the pool, then toward the woods and the springs. Passing Frank and Beverly's place, he heard a voice whisper, "Kevin?"

He walked over to find Frank sitting on the steps to the deck, so he sat down beside him. They stayed there for a while, neither speaking, until Kevin reached over and took Frank's hand. They both squeezed several times before resting their arms on their legs, still not letting go.

"I just don't know what to do," Frank whispered.

Kevin shook his head. "I don't either, Frank." Then, after a minute, he added, "Yeah, I guess I do. I know what you can do, and I know what I'm gonna do, too."

Barely visible in the faint moonlight, Frank looked up at him. "You got a plan, hoodlum?"

"Yeah. You know, when I was little, I used to think you could fix anything. Then when I got a little older, I figured out you couldn't. But you *did* do everything you could. That's something I've always counted on. Frank, what you did was stand by me and help me face whatever came my way. You went through it with me. That's what you're gonna do for Beverly. That's what I'm gonna do for both of you."

Kevin could feel his friend's hand tremble. Frank looked down again, whispering, "What if the treatments don't work?"

"We'll help Beverly through it, whatever the outcome."

Tears traced lines down Frank's cheeks, reflecting the faint light. He tried to speak, but couldn't find his voice. Finally, he managed to say, "Kevin, I—" He paused to catch his breath, then so faintly it could barely be heard, finished, "I need your help."

They sat there for a long time like that, both with too much to say, friendship finding a way to say it without words.

The night filled their world with sound, the chirrups and slithers and rustles and, in the midst of it all, the sniffles of Beverly's men steeling themselves to face uncertainty, each in his own way . . . determined to face it together.

The next year and a half presented many challenges for Beverly and her "family," as she called them. Still, she refused to miss out on enjoying her life, always cherishing and appreciating every moment. Through it all, as Linda had taught, she collected a lifetime's worth of memories and beautiful images, many of them captured on film by little Jared or Lucas or even sometimes Kevin.

Click. The groundbreaking ceremony for the second animal hospital, Beverly in a wheelchair gingerly holding the silver shovel, Frank hovering over her to help. Click. Beverly trying on her new wig, Ruth making some final adjustments, both pausing to mug for the camera. Click. Kevin and Lonnie clad in suits, both with a few drinks in them, hanging little cheese snots from their noses for the photographer. Click. Cynthia sneaking up behind the guys to make horns over their heads.

Click. Beverly holding hands with Loretta beside Linda's and Marshall's graves, new silk flowers, sad geese in the background looking on. Click. A group picture, smiling in the sunshine, splashed by the surf, cruising on the *Fine Print.* Click. Frank and Kevin and Doug and Junior at the opening of a new store in Lapeer, Michigan. Click. Lucas sleeping in the hollow log, dreaming about a talking caterpillar that someday would delight millions of children. Click. Kevin asleep on the couch, Frank dozing in the chair beside him.

Click. Frank and Beverly caught slow dancing in the entertainment room, mes-mer-ized, swaying, her weight supported by her loving husband. Click. Beverly, sitting in her wheelchair, frail and weak, holding a framed montage of precious photos given to her for her birthday, smiling for the camera, surrounded by the people in her life, the people she loved, the people who loved her.

CHAPTER 41

On a hot, muggy morning, Kevin stood in the sandy clearing next to the springs, looking across the water with both arms raised in the air, a photograph of colored lights in his right hand. He stood there like that for a full ten minutes, then walked over to the woods and assumed the same position. After another ten minutes, he climbed on top of the big hollow log and raised his arms again. The creatures who lived in and around the springs all ignored him. The real world carried on, oblivious to the frustration and pain of a young man balancing precariously in the air.

"Are you here?" he called out. "Where are you? Don't ignore me! We have more to learn!" The unexpected noise quieted some of the insects and small animals only briefly before the cacophony resumed. Frustrated, he sat on the log and rubbed his face with his free hand. He studied the photograph, then looked out across the water again. This wasn't going to work. It was time to give up.

A single pinpoint of magenta-colored light swirled around in the water behind him, rising slowly into the air, curiously watching the young man. Then it moved over beside him and lightly brushed against his cheek.

Startled, Kevin sat upright and looked about, relieved when he noticed the sparkle hovering a few feet away.

He reached out slowly toward the shimmering light, gently cupping it in his hand. He guided it close to his body, then gingerly used his other hand to touch his brow. The light slowly explored his face, then started to swirl around, drawing patterns on his forehead.

Then, suddenly, the light was gone.

Frank and Kevin sat beside Beverly's bed there in one of the condo's spare bedrooms, which had been outfitted as a makeshift hospice. The nurse added a dose of morphine to Beverly's IV, then checked her vital signs. Beverly's stiffened limbs relaxed, her breathing slowed, and she seemed to drift off to sleep.

"She's resting now, Mr. Tanyon. It's time for me to go. Remember, Tracy will come take over in two hours." Frank nodded absently. She packed up her things and let herself out.

"Frank," Kevin started, reaching up and putting his arm around his older friend's shoulders, "I've got a list of things we need. I was going to go out and pick them up, but I want you to go instead."

Frank looked at him, the sadness in his eyes strengthening Kevin's resolve. He knew how to make Beverly comfortable, but to help Frank, the answers were not so obvious.

"I need to watch her—" Frank started, his eyes drifting to the woman he loved more than life itself. So many times he had wished he could trade places with her. So many times he had wished he could trade his life if only to ease her suffering for a moment. "I need to make sure it doesn't hurt."

Kevin reached over and lifted him gently but firmly. "I'll stay with her, Frank. You need to stretch your legs and get some fresh air. Go pick up these things, then stop and get us something for dinner on your way back."

Frank looked lost, but he seemed to recognize something reassuring in Kevin's eyes. He nodded, knelt beside Beverly, and kissed her on the cheek, whispering, "I'll be back soon. You get some rest—I'll be back."

Kevin led him to the door, reminding him about the list, and sent him on his way. He returned to the bedroom, moved his chair to the other side of the room, and settled in to continue the vigil.

"Mama?" she whispered. "Mama? Are you awake?"

"Linda?" Beverly mouthed, gingerly opening her eyes and peering about. "Is that you?"

"I'm right here, Mama." Linda reached over and held her mother's hand.

Beverly struggled to sit up. "Oh, Linda, I knew I'd see you again."

"Be still, Mama. Don't strain yourself. I'm right here."

"I knew you'd come back."

"You know I've been with you all along. Your love was so strong that you refused to let me go."

"Yeah . . . I could feel you. I hope you're proud of all the things we did . . ."

"*Very* proud—*so* very proud."

"I kept your memory alive, you know," Beverly told her, having some difficulty finding the strength to speak.

"Was it good, Mama? Was it all good?"

"Oh yes. Nobody could have been loved more than me. That little Kevin—you should see him now, he's a fine, handsome young man so in love with his new wife that it's a wonder he still comes around to pester us old folks."

"I told you he was special, didn't I?"

"Yeah." Beverly smiled, recalling a million images of the lovable little boy, the gangly teen, the high schooler, collegian, businessman, friend . . .

"I made the right call on that Frank feller, too, didn't I?"

"You sure did." Images of Frank flooded her mind—at the helm of his boat, helping with animals, stripping to his drawers to climb in and stretch her leg, proposing amid a million twinkling lights, waiting for her to walk down the aisle, a hundred times driving her back and forth to the hospital, holding her while she got sick, then cleaning up the mess, embracing her while they danced into a world all their own . . .

"You know," Beverly continued, memories giving strength to her words, "I came down here to Florida feeling like my life was over. Yet, the people who mean the most to me now, many of the best parts, they all happened here. I had nearly given up, but you and Kevin and, yes, Frank—you all kept me on track. It's never too late for new experiences—" She grew quiet, trying to catch her breath. "It's never too late for love."

"And Frank loves *you* with all his heart," Linda agreed.

"I just hate to leave him," she whispered, starting to cry softly. "I know how hard it will be for him." She tried to catch her breath. "I wish he didn't have to hurt."

"Don't worry, Mama. You're leaving him more than you can imagine."

"Yes," she said, closing her eyes. "I sure do—cherish that—man." She reached out for a moment, took one last breath, then laid her hand gently at her side. Kevin rushed over, but stood helplessly by.

Linda touched Beverly on the cheek and whispered, "I love you, Mama."

Frank drove down the private road toward the condos. He felt panic when he saw several unfamiliar cars, a police cruiser, and a county van parked along the side of his driveway. Several neighbors milled around outside, whispering, watching, waiting. He jumped out of his van, ran to the door, and rushed inside. Before he could cross the living room, Kevin emerged from the hallway and grabbed him bodily. Frank twisted and flailed, trying to break free, wanting to rescue Beverly, reaching out.

Kevin held tightly, softly repeating, "Frank— Frank— There's nothing you can do. Listen to me, Frank, be still. Frank . . ."

Finally, the older man quit struggling. He stood there panting, exhausted, trembling, crying softly. "I need to see her," he said.

Kevin turned and, with a supporting arm still around his friend, gently walked him down the hallway to where Beverly lay. Several people stood around helplessly, looking awkward and uncomfortable. The medical examiner sat in a chair beside the bed, recording information on a clipboard. After a gesture from Kevin, they all filed quietly out to the hallway, the examiner closing the door behind himself.

Frank knelt on the floor beside Beverly, reaching out to touch her—her hand, her face, looking for some sign, anything to convince him she might still be there.

Behind him stood Kevin holding his friend's shoulders. Frank held her lifeless hand to his own cheek, then buried his face in the bed and sobbed.

After a few minutes, Kevin lifted him up, turning him around. He wrapped his arms around him protectively, reminding him he wasn't alone, then guided him across the room where they paused to stand, still holding on to each other. The attendants came in and carefully moved her to a stretcher, covered her, then wheeled her out to the van.

Frank tried to follow her out, but Kevin held on, refusing to let him go.

As he watched them take her away, many images flashed through Kevin's mind. The one that endured strongest was her reassuring smile, the one she gave him that awful day the social worker took him, a scared little boy, away from her. Through tearful eyes, he had seen her smile before gathering him into her arms and *promising* she would come "rescue" him and bring him back home. She told him to carry that hug with him for whenever he needed it—something he did for many years.

He needed it now . . .

Still holding on to Kevin, Frank remembered how it felt to dance with Beverly at their wedding, everybody watching to see if her injuries would prove too great. He recalled how confident he felt that night, so in love and so happy that nothing else mattered. He would hold on to her tightly, support her, help her dance—even if it meant carrying her. In the strong arms of the man she loved, she would see that nothing could interfere with their moment of magic.

Now she was gone, and it was Kevin who held and supported him.

Two friends shared their moment of profound grief, remembering how much Beverly had meant to them, to Linda, to all the people whose lives she touched.

As word spread that evening, they came from every direction to see Frank, to pay their respects, all feeling helpless, seeking others who would understand. Cynthia, or maybe Ruth, or even Lonnie met them at the door. Loretta was there, talking when she could, retreating to a private room with Henry when she felt overwhelmed. Kevin stayed near Frank, sometimes moving around, sometimes sitting and letting people approach them.

There were friends and family, many bringing food, all feeling a deep loss, not sure what to do, wanting to show how important Beverly had been to them—and that Frank always would be. Everyone wanted to take a piece of the hurt away, to ease

Frank's pain, to give him strength—but each had to carry his own grief. All they could do was be there, together, with others who understood.

Kevin remembered how both he and Frank had once been lonesome. He had taken his mother for granted as much as Frank did with Henry. Kevin and Frank had each other at the time, but didn't understand how important that should be. Each believed all he would need was a friend or a lover or a family all his own. It wasn't until Beverly filled that gap that either understood the give and take, the sadness that comes with being happy, the sorrow that offsets the joy. Kevin always wondered how true love would feel, yet he had to learn that he'd had it all along. Beverly's love and the adversity of a harsh world gave perspective to his tender feelings.

Kevin decided he and Frank had been very lucky—lucky enough to find the right people—lucky enough to find each other. They had learned to give of themselves, to share with others, to care. Because Frank was that kind of man, because Beverly had been that kind of friend, these people they touched were drawn here . . . hurt by the loss, to care for those left behind.

The more it hurts, the more it meant, the luckier you are, Kevin thought.

The hour grew late and everybody left except Kevin and Cynthia. Frank was exhausted, still numb, not sure how he could go on. Kevin kissed Cynthia, holding her like he never dared let go, but then sent her home, telling her he was going to sleep over. That old tradition between friends would continue, but this time it would be to help his older buddy get through the night.

Through his grief, Kevin decided he really *did* have a good life. There were so many things to learn, experiences to cherish, important moments and people to remember, opportunities to share, time enough for love. There were friendships like his and Frank's, unconditional, sometimes one needing from the other, often the other way around. He had asked so much of Frank, yet had received substantially more. Tonight, he would give his friend something back.

"Frank," Kevin said softly, guiding him over toward the stereo. "Will you play that song from the night you and Beverly got engaged?"

"What was?—oh, yeah. She sure did love that song."

Frank walked over and located the proper CD. He tried to put it in the player, but his hands shook too badly. Kevin started to take it from him, but decided instead to hold Frank's hand steady and help him do it for himself.

As the music started, Frank turned and . . . *there she was!*

Kevin smiled, a twinkle in his eyes, and with a tip of his imaginary hat, he retreated into the night.

Frank and Beverly gazed lovingly at each other; then he reached down and took her by the hand.

She drawled, "Would the kind gentleman be willing to help a lady fill her dance card? It seems the rest of the slots are still available."

"For *you*, madam, it would be an honor!" he drawled back. Then in his own voice, he added, "I've *always* had the hots for *you*!"

There would be a funeral to plan the next day, a marker to order, affairs to settle, but that night—and many more nights in the years to come—Frank put aside his grief and remembered.

If death is a part of living, then it's memory that bridges the chasm between the two.

Frank and Beverly held each other tightly, swaying gently to the rhythm, unencumbered by injury or pain, overwhelmed by love, surrounded by a million pinpoints of light, every imaginable color swirling around and through them as two people who would always be in love danced the dance of life.

The Fresh Ink Group

Publishing
Memberships
Share & Read Free Stories, Essays, Articles
Free-Story Newsletter
Writing Contests

Books
E-books
Amazon Bookstore

Authors
Editors
Artists
Professionals
Publishing Services
Publisher Resources

Members' Websites
Members' Blogs
Social Media

www.FreshInkGroup.com

Email: info@FreshInkGroup.com

Twitter: @FreshInkGroup

Google+: Fresh Ink Group

Facebook.com/FreshInkGroup

LinkedIn: Fresh Ink Group

About.me/FreshInkGroup

www.ingramcontent.com/pod-product-compliance
Lightning Source LLC
Chambersburg PA
CBHW020552260626
47157CB00003B/673